Angie

A Gentle Taming

"I want you to look me in the eye," Alec said slowly, "and tell me that you didn't enjoy our lovemaking."

The heat from his gaze pulsed with undisguised passion, and Lauren felt her will to resist him slip a notch. "Please, I have to go—"

A look of triumph flickered behind his eyes. He tilted her face toward his and a tremor rippled through her as his lips claimed hers.

She groaned and leaned into his embrace, returning his kiss with a hunger that came from deep within her soul.

Alec dragged his mouth away from hers. "Look at me, Lauren, and tell me you want me to stop," he commanded.

Her lips still burning from his kiss, she swallowed hard and shook her head. "I-I can't . . ."

Other **AVON ROMANCES**

BELOVED PRETENDER *by Joan Van Nuys*
DARK CHAMPION *by Jo Beverley*
FLAME OF FURY *by Sharon Green*
FOREVER HIS *by Shelly Thacker*
OUTLAW HEART *by Samantha James*
SCANDALOUS *by Sonia Simone*
TOUCH ME WITH FIRE *by Nicole Jordan*

Coming Soon

TENDER IS THE TOUCH *by Ana Leigh*
PROMISE ME HEAVEN *by Connie Brockway*

And Don't Miss These
ROMANTIC TREASURES
from Avon Books

ANGEL EYES *by Suzannah Davis*
FASCINATION *by Stella Cameron*
LORD OF FIRE *by Emma Merritt*

A GENTLE TAMING

ADRIENNE DAY

AVON BOOKS NEW YORK

A GENTLE TAMING is an original publication of Avon Books. This work has never before appeared in book form. This work is a novel. Any similarity to actual persons or events is purely coincidental.

AVON BOOKS
A division of
The Hearst Corporation
1350 Avenue of the Americas
New York, New York 10019

Inside cover author photograph by William E. Baker, Jr.
Published by arrangement with the author
Library of Congress Catalog Card Number: 93-91642
ISBN: 0-380-77411-9

First Avon Books Printing: January 1994

Printed in the U.S.A.

RA 10 9 8 7 6 5 4 3 2 1

Chapter 1

Arizona Territory, 1890

One by one, the hammers fell silent as the men laying new shingles on the roof of the Millerville Rooming House stopped to watch the newcomer ride into town. On the front porch, the swing where Jake Hanby could be found courting Martha Sikes every Saturday night stilled, and Alma Sikes, Martha's aunt, put on her reading glasses so she could get a good look at the man. Behind her, the screened door slammed as Martha, drying her hands on a dish towel, stepped onto the porch.

Two doors down, Arminta Larson, who hadn't done a lick of housework since the day her husband hired a Mexican girl to help with the cleaning, appeared on her front steps to shake out one of the scatter rugs that lay in her front hall.

Nor did the curiosity diminish when the newcomer turned his horse down Main Street. The poker game that had been going on in the back of Burroughs' Feed Store came to an abrupt end, the players spilling out into the street to loiter as if they had nothing better to do. And the boardwalk in front of Hawthorne's Drugstore, which had already been swept once that morning, suddenly needed sweeping again. Everyone within a hundred miles of Millerville had heard about the newcomer, Alec MacKenzie, but few had actually seen him.

Until today.

In front of the Millerville Mercantile, Lauren Cooper was hefting the last sack of flour into the bed of the wagon when her fourteen-year-old brother, Bubba, grabbed her arm. "Hey, Coop, look! There's that man Cal told us about. That foreigner who bought the Williams place."

Lauren dusted her hands on her britches and turned to look as Alec MacKenzie tied his horse's reins to the hitching post across the street and started walking straight toward them.

Lauren's breath caught. The man was well over six feet tall, with a powerful, well-honed body that commanded respect. His dun-colored coat fit across his wide shoulders as if it had been tailor-made for him, and his jeans hugged his narrow hips and long, muscular legs. He wore a black hat and expensive fancy-stitched black boots. At his waist, a broad silver and turquoise belt buckle flashed in the sun when he moved. He walked with the ease and confidence of a man who was accustomed to getting what he wanted, be it power or possessions or—Lauren's pulse quickened—women. His bold gaze swept over her, and for one agonizing second, she had the horrible feeling that he could read her mind.

Noticing that Bubba was gawking at the man, Lauren jabbed him in the ribs with her elbow. "Close your mouth before you swallow a fly!"

Bubba snapped his mouth shut. Shoving his hands into his pockets, he kicked idly at a loose board and pretended not to notice the Scot as he stepped up onto the boardwalk. Alec MacKenzie stopped, his feet apart, and removed his hat. "Good morning, lad." The accented words rolled off his tongue like notes off a mouth harp.

Bubba lifted his gaze, then his entire head, tilting it back as far as his neck would stretch, until he was looking straight up at the tall, broad-shouldered man who towered over him. Bubba swallowed hard, the Adam's apple that protruded through his skinny neck visibly bobbing. Beneath a shock of wheat blond hair, the tops of his ears turned a brilliant red. He couldn't have spoken if his life depended on it.

Alec MacKenzie's gaze shifted to Lauren, his warm brown eyes sparkling as they locked intimately with her blue ones. The sun reflected off his tawny hair, making it shine like dark, polished bronze. A peculiar warmth ignited in the pit of her stomach and spread through her limbs, making her feel like she did when she ate too much watermelon: just a little bit sick, but not so miserable she wouldn't do it again.

Almost against her will, her lips curved into a hesitant smile.

Suddenly Alec MacKenzie reached out and brushed his tanned knuckle across her cheekbone, and Lauren thought for certain she was going to swoon right there on the boardwalk in front of the Mercantile. "You have flour on your face, lass."

Lauren's smile vanished.

Alec MacKenzie winked at her, then dropped his hand and continued on into the Mercantile.

Lauren's hand flew to her face. "Oh, hell!" she mumbled as she scrubbed at her cheek. She could feel her face turning as red as her brother's ears. She wanted to crawl under the boardwalk and die. "Why didn't you tell me I had flour all over my face?" she demanded of Bubba.

"You didn't ask."

Flashing him a retaliatory glare, Lauren turned to go back into the store. "Stay here. I'll be right back."

"Where are you going?"

"Just stay with the wagon."

Alec MacKenzie was at the counter, talking with Mr. Edrich, the owner, when Lauren slipped back inside the store. She ducked down the aisle where the piece goods were displayed and pretended to study a bolt of pink calico. She strained her ears to listen. Since Alec MacKenzie now owned the ranch bordering theirs, it paid to know as much as possible about their new neighbor.

"Your order will arrive in Tucson at the end of the week, Mr. MacKenzie," she heard Mr. Edrich say. "You may pick it up yourself, or you can arrange with one of the transport companies to deliver it. I'd recommend Bartlett & Ochoa. They handle much of the shipping for Fort Huachuca. They're fairly reliable, and you won't have to worry about making sure you have enough wagons to carry back all that wire."

"I'll look into it. Also, I'll need extra help if I'm to get those fences up in time. I'll give fair consideration to anyone willing to put in an honest day's labor. Do you know of anyone who can use the work?"

Fences! Lauren bit her tongue to keep from blurting out the obscenity that sprang to her lips. Why, that mangy coyote! None of the ranchers in the valley used fences. They just let their cattle roam, then branded the calves and divided up the mavericks during the spring roundup. If Alec MacKenzie fenced off the range for his own use, plenty of ranchers were going to be furious—Pa included.

"Try the mine," Mr. Edrich said. "They've laid off plenty of men since the price of silver started dropping."

Lauren moved around the end of the aisle and focused her attention on the cans of fruit stacked on the shelves at one end of the counter. Her back was still toward Alec MacKenzie, but she was closer now and could hear better. Fences, indeed! It was obvious the man didn't know what was good for him.

"With whom should I speak at the mine?"

"Harland Summers. He's the superintendent." Mr. Edrich's voice trailed off, then he asked sharply, "Are you looking for something in particular, Miss Cooper?"

Lauren whirled around. Instead of Mr. Edrich, however, she found herself staring into Alec MacKenzie's amber-flecked eyes. The intensity of his gaze threw her off guard, piercing her defenses and making her forget where she was. There was a stubborn set to his chin, but his mouth was wide and generous, and his eyes radiated a golden warmth. She realized with a start that he was the most handsome man she had ever seen.

One tawny eyebrow lifted questioningly, and her own delicately arched brown ones dipped in annoyance. *Arrogant foreigner,* she thought. He was probably one of those prissy English gents who were coming over from London in droves and buying up all the available rangeland—with other people's money—and trying to impress their friends back home with tales of how they fought wild Indians in the untamed West. Ha! Except for the Papago, who slipped off the San Xavier Reservation now and then and tried to stir up trouble, there hadn't been any Indians in the valley since Geronimo surrendered to the Army four years ago and got carted off to Fort Marion.

"Miss Cooper, I asked you a question," Mr. Edrich snapped, his impatience mounting. "Are you looking for something in particular?"

Tearing her gaze away from Alec MacKenzie's, Lauren plucked a tin off the shelf and marched up to the counter. "Peaches," she said firmly. In spite of her show of self-confidence, her knees felt like jelly.

Mr. Edrich's eyes narrowed. "Peaches weren't on the list you brought in, young lady."

"I know that. But Pa's been talking about peach pie, and there's none in season. I thought I'd surprise him." She fished in her pants pocket for what remained of the money Pa had given her for the supplies.

Mr. Edrich's lips thinned in annoyance, but he said nothing.

Before she could get the money out of her pocket, commotion erupted in the street. Lauren glanced up at the window just in time to see her wagon take off as if it had been shot out of a cannon. Bubba burst into the store. "Coop, you gotta come quick! Sam just drove off our team!"

Forgetting both Mr. Eldridge and Alec MacKenzie, Lauren bolted for the door.

When she reached the boardwalk, Sam Luttrell and Eliot Dandridge, perched high on their horses, were walking their mounts back and forth over the bags of flour and cornmeal that had fallen off the back of the wagon. Flour engulfed them like a great white cloud.

Lauren felt sick. Pa was going to have her hide for letting the horses run off with their supplies. "Damn you, stop that!" she shouted.

Sam leered out at her. "Consider that a warning, Coop. If your old man don't stop cutting Dandridge's herd, you're going to lose more than a couple bags of flour."

Lauren bristled. "Pa didn't steal your cattle!"

"Well, there's an awful lot of calves with Bar-T brands trailing after Diamond Cross cows that says different."

"He's right," Eliot cut in. "If you don't want my father to take matters to the law, Frank Cooper and his men had better stay off Diamond Cross land."

At nineteen, pale, sickly Eliot Dandridge was the same age she was, although he looked younger. He was also a yellow-bellied coward if

Lauren had ever seen one. That was why he took Sam Luttrell with him everywhere he went. Sam was twenty-two, a bully, and a card cheat. According to rumor, he had even marked one of Miss Chloe's "girls" with a branding iron so he wouldn't have to share her. With his dark, curly hair, he might have been handsome if his left eye didn't wander disconcertingly when he looked at you. Lauren ignored him. "Now, listen here, Eliot Dandridge. You can just go and tell your father—"

"No, you listen here," Sam interrupted. "We've had enough of Cooper trash rustling cattle in this valley. You better keep your noses clean, or you're going to regret it." He turned his horse and started to ride away.

Lauren's temper soared. No one called the Coopers trash and got away with it. Remembering the can of peaches in her hand, she drew back her arm and hurled the can at Sam Luttrell's departing back. Sam yelped as the can struck his shoulder.

Swearing savagely, he turned his horse around and spurred him back toward the Mercantile. Fear constricted Lauren's heart as he leapt down from the saddle, his face dark with fury.

Before she could run, he seized the front of her shirt and dragged her off the boardwalk. He raised his fist, and she ducked, but not quickly enough. A blinding pain exploded inside her head. She reeled backward, unable to catch her balance, and landed on her back in the middle of the street.

"Coop!" Bubba's shrill scream pierced her daze.

Struggling to sit up, Lauren forced open her eyes. Through a curtain of pain, she saw Bubba running toward her. Then she saw Sam stick out his foot, tripping the boy and sending him sprawling.

Lauren staggered to her feet. Her head was pounding and bright white lights were moving in front of her eyes, but she would be damned if she was going to let anyone lay a finger on her baby brother. It was time someone taught the mighty Sam Luttrell a long overdue lesson. Doubling up her fists, she broke into a run.

"Sam, watch out!" Eliot Dandridge yelled.

Sam turned, and Lauren plowed headfirst into his belly, striking him with an impact that knocked him off his feet. He went down, dragging Lauren with him.

She clawed at his face. She dug her fingers into his eye sockets. Sam grabbed her wrists and jerked her hands down. She threw her head forward, bashing him in the mouth with her forehead. Cursing, Sam shoved her off him, then dived after her. They rolled in the dirt. Finally managing to straddle him, Lauren sank both hands into his thick dark hair and banged his head against the ground. She heard yelling, as if onlookers were cheering them on. For one glorious second, she had the upper hand. Then they rolled again and he was on top of her, pummeling her with his fists.

Suddenly the weight lifted as Jack Corrigan, the bartender from the Shady Lady, and two men Lauren did not recognize pulled Sam off her. But even three men were having a hard time restraining him, and for a minute it looked as if Sam might break free. Still too angry to think clearly, Lauren scrambled to her feet and lunged at him.

A pair of strong arms locked around her middle, jerking her back against a broad chest as hard as a slab of granite. Lauren struggled fiercely, but to no avail. Her arms were pinned at her sides, and she couldn't get enough leverage to issue an effective kick. "Blast you! Let go of me!"

The powerful arms tightened around her. "Easy, lass," a deep, melodious voice murmured in her ear.

Lauren swore aloud. She tried to wrest out of Alec MacKenzie's hold, but he was too strong for her and she ended up squirming futilely.

A crowd was quickly gathering around them. "Hey, Luttrell!" one man taunted. "Picking fights with little girls now?"

Laughter erupted in the crowd.

Sam's face turned a menacing shade of dark red.

Jack Corrigan held Sam firmly by the collar. "You'd better ride out of here before I summon the sheriff. You were warned what would happen the next time you picked a fight in town."

"She started it! She threw that goddamned can at me!"

"You ran off my team and trampled my supplies!" Lauren shot back. She could feel something warm and wet dripping from her nose, but because Alec MacKenzie was restraining her, she couldn't wipe it away.

"Get out of town, Luttrell," Jack said. "I don't want to see you around here until you've cooled off."

The men released Sam. He picked up his hat and knocked it against the side of his leg, sending up a thick cloud of dust. The glare he sent Lauren told her this was far from over.

She surged toward him, but Alec held her back. Sam Luttrell mounted his horse, and he and Eliot Dandridge rode away. Twisting in the Scot's arms, Lauren shouted after them, "And don't come back, you pea-brained heaps of cow dung!"

Alec gripped Lauren's shoulder. "That'll be enough of that, lass."

Lauren shrugged off his hand. "Go suck an egg!" She dragged her arm across her nose, and a loud curse burst from her lips when she saw the blood on her sleeve. A terrible stinging pain shot up the back of her nose and into her eyes. "Holy hell! That son of a bitch broke my nose!"

Alec reached for her. "Let me see."

Lauren slapped his hand away. "Leave me alone."

Bubba gaped at her. "You're bleeding to death, Coop!"

Lauren shot him a pained look. "I'm not bleeding to death," she mumbled through the hand she was holding over her mouth and nose. Blood seeped between her fingers and ran down her chin.

"Bring her into the saloon," Jack Corrigan

said. "I just got an ice delivery. We can chip off a piece to put on her nose."

"I don't need any ice," Lauren protested, but Alec had already taken her arm and was steering her in the direction of the Shady Lady. The crowd parted to let them pass.

The interior of the saloon was cool and dimly lit. Since it was the slow time of the day, only two customers sat at the bar. They stared while Alec pulled out a chair at one of the tables and guided Lauren into it. Her light brown hair had come unbraided and tumbled down her back, reaching to her waist. She was still holding her nose, but the flow of blood had not lessened.

"Tilt your head back, lass," Alec ordered.

Lauren was beginning to be afraid. She hadn't seen this much blood since one of their hired hands got jumped by a cougar. Not knowing what else to do, she did as he instructed, only to find herself staring directly at a bigger-than-life-sized painting over the bar of a completely naked woman lounging on a chaise. Her eyes widened. So *that* was what Miss Chloe looked like with her clothes off!

Apparently realizing what she was looking at, Alec strategically placed himself between Lauren and the painting.

Lauren glowered at him over her blood-covered hand. She didn't know what he thought he was protecting her from. She saw more than that every time she took a bath. At least *she* didn't have a tattoo of a rose on her hip!

Jack Corrigan brought some ice chips wrapped in a towel, and several wet cloths. Alec pulled up a chair and sat down. He grasped Lauren's chin and she tried to pull away. "I don't need your help."

Alec tilted her head back farther. "I want to make certain your nose isn't broken, lass. You'll need to move your hand."

Against her better judgment, Lauren obeyed. The feel of Alec MacKenzie's work-roughened fingers on her skin was disconcerting. Since when did prissy English gents have calluses?

She watched him from beneath her lashes as he wiped the blood off her face. He was fair enough to look at, she thought peevishly, not knowing why that should irritate her. He appeared to be older than Sam Luttrell, but not as old as Jake Hanby, who turned thirty-two his last birthday. And he had obviously gotten a bit more sun than he was used to, because his nose was peeling. The tanned skin around his eyes crinkled at the corners, making him look as if he was smiling even when he wasn't. His hair was a rich golden brown with just a hint of red, like a lion's mane. And, like a lion's mane, there was plenty of it. Alec MacKenzie wasn't in any danger of going bald, no matter how old he was.

Alec's eyes narrowed in concentration as he felt along the bridge of her nose.

Lauren turned her gaze back up toward the ceiling. Her face was starting to hurt something fierce. Tears smarted in her eyes, blurring the pattern embossed in the tin ceiling panels. "I wish you'd hurry up," she managed to get out without gasping. "I'm getting dizzy."

"Your nose isn't broken, lass, but there is some

swelling. You're going to be sore for a few days."

Suddenly it felt as if someone had stuck a knife between her eyes.

Lauren shrieked and started up out of the chair. "You sorry son of a—"

Springing to his feet, Alec placed his hands on her shoulders and pushed her back down. Concern darkened his warm brown eyes. "It's all right, lass," he said gently. "It's over now."

Holding both hands cupped over her nose, Lauren glared up at him through her tears. "You bastard! What the bloody hell were you trying to do? Blind me?"

Annoyance flickered in Alec's eyes as he picked up the ice pack. "I'd appreciate it if you wouldn't use profane language, lass. It's unbecoming in one so young and pretty. Now, tilt your head back."

Lauren snatched the ice pack out of his hand and held it alongside her throbbing nose. Scalding tears streamed down her cheeks. Annoyed that he should see her cry, she gave them an angry swipe with her sleeve. "I don't give a damn what you think, mister! I didn't ask for your help. Why don't you just go back to your ranch and put up your bloody fences?"

Understanding dawned in Alec's eyes. Planting a foot on the seat of the chair he had just vacated, he rested his forearm across his thigh and studied Lauren through half-closed eyes. "So that's what this is about. The fences. I gather you overheard me talking with Mr. Edrich about my shipment of wire?"

Lauren fidgeted and averted her gaze. No one had ever told her she was pretty, and she didn't know if he really meant it, or if he was being condescending. Her attention drifted toward the turquoise nuggets embedded in Alec's silver belt buckle, then lower still to the distinct masculine bulge that strained against the fabric of his slim-fitting jeans. Her cheeks flamed as she realized too late where her gaze had strayed. She jerked her eyes up to his face and met his questioning gaze with a look that was blatantly accusing. "Just where are you putting up those fences?"

"What concern is that of yours, lass?"

"It concerns me plenty, mister. If you start fencing off all the good grazing land and watering holes, you're going to drive the rest of us right out of this valley!"

Bubba burst through the swinging doors of the saloon. "Jake caught our horses and brought the wagon back—" He broke off and gaped at his sister. "Wow! Look at that shiner!"

Again Lauren felt her face growing hot. *Why, that lying polecat!* She wanted to kick herself for going all soft inside when Alec MacKenzie said she was pretty. She should have known he didn't mean it. No one was pretty with a black eye and a bloodied nose and God-only-knew what else. She stood up. "Come on, Bubba. Let's go home."

Slapping the ice pack down on the table, she raked her gaze down Alec MacKenzie's towering frame and back up again. "Thanks for nothing." Giving her disheveled locks a haughty toss, she pivoted and walked away.

Alec watched her leave, his gaze drawn to the saucy sway of her backside as she marched out of the saloon. Bubba trotted after her.

Alec gave his head a stern shake as though to clear it. He had always known that American women were more independent than their European counterparts, but one who could make even a seaman blush with her swearing was a phenomenon he had previously encountered only in places most women wouldn't dare tread. "That one could stand to have her mouth washed out with soap," he said, returning the soiled towels to the bar.

The barkeep chuckled. "Lauren's not a bad kid. And she's not as tough as she pretends to be, so don't let her fool you."

Lauren. A pretty name for a lass as prickly as a thistle, Alec thought. "Who is she?"

"Frank Cooper's her father. The towheaded youngster with her is Frank, Junior, but everyone calls him Bubba. They're your nearest neighbors."

Remembering that they had not been introduced, Alec extended his hand. "The name's Alec MacKenzie. Thanks for your help out there. I was afraid that big fellow was going to beat the lass to a pulp."

The men shook hands. "Jack Corrigan." Jack poured a glass of Scotch whiskey and pushed it across the bar to Alec. "It's on the house.

"That would be Sam Luttrell," Jack continued, wiping glasses with a towel and stacking them on a shelf behind the bar. "He works for Martin Dandridge. When Sam's not occupying a jail cell, he and Dandridge's son are usually out looking for trouble. If they can't find any, they start some. You'd do well to steer clear of both of them."

Alec's expression was thoughtful as he swirled the whiskey around the bottom of the glass. He noticed the blood on his coat sleeve and the cuff of his shirt, and a bad taste filled his mouth. Any man who would beat up either a woman or a child deserved to be horse-whipped. "Did you say he works for Martin Dandridge?"

"That's right. At the Diamond Cross ranch on the south side of Beaver Creek. If you stick around long enough, you'll meet him. Dandridge is involved in just about everything that goes on in this town. By the way, in case no one's told you yet, welcome to Millerville."

Alec downed the whiskey and set the glass on the counter. "Thanks for the drink. I owe you one. If you'll excuse me, I need to wrap up my business at the Mercantile."

And then I intend to pay Martin Dandridge a visit, he added to himself.

As Alec started to leave, his gaze rested on the painting over the bar. He noticed the rose tattoo on the woman's hip, and immediately he thought of Lauren Cooper. Not a thistle, he mused, remembering her long-lashed blue eyes, soft brown hair, and enticing figure. A rose. A wild rose, delicate and lovely and full of thorns.

And in dire need of taming.

Frank Cooper's face was livid. "Damn you! I send you into town for supplies, and you get into a brawl. Can't I count on you to do anything right?"

"Pa, it wasn't my fault!" Lauren's voice wavered. "Sam Luttrell deliberately spooked the horses and—"

"Don't talk back to me, girl. If you'd stayed with the wagon like I told you, none of this would've ever happened. I swear, you're as worthless as tits on a boar hog. Now, go wash up and get dinner on the table. I got some hard-working men waiting to be fed. And stop your sniveling, or I'll give you something to cry about."

Hoisting his crutches beneath his arms, Frank hobbled from the kitchen.

Lauren wiped her eyes with her fingertips as she watched him go. She waited until she heard the screened door slam after him before venting her anger on the leg of the kitchen table with a fierce kick. It wasn't fair! Every time something happened, Pa blamed her, regardless of who was responsible.

Bubba stuck his head in the kitchen doorway. "Is it safe to come in now?" he whispered.

Lauren felt a prick of resentment. Bubba always managed to disappear whenever Pa was on the warpath. Not that she faulted him. But she wished that just once he'd stay to share the blame with her. "It's safe. Pa went outside."

Bubba released his breath in a sigh of relief. He pulled a chair away from the table and straddled it. "Sam really popped you a good one, didn't he?"

Going to the sink, Lauren covered the drain and began working the pump handle. "Yeah, well, it's real easy to beat up on someone half your size." She winced as she glanced in her father's shaving mirror over the sink. Sam Luttrell sure hadn't done her any favors. An ugly black and purple bruise completely encircled her left eye. Her bottom lip was split. And she could swear that her nose, in spite of Alec MacKenzie's assurances that it wasn't broken, canted to one side.

"Why'd you have to throw that can at him?" Bubba asked. "You could have just let him ride off."

"Because he called us trash, that's why. We might not be rich like Mr. Dandridge, but that doesn't make us trash. And he said Pa was stealing Diamond Cross calves."

"That's crazy! Pa's no cattle rustler!"

"You know that, and I know that, but all Sam Luttrell knows is that the fastest way to get a man hanged around here, short of calling him a horse thief, is to accuse him of stealing cattle. But that's not important. We have another problem on our hands." Lauren's voice dropped to little more than a whisper. "That new fellow, MacKenzie? He's putting up fences."

"Fences!"

"Shhh! I don't want Pa to hear." Lauren glanced at the doorway, half expecting to see their father standing there. "I heard him talking to Mr. Edrich. He's having a load of wire delivered from Tucson. A big load. And he's looking to hire extra men just to help with the job."

"You think he'll fence off Six-shooter Canyon?"

"It's on his property."

"But that's the best grazing land in the valley! Pa's gonna be mad as a hornet."

"He's going to be more than that. Bubba, we can't survive if Mr. MacKenzie fences off that canyon. The only decent grass on the Bar-T is in that meadow we cut for winter feed."

"What are we gonna do?"

"What we're *not* going to do is tell Pa. You know how he gets. He'll go over to MacKenzie's and raise a ruckus, and probably wind up getting himself shot."

"It's gonna be awful hard keeping it from him once them postholes start getting dug."

"Promise me you won't say anything. I don't want Pa upset."

Bubba waved her aside. "You worry too much, Coop."

"Bubba!"

"All right, I promise!"

By the time dinner was on the table and the hired hands trooped into the house, Frank Cooper's temper had abated little. "It's about time," he complained as he propped his crutches against the wall and lowered himself into the chair at the head of the table. "A man could starve around here just waiting for a decent meal."

Lauren bit her tongue. It was useless arguing with Pa when he was like this, and she'd already angered him enough for one day.

"That sure is a walloping bruise you got there," Bernie Wintz said as he helped himself to the green beans. "I hope you gave Sam Luttrell a souvenir of his own."

Feeling her father's disapproving gaze on her, Lauren gave Bernie a sheepish half smile, but said nothing.

"You should've gone to the sheriff," Cal Hoagland said. "The only reason Luttrell keeps getting away with these stunts is because everyone is too scared of him to—"

"You leave the sheriff out of this," Frank interrupted. "I don't want the law out here snooping around and asking a bunch of nosy questions."

Lauren saw Cal and Bernie exchange glances.

"I hear our new neighbor from over at the Williams place was in town today," Jimmy Smith said.

Bubba's face lit up. "Yeah, he broke up the fight between Coop and Luttrell. He talks funny too!"

Jimmy stopped with his fork halfway to his mouth. "What do you mean, he talks funny?"

"I don't know. Kinda like it's American, but it's not. Hell, ask Coop. She can tell you."

"Arch told me he's from Scotland," Cal said. "I wonder if he's with one of them big English cattle companies like that Mountain States Corporation that bought up all the land east of Pinal."

"If he is," Frank said, "he'll have a fight on his hands. No damned foreigner is going to get away with coming in here and taking over our land."

"Maybe we should go pay him a visit," Jimmy suggested. "Find out what he's up to."

"I don't want any trouble," Frank warned.

Jimmy speared a slice of ham with his fork and lifted it to his plate. "There won't be no trouble. We'll just have a look around. See what he's doing with the Williams place."

"What we need to be doing," Cal reminded him, "is hiring extra hands to help with the roundup. If we wait too long like we did last year, Dandridge is doing to get all the good hands before anyone else has a chance to—"

"No."

Everyone turned to stare at Frank.

"No?" Cal asked. Cal Hoagland was the ranch foreman. He and Bernie and Jimmy were the only permanent employees. Extra hands were hired only when needed, usually for the spring roundup.

"We're not hiring anyone from the outside this year," Frank said tersely. "Bubba's old enough now to pull a man's load, and Coop can get her tail out there and earn her keep. We'll make do."

Bubba's eyes widened. "You mean I can get out of school?"

Frank glowered at his son. "Shut up and eat."

Cal frowned into his coffee mug. "Frank, there's a good five hundred head of cattle in them hills. Even with the young'uns helping out, we'll need at least two more men."

"I said, we'll make do," Frank snapped.

"Pa, you can't take Bubba out of school," Lauren said. "He's almost caught up to where he should be. If he falls behind again, Mr. Gates will set him back a grade."

Beneath the table, Lauren barely had time to jerk her leg out of the way before Bubba's foot connected with her shin. She glared at her brother. Bubba stuck out his tongue.

"Bubba's wasted enough time at that school," Frank said. "He can read and write and do sums. That's all he needs to know. Right now, the roundup is more important. Besides, he's going to be taking over this place someday. It's time he learned how to run it."

Lauren stared at her father in disbelief. She could not believe her ears. Before Mama died, she had made Pa promise that Bubba would finish school. He had *promised*.

Frank started to refill his coffee cup and realized the pot was empty. He gave his daughter a look of exasperation. "What are you gawking at? Don't just sit there. Go put another pot on."

Lauren opened her mouth to plead with Pa not to let Bubba drop out of school, but Frank's hard gaze bored into her, and the words died in her throat. Mumbling a hasty "Yes, sir," she pushed her chair away from the table and took the blue enameled coffeepot into the kitchen.

She should have said something while she had the chance, she thought as she filled the pot with fresh water. Even if Pa hadn't made that promise to Mama, it would be a mistake to let Bubba quit school. Ranching was no longer an uneducated man's business. Ever since wealthy ranchers like Martin Dandridge began upgrading their stock with Hereford and Brahman bulls, the buyers had stopped paying good money for scrub *corriente* cattle. Nowadays, a man had to know about things like crossbreeding and marketing and veterinary medicine. If Bubba was going to compete with the likes of Martin Dandridge and Alec MacKenzie, he needed to finish school, maybe even go on to the university. Otherwise, Bubba was going to find himself struggling like Pa, year after year, with nothing to show for his hard work except a mountain of debts and a few acres of overgrazed range land.

Or worse, Lauren thought dismally, he could turn into a shiftless troublemaker like Sam Luttrell.

There was a loud scraping of chairs on the floorboards in the dining room. Then Lauren heard Cal say, "Uh, oh. Here comes trouble."

Putting down the coffeepot, she went to the sink and pulled back the corner of the curtain to look out the kitchen window.

The air froze in her lungs.

Three men were riding their horses up to the house: Martin Dandridge; his son, Eliot; and Sam Luttrell.

Chapter 2

Frank and Bubba and the hired hands went out onto the front porch. The riders reined in their horses. "Good afternoon," Martin Dandridge called out.

Frank leaned on his crutches. "'Afternoon, Martin. What brings you out this way?" In spite of his welcoming greeting, suspicion showed in his narrowed eyes.

"I won't beat around the bush, Frank. Your new neighbor, MacKenzie, came to see me today. He told me about the trouble my boy and Sam here caused for your daughter."

Eliot Dandridge shifted uneasily in the saddle.

"I want you to know, Frank," Martin continued, "that whatever our differences, I won't stand for the kind of behavior MacKenzie witnessed from these two. That's why they've come to apologize to her. Is she here?"

Frank turned his head and yelled over his shoulder, "Coop, get your tail out here!"

Lauren, who had been standing in the hall, just out of sight of the doorway, listening to the exchange, swore silently. *That blasted foreigner!* Didn't he know how to mind his own business? Maybe they did things differently where he came from, but here a man knew to stay out of another man's fight. Now she wouldn't be able to ride anywhere without having to worry about Sam Luttrell waiting to jump her. Taking a deep breath, she went out onto the porch.

Martin's mouth thinned when he saw the bruises on Lauren's face. "You do that?" he demanded of Sam.

"She asked for it."

"Answer my question!"

Revenge sparkled in Sam's dark eyes as he met Lauren's accusing gaze. "Yeah, I did it."

Martin muttered a curse under his breath. "Damn it, Luttrell, one of these days you're going to push me too far." He jerked his head toward the house. "Get down," he ordered. "Both of you."

Eliot dismounted and stood awkwardly by his horse. Sam reluctantly followed.

"Well, what are you waiting for?" Martin barked.

The men removed two one-hundred-pound sacks of flour and a sack of cornmeal from the backs of their horses and carried them to the porch.

"We're replacing the supplies you lost," Martin said. "I've also made it clear to these two that they're to keep their distance from your daughter."

Sam and Eliot started to return to their horses.

"Where in the hell do you think you're going?" Martin snapped. "You're not through yet."

Dragging their feet, Sam and Eliot returned to stand in front of Lauren. Eliot removed his hat. He avoided Lauren's gaze. "I'm sorry, Miss

Cooper, about the trouble Sam and me caused you. It won't happen again."

Lauren started to tell him that it was all right, to forget about it, but she bit her tongue. It *wasn't* all right. Furthermore, she knew that Eliot's promise that it wouldn't happen again would last only until they were out of Martin Dandridge's sight.

"Luttrell," Martin bit out.

"Sorry," Sam mumbled.

"Luttrell!"

Sam flashed his employer an angry glance, then turned back to Lauren. "I'm sorry for the trouble I caused you." His wooden tone belied the venomous look in his eyes.

Lauren's stomach knotted, and she glanced away. She had seen that look before and she knew what it meant.

Frank glared at her. "What's wrong with you, girl? These men came to make their apologies. The least you can do is show some manners."

Lauren swallowed her resentment. "Apology accepted," she mumbled ungraciously, not looking at the men. She could not help but feel that she was being turned into the villain here. Pa sure wouldn't be so quick to forgive if he'd been the one to get his face ground into the dirt.

Sam and Eliot mounted their horses.

"If these two give you any more trouble, Frank," Martin said, "I want to know about it."

The three men rode away.

Cal chuckled. "For a minute there, I thought Dandridge was going to make them boys get down on their knees."

Bernie hitched up his suspenders. "Would've served them right if he had. Well, I need to get back to mending the corral fences." He nudged Bubba. "Lend me a hand, kid."

Bubba trotted close on the older man's heels. His eager voice drifted across the yard as they headed toward the corral. "Bernie, do you think Pa will let me go on the drive this year?"

Cal hoisted a sack of flour onto his shoulder. "Show me where you want these, Coop. Jimmy and me, we'll carry them into the house for you. Jimmy, grab one of them sacks."

Lauren held open the screen door. "Thanks. I appreciate the help."

A grin split Jimmy's weathered face from ear to ear. "Figured it's the least we can do for the only person in the valley brave enough to clobber Sam Luttrell with a can of peaches."

"Fool enough, you mean," Cal said as he carried the flour into the house. "You stay away from him, Coop. That boy is trouble, plain and simple." He shook his head. "Can't get over that MacKenzie fella going to Dandridge. The man's barely had time to get the traveling creases out of his clothes, and already he's made an enemy of Luttrell. Now, if it had been up to me, I would have made sure something happened to Sam on his way home some night when he least expected it. And I sure as hell wouldn't let him know who done it."

If Alec MacKenzie doesn't quit interfering where he's not wanted, Lauren thought, something is liable to happen to *him* on the way home one night.

After Cal and Jimmy had stored the sacks in the pantry and gone back outside, Lauren put on the coffee. As she filled the washbasin with water at the sink pump, she pushed her anger at Alec MacKenzie to the back of her mind and tried to concentrate on how she was going to approach her father about Bubba. Frank Cooper didn't set much store by schooling, having dropped out himself halfway through the sixth grade, and he had never understood his wife's insistence that both their children get as much of an education as possible. As far as he was concerned, he'd done just fine without it. He couldn't see that times had changed since he was a boy.

Frank was sitting at the table alone when Lauren carried the coffeepot into the dining room. She stopped short, her stomach clenching at the sight of the opened bottle of whiskey on the table and the glass in her father's hand. It had been a good two weeks since he'd had a drink. She had hoped the dry spell would last longer this time. Taking care not to make a sound, she turned and tiptoed back into the kitchen. When Pa started drinking, it was best to stay out of his way.

Alec knew when he was cornered. And he knew he had no chance of escaping gracefully. His mouth breaking into a wide smile, he clicked his heels together and bowed slightly at the waist. "Madam, I would be delighted to join you and your friends for luncheon."

Arminta Larson beamed. "We've been meaning to welcome you to Millerville long before this, but you're a hard man to track down, Mr. MacKenzie. Isn't he, ladies?"

Four heads nodded vigorously in agreement.

They were standing in front of the Wells Fargo Bank. Alec was certain the women had been lying in wait for him while he was inside the bank conducting his business; they had pounced on him the instant he exited the building. "I do have an enterprise to run, as well as numerous stockholders to answer to. I must keep busy lest my investors begin to fear I am squandering their money."

A murmur rippled through the group. "Investors?" Arminta made a show of patting her upswept coiffure to assure that every glossy black strand was in place. "It sounds so *important*. You must tell us all about it. Amy writes the social column for the *Millerville Gazette*. I'm sure she would love to do a piece on—"

Arminta broke off, then continued breathlessly, "Oh, I do forget my manners. Mr. MacKenzie, allow me to introduce my fellow officers in the Millerville Women's Junior League. This is Amy Taylor. She's the vice president. As I was saying, Mr. MacKenzie, Amy writes for the *Gazette*. She could do an article on you as a way of introducing you to everyone in the valley. But we can discuss that later."

Amy Taylor was a plump, pink-cheeked woman who appeared to be in her mid-thirties. She giggled when Alec bent over her outstretched hand.

"I'm pleased to meet you, madam."

"And this is Martha Sikes, our treasurer."

Alec recognized Martha, or rather, the wispy brown hair that refused to stay pinned in the knot at her nape. Martha had come out onto the front porch of the boarding house the day he had ridden into town to inquire after his order of fencing wire and ended up breaking up a fight in the middle of Main Street. Martha's cheeks were two bright spots of color, and she refused to meet his eyes when the other women gave her a tiny shove forward. Alec noticed that she was not wearing a wedding ring. He wondered if a bit of matchmaking was going on here.

"This is Meredith Tribble, our secretary, and Cissy Page, who is in charge of fund-raisers." Arminta glanced at her watch. "Oh, my, we are going to be late if we don't hurry, and I don't want to lose our reservations. Have you had the opportunity to dine at the Silver Nugget Hotel, Mr. MacKenzie?"

"No, madam, I have not."

"Well, you are in for a real treat. The Silver Nugget serves up the finest dishes in the county. And it is so hard to get reservations when you want them. We had requested a table for six, but Caroline Magruder, who helps Cissy with the fund-raisers, wasn't able to be here, so it was such a lucky thing we ran in to you in town today."

Lucky for whom? Alec wondered, his expression guarded. Still, this luncheon might prove to be worth his time after all, he told himself. People loved most to talk about themselves. After that, they loved most talking about each other. If he played his hand right, he could learn a great deal about the residents of Millerville while divulging relatively little about himself. He bent his arm toward Arminta. "Let it not be said, madam, that I caused you to lose your table," he said cheerfully. "Shall we?"

Arminta turned twenty shades of red as she put her hand on Alec's elbow. "By all means, Mr. MacKenzie. Ladies?"

Standing on the corner of Broad and Willow streets, the three-storied Silver Nugget Hotel was a handsome sandstone and marble relic of grander times, when Millerville was a boomtown with a shiny future, before it became apparent that the valley's economy would be built on cattle rather than silver. Crystal chandeliers hung from the vaulted ceiling of the paneled dining room, and the linen-draped tables were adorned with costly displays of hothouse orchids.

As Alec perused the menu, he noticed that he and his party seemed to be drawing an inordinate amount of attention. "Is it my imagination," he asked offhandedly, "or are we being stared at?"

As if on cue, five feminine heads turned at once. The two gentlemen seated at the next table, caught staring, suddenly looked away.

"Oh, them," Arminta said, a note of disgust in her voice as she turned back around. "That's Clyde Croswell and his son, Norman. They own the lumber mill over near Patagonia. Norman married Jenny Buchanan last summer, and he wasn't at all pleased about being forced into it." Her voice dropped conspiratorially. "The baby was born six months after the wedding."

"Minta!" Cissy Page looked horrified. "Mr. MacKenzie is going to think we are a bunch of gossips." She turned to Alec. "We really are involved in worthwhile projects, Mr. MacKenzie. In fact, just last month, we raised enough money to send one of our town's brightest young men to the university. He is going to become a doctor and return here to take over Dr. Blakely's practice when Dr. Blakely retires. Of course, there is one fund-raiser for the new firehouse that you might be able to help us with, Mr. MacKenzie . . ."

Throughout the luncheon, Alec found himself dodging both questions about himself and commitments to any of the many charitable endeavors sponsored by the Millerville Women's Junior League. He agreed to attend the town's Fourth of July celebration after Martha Sikes blushingly informed him that he could bring a guest; he was very careful not to say anything that might give Martha the mistaken idea that she was to be his chosen guest. "My sister and her husband will be visiting then," he said noncommittally. "Perhaps I will bring them."

"I hope Sam Luttrell doesn't cause any trouble this year," Amy Taylor said. "Last year, he blew up the fireworks display while everyone was watching the parade. We thought there had been an explosion at the mine."

"Ah, yes. Sam Luttrell," Alec said. "The man who engaged in a bout of fisticuffs with a young lady in the middle of Main Street a couple of weeks ago."

Arminta rolled her eyes. "Lauren Cooper is no lady, Mr. MacKenzie. Trouble asking for trouble is what she is. I wish just once someone would take that girl in tow and show her the proper way to dress."

"It's not the child's fault she has nothing decent to wear," Meredith Tribble piped up in Lauren's defense. "I feel sorry for her, stuck out there on that run-down ranch, trying to do right by her brother as well as take care of an invalid father."

Arminta snorted. "If Frank Cooper is an invalid, he has only himself to blame. He was drunk when that horse threw him. He's lucky he wasn't killed. But that Lauren, now, she's trouble in the making, running around in men's pants and *swearing*. I've never heard anything the likes of what comes out of that girl's mouth. Alice Donovan used to pray Lauren would quit school. She couldn't control her. Lauren was always disrupting the class. She stuck a piece of taffy on my Harold's chair, and it got all over the seat of his new trousers. Now, if Mr. Pruitt had been teaching then, he would not have hesitated to take a switch to that girl, and not let her get so out of hand."

"Oh, Minta, that was years ago," Cissy admonished. "Lauren was just a child, and your Harold was no angel himself."

Arminta looked flustered. "Well, there's no denying that the Coopers have been nothing but a blight on this town, what with Frank and his drinking, and Frank, Jr., following right in his footsteps. Why, just last Saturday, Alma and I saw that boy trying to steal cigars from Hawthorne's Drugstore."

None of the Coopers seemed to have endeared themselves to their neighbors, Alec thought. He had not seen Lauren since the day of the fight between her and Sam Luttrell, but he certainly had not forgotten her. Judging from the reactions of the individuals in Millerville whom he had met thus far, it would appear that Lauren Cooper made a lasting impression on all whose lives she touched.

No one escaped being pricked by the rose's thorns.

Two and a half hours later, Alec managed to extricate himself from the clutches of the Millerville Junior Women's League and slip into the Shady Lady Saloon for a brief respite before going home.

Jack Corrigan greeted him with a knowing grin. "How was lunch?"

Alec placed a bank note on the bar. "News travels fast," he said dryly.

Jack chuckled. "It always does around here." He opened a bottle of Scotch and poured Alec a glass.

Two more men entered the saloon. They nodded at Alec, then went to the other end of the bar. "How about a cold one, Jack?" One of the men called out.

"Coming right up."

Alec took a drink of the whiskey and looked

at the painting over the bar. The woman reclining on the chaise had a generous, shapely figure, an abundance of lustrous red hair, and full red lips. There was no slyness in her dark doe eyes, but neither was there any trace of youthful innocence. The artist had perfectly captured the expression of someone who had experienced a great deal of living without becoming embittered by it. She was the kind of woman who could satisfy both a man's body and his soul, but would never allow herself to be owned by him.

His gaze drifted to the rose tattoo on her hip, and he smiled as the memory of guileless blue eyes widening in surprise flickered through his thoughts.

A throaty voice broke through his musings. "Do you appreciate fine art, Mr. MacKenzie?"

Alec turned. Across the saloon, seated at one of the tables, was a handsome woman. He was surprised he had not seen her when he came into the saloon. She was modestly attired in a teal-colored riding skirt and fitted jacket, but there was nothing demure about the assessing gaze that she fixed on him. Recognition dispelled his frown of puzzlement. It was the red hair, carefully dressed in stylish curls, that gave her away. He raised his glass to her. "I appreciate beauty," he corrected.

The woman smiled and inclined her head, graciously accepting the compliment.

Unrelieved longings reminded Alec that he had gone too many months without a woman.

Carrying his glass, he crossed the saloon. "May I join you?"

She motioned toward a chair. "By all means, Mr. MacKenzie."

Alec pulled out a chair and sat down. "You have me at a disadvantage, madam. You know who I am, but I'm afraid I can't return the courtesy."

"That's easily corrected. I'm Chloe Roberts."

"Chloe Roberts," Alec repeated. Up close, the woman looked older than she did in the painting. There were fine lines at the corners of her kohl-enchanced eyes, and the skin around her mouth had lost its suppleness. Still, her hair was naturally red, and she had an enviable figure. She was a fine-looking woman. He motioned to Jack Corrigan, then nodded toward the painting over the bar. "May I ask how you came to occupy the place of honor?"

Chloe chuckled. "I donated the painting," she said. Her voice was deep and pleasant. "It's good for business."

Alec regarded her through narrowed eyes. "For the saloon?"

She smiled meaningfully. "And for me."

Jack came over to the table.

Alec looked at Chloe. "What are you drinking?"

"Same thing you are."

"Bring us a bottle," Alec told Jack.

"Oh, hell. How'd you get caught in there?" Lauren dismounted and walked over to the white-faced calf that was trapped in a patch of prickly pear.

"Where's your mama, little fella?" she asked. Shielding her eyes from the sun with her hand, she peered across the pasture where scattered cattle were peacefully grazing on the young spring grass.

Unable to move, the calf eyed her woefully and bleated.

"All right, all right. I'll get you out." Lauren shook her head. "For the life of me, I can't see how you got in there in the first place."

She retrieved a rope from her horse. She wished she had a machete or some other knife, but the rope would have to do.

She tied a slipknot in one end of the rope, then looped it over the top of one of the cacti and pulled it tight. While she worked, she talked softly to the calf so he wouldn't spook.

Bracing herself, she pulled hard.

The cactus moved only slightly.

Swearing under her breath, Lauren tried again. The calf's bawling shook her confidence. She feared he would panic and lunge into the prickly pear spines.

Suddenly there was a loud *snap,* and she staggered backward as the cactus broke away.

The calf bawled louder.

"Hush, fella. It'll be all right." Lauren yanked the broken prickly pear out of the way and bent down to loosen the rope.

"Need help, lass?"

Fear exploded in her chest. She shot upright

and whirled around. Alec MacKenzie was sitting on his horse only a few yards away.

Relief, then anger, surged through her. "You scared the hell out of me. Don't you know better than to sneak up on someone like that?"

"I thought you saw me. I waved to you."

"If I'd seen you, I wouldn't have jumped halfway out of my skin," Lauren retorted.

Amusement twinkled in Alec's eyes. "*Touché.*"

Annoyed that he should be enjoying himself at her expense, Lauren bristled. "What does that mean?" she demanded.

"It means, lass, that you have a valid point."

She eyed him warily, skeptical of his explanation. Her nerves remained on edge as he dismounted and walked toward her.

He was taller than she remembered, his strides more forceful, more confident. He was not wearing a coat. His white shirt was open at the neck, and his sleeves were rolled up, revealing forearms that were tanned and sinewy and covered with red-gold hair. The memory of those strong arms around her, holding her, returned full force, causing her pulse to quicken. She glanced away before he could see the rush of color to her face.

Alec removed a knife from the leather sheath he carried on his belt. "I'll help you cut him loose."

Lauren unthinkingly took a step backward, then caught herself, both annoyed and perplexed by her reaction to him. She glanced at his face to see if he had noticed her jumpy retreat. If he did, he gave no sign. Some of the tension left her, but not all. She still remained edgy and disturbingly aware of his presence.

Alec hunkered down next to the prickly pear. He eased his hand into the thorny tangle and began slicing through the fleshy cacti with the knife.

Lauren fidgeted. "What can I do?"

"Nothing, yet," he said over his shoulder. "Just stay out of the way in case this falls."

Not certain whether she was more annoyed or relieved that he had taken over the task of freeing the calf, Lauren stood awkwardly to one side while Alec worked.

The day was unusually hot for so early in the season. Lauren squinted up at the sun, feeling its warmth on her face. The distinctive chatter of a cactus wren disturbed the stillness. A bee buzzed past her, then returned to hover around her head. She slapped it away.

Sweat caused Alec's shirt to cling to his back in a long vee between his shoulders. Lauren stared at the spot, then at his broad back, mesmerized by the flexing muscles beneath the fabric. Her heart began to hammer. She nervously moistened her lips. He's just a man, she reminded herself. Flesh and blood, bone and sinew, and . . . and . . . something else. Something she could not define, but which affected her deeply nonetheless. Her gaze drifted down his back to the place where his shirt was tucked into his jeans, then lower, over his buttocks, and something warm and unsettling quivered in the pit of her stomach.

She shifted uncomfortably, not realizing until

she did so that she had been pressing her legs together in a futile attempt to repress the hot ache that had begun to pulse at the very core of her being. She squeezed her eyes shut and fought to regain control. "Oh, God," she whispered.

"What's wrong?" Alec asked.

Her eyes flew open. "Nothing," she said quickly. Too quickly. Her face flamed. Surely she hadn't spoken aloud?

Alec cast her a curious glance. He pulled a large section of prickly pear away from the thicket. "Take this," he ordered. "Don't stick yourself."

Relieved to finally have something to occupy both her hands and her mind, Lauren jumped to do his bidding. She gingerly picked up the cactus and dragged it out of the way, then returned for the next section that Alec had cut free.

Within minutes, an opening gaped in the stand of prickly pear. The calf bolted from his thorny prison and lumbered across the pasture toward the herd.

Alec straightened, returning the knife to its sheath.

Feeling more awkward and self-conscious than ever, Lauren brushed her hands on her pants and feigned nonchalance as she looked out across the valley. She couldn't bring herself to look at him; she didn't *dare* look at him. "Thanks," she mumbled stiffly.

"We're neighbors, lass. I would expect the same in return."

There was a peculiar tightness in Lauren's

chest that refused to go away. "Ordinarily, I would agree with you," she said, still avoiding his gaze. "Unfortunately, your help has a way of turning sour on me. I'd be obliged if you just left me alone in the future." Her voice wavered.

She picked up her rope and started toward her horse, but Alec caught her arm, stopping her. "Whoa, lass. Not so fast. What are you talking about?"

The feel of his hand on her arm sent a jolt of awareness through her. She jerked out of his grasp and met his penetrating gaze with a look that was part defensive, part defiant. "I'm talking about your visit to the Diamond Cross. Do you have any idea how much trouble you've created for me?"

For a moment they just stood there, their eyes locked in silent battle, an undeniable energy charging the air between them. If he touched her again, Lauren thought she might explode.

"What happened?" he asked.

Attributing the impulse to vanity, Lauren resisted the temptation to cover the fading remains of her blackened eye with her hand. "What happened is that Martin Dandridge made his son and Sam Luttrell apologize to me."

"Good."

"Good?" Her eyes widened in disbelief. "Mr. MacKenzie, he *made* them apologize. And they're not going to forget it!"

"Nor would they forget getting away with their crime. And that, lass, is a far more dangerous prospect."

Inwardly, Lauren knew he was right, but she

was not about to admit it. "What I'm trying to explain is that I don't want you interfering in matters that don't concern you. I appreciate your help with the calf, and I suppose I also appreciate your pulling Sam off of me, but that's where it has to end. Out here, a man fights his own battles."

A muscle in Alec's cheek knotted. His gaze traveled suggestively down the length of her, lingering where decorum dictated it should not, then returned to capture hers. "And a woman, Lauren?" he asked softly, his accented voice as smoothly seductive as whiskey and cream. "Is she also expected to fight her own battles?"

Lauren stared at him, her gaze locked so tightly with his that she felt as if she were caught in a trap. No one had ever looked at her like that before, or had such a devastating effect on her sensibilities. Every one of her instincts told her to get the hell out of there before she did something utterly foolish, not because she didn't know better, but because she couldn't help herself. "I have to get home," she said shakily.

"I'll escort you."

"No!" Realizing how sharply she had spoken, she hastened to explain. "It's not a good time. I have a mountain of chores to do to get ready for the roundup. Besides, Pa's not in the best of moods." She bit down on her bottom lip, acutely aware that Pa's moods were none of Alec's business.

He did not press her. "As you wish," he said,

his even tone betraying nothing of what he was thinking.

Lauren coiled her rope and hung it from her saddle horn. She could feel Alec watching her as she mounted her horse. Taking a steadying breath, she forced herself to meet his disarming gaze. "Good day, Mr. MacKenzie."

His eyes never left her face. He inclined his head. "Good day, lass."

Lauren dug her heels into the gelding's sides. She did not slow down until she was well out of Alec MacKenzie's sight.

She could not stop shaking. For as long as she lived, she would never forget the way he had looked at her, as if he were undressing her with his eyes. His gaze had been as tangible as a touch, the memory of it causing her skin to tingle as his words, hauntingly suggestive, echoed in her mind. *And a woman, Lauren? Is she also expected to fight her own battles?*

"You're crazy," she muttered, trying to calm herself by speaking aloud. "It's all in your imagination. What man in full possession of his faculties would be interested in you?"

She was halfway home before it occurred to her to wonder where he had learned her name.

On foot, Grady Wright from the Diamond Cross led his horse up the side of the mountain. Five more hands formed a single line behind him, each man holding on to the tail of the horse in front of him. Lauren brought up the rear. Like the others, she gripped the tail of the horse ahead of her, letting the animal pull her up the steep incline while she led her own horse by its bridle. She slipped on the rocky ground, but quickly regained her footing and kept climbing.

The spring roundup was one of the few occasions when the local ranchers worked together, rather than in competition with each other. In the morning, riders combed the hills, searching out cattle. In the afternoons, the calves would be marked with their mothers' brands and the unbranded strays would be divided up among those ranches that took part. Evenings usually found the tired cowboys gathered around the chuck wagons, playing poker or monte, and stretching the limits of credibility as each tried to top the others' tall tales.

Nothing more had been said about Bubba staying in school, and Lauren had not dared broach the subject again. He had gone to school on Monday, but had left in the middle of the morning after being reprimanded for throwing spitballs. It weighed heavily on Lauren's conscience that he was not likely to return, but she felt powerless to do anything about it. He was down at the main camp now, guarding the saddle horses and packhorses.

When the incline leveled out, the hands remounted their horses. "Harden, I want you and O'Reilly to go east," Grady instructed. "T.J. and Coop, you head south. Ramon, you stick with me. T.J., when you head up Six-shooter, keep an eye out for those mustangs Ruiz saw."

Those were the only orders given. Each person knew what was expected of him. Tucking her braids up beneath her hat so her hair wouldn't snag on the mesquite thorns, Lauren rode after Thomas Jefferson Powell, known as T.J., who worked for Jim Lassiter over in Cochise County.

It wasn't long before they spotted the strays. Most of the steers were young, less than three years old, and had ventured up into the hills for the fresh young grass that sprouted as soon as the weather started warming in early spring. Lauren removed her coiled rope from around her saddle horn.

T.J. spoke over his shoulder at the same time that he motioned with his hand. "You go that way, and I'll go around here." A rebel yell tearing from his throat, T.J. spurred his horse.

Lauren headed in the opposite direction, yelling and smacking the coiled rope against the creosote bushes and scrub oak as she rode by. The object was not to capture the strays, but to drive them down into the valley, where they would be roped, and the mavericks branded. At that time, any young males not selected to be used as range bulls would also be castrated. In the fall, the roundup would be repeated, only this time the adult steers, the three- and four-year-olds, would be driven to markets in Tucson.

The sun was high when T.J. and Lauren stopped to rest. They had been working the brush since dawn. T.J. removed his hat and dragged his sleeve across his forehead. His hair was drenched with sweat and plastered to his head. He squinted across the valley. "Take a look at that. MacKenzie doesn't waste any time."

Lauren looked in the direction he pointed. Sure enough, along the arroyo that marked the northwest boundary of Alec MacKenzie's land, fence posts had been erected. The wire hadn't been strung yet, but once it was, they would be denied access to Six-shooter Canyon.

She hadn't seen Alec since the day he had helped her rescue the calf, but she hadn't been able to stop thinking about him. She could not dispel the image of intense brown eyes that seemed capable of probing her secrets, or forget the rough-gentle feel of his hands on her skin, or the sheer strength in his powerful arms.

Even sleep provided no relief. The past two nights, she had jerked awake from dreams she could not remember, her body drenched and her heart racing and a smoldering ache between her thighs. She knew instinctively that Alec had been there, in her deepest thoughts, invading even her dreams.

Hoping T.J. didn't sense how nervous talking about Alec made her, she said offhandedly, "Bernie said he heard in town the other day that MacKenzie is buying up a lot of land along the San Pedro River. Do you think he'll fence that in too?"

"More'n likely he'll hold on to it a year or so, then sell it. There's been talk about expanding the railroad down that way. If that happens, he should be able to turn a pretty profit." T.J. wet his bandana with water from his canteen and used it to mop his neck. "I haven't seen any sign of those mustangs Grady was talking about. Have you?"

Lauren sat down on a rocky outcropping and uncapped her own canteen. "None at all. Do you want to go up into the canyon and look for them?"

"Might as well. I don't think we're going to find many more strays down here. And this might be our last chance to ride up there before MacKenzie fences it off."

A small seasonal creek ran through Six-shooter Canyon. During the summer, it was either bone-dry or a raging torrent, depending on how much rain fell in the mountains. In the spring, though, it was a steady trickle that flowed clear and cold through the wooded ravine. Towering cottonwoods, their pale green leaves providing a startling contrast to the darker green of the surrounding oaks, formed a broad canopy over the creek, turning it into a refuge for man and beast alike. A tingle of fear raced down Lauren's spine. It was here that the cougar had jumped one of their seasonal hires, nearly killing him.

T.J. dismounted and hunkered down by the water. "See that?" he said, indicating the tracks. "The mustangs have been here. Probably as late as yesterday. Looks like they headed upstream."

Lauren pushed back her hat and looked around. "It's quiet up here," she said. Her voice sounded unnaturally loud. Even the birds seemed to have been silenced. The only sound to break the stillness was the gurgling of the water as it skimmed over the pebbles in the creek bottom.

T.J. stood up. "Do you want to keep going?"

Lauren shrugged. "I'm game if you are." She felt uneasy, but if T.J. thought it was safe, then it probably was.

They rode for another hour, following the clearly marked trail across the high pasture where the cattle could always find good grass even in midsummer—grass that would no longer be available if Alec fenced off access to the canyon—and higher into the mountains. The air was much cooler here. The juniper and piñon that dominated the lower slopes gave way to dense stands of ponderosa pine, which blocked out the sunlight and carpeted the ground with a thick layer of long needles that obscured the trail they were trying to follow. Although she said nothing, several times Lauren felt the fine hairs on the back of her neck lift. She could not shake the eerie feeling that they were being watched.

Finally, T.J. reined in his horse. Motioning to her to be silent, he pointed.

Lauren's breath caught in her throat.

There must have been more than a hundred and fifty outlaw horses in the herd—horses that would bring a good price on the open market. They were standing in a clearing, peacefully grazing, unaware that they were being watched. The leader of the herd, a black stallion, lifted his head as though he'd caught a scent. He stood unmoving for several minutes, then went back to eating.

Lauren slowly released her breath.

"We're going to need help," T.J. whispered. "I

want you to go back and find Grady while I slip around to the other side and see what I can do to block their escape up the canyon."

Lauren nervously moistened her lips. By the time she got down to the camp and back, it would be dark. They would have to round up the horses in the pitch-black. Up here, that could be dangerous. "It'll be night soon," she said. "Maybe we should come back tomorrow."

T.J. shook his head. "I don't want to take a chance on someone like Luttrell claiming these. At least Grady is fair. He'll divide the herd evenly."

Lauren didn't know why she felt so uneasy. It wasn't as if they still had to worry about Chiricahua Apaches hiding out in the hills. It was probably safer now than it had ever been. "I'll be back as soon as I can," she said. "You be careful. And don't try corralling that herd by yourself."

"Don't worry. I won't do anything stupid. I'm keeping an eye on that big stallion though. I want him for myself."

Moving slowly so she wouldn't startle the mustangs, Lauren turned her horse and headed back down the slope in the direction they had come.

She had not gone more than a hundred yards when a gunshot rang out, spooking her horse. She gripped the reins and fought to get the gelding back under control. The thunder of hooves as the mustangs took flight filled the canyon with its horrible roar. *"T.J.!"* she yelled, but her voice was smothered in the din of the stampeding herd.

Digging her knees into the gelding's sides, she urged him back up the hill. "T.J.! Do you hear me?"

When she reached him, she leapt from the saddle. His horse was gone and he was lying facedown on the ground. Kneeling beside him, she grabbed his shoulder and rolled him over. "T.J.?" Panic quivered in her voice. His eyes were closed and a crimson stain was spreading rapidly across the front of his shirt from the bullet hole in his chest.

Chapter 3

"T.J., for crying out loud, don't you dare die on me!"

T.J. groaned and a grimace of pain distorted his face. "Son of a . . . bitch . . . shot me," he choked out.

"Did you see who it was?"

He shook his head. The effort cost him. His face was the soapy gray of wood ashes.

Lauren's heart thundered against her ribs. She nervously moistened her lips and glanced around. T.J.'s horse was gone, and she had to get him to a doctor. He was pumping blood—fast. Not knowing what else to do, she hastily removed her shirt, yanking the tails out of her pants with a vengeance. Her white cotton camisole, damp with sweat, clung to her skin. Pale gold freckles dusted her bare shoulders. "This isn't the cleanest thing in the world," she said as she turned the shirt inside out and folded it into a thick pillow, "but it's all we got."

T.J. made no protest as Lauren unbuttoned his shirt and tucked the makeshift compress between his shirt and his chest. For the second time in as many weeks, more blood than she was prepared to handle gushed over her fingers, and her stomach rebelled. Gritting her teeth, she pulled the front of T.J.'s shirt closed over the compress and fastened the buttons. It was a tight fit, but that was good. It would keep the compress from shifting and help stanch the flow of blood. Her hands trembled.

T.J. took several deep breaths and swallowed dryly. "You got . . . your canteen?"

Wiping her bloodied hands on her pants, Lauren went to her horse and retrieved her canteen. Uncapping it, she knelt beside T.J. and held it to his lips. He lifted his head, and she braced one hand beneath his neck to steady him while he drank. Finally, he lay back and closed his eyes. Some of the color had returned to his face and he was breathing easier. "I must've swallowed a pint of dust when I hit the ground," he joked feebly.

Lauren sat back on her heels, her brow furrowing as she noticed the lengthening shadows. There wasn't much daylight left. "MacKenzie's place isn't more than three or four miles from here as the crow files," she said. "If we can get you that far, I can ride into town for the doctor. Do you think you can mount my horse?"

"I can try."

After what seemed an eternity, Lauren managed to get T.J. into the saddle. She climbed up behind him.

The going was slow. With T.J. sitting in front of her, blocking her view, Lauren had to bite her tongue to keep from expressing her frustration at not being able to see where they were going. By the time they were down off the mountain, however, it no longer mattered. T.J. had lost consciousness and was slumped forward. It was all

Lauren could do to keep him from falling off the horse.

It was almost completely dark by the time they reached the end of the long drive leading up to the main house. The old *Valle Verde* sign that had hung over the gate for as long as Ned Williams owned the ranch had been replaced by a new one that read *Duneideann*. The bold letters that had been burnt into the raw pine were barely legible in the dusk.

Lights burned in the main house and in the bunkhouse. The remaining outbuildings were dark shadows against the surrounding hills. Lauren guided the gelding into the yard. Placing one hand alongside her mouth, she called out, "Hallo! Is anyone home? Hallooo!"

The front door of the main house swung open, and Lauren saw the tall figure of a man silhouetted against the light that spilled out into the yard. Somewhere else, a door slammed. Suddenly, the previously deserted yard was swarming with people.

"What the hell?"

Lauren recognized the speaker as Sly Barnes. Sly had worked as foreman for Ned Williams. She was surprised to see that he was still here.

"It's T.J. Powell," she said. "He's been shot." She slid off the horse's back and scampered out of the way as Sly and another man reached up and caught T.J. just as he started to topple. They eased him to the ground.

"What's going on here?"

Lauren whirled around at the sound of that deep, rich voice and found herself facing Alec

MacKenzie. In the darkness, she could feel his gaze burning into her, expertly dismantling her defenses. Instantly, her guard went up. She didn't trust him. Worse, she didn't trust herself when she was with him. He had a way of making her feel and say and do things that she otherwise wouldn't. "We were hunting strays up in Six-shooter Canyon," she said, deciding at the last second not to say anything about the mustangs. Since the canyon was on his land, he might decide the herd belonged to him. "Someone shot T.J. I don't know who. We didn't even get a look at him."

Alec barked an order to his men. "Take him into the house. There is a spare bedroom at the top of the stairs. Second door on the left."

"Be careful with him," Lauren worried aloud as they bent to lift the wounded man. "He's lost a lot of blood." As the men carried T.J. toward the house, she gathered the gelding's reins and put her foot in the stirrup.

"Just where do you think you're going, lass?"

"To get Doc Blakely."

"You'll stay here. It's too dangerous for a lass to be out and about after dark."

"Don't be ridiculous. I've lived in this valley all my life. I could find my way to town blindfolded."

"I'm sure you could. However, I'll send someone else into town for the doctor." Before Lauren could object, Alec gripped her elbow, preventing her from mounting her horse, and turned to one of his hired hands, who had come out from the bunkhouse to see what all the fuss was about. "I want you to ride into town, Simms, and fetch both the doctor and the sheriff. Tell them a man has been shot."

"Yes, sir."

As Simms hurried off to do his employer's bidding, Alec gave further instructions for Lauren's horse to be rubbed down and watered. Still holding her elbow as if he feared she might try to flee, he steered her toward the house.

Lauren had to trot to keep up with Alec's long-legged strides. "Damn you," she bit out. "Who gave you the right to shove me around and tell me what I can and can't do? You're not my employer. You're not my father. And you're sure as hell not my—" She broke off, horrified to realize that she had been about to say *husband*. "My . . . my employer," she finished lamely. She tried to pull free, but he merely tightened his grip.

"You'll need to stay here to answer the sheriff's questions," he said. "Then either he or I will escort you back to wherever you need to go."

Lauren balked. "Oh, no, you don't. You're not getting me to talk to Sheriff Early."

Alec came to an abrupt stop. He spun Lauren around to face him. "Why?"

Although she couldn't think of a reason, Lauren didn't think Sheriff Early would have any trouble coming up with one. The Coopers weren't exactly on the sheriff's list of best-liked people. She squirmed beneath Alec's probing scrutiny. "I just don't like him, that's all. Besides, the person who shot T.J. is probably long gone by now."

"Possibly," Alec said slowly, deliberately. "But if a man is shot while on my property, 'tis my duty to report the incident."

Something in his tone struck a nerve. Lauren stiffened. He thought she was hiding something! "Go ahead and send for the sheriff, if that's what you want," she snapped. "He won't do anything. You'll just be wasting your time. You'll see."

"Let me be the judge of that," Alec said curtly. He continued walking toward the house and up the front steps, pulling Lauren along with him.

The front door opened to a wide central hallway tiled with black-and-gray marble. A glittering chandelier cast a warm glow over walls that were adorned with an impressive array of portraits in gilded frames. At the top of the curving staircase, Lauren saw Sly Barnes and the other man carry T.J. into one of the bedrooms. She stared around her in wonderment, her annoyance with Alec momentarily forgotten in the presence of such overwhelming luxury. She had heard once that this house had six bedrooms and *two* privies, but she hadn't believed it. Until now.

A stout man with bushy gray sideburns closed the front door after them. He was dressed in a black coat and sharply creased black trousers that Lauren considered far too fancy for everyday wear, and she wondered if he were an important guest.

Alec released her arm. "Galston, take Miss Cooper into the kitchen so that she may wash up, then show her to the library. I'm going to check on the wounded man." He started toward the stairs, then stopped and turned back. His gaze dropped to Lauren's chest, and a look of pained regret flickered across his face. "And, Galston, please find something for her to wear."

Lauren followed Alec's gaze, and a rush of heat consumed her cheeks as she realized what Alec was looking at. In the light of the chandelier, her nipples were clearly visible through the dirt and blood-streaked camisole that clung to her breasts, revealing more than it disguised. She had forgotten that she had removed her shirt. Goose bumps broke out on her bare skin as she self-consciously hunched her shoulders and crossed her arms in front of her. Thoroughly embarrassed, she glanced up at Alec, but he had already turned away and was walking toward the stairs.

The man with the gray sideburns coughed slightly. "This way, Miss."

Puzzled, Lauren followed him toward the rear of the house. For a guest, he sure was going out of his way to wait on her.

The kitchen was almost as big as the entire downstairs floor of the Coopers' house. Lauren stared around her in amazement. The huge black cast iron stove that was nestled into its own alcove was three time the size of the stove at home. And it had two ovens!

Galston brought her a thick white towel and washcloth, and a large chunk of soap that smelled like freshly cut spruce, and showed her how to operate the spigots at the sink to get just the right mix of hot and cold water. Lauren felt a twinge of envy. What she would give not to have to heat water in a kettle on the stove!

After scrubbing herself as clean as she was liable to get without stripping naked and climbing into a tub, Lauren put on the man's blue shirt Galston had brought her. The shirt was large on her, but at least it was clean. There was not much that could be done about her pants, however, except rub off the worst of the grime with the damp towel, and wait for the next washday. She tucked the long tails of the shirt into her pants and rolled up the sleeves.

When Galson saw the condition of the once-clean towel and washcloth, a mortified look crossed his face. He gingerly picked up the items by the corners and carried them out the back door. Lauren wasn't certain whether she felt amused or insulted. She could already visualize him ordering the offending articles burned.

Galston escorted her to the library. Lauren wasn't sure what to expect. The only library she had ever seen was the Free Lending Library in Millerville, which smelled like mothballs and wasn't exactly free since it cost two cents to check out a book for a week. He swung open the double doors. "Please wait in here, Miss Cooper. Mr. MacKenzie will join you shortly."

Clutching her battered black hat, Lauren stepped through the doorway. Her breath caught in her throat.

Never in her life had she seen such a beautiful room. Bookcases that reached almost to the ceiling spanned the length of two walls, and were filled with more leather-bound volumes than

Lauren had thought existed in the entire world. On the wall opposite the door, flanked by tall windows, a massive stone fireplace offered a welcoming blaze. The fourth wall housed a collection of armor and muskets and other weapons. A sofa and several comfortable-looking chairs covered in cordovan leather were arranged before the fireplace. And an account ledger lay open on top of a large desk that was fashioned of a wood so dark it looked black.

Uncertain whether it was permissible to step on the carpet that covered the polished wood floor, Lauren turned to ask the man who had brought her here, but he was already gone. Not wanting to take any chances, she avoided the intricately patterned carpet entirely as she moved cautiously around the perimeter of the room toward the hearth.

Tucking her hat beneath her arm, Lauren extended her hands toward the fire. Because it was early spring, the nights were still brisk, and the heat felt good.

Over the fireplace hung a huge painting of a man in full Highland dress. He was wearing a dark green kilt and matching plaid hose. His green jacket had deep cuffs, which were turned back to reveal a red lining and were fastened in place with brass buttons. The waistcoat over his white shirt was also red. A dirk was suspended from his belt and a sprig of holly tied with white ribbon was secured to his hat.

Lauren frowned. The portrait bore a strong resemblance to Alec, although upon closer inspection she realized that the similarity lay less in the man's rugged features than in his bearing. She wondered wryly if arrogance and overblown self-assurance were Scottish traits or MacKenzie traits.

She wandered around the room, studying the books that lined the shelves. Some of them appeared to be quite old. She did not dare touch any of them, however, and was careful to keep her hands locked on her hat so she would not be tempted.

She was so engrossed in looking at the books that she did not hear Alec come into the room, and he had a moment to watch her unobserved.

Thank God Galston had found a shirt for her to wear, he thought. A big shirt, roomy enough to leave something to the imagination. Although the sight of her breasts through her thin undergarment had been a pleasant diversion, he had not been prepared for his body's immediate response. Usually he had better self-control than that.

He could not help noticing, however, that she was still clad in those damnable britches that clung so snugly to her bottom they looked as if she had donned them when she was twelve and grown into them. Her light brown hair hung down her back in two thick braids that had long since lost their tidiness. Unexpectedly, he caught himself remembering how her hair had looked that morning in town when it had come unplaited and spilled around her shoulders. It had appeared so soft, so inviting, that he had barely restrained himself from reaching out to touch it. He wanted to touch it now. He wanted to unbraid it and bury his hands in it and feel its silken softness against his skin, on his lips. . . .

He swore silently.

Knotting his hands as if it were the only way he could prevent himself from doing anything untoward, Alec started across the room. "I see Galston found something for you to wear."

Lauren started guiltily at the sound of his voice and whirled to face him. She unthinkingly brought her hand up in front of her to shield her breasts from his view, then remembered that there was no need. Embarrassed by what she had done, and annoyed with Alec for scaring the daylights out of her, she lowered her hand. "I wish you wouldn't do that," she said testily. "One of these days you're going to sneak up behind the wrong person and get yourself shot."

Amusement shone in Alec's eyes. "Then I shall have to be more careful," he said.

He came toward her, all too quickly closing the distance between them, and Lauren's heart began to pound. The raw masculine strength that emanated from his powerful form seemed to fill the room, diminishing everything in it, herself included, and making her acutely aware of her much smaller frame, and her vulnerability.

She nervously moistened her lips. "How's T.J.?"

"He's alive."

"Can I see him?"

"Not yet. My foreman is with him now. Your friend is in good hands."

"But I just wanted to—"

"No," Alec said firmly. "You'll only be in the way." He motioned to a chair by the hearth. "Please, sit down. Galston will bring tea shortly. We may have a bit of a wait before the doctor and the sheriff arrive."

Alarm surged through her. "Is he going to be all right?"

"We'll know more after the doctor has seen him. Until then, all we can do is wait."

Not knowing what else to do, Lauren went to the chair he indicated. Her feet sank deeply into the carpet as she crossed the room. She eased herself onto the oversized seat. "You sure do have a lot of books," she said, letting her gaze travel around the room.

Alec fed another log to the fire. "Do you like to read?"

Lauren shrugged. "I don't know. I guess."

Alec braced one elbow against the mantel and regarded her thoughtfully. "I am assuming you do know how to read."

Lauren's head snapped around. "Of course I know how to read. I'm not ignorant."

"I never said you were."

Lauren felt her face grow warm. "It's just that I've never had a chance to read much except for my schoolbooks," she said, trying to amend her outburst with an explanation.

At that moment, the man with the gray sideburns arrived with a silver tray laden with dainty cakes and pastries and a delicate bone china tea service. Galston, Lauren was beginning to realize, was not a guest but a servant. He set the tray down on a low round table in front of her, and after a glance at Alec for instructions that came in the form of a barely perceptible nod, he left the room.

Alec pulled up a chair and sat down. "Will you do me the honor of pouring?" he asked.

Lauren stared at the tea service in horror. Made of the most delicate porcelain she had ever seen, the pieces were covered with peacocks and roses and were rimmed with narrow bands of gold. She couldn't believe they were actually meant to be *used*. "You m-mean, that thing?"

"That is a teapot, lass."

"That's no teapot. That's an accident looking for a place to happen! What if I break it?"

Rising from deep inside him, Alec's laugh was as rich and marvelous as his voice. His brown eyes sparkled with genuine good humor, and Lauren felt as if he were laughing with her instead of at her. "I doubt you would break it, Lauren," he said when he finally caught his breath, "but if you prefer, I'll pour."

The way her name sounded when he said it did funny things to Lauren's insides. "I think you'd better," she said shakily.

While Alec poured the tea, Lauren looked around her at what seemed like miles and miles of books on the shelves. "Miss Donovan used to bring her own books to school sometimes and let us look at them during recess," she said. "She wouldn't let us take them home because she was afraid we might damage them. Then she got married and moved to Tucson, and took her books with her." At Alec's bemused expression,

Lauren shrank back in her chair and eyed him sheepishly. "I talk too much. Pa says I could cause the cattle to stampede with my jabbering."

Alec handed her a cup of tea. He picked up the platter of cakes and offered it to her. "Tell me about your family."

The cup rattled in its saucer as Lauren set it on her lap. She selected a tiny, chocolate-iced cake decorated with a pink sugared rosebud so delicate she could almost see through it. "There's not much to tell," she said, holding the cake up to the light so she could see how the flower had been made. "Mama died when I was thirteen. Now there's just Pa and Bubba and me. You sort of met Bubba in town that day you . . . er . . . helped me out with Sam Luttrell. Pa doesn't get into town much any more since the accident. He got thrown and trampled last spring, so now it's hard for him to get around." Lauren picked off a rose petal and put it into her mouth. The confection dissolved on her tongue. She took a bite of the cake.

"Tell me, lass, what is the real reason you and your friend were in the canyon?"

The question caught her like an Indian ambush. She swallowed without chewing and the cake went down in a single audible gulp. "I beg your pardon?" she choked.

Alec leaned forward and rested his forearms on his thighs. He was so close to her that she could see the life pulsing through the vein in the side of his throat. He wasn't smiling. "Don't play games with me, lass," he cautioned in a dangerously silky voice. "There is naught I dislike more than deceit and trickery. If we are to get along, I expect you to be honest with me."

The color siphoned from Lauren's face. What was she going to do now? She didn't know what T.J. might have told him—if anything—but she didn't think he would want her to give away the location of the mustangs. They were too valuable. She set her teacup and saucer on the table. "I'd best be getting back. Everyone's going to worry that T.J. and I haven't shown up for supper." She started to stand.

Alec's hand shot out and snapped around her wrist. His gaze captured hers. "I wasn't trying to frighten you, Lauren. All I'm asking of you is the truth."

He wasn't holding her tightly, but the feel of his strong fingers around her wrist caused her knees to turn to pudding beneath her, and she sank back down into the chair. She could not have fled if she had wanted to. It had nothing to do with the hold he had on her wrist. Instead, it was as if some power greater than she was *willing* her to stay.

The intensity of his gaze made her uneasy. "We were looking for strays," she said. Then, realizing that he was probably going to find out the truth anyway, she added testily, "And then we went up into the canyon to look for a herd of mustangs that one of the hired hands saw. We found them too. I'd just started to go back to camp for help when T.J. got shot."

"Is that all?"

Lauren pinned him with a disbelieving glare and jerked her hand out of his grasp. "Of course that's all. You want me to swear on a stack of Bibles or something?"

Leaning back, Alec braced his elbows on the arms of his chair and brought his hands together in front of him, steepling his fingertips. He studied her thoughtfully. "Did you think I would object to your search for the wild horses?"

"Hell, I don't know what to think. For all I know, you intend to have us both arrested for trespassing."

"Until the boundaries of my property have been surveyed and the fences installed, you have every right to use the canyon, as long as you're not breaking the law."

Lauren fidgeted. After an awkward moment of silence, she spoke again. "Does this honesty stuff pertain to both of us, or am I the only one required to tell the truth here?"

"Meaning?"

"Meaning, just why are you putting up those fences?"

"Ah, I thought you might ask that."

"Well?"

"The truth, lass, is that I am importing some expensive bulls from Scotland, to be used for crossbreeding. I would hate for my investment to turn up on someone else's land, wearing an altered brand. Therefore, I am taking the necessary precautions to prevent that from happening."

"You sure don't have much faith in your neighbors, do you?"

"I don't have much faith in human nature,"

Alec corrected her. " 'Tis one of my biggest failings."

It occurred to Lauren that if caution was a failing, then Alec MacKenzie's slate must be damn near spotless. "I hope you're aware that you're going to run the rest of us out of business."

"Lauren, I was honest with you regarding the fences. Now I'm going to be honest with you again and tell you that I have no intention of indulging you with any further discussion of the matter. Is that understood?"

"I understand it," Lauren said peevishly. "But I don't have to like it."

"I respect that."

Lauren's eyes narrowed. "You mean, you're not angry?"

"Should I be?" She was looking at him with such undisguised skepticism that Alec was hard-pressed not to crack a smile. Her defensiveness puzzled him. He could not help wondering why she kept thrusting a wall of thorns between them. When she remained stubbornly silent, he said gently, "I'm not angry, lass."

Lauren visibly relaxed. Her gaze darted away from his, but not before Alec witnessed the relief and confusion that clouded her eyes.

Dr. Blakely and the sheriff arrived a short time later. They were with T.J. for the better part of an hour before the sheriff returned downstairs to question Lauren about the shooting. She told him everything she had told Alec, including the part about finding the mustangs.

Sheriff Early frowned as he studied the bullet

Dr. Blakely had given him. It was a standard .44 caliber, so common as to be of no help at all. Most men in these parts who carried a gun used one with either a .44 or a .36 caliber bore. "So you didn't get a good look at the man who shot Powell?" he asked.

"I didn't get *any* look at him. The shot came out of nowhere. T.J. didn't see him either."

The sheriff eyed Lauren closely. "Do you know where Sam Luttrell was today?"

Lauren shrugged. "I-I don't know. He was in camp this morning. I think he went out with Bernie's crew."

After a few more questions that led nowhere, Sheriff Early finally said, "It's getting late. Come on, I'll take you back to camp."

Dr. Blakely was just coming down the stairs with his battered black medical bag when Lauren and Alec and Sheriff Early went out into the hall. "Mr. Powell is conscious, but he's in bad shape," the doctor said. "He needs to stay in bed and keep that dressing dry."

"He's welcome to stay here while he recuperates," Alec said.

"Good. I'll be back in the morning to check on him. In the meantime, if he starts running a fever and getting delirious, send someone for me right away."

While Lauren went to get her horse, Sheriff Early hung back to speak with Alec. "I hear you broke up a fight between the girl and Sam Luttrell a couple of weeks back."

Although he had spoken casually, something

in the sheriff's tone struck a nerve. "Aye," Alec said slowly. "I intervened."

The sheriff scratched the side of his head. "Not meaning to tell you your business, MacKenzie, but you might want to keep your distance where the Coopers are concerned. Riff-raff, you could say. Always looking for a fight. Give them half a chance, and they'll steal the shirt right off your back."

Alec found himself fighting the urge to plant his fist in the sheriff's heavy-jowled face. His eyes narrowed dangerously. "What, specifically, have the Coopers done to warrant such blanket disapproval, Sheriff?" he asked.

"It's not any one thing. It's the overall situation. Frank now, he's more often than not to be found with his nose in a bottle. And the boy, well, that's a story-and-a-half right there. Sticky-fingered little tyke. Heading down the road to ruin, just like his old man." The sheriff shook his head. "Frank's wife, now, she was a lady. A Cooper, yes, but a lady nonetheless. A shame when she died."

"And Lauren?" Alec asked icily.

The sheriff shook his head. "That one is about as tetchy as a bear with a burr in its paw. Can't open her mouth without offending someone. Besides, you know what they say about the apple not falling far from the tree. Were I you, I'd take inventory of the family silver after we leave."

Alec decided then that he did not like Sheriff Early.

"Coop! We've been looking all over for you ever since T.J.'s horse came back without a rider," Grady Wright said. "Where have you been? Where's T.J.?"

Lauren and Sheriff Early dismounted. By the time Lauren finished relating to Grady what had happened, a crowd had gathered around them.

"T.J. gonna be all right?" one of the hands asked.

"A day in bed and he'll be chafing at the bit to get back in the saddle," Sheriff Early said. Excusing himself, he worked his way through the crowd toward Archer Kendrick, Martin Dandridge's foreman. An uneasy feeling fluttered in Lauren's stomach as she watched them move out of earshot.

Bubba squeezed his way between two of the men. "Hey, Coop! Guess what? Cal says I'm doing such a good job as wrangler, he's gonna let me go on the cattle drive this fall!"

Bernie's hand descended on the boy's shoulder. "Give your sister a chance to catch her wind," he said. He looked at Lauren. "You hungry?"

"I ate earlier. Right now I just want to turn in." The ride back to camp from Alec MacKenzie's ranch had been strained. Sheriff Early had attempted to be pleasant, but his dislike of her kept showing through his veneer of civility, and when she failed to respond to his overtures with what she figured he would consider sufficient gratitude, he stopped talking to her altogether.

The crowd broke up as the men began returning to their campfires and bedrolls. Bernie took the reins of Lauren's horse and passed them to Bubba. "You unsaddle Popcorn and make sure he gets some oats."

"Aw, do I have to?"

"It's one of a wrangler's duties, kid. You don't want someone else to beat you out of a job come fall, do you?"

After Bubba led the gelding away, Bernie turned back to Lauren. "You sure you're okay? You're awfully quiet."

"I'm just tired." Lauren's voice shook. "It scared the bejesus out of me when T.J. got shot. I thought he was going to bleed to death before I could get help."

"Well, you did just fine, and don't let anyone tell you different."

Lauren didn't know if it was relief or exhaustion or what, but she suddenly had the urge to sit down and bawl her eyes out. Her throat tightened. "Thanks, Bernie," she whispered hoarsely.

As she was shaking out her bedroll behind one of the supply wagons, the sounds of arguing reached Lauren's ears. She couldn't make out what the men were saying, but one of the voices sounded like Sam Luttrell's.

She was just pulling off her boots when Sheriff Early stopped by to let her know that if nothing turned up in the meantime, he would be back in the morning to have her take him up into Six-shooter Canyon and show him exactly where the shooting took place.

After the sheriff left, Lauren crawled beneath the blanket. Every bone and muscle in her body ached, and she could not recall a time when she had felt as tired as she did tonight. She was thankful that T.J. was all right. She couldn't bring herself to think about what would have happened had she let him die.

Suddenly a hand fastened around her upper arm in a painful grip, and she was hauled roughly to her feet. Sam Luttrell shoved her against the wagon. "You conniving little bitch! Why'd you put the sheriff on my tail?"

Lauren's mouth dropped open. She started to shake her head. "I didn't . . ."

"You told Early I was the one who shot T.J.!"

"I didn't!"

Sam knotted his fist in Lauren's hair, bringing stinging tears to her eyes. He forced her head back. "It won't do you any good to lie about it, Cooper."

"Ow! I'm not lying!"

Cal Hoagland, the Coopers' foreman, suddenly appeared behind Sam. He put his hand on Sam's shoulder. "Let her go, Luttrell."

Sam shrugged off Cal's hand. "Like hell I will! First she gets MacKenzie to complain to Dandridge about me, and then she fills Early's head with suspicions about me!"

"I did not!"

"I said, let her go!" Anger shook in Cal's voice.

Sam shoved Cal back with his free hand. "Back off, old man. This isn't your fight."

"I didn't do any—*ouch!*" Lauren clawed at the hand that gripped her hair.

Cal seized Sam's shirt and yanked him back. "I said, let her go, you son of a—"

Sam released Lauren and swung. Cal ducked, barely dodging Sam's fist.

Jerome Carter and Grady Wright grabbed Sam from behind. "Knock it off, Luttrell," Grady ordered. "Kendrick warned you about fighting."

Bernie grabbed Lauren's arm and yanked her out of the way.

Sam lunged toward her, but the two men held him back. Sam unleashed a string of obscenities and tried to break free of the hold the men had on him.

Archer Kendrick's voice interrupted Sam's tirade. "That's enough, Luttrell!"

Sam was breathing hard. He turned an accusing glare on Lauren. "She told Early that I shot T.J."

Kendrick looked at Lauren. "Did you?"

"No, I didn't." Lauren had to fight hard to keep the quiver from her voice. The last thing she wanted to do was humiliate herself by crying in front of close to a hundred men.

"Then why was the sheriff asking me all those questions about where I was today, and who I was with?" Sam demanded.

"The hell if I know!" Lauren retorted. "He even asked *me* where you were today, and I told him you were with Bernie."

"All right, you two. I've heard enough," Archer Kendrick said. "Luttrell, I'm going to tell you one last time: any more fighting, and you can pick up your pay and get out of here."

"Aw, c'mon, Arch. You can't mean that!"

"I mean it. You've been pushing your luck for

the past year. I won't tolerate it. Any more trouble, you're fired."

Sam's face was twisted with anger, but he said nothing. Jerome and Grady let go of him, and he stomped away.

After Sam had gone, Archer Kendrick leveled a warning finger at Lauren. "I don't know what you did to set him off, but I wish you'd keep your distance from Luttrell. I have enough to worry about without having to referee your damned squabbles."

Before Lauren could say anything in her own defense, Kendrick turned and stalked away. She swallowed hard against the tears that clogged her throat. "Damn it all," she swore aloud.

"Don't fret about it, Coop," Bernie said. "You've had a bear of a day. Get some sleep. Everything will be forgotten in the morning."

Morning proved Bernie wrong.

Cal kept Lauren back until after the other hands had ridden out. Only a half dozen men remained in camp—the chuck wagon cooks, Cal, Bubba, and one other boy who was helping Bubba tend the horses. Ignoring the curious stares of the cooks, Cal took Lauren aside. "Arch and me, we was talking," he said, "and we decided it would be best if you went home."

Lauren felt as if he had punched her between the eyes. "Why? I didn't do anything. Sam started it. I was minding my own business, and *he* came after *me*."

"I know that, Coop. I was there, remember? But having you and Luttrell in the same camp is like poking a hornet's nest with a stick and expecting not to get stung. As long as there's this bad blood simmering between you two, it's best if you just go home and stay out of his way."

Lauren stared at him in disbelief. Her chin quivered, and she had to grit her teeth to steady it. "It's not fair," she choked. "Sam's the one who started the trouble, and *I* get punished for it."

Cal shook his head. "That's not the way of it, Coop. It's for your own safety."

Lauren clenched and unclenched her fists. "Yeah, well, thanks an ever-loving lot, Cal Hoagland. Of all people, I thought you'd be the last one to side with Luttrell." Pivoting, she marched back toward the camp.

"I'm not siding with Luttrell," Cal called out to her departing back. "I'm trying to keep you from getting your blasted skull bashed in!"

Acutely aware of the curious stares that followed her, Lauren packed up her bedroll and laid it on the ground next to her saddle and the rest of her gear, then went to get her horse. There was a terrible ache in the middle of her chest, and tears blurred her eyes, but she blinked them back, determined not to cry until she was alone and no would see her.

Bubba untied one of the ropes that formed the makeshift corral, and went in to get Popcorn. "You going home?" he asked when he brought the horse to her.

Lauren slipped the bridle over the gelding's head. "How'd you know?"

Bubba shrugged. "Everyone knows. We heard Cal and Mr. Kendrick talking last night. Mr.

Kendrick says having a female along on a roundup is inviting trouble."

The smugness in her brother's voice when he repeated Archer Kendrick's remark hurt more than the words themselves. Lauren gripped the gelding's reins. "I'll see you when you get home." Her voice cracked.

No one spoke to her as she saddled her horse. It was just as well. With the way she felt, she was liable to snap off someone's head. She placed her foot in the stirrup and swung up into the saddle. *Good riddance to all of you,* she thought as she dug her heels into the horse's sides.

She was well away from camp when she finally slowed the gelding to a walk. Tears streamed down her face. It wasn't fair. Sam Luttrell was the one who started the trouble. Why didn't Archer Kendrick send *him* away?

She was so engrossed in trying to make some sense of the situation that she failed to notice the approaching riders until they were less than a quarter of a mile from her. There were two of them, both men. Judging from their clothes, they might have been participating in the roundup, but she couldn't be sure. She fumbled in her pockets for her handkerchief, but couldn't find it. She sniffled and dried her eyes on her sleeve.

As the men neared, her heart began to pound unnaturally fast. They were riding straight toward her. Had they merely been working, they would have just waved from a distance.

Suddenly she recognized their horses, and then the men. Her stomach knotted. The riders were Sam Luttrell and Eliot Dandridge.

Chapter 4

The two men reined in their horses. Sam Luttrell pushed back his hat and grinned at her. "Fancy seeing you here, Cooper. A little far away from the roundup, aren't you?"

Panic unfolded in Lauren's gut. "There's no need pretending you don't know that Cal and Mr. Kendrick sent me home. Everyone else knows it, and I'm sure you were among the first ones to get wind of the good news."

Sam and Eliot exchanged glances. "Well, now," Sam drawled, "I don't know if Eliot and me would call it good news exactly. I mean, we were looking forward to having us a little fun. You know, just to show you there's no hard feelings about you setting the sheriff after me."

Lauren's mouth felt as dry as wheat chaff. "I told you, Sam, I didn't tell the sheriff anything. He was the one who asked me about you."

Sam leaned forward and rested his arm against his saddle horn. "Now, you don't expect us to believe that, do you? Do you believe it, Dandridge?"

Eliot grinned. "Nope."

"If you don't believe me, go ask Sheriff Early. Or better yet, go ask Mr. MacKenzie. He was right there when the sheriff questioned me, and he heard everything I said."

A dangerous light glinted in Sam's eyes. "You expect me to go visit MacKenzie after what he did to me, getting the boss all riled up about that little fight we had? I'll pay MacKenzie a visit all right, when I'm good and ready, and it sure as hell won't be to chat."

Luttrell was up to something, and Lauren knew that if she didn't get out of there quick, she was liable to find out the hard way just what that something was. "Listen, Sam, last night I was too worried about T.J. to give any thought to turning the sheriff's ear with tales about you. Whatever he's got on you, it came from someone else. Not from me."

"I don't believe you."

"I don't care what you believe. Right now, I just want to go home. So if you'll kindly get out of my way—"

"Now, why would we want to do a thing like that?" Sam asked.

"Why, indeed?" Eliot echoed.

Lauren glanced from one to the other. She wished Cal were here. Or Bernie. She didn't like this one bit.

Sam lifted his coiled rope from his saddle horn. "You don't listen too good, Coop. *I already told you,* Eliot and me, we aim to have us some fun."

The realization of what they had planned hit Lauren like a dose of skunk spray. She jerked on her reins, bringing Popcorn around sharply, and dug her heels into the gelding's sides.

The horse lurched forward.

The valley floor was rocky and uneven, and it

was all Lauren could do to keep Popcorn from running into a patch of prickly pear. Hoofbeats thundered in her ears, echoing the furious pounding of her heart. She glanced back over her shoulder. Sam and Eliot were gaining on her. Sam was whirling his rope over his head. If she could just get within sight of the camp . . .

The rope smacked painfully against her head, causing Lauren to cry out in surprise, then slithered down over her shoulders and jerked tight, pinning her arms at her sides.

The reins ripped through her hands. She went down, landing on her shoulder on the hard ground. Because one end of the rope was tied to Sam's saddle horn, she was jerked about like a rag doll and dragged several feet before he brought his horse to a complete stop.

Sam jumped down from his horse.

Lauren groaned and tried to sit up, but the effort sent a burning pain shooting through her body, and she collapsed.

Sam grabbed her feet, and quickly wrapped the rope around her ankles and legs.

Lauren tried to kick him, but the strength seemed to have been knocked out of her, along with her breath. Tears stung her eyes. "Damn . . . you . . ." she choked, gasping for air. Her body felt as if it were on fire.

Sam straightened. "Hurry up, Dandridge!" he shouted.

Eliot Dandridge, who had ridden after Lauren's horse, returned with the gelding in tow. He grabbed Lauren's rope, made certain it was securely attached to her saddle horn, then tossed the free end to Sam.

Sam dropped down on one knee and seized Lauren's hands. She managed to wrench one free. Sam grabbed for it, and Lauren raked her fingernails down the side of his face. Swearing, he caught her hand and yanked it down.

He wrapped the end of the rope around her wrists, binding them together, and knotted it. "I'll teach you to mess with me," he bit out.

Lauren tried desperately to work her hands free, but the rope was too tight. Never before in her life had she felt so defenseless. A sob broke in her throat. "You won't get away with this, Sam Luttrell. If you think the sheriff was suspicious of you before, just you wait. He won't have to ask any questions this time. He'll *know* you did it."

Sam stood up and jerked his head toward Lauren's horse. "Get up there," he ordered Eliot.

Eliot Dandridge looked baffled. "Me?"

"You heard me. Get on that horse."

Nervously moistening his lips, Eliot got down off his own horse and mounted Lauren's. The enthusiasm had gone out of his movements. He didn't like Lauren Cooper, but what Sam had in mind was a bit much, even for him. Still, he didn't dare go against Sam, or he was liable to be Sam's next target.

Sam pulled his own rope, unwinding it from Lauren's legs, then released the noose from around her body. Coiling the rope around his hand, he smacked it hard against Popcorn's flank and yelled, "Make it good, Dandridge!"

* * *

T.J. Powell pushed his breakfast tray away and rubbed his hand across his full stomach. He grinned sheepishly. "A man could get used to this," he said. "Thanks, MacKenzie. I owe you one."

Galston took the tray away.

"Do you feel up to having a visitor?" Alec asked. He handed T.J. a shirt to wear while his clothes were being laundered. "The sheriff wants to ask you some questions."

"Sure. Let me get this on—" T.J. winced at the pain that stabbed his chest when he tried to get out of bed.

Alec helped him put on the shirt. "You had best stay in bed, Mr. Powell. You lost a great deal of blood yesterday."

T.J. slumped back against the pillows. His face was ashen. "You're right. Maybe you'd better send Sheriff Early up here."

Alec went downstairs.

Roy Early was waiting in the library. "Mighty impressive collection of books you have here," he said when Alec entered the room. "Have you read them all?"

"Many times. Do you read, Sheriff?"

"Not unless I have to."

Alec's expression revealed nothing of the dislike he felt for the man. "You may go upstairs to see Mr. Powell. Try not to keep him long. He's still weak."

"I won't be more than a few minutes. I just need to ask him where he was when he got shot."

"Why don't you ask Lauren? She could take you right to the spot."

"She's nowhere to be found. Kendrick sent her home, but when I went to the Bar-T, Frank hadn't seen her."

Alec frowned. "Isn't Kendrick Martin Dandridge's foreman?"

"The same."

"Why did he send Lauren home? I thought she was going to stay for the entire roundup."

"Because she can't keep her nose clean, that's why. She and Luttrell went after each other again last night." Early motioned toward the door. "Powell in the same room?"

"Sheriff, did you search for Lauren Cooper at all?"

A look of annoyance crossed Early's face. "Mr. MacKenzie, Lauren Cooper is the last person anyone needs to worry about. When she's through sulking, she'll go home."

Although Alec did not agree with the sheriff, he said nothing. He waited until after Sheriff Early had gone, then he went upstairs to speak with T.J. himself.

"Mr. Powell, may I have a few minutes of your time?"

There was a crack in T.J.'s grin. The pain was starting to get to him. "I'm not going anywhere soon."

Alec pulled a chair up alongside the bed and sat down. He told T.J. what Sheriff Early had relayed to him. "I don't know Lauren very well," he said when he had finished. "Is it like her to disappear without telling anyone?"

T.J.'s brows drew together as he pondered Alec's question. "She might have if she was mad enough about being sent home, but . . ." T.J. shook his head. "I don't know. That just doesn't sound like Coop."

"Do you think she could be in trouble?"

"You mean Luttrell?"

"Yes."

"I'd believe that before I'd believe that Coop ran off."

Alec could not shake the image that had taken root in his mind of Lauren out in the desert, hurt and alone. He kept seeing her the way T.J. Powell had been last night when Lauren brought him to Duneideann, bleeding profusely from a bullet wound for which no one was likely to claim responsibility. He stood up. "Thank you," he said.

"What are you going to do, MacKenzie?"

Alec moved the chair back to its original location. "I'm going to look for her."

This was the first time since his initial inspection of the property that Alec had ridden the boundary between Duneideann and the Bar-T. He had three men with him: two former silver miners whom he had hired to help put up the fences, and Sly Barnes. Sly had returned from the roundup earlier that day and had confirmed Sheriff Early's report of a disagreement between Lauren Cooper and Sam Luttrell. Most of Alec's hands were still at the roundup.

Surrounded completely by mountains, the open expanse of the valley floor was broken by thick stands of prickly pear and mesquite and creosote bush. An occasional saguaro rose above the low-growing vegetation, pointing a thorny finger into the sky.

The riders spread out to cover more ground. Each staying within sight of the man closest to him, they rode parallel to one another. They walked their horses so they wouldn't miss anything—a trail, a scrap of clothing, a splatter of blood.

The sun beat down on them. Even Alec, who often chose to work bareheaded, wore a hat for protection, along with long sleeves and sturdy jeans to shield his arms and legs from the ever-present thorns and sandburs.

They rode for hours without seeing anything out of the ordinary. If anyone had ridden this way recently, there was no sign of it. Suddenly, one of the former silver miners called out, "Hey, Mr. MacKenzie! Come take a look at this!"

Alec turned his horse and rode toward the man.

The grass and brush here were beaten down, as if something had been dragged across them. Alec was just starting to dismount to get a closer look when Sly yelled, "I found something!"

When Alec reached Sly, the foreman had dismounted and dropped onto his haunches.

"What is it?"

Sly motioned toward the rope lying on the ground. It was a grass rope, about sixty feet long, and showed moderate wear. Judging from the way it lay, it appeared to have been flung there, rather than dropped or put down and forgotten. "I don't know how it is where you come from, Mr. MacKenzie," Sly said, "but out here, a man's rope is his lifeline. He wouldn't be caught dead without it."

Unless he—or she—was already dead, Alec thought uneasily.

Sly picked up the rope and coiled it, looping it around his hand. He nodded his head toward the other rider. "What did Colin find?"

Alec looked around. The man who had spotted the flattened grass was guiding his horse slowly toward them. He kept his gaze fixed on the ground and seemed to be following a trail. "The grass is trampled," Alec said.

When the man drew close to them, he called out, "It seems to be leading toward the wash, Mr. MacKenzie."

Alec mounted his horse. "Let's hope it's nothing."

The trail Colin was following led toward the wash, then away from it. Then another ribbon of trampled grass crossed over the first. Soon they came upon an open area where the grass and brush were bent down all around them. The ground was freshly broken in places.

"Stampede?" the other miner asked.

Sly pushed back his hat and scratched his head. "Looks more like something was dragged."

Then they saw the vultures. There were two of them, circling slowly above the wash, about a quarter of a mile away.

Alec spurred his horse.

The second miner began shouting and frantically waving his arms. He turned his horse and rode down the bank into the wash. Alec rode after him, bringing his horse to an abrupt stop when he reached the cracked, dry bottom of the riverbed.

At the far side of the wash, in the shadow of the sandy bank, a body lay unmoving, face downward in the dirt.

Alec's stomach clenched.

It was Lauren.

Sly Barnes bounded up the front steps of the main house and opened the door. Behind him, Alec moved more slowly, carrying Lauren in his arms. She was unconscious.

Galston met him at the door. "Get towels and antiseptic and a pair of scissors," Alec ordered. "Sly, send someone for Dr. Blakely."

Alec carried Lauren up the stairs and into his bedroom, where he laid her on the bed.

Lauren's head rolled to one side. Her braids had come undone, and her hair was snarled. Alec removed a twig from a soft brown strand and lifted it away from her face. He winced. The left side of her face was scraped and bruised, and blood had crusted over a gash above her eyebrow. Her eyes were closed, and her lips were cracked and dry.

"My God! Where did you find her?"

Alec turned to see T.J. standing in the doorway. He was clad only in his borrowed shirt, and his face was pale. He clutched the doorjamb for support.

"Encina Wash."

"Is she going to be all right?"

"I don't know. Whoever did this to her left her to die. Mr. Powell, you had best get back into bed. I'll take care of the lass." Alec began removing Lauren's shoes.

Just then, Galston appeared with the items Alec had requested, and T.J. moved out of his way.

While Galston went into the adjoining bathroom to run a basin of hot water, Alec used the scissors to cut away Lauren's clothes. They stuck to her skin where the blood had dried, and although Alec tried to be careful, several of the deeper cuts began to bleed again.

What he saw made him physically ill.

There wasn't a place on Lauren's body that wasn't bruised. Her left hip and the front of her thighs were scraped raw, and in the places where her clothes had shredded, dirt and debris were embedded in the torn flesh. There were rope burns on her wrists, validating Sly's theory that she had been dragged.

Alec clenched his teeth. He wanted to kill the man who had done this to her; he was certain it was a man, and he was certain it was Sam Luttrell. But until Lauren regained consciousness and told him what had happened, he could not rightfully accuse anyone.

With Galston's help, Alec cleaned Lauren's cuts and washed the dirt from her body. He had just finished bathing her injuries with the Lister's antiseptic Galston had provided when Lauren began to stir.

Alec carefully slid one arm beneath her shoulders and the other behind her knees, then lifted her off the mattress.

Galston stripped off the wet coverlet and turned back the sheet, and Alec lowered Lauren. He drew the top sheet and a blanket over her.

Her eyes fluttered open. Panic and pain darkened their blue depths. "It . . . hurts," she gasped.

" 'Tis all right, lass. You'll be safe here. I won't let anyone hurt you."

He lifted her head and held a glass to her lips. Tears filled her eyes when the glass bumped her cracked lips, and she pulled away. After several unsuccessful attempts to get her to drink, Alec lowered her to the pillows. He sat down on the edge of the bed. "Lass, who did this to you?"

Lauren turned her head away. Tears clung to her lashes. She swallowed several times, and Alec saw her throat working as she struggled not to cry. His stomach clenched. "Was it Sam Luttrell?"

Lauren squeezed her eyes shut. A tear slipped down her cheek.

Alec's anger hardened into something unforgiving and dangerous. "Was Luttrell the only one?"

A sob broke in Lauren's throat. She shook her head.

"Who else, Lauren? Who was with him?"

"El-iot," she choked.

"Eliot Dandridge?"

Lauren swallowed hard and nodded.

"Anyone else?"

"N-no . . ."

Alec fought to keep his temper under control. *Damn those two!* He could see now that going to Martin Dandridge had been a mistake. The Coopers had gotten back the supplies that Sam and Eliot had destroyed, but at what cost?

This time, he decided, they were going to pay for what they had done to Lauren.

After the doctor left, Alec returned to see Lauren. The curtains had been drawn against the harsh afternoon sun. Dr. Blakely had given her something to dull the pain, and she seemed to be resting peacefully.

Alec went to stand beside the bed. Her hair was spread across the pillows and her eyes were closed, her long lashes dark and thick against her cheeks. For the first time, Alec realized how delicate her features were, and the discovery took him by surprise. Her cheekbones were finely chiseled, her nose straight, and the arch of her brow naturally elegant. Had his first encounter with her been in a London drawing room instead of on a dusty Arizona street, he would have assumed she was a lady of quality.

The type of woman one married.

Alec frowned, annoyed with himself for even thinking such a thing. Lauren Cooper was hardly the type of woman he would choose for a wife. The woman he married would be wellborn, socially adept, and capable. If she was pleasing to the eye, so much the better. He did not expect her to satisfy him in bed; those needs could be met elsewhere. He wanted someone who would bear his children and run his household and help entertain his clients, without causing him either public embarrassment or private scandal.

When the time was right, he thought, he would return to Edinburgh and select a wife. In the meantime, he had a ranch to run and numerous business ventures to occupy both his time and his thoughts.

He also had one defenseless, intriguing, and undeniably pretty girl asleep in his bed.

"What am I going to do with you, lass?" he murmured. Bending down, he kissed her cheek. The unexpected softness of her skin against his lips triggered a stirring in his loins. He pulled back, his brows drawing together in bewilderment as he stared down at her. While the kiss had been innocent enough, his body's reaction to it was not.

He straightened and took a deep breath, suppressing the unbidden longings. Lauren was a guest in his house, he sharply reminded himself. A neighbor. The daughter of a neighbor.

Nothing more.

Alec ordered his horse saddled and rode into town. He went to the sheriff's office, but Early wasn't there. After several inquiries, he finally caught up with him at Arminta Larson's house.

A thin, brown-skinned girl who didn't appear to be any older than Lauren opened the door. In halting English, she invited Alec into the parlor, then disappeared down the hall toward the dining room. A few minutes later, Sheriff Early stepped into the parlor. Arminta Larson was right on his heels.

"Mr. MacKenzie," Arminta cooed. "How wonderful to see you again! Please join us for dinner."

Alec managed to conceal his dislike of Arminta Larson behind a warm smile. "I appreciate the offer, madam, but I must decline. And I apologize for interrupting your meal, but I need to speak with the sheriff regarding a matter of some urgency."

Arminta fluttered her eyelashes and patted her hair. "Of course, Mr. MacKenzie. I understand completely. However, you absolutely must agree to accept a dinner invitation for some time in the near future. There are many prominent townsmen whom you should meet in order to facilitate your integration into Millerville society."

Knowing that Arminta Larson might prove invaluable in helping establish contacts for his planned business ventures, Alec refrained from saying what he was thinking. "You are very kind," he said instead. "I would be delighted to accept an invitation in the future, when my schedule allows."

"Why, that's wonderful! Let's see, on the thirtieth I am hosting a birthday dinner for Mr. Larson—"

"Mrs. Larson, I need to speak with the sheriff."

Arminta was not so obtuse that she did not detect the impatience in Alec's voice. "Do pardon me, Mr. MacKenzie. I know you are a busy man. If you will excuse me, I will leave you two gentlemen alone so that you may conduct your business in private."

Arminta pulled the double doors closed as she backed out of the parlor.

As the sound of her footsteps faded down the hallway, Sheriff Early shook his head. "I swear, that woman never shuts up. She was like that throughout dinner. So tell me, what is so urgent that it can't wait until morning?"

"Lauren Cooper."

Roy Early held up his hand in a silencing gesture. "I know what you're going to say: it's nearly dark, and she hasn't come home. And I'm going to tell you the same thing I told you this morning."

Alec's temper flared. "My men found her in Encina Wash. Eliot Dandridge and Sam Luttrell had tied her hands together and dragged her across the desert. She was barely alive."

Sheriff Early drew back in disbelief. "Listen here, MacKenzie, that's a mighty stiff charge to go around making without any proof."

"When Lauren regained consciousness, she identified the men. As for proof, perhaps you should come out to Duneideann and see for yourself how badly beaten she is." Alec made no attempt to soften the sarcasm in his voice.

"I'm not saying I don't believe you. But what it boils down to is Miss Cooper's word against theirs. And unless there is an outside witness to corroborate her story, it's going to be near impossible to make any charges stick."

"Meaning?"

"Meaning, Martin Dandridge is a powerful

man in this valley. He has access to the finest legal counsel in the Territory. If Lauren Cooper tries to press charges against Dandridge's son, they'll tear her apart in a courtroom. I'm sure you don't want Miss Cooper's name dragged through the mud over some petty incident that is likely to be forgotten in a few months."

Black rage tightened every muscle in Alec's body. He was tempted to take a swing at the sheriff. "You're right," he said with carefully measured deliberation. "Pressing charges against Eliot Dandridge and Sam Luttrell is not a viable solution to the problem." He started toward the door.

Sheriff Early was suddenly suspicious. "Don't you attempt to take the law into your own hands," he warned.

Alec stopped, one hand on the door and turned back. His expression was thoughtful. "I am not overly familiar with some of your American customs, *Sheriff,*" he said, emphasizing the word. "Perhaps you can answer a question for me. Is this an election year?"

Sheriff Early bristled. He wasn't stupid. He knew exactly what Alec MacKenzie was trying to do. "It's not," he said stiffly. "Ninety-two is the next election year."

Alec's smile did not extend to his eyes. "I'll keep that in mind. Good night, Sheriff."

By the time Alec reached the valley where the men participating in the roundup were camped, it was well past the dinner hour, and many of the men had already settled in for the night. Although dozens of pairs of eyes followed him as he rode into camp, no one tried to stop him. A few inquiries yielded exactly what he wanted to know. He dismounted, tied his horse to one of the chuck wagons, and headed straight toward the central campfire.

Eliot Dandridge was sitting by the fire, eating his supper and laughing over a joke Jerome Carter had just told. He was just about to take a drink of coffee when a strong hand grasped the back of his shirt and hauled him to his feet.

Coffee and pinto beans went flying as his dishes clattered to the ground.

The other men around the campfire scrambled out of the way.

Alec swung Eliot around with his left hand and drew back his right. Eliot's eyes widened with fear and recognition, and he threw his hands up to protect his face. "I didn't mean to hurt her! Sam and me, we just wanted to have some fun."

Alec shook Eliot so hard the young man's feet cleared the ground. "You nearly killed her. Do you call that *fun?*"

Eliot cringed. "I didn't want to do it. It was Sam's idea. I thought we were just going to stick a cactus pad under her horse's tail and make him buck her off."

Disgust burned in Alec's eyes. "You stinking little coward," he bit out. "I'm tempted to give you a taste of what you did to that girl, but you're not worth going to jail for."

Behind Alec, a man asked, "Who's goin' to jail?"

Alec did not need to see the man to recognize his voice. With a strength born of rage, he lifted Eliot Dandridge off the ground and turned. He hurled Eliot into Sam Luttrell, sending both men sprawling.

Sam rolled to his feet and went for his gun, but a half dozen other men sprang into action at once, grabbing him and pinning his arms back. "Don't, Luttrell," one man warned. "You remember what Kendrick told you about fighting."

Archer Kendrick and Cal Hoagland pushed their way through the crowd that had formed. "What's going on here?" Kendrick demanded.

"He started it," Sam said, jerking his head toward Alec. "He just rode in here and started knocking me and Dandridge around."

Kendrick looked at Alec, recognizing him from the day he had come to the Diamond Cross ranch to see Martin Dandridge. "Is that true, Mr. MacKenzie?"

Alec stared hard at Kendrick. "Who are you?"

"Archer Kendrick. I'm the foreman at the Diamond Cross."

Alec wished he had gotten a good punch at Luttrell before the others had intervened. "I would like to break every bone in their miserable bodies; and if they don't keep their distance from Lauren Cooper, Mr. Kendrick, that is precisely what I intend to do."

"What happened to Coop?" Cal Hoagland demanded.

"Ask them," Alec said curtly.

Kendrick turned to Sam. "What's he talking about?"

"Nothing. He's all riled up over nothing. The man's worse than Arminta Larson, always sticking his nose where it don't—"

Sam broke off as Archer Kendrick grabbed the front of his shirt, nearly yanking him off his feet. "Don't give me that *nothing* crap, Luttrell. Tell me what you and Dandridge did to Frank's daughter, or *I'll* break every bone in your body."

Sam's left eye strayed, making it appear as if he was looking past Kendrick. "We just had us a bit of fun, is all."

"Answer me!"

Behind Sam, Eliot fidgeted. "We hog-tied her and took her for a ride," he said hesitantly.

Kendrick's face turned menacing. "You did *what?*"

"Aw, c'mon, Arch," Sam protested. "She deserved it, after telling Early I was the one who shot T.J."

Kendrick shoved Sam away from him. "Get your gear together and get out of here. You're both fired."

"Fired!" Sam's mouth dropped open.

"Mr. Kendrick, you can't do that!" Eliot protested. "My father won't let—"

"How Martin chooses to deal with you is his business," Kendrick said. "But hell will freeze over before you work for me again."

Sam's face twisted with rage. He lunged toward Alec, but several men caught him and pulled him back. He tried to break free. "I'll get you, you rotten son of a bitch!" he shouted at

Alec. "What we did to Coop won't amount to half of what I'll do to you! I'll kill you! I'll kick your rotten hide all the way back to the cesspit you came from!"

"Get him out of here," Kendrick ordered. Then to Sam and Eliot, he said, "You can pick up your wages when I get back to the ranch. And stay away from the Coopers!"

The men started to drag Sam away, but he shrugged them off. "I can walk," he snapped. He glowered at Alec and opened his mouth to say something, then clamped it shut again. He pivoted and stalked off, shoving aside anyone who happened to be in his path.

Eliot Dandridge hesitated. He glanced uncertainly from Kendrick to Alec and back again. "Mr. Kendrick, it wasn't my fault. I didn't want—"

"Get out of here," Archer Kendrick said.

"I didn't want to do it! Sam made me."

"I said, get out of here."

Eliot swallowed hard. He looked like he was going to cry. His shoulders slumped in defeat, he followed Sam Luttrell.

"Mr. MacKenzie, I'm Cal Hoagland, the foreman at the Bar-T. Is Coop all right?"

Alec studied Cal for a moment without speaking. Finally, he decided that the man was genuinely concerned about Lauren. "She was hurt badly, Mr. Hoagland. She'll mend, but it will take time. I'll be keeping her at Duneideann until she is recovered enough to return home."

Cal muttered an oath under his breath and shook his head. "Poor kid. If I'd known something like this was going to happen, I wouldn't have sent her home this morning."

Alec's jaw knotted. "You knew. So did you, Mr. Kendrick. Unfortunately for Lauren, you chose to ignore the signs."

Alec turned and headed back toward his horse.

Cal shifted uneasily, but he did not dispute Alec's accusation. "Tell Coop I'll come see her in the next day or two," he called out. "Soon as I can break away from here for a couple of hours."

Alec lifted his hand in acknowledgment, but did not look back.

Kendrick followed Alec. "I hope you're aware that you've made yourself a couple of enemies," he said.

"Aye, I'm aware of that."

"Just so you know to keep your back guarded."

Alec put his foot in the stirrup and swung up into the saddle. "You might pass on something to the rest of the men here, Mr. Kendrick: I'll kill the next man who hurts Lauren."

Chapter 5

Summoning every ounce of strength that she had, Lauren tried to sit up, but the pain was too great and she fell back on the pillows. She took a shuddering breath, and then another. Every muscle in her body hurt. She felt as if she had been trampled in a stampede.

For several minutes, she just lay there, focusing her gaze on the shadows and shapes in the darkened room and trying to remember where she was and how she had gotten here. The last thing she recalled was being sent home from the roundup.

Beneath the covers, her hand came into contact with something sticky. She touched her left hip. It too was sticky, and it hurt like hell. The smell of camphor filled the air, and she wrinkled her nose in disgust.

She cautiously moved her hand down her leg, then back up toward her neck. Then it struck her: she was *naked!*

Dear God, where were her clothes?

Suddenly the bedroom door opened, and Alec entered, carrying a tray. His silhouette in the light from the hallway was tall and lean, his close-fitting jeans emphasizing the powerful muscles of his long legs. His rumpled white shirt was open at the neck, and the sleeves were rolled up. His tawny hair had fallen forward over his forehead. He set the tray on the table beside the bed. "I thought you'd be awake, lass. You were starting to stir when I left you a few minutes ago. Do you feel up to having some hot tea?"

Suddenly she remembered where she was.

She remembered Sam Luttrell and Eliot Dandridge trying to kill her.

She remembered Alec MacKenzie taking off her clothes . . .

She clutched the covers high up under her chin and fought the surge of humiliation that threatened to overwhelm her. "Where are my clothes?"

"I'm afraid they were beyond salvaging, lass. I'll go out to the Bar-T in the morning and get some others for you to wear."

Lauren eyed him suspiciously. "Who else saw me naked?"

"Galston helped me clean your cuts—"

Lauren groaned.

"Galston is very discreet. Without his help, it would have been impossible for me to undress you without hurting you any more than you already were."

She wanted to crawl into a hole somewhere and die. It was bad enough that she was stuck here in bed, too sore to move and naked as a jaybird; the fact that anyone had actually seen her naked was more than she could bear. "Why didn't you just sell tickets? Then everyone in the Territory could've watched the sideshow." In spite of herself, her voice wavered.

"It was not my intention to embarrass you. I'm sorry if you think it was." When she didn't respond, Alec added quietly, "I'm your friend, Lauren. I would never intentionally do anything to hurt you. You can trust me."

A painful lump crowded Lauren's throat. Who else *could* she trust? Pa would just say she must've done something to bring trouble upon herself. Bubba was too young to understand. And Cal was the one who had sent her home from the roundup. If she couldn't count on the people she loved most, then who else was there?

She swallowed hard, but the lump wouldn't go away. "I tried to get away," she whispered achingly, "but they were too fast. I couldn't even outride them." Her voice caught. "I can't outride them. I'm not strong enough to fight them off. What am I supposed to do? Start carrying a gun?"

"A gun is not the answer."

"I suppose you have a better idea?"

"I'm afraid not. Not at the moment anyway." Taking care not to hurt her, Alec helped Lauren sit up.

She held the covers tightly in place over her breasts and tried unsuccessfully to ignore the feel of his hand on her bare back, bracing her. His touch seemed to burn into her skin, like a brand. He handed her a cup of tea and held her fingers steady while she took a sip. When she had had enough, he returned the cup to the tray.

Lauren lay back down and closed her eyes and waited for the tea to spread its soothing warmth throughout her body. The place on her back where Alec had rested his hand still tingled. Unbidden images flickered through her mind: images of Alec carrying her into the house and up the stairs; images of Alec holding her, telling her that everything was going to be all right; images of Alec taking off her clothes; images of Alec kissing her—

He bent down and adjusted the covers around her.

Lauren's eyes flew open.

He slipped his hand beneath her head and lifted it slightly to straighten the pillow. Lauren's pulse leapt unexpectedly. "The tea will be here beside the bed should you want more," he said when he had finished. "I'll return later to look in on you."

Lauren stared up at him. Her heart pounded and she was uncomfortably aware that the warmth seeping through her limbs had nothing to do with the hot tea. "You're leaving?"

"I'll be close by. Try to get some sleep." Alec started toward the door.

"Mr. MacKenzie?"

"Aye?"

She nervously moistened her lips. Her heart was still racing. "When you took my clothes off . . . did you *look?*"

Alec chuckled softly. "Good night, lass."

He pulled the door shut after him.

"Mr. MacKenzie!" Lauren stared at the closed door, willing it to open, but Alec did not return. "Damn you," she muttered under her breath, although she wasn't certain what she was swearing at. Of course he had looked; he was a man, wasn't he? He had probably gotten himself a royal eyeful too.

Tears stung her eyes as she tried to roll onto her side. She wished Dr. Blakely was here to give her some of that elixir he had given Pa after his accident to make the pain go away, then immediately rescinded that wish. She had hurt worse before, and she'd managed to live through it. She just couldn't remember when.

Frank Cooper squinted through the screen door at the tall figure framed by the sunlight. "What the hell do you want?"

"I'm Alec MacKenzie, your new neighbor."

"I know who you are."

"May I come in?"

"Why?"

"It's about your daughter, Mr. Cooper."

"Damn it all! I knew that girl was up to no good. The sheriff was here yesterday looking for her. What did she do?"

"She didn't do anything. She's been injured."

"Injured! How in the hell did she manage that?"

"Mr. Cooper, I refuse to talk with you from opposite sides of the door. If you aren't going to invite me in, please do me the courtesy of coming out onto the porch."

Grumbling, Frank pushed open the screen door. "You might as well come in," he said. Leaning heavily on his crutches, he turned and hobbled into the parlor. Alec followed him.

Frank picked a shirt up from a chair. "You can sit here."

Alec was not unfamiliar with the sour odor that permeated the room; he had smelled it often enough in the cheaper alehouses and roadside taverns. "I'll stand, thank you. What I have to say won't take long."

"Suit yourself." Frank propped his crutches against the chair and put on the shirt.

Alec tried to find some resemblance between Frank Cooper and his daughter, but he saw none. Frank was a big man, both in bone structure and in girth, whereas Lauren was small-boned and slender. Both Lauren and her brother must take after their mother, he thought. "Mr. Cooper, Sam Luttrell and Eliot Dandridge tied up your daughter and dragged her across the desert. By the time my men found her, she was barely alive."

Frank shoved the tails of his shirt into his pants. "She did *what?*"

The muscle in Alec's jaw knotted. It was becoming apparent that Frank Cooper was going to blame Lauren for what had happened, no matter who was really at fault. "Have you no concern at all for Lauren's welfare?"

Frank's expression was a mixture of annoyance and bewilderment. "What the hell is that supposed to mean?"

"You have known for several days that your daughter was missing. I told you just now what happened to her. Yet not once have you asked me how she is faring or how badly she was injured. I am beginning to think you don't give a damn about Lauren."

"Now, you listen here, MacKenzie. I don't

know who gave you the right to come waltzing into my house and spouting off about how I raise my kids, but you can get right back down off your pulpit and—" Frank broke off and his face turned red. "Don't you dare walk away while I'm talking to you!"

Alec stopped in the doorway and turned back toward Frank Cooper. His usually warm brown eyes were cold as ice. "Where is Lauren's room? I wish to take her some clothes back to Duneideann with me."

"Like hell you are! Lauren's going to get her butt home where she belongs!"

"Dr. Blakely instructed that she not be moved for several—"

"Doc Blakely! I don't have the money to pay for no doctor!"

"You need not concern yourself with paying for the doctor's services, Mr. Cooper. I've already taken care of it. Now, if you will kindly direct me to Lauren's room—"

"The Coopers don't accept charity, MacKenzie."

"Good," Alec said curtly. "I'm not inclined to dispense any." He started up the stairs.

Frank swore under his breath. "It's the room at the back," he called out. "And you better not take anything that don't belong to her, or I'll have the law after you for thievery."

Alec shook his head. Frank Cooper was unbalanced.

Even if he hadn't been told which bedroom was Lauren's, he would have had no trouble finding it. The instant he entered the room, he could feel her presence there. A narrow iron bedstead covered with a clean but faded patchwork quilt stood against one wall. Next to it, on the scrubbed pine floor, was a braided rag rug. Beside the door was a three-drawer bureau. A crocheted doily protected the top of the bureau. On top of that was a mismatched pitcher and washbasin. The blue and white porcelain pitcher had a chip in the fluted rim and a crack running down one side. A thin coating of dust covered everything.

There were no closets or wardrobes in the room. Instead, a narrow board fitted with wooden pegs ran the length of one wall. A pair of pants, a flannel shirt, a man's winter wool half-coat, and a white cotton nightgown hung from the pegs. Beneath them, on the floor, was a pair of galoshes.

In the bureau, Alec found another pair of pants and more shirts, as well as underdrawers, camisoles, and socks, all neatly folded and placed in separate piles. In the back of the top drawer, beneath the white cotton camisoles, he found a cigar box.

Curious, he opened the box.

Inside were a pink hair ribbon, a sea horse, a half dozen shiny black seeds the size of small peas, a card with the Lord's Prayer on one side and a picture of London Bridge on the other, and several strands of pale brown hair enclosed in a silver locket. Alec started to smile at the odd assortment when it suddenly struck him that he was looking at Lauren Cooper's entire collection of worldly possessions.

Alec closed the box and looked around the sparsely furnished room, seeing it with new eyes.

Aside from a few changes of clothes, everything Lauren owned was contained in that cigar box.

She didn't even have a dress.

Alec took a deep breath, uncertain why he was so shaken by the discovery. It was not as if Lauren were living in abject poverty; he simply wanted her to have more. He wanted her to have all the niceties and refinements that he had always taken for granted. He wanted to see her in a dress. A pretty gown, with soft kid shoes to match. He wanted to see her with her hair pinned up, so that he could remove the pins and let her light brown hair fall down over his hands. He wanted—

Alec shook his head. Where Lauren Cooper was concerned, his thoughts were taking a dangerous turn. He had begun thinking of her as if she were a beautiful, desirable woman rather than the ill-mannered hoyden that she really was.

And it was all because of that unexpected question she had asked him earlier this morning: *When you took my clothes off, did you look?*

With that question, she had unleashed a demon in his mind. Suddenly, he could think of nothing else. Suddenly, it was not her scrapes and bruises that occupied his thoughts. It was the slenderness of her waist. The rounded fullness of her breasts with their pale pink tips. Her long, shapely legs. Lauren had beautiful legs. He wanted to see those legs again. He wanted to touch them, to feel them wrap around him—

He swore inwardly. If he wasn't careful, he was going to find himself doing more than just entertaining a host of pleasant desires; he was liable to act on them.

He removed the pants, two shirts, and several changes of undergarments from the bureau and closed the drawers. After one final look around, he left the room.

Frank Cooper was waiting for him at the bottom of the stairs.

Frank regarded with suspicion the pile of clothes Alec was carrying. "Why'd you get so many?" he asked. "Just how long are you planning on keeping her there?"

"Lauren will stay at Duneideann until I feel she is ready to return home."

Frank opened his mouth to object, then abruptly shut it again. "Suit yourself," he said instead. "You'll find out soon enough that the girl's nothing but trouble, always mouthing off about things that don't concern her. I warned her about keeping away from Luttrell, but she wouldn't listen. She doesn't listen to a damn thing I tell her, and she sure as hell won't listen to you. You can bank on that, mister."

Alec stopped in the hallway, an arm's reach away from Frank Cooper. The cold sparks that snapped in his eyes barely hinted at the anger and revulsion that smoldered inside him. In his entire life, he had never met anyone who repulsed him the way Lauren's father did. Not the sheriff. Not even Sam Luttrell. The anger he felt toward those two did not come close to matching the choking rage he felt toward Frank Cooper. "I'll tell Lauren you send your regards," he said icily. He opened the screened door and left the house.

"You tell her to get her butt home," Frank shouted.

Alec did not look back. If he did, he was liable to do the unthinkable and flatten a man on crutches.

Alec spent the ride back to Duneideann trying to come up with a way to remove Lauren from her father's influence.

He could offer her a job, he thought. But where? Duneideann was out of the question. He already brought in sufficient day workers from town to help Galston with the cleaning and the laundry. Furthermore, something inside him rebelled at the idea of Lauren's working as a servant in his house. It was not that he considered the work demeaning; he simply didn't want Lauren waiting on *him*.

Some of the business ventures he was developing would offer opportunities for employment. Unfortunately, they were still a long way from implementation; it might be months before anything that Lauren was qualified to do became available.

Something will turn up, he thought. If nothing else, perhaps he could find someone in town who was not already prejudiced against her and would be willing to hire her.

At the house, T.J. Powell was sitting on the

front steps. He was dressed, and his horse was saddled. He got to his feet, his movements slow and cumbersome.

Alec dismounted. "Leaving us already?"

"Yes, sir. This lying in bed all day is wearing on me. I need to get back to work, although I probably won't be able to do much for a while. I just wanted to thank you for putting me up these last couple of days."

" 'Twas my pleasure, Mr. Powell. I'm just sorry your stay wasn't caused by more favorable circumstances. Are you sure you're up to the ride?"

"The doc says it'll be all right as long as I take it slow. He stopped by this morning while you were gone. Besides, Sly is riding with me as far as Encina Wash. If I can make it that far without falling off my horse, I can make it the rest of the way." T.J. paused. "How's Coop holding up?"

"When I looked in on her earlier, she was sleeping soundly. She'll mend. It will just take time."

"I know what some of the folks around here say about her, but Coop's a good kid. She's never done anything to anyone that wasn't deserved. I hope she's all right."

"I'm sure Lauren will appreciate your concern. I wish her father showed as much."

T.J. snorted. "I wouldn't hold my breath. Frank Cooper never gives a thought to anyone but himself. But that's just my opinion. Don't let me sour you on the man before you've had a chance to meet him and form your own judgments."

"I've already met Frank Cooper, and there's nothing you can say that will change my opinion of him."

Sly Barnes rode into the yard. "You ready to go?"

T.J. put his foot in the stirrup and eased himself up into the saddle. "Thanks again for your hospitality, MacKenzie. When Coop wakes up, tell her I'm pulling for her. Let me know if she needs anything, will you?"

"Thank you for offering, Mr. Powell."

"Coop saved my life. It's the least I can do."

After T.J. and Sly rode away, Alec retrieved Lauren's clothes from his saddlebags and carried them into the house.

Upstairs, he found Lauren curled up in a chair by the window, rubbing her hair dry with a towel. She was wearing one of his silk dressing robes, and the dark green color was flattering to her. Her legs and feet were bare. At the sight of them, the sudden memory of how shapely and well-formed she was shot through him, making the blood surge into his loins.

Damn! Alec paused in the hallway and took a steadying breath. His inability to control his body's reactions where Lauren was concerned was becoming more than a minor nuisance. No woman had ever affected him so powerfully.

And that scared the hell out of him.

Lauren lowered the towel to her lap and shoved her damp hair away from her face. Her gaze rested on the bed, and her pulse quickened. She had learned from the day worker who came in to straighten the room that this was not one of the guest rooms. Alec had put her in his own bedroom. She had slept *in his bed.*

Only half-aware of what she was doing, she brushed the sleeve of his robe against her cheek, marveling at the luxurious softness against her skin. She had never before worn anything made of silk, and had no idea that anything could feel so wonderful. Or so decadent. The fleeting scent of a man's cologne tinged the air whenever she moved. Holding the sleeve up to her nose, she closed her eyes and breathed deeply, trying to identify the elusive scent. It reminded her of Alec.

From the doorway, Alec coughed.

Lauren's eyes flew open, and she yanked down her arm, mortified at being caught doing something as silly as *smelling* Alec's robe. Color flooded her face.

Alec crossed the room and placed her clothes on the foot of the bed. "I'm surprised to see you up and about, lass. How do you feel?"

Acutely aware that she was completely naked beneath the robe, Lauren clutched the robe closed at her throat with one hand and at her waist with the other. "Like I got run over by a train."

" 'Tis to be expected." He went to her and placed his hand against her forehead.

The feel of his warm, callused palm on her skin did funny things to Lauren's stomach. Every nerve in her body quivered with a tingling awareness of him, of his closeness.

Of the fact that she had spent the night in his bed.

Again she smelled the cologne. It was a subtle, masculine scent. Alec was wearing it. She stared at his belt buckle, trying desperately not to let her gaze drop any farther than was decent, and took a shuddering breath. "Am I going to live?" she asked.

Alec chuckled. "It certainly appears that way, lass. At least you're not feverish." He sat down on the edge of the bed. "Did Dr. Blakely give you permission to take a bath?"

"He said it was all right. Besides, I needed one. The water stung like mad when I first got in, but once I got used to it, it felt good. I stayed in it so long my fingers and toes puckered up." She nervously bit her lip and cast Alec a shy glance from beneath her lashes. "Are you aware that your bathtub is even bigger than Miss Chloe's?"

Alec eyed her skeptically. "Now what would a good lass like you be knowing about a place like that?"

Lauren clutched the robe tighter. Her face was so hot it felt as if it were on fire. "Actually, it was sort of a dare. Harold Larson told everyone at school that Miss Chloe had red satin sheets on her bed, and no one believed him. To prove him wrong, *somebody* had to sneak into her house and look."

Alec's eyes darkened as he regarded her. "And you were that someone?" There was an odd husky note to his voice that caused prickles to erupt on Lauren's skin.

She grinned sheepishly. "I drew the short straw."

"I see."

She swallowed hard. If the room got any hotter, she was going to faint. She nodded toward the clothes on the bed. "Thanks for bringing my clothes. I-I didn't have anything to wear after my bath, so I borrowed your robe. I hope you don't mind."

Alec's gaze drifted the length of her before returning to her face. "Of course not," he said thickly. "It suits you far better than it ever did me."

Lauren's heart missed a beat. He had given her *that look* again, as if he were mentally peeling off her clothes, only this time there wasn't much to peel away. And he knew it; she could see it in his eyes. She shifted slightly and moved her arm in front of her in an awkward attempt to hide the outline of her breasts beneath the silk.

They were interrupted by a knock at the door. Galston stood in the doorway. "Mr. MacKenzie, you have a visitor. A Mr. Martin Dandridge."

"Oh, hell," Lauren muttered.

"Tell Mr. Dandridge I will be down shortly," Alec said.

"Yes, sir." Galston left.

"You can't tell Mr. Dandridge what happened," Lauren pleaded. "I don't even want him to know I'm here."

"I have a feeling, lass, that Martin Dandridge already knows what happened."

"That's impossible! It only happened yesterday. How could he have found out so—" Lauren broke off, and her eyes grew wide. "Good God, you didn't! *Please* say you didn't tell Mr. Dandridge."

"I didn't tell him. I confronted his son and Sam Luttrell. Eliot Dandridge confessed."

Lauren groaned. "Mr. MacKenzie, I know you mean well, but your interfering is only making matters worse for me. I wish you'd mind your own business."

"Had I minded my own business, lass, you would at this moment be lying in the bottom of a wash, having your carcass picked over by vultures."

"That's not what I meant. I'm grateful that you saved my life, but Sam Luttrell—"

"Anything that involves Sam Luttrell involves me. He knows he will have to deal with me if he bothers you again."

Lauren shook her head. Confusion clouded her eyes. "I don't understand you. No one else in this valley will lift a finger to help a Cooper, yet here you are, sticking your neck out and stepping in shi—I mean cowflop—up to your ears over something that doesn't even concern you. Why?"

Alec stood. "I need to go talk with Martin Dandridge," he said firmly.

"You haven't answered my question."

"Nor do I intend to." Alec softened the curtness of his words with a warm smile. "I'm glad to see you're doing better, lass. I was worried about you." He turned toward the door.

"Mr. MacKenzie, wait!"

"Aye, lass?"

Lauren plucked nervously at the edge of the

towel. "It's not right that you keep fighting my battles for me. I should be the one to go talk to Mr. Dandridge."

Alec was silent a moment before responding. "Are you certain you want to?"

"No. But I'm going to run into him sooner or later, and I'd rather face up to him here where I have you by my side than somewhere else where I'm liable to be pressured into retracting my story. Even Pa isn't likely to believe I didn't do something to bring this on myself. In my whole life, you're the only person who has ever stood up for me."

A long-forgotten incident tugged at Alec's memory. When he was fourteen, he was wrongly blamed for breaking one of the stained glass windows at St. Vincent's Church. His pleas of innocence went unheeded and he was punished for the deed. Although his anger and resentment at being falsely accused soon passed, he had never forgotten the pain he had felt at not being believed. And yet that had been a single incident. Alec could not fathom spending a lifetime fighting falsehoods and misconceptions. It was no wonder Lauren tended to bristle like a porcupine at the slightest provocation.

"All right, if you wish to speak with Martin yourself, I'll respect that wish. I'll wait downstairs while you get dressed. Do you want me to send someone up to help you?"

Lauren shook her head. "I can manage."

Alec started to turn away, then hesitated. His expression was solemn. "I think you will find Martin Dandridge a fair man, lass. However, regardless of what happens, I'll stand behind you. You have my word on that."

Lauren bit down on her lower lip. More than anything she wanted to believe him. She had no reason to. Nor did she have a reason not to. "Thanks, Mr. MacKenzie."

Martin Dandridge was studying an antique claymore when Alec entered the library. "Pretty impressive collection you have here. Family heirlooms?"

"Some of them. Most were acquired. May I get you a drink?"

A wishful look crept into Martin's expression. "You wouldn't happen to have any Glenlivet on hand, would you?"

Alec chuckled. He went to a small upright chest and unlocked it. He could almost hear Martin Dandridge salivating as he withdrew the crystal decanter of twenty-five-year-old Scotch whiskey from the chest.

"Did you say your family is from Edinburgh?" Martin asked.

"Duneideann originally, in Wester Ross. My father moved to Edinburgh before I was born." Alec poured a small amount of whiskey into each of two glasses.

"Mine came from Surrey. Still have relatives there, although I haven't seen any of them in more than twenty years."

Alec carried the glasses across the room and handed one to his guest. "Please, sit down."

Martin lowered his large frame into a chair and set his hat on the low table in front of him.

Leaning back in the chair, he stretched out his legs and raised his glass in a toast. "To men of uncommon tastes."

A look of ecstasy melted over Martin's features when he tasted the Scotch. "Damn, this is good. Last time I had this was in Boston at the victory dinner celebrating Samuel Orrin's election to the Massachusetts State Legislature." He laughed. "That was back when I had more hair and less girth."

Alec sat down across from Martin. The pleasantries continued for a few more minutes before Martin Dandridge got around to the real reason for his visit. "Roy Early rode out to the Diamond Cross this morning and told me he thought Eliot might have gotten himself into some kind of trouble yesterday. Roy wouldn't elaborate; he just said that it involved Frank Cooper's daughter. I went out to the roundup to look into it, only to find out that Kendrick had fired both Luttrell and my son. When Kendrick told me what they had done, I wanted to wring their miserable necks."

"They nearly killed her, Martin. If my men hadn't found her, I doubt Lauren would have survived the night."

"I don't know what's gotten into that kid. He never gave me a lick of trouble until he started taking up with Luttrell." Martin scowled down at the caramel-colored liquid in his glass. "I've decided to send him back East to school. He won't be too happy about my decision, but he'll learn to live with it. And he has relatives back there, so he won't be among strangers."

"I'm sorry it came to this."

"So am I. That boy is my life. Ever since his mother died—well, that's another story. I hope the change of scenery will be good for Eliot. He needs to get away from Luttrell—and from me. Unfortunately, I've spent the past few years making excuses for him when I should have been tightening the reins. Eliot needs to learn to do things on his own and to take responsibility for his actions."

"I hope it works out for you. For both of you."

"How's the girl doing?" Martin asked.

"I'll live," Lauren said from the doorway.

Both men surged to their feet.

Lauren clutched the doorjamb for support. She had put on a pair of jeans and a faded brown shirt. Her feet were bare, but her now dry hair had been pulled back and secured in a loose braid. The color had drained from her face, making her cuts and bruises stand out in garish contrast to her pale skin.

Alec hastened to Lauren's side and caught her arm to steady her. "You should have called me, lass, rather than risk falling down the stairs."

"I'm fine. I just got a little dizzy is all."

"My God," Martin said in a strangled voice.

"I'd show you the rest," Lauren said, "but I'm not about to take my clothes back off after all the trouble I went through putting them on."

Alec led Lauren to the chair he had just vacated and helped her sit down. In spite of her outward hostility, her eyes were wide and dark, and perspiration had beaded across her upper lip, betraying the pain she was attempting to hide with her sarcasm.

Martin sat down on the edge of his chair. He leaned forward, his hands on his knees and his gaze fixed on Lauren's bruised face. He shook his head in disbelief. "When I get home, I'm going to tan that boy's hide," he said.

"I don't care what you do to Eliot, Mr. Dandridge. Or to Sam, for that matter. All I want is for them to stay away from me and leave me alone. I didn't even do anything to them. I got sent home from the roundup because Sam started a fight. I was on my way home when they waylaid me."

Martin's expression was grim as he pondered what Lauren had just told him. "There's not too much I can do about Luttrell since he no longer works for me. I will, however, put out the word that he's off-limits. Once he realizes no one in the valley will hire him, maybe he'll head back toward Mesilla where he came from. We can always hope.

"As for Eliot, he won't be giving you any more trouble. That I can promise you. He'll be leaving at the end of the week. I'm sending him back to Boston for a while."

Lauren eyed the rancher warily. "I didn't think you'd believe me."

"No one wants to believe that his own son is capable of doing something like this. But with the evidence staring me in the face, I have little choice."

Lauren toyed with one of the buttons on the front of her shirt. "I don't know if it'll make any difference to you, Mr. Dandridge, but Eliot didn't want to do it. Sam made him."

"That's very kind of you. All the same, Eliot is old enough to start developing some backbone and stop letting Luttrell push him around." Martin stood up and picked his hat up off the table. "Well, I've said what I came here to say. If you have any trouble at all with Luttrell, you let me know. There's no excusing what he and my son did to you."

"Thank you for believing me, Mr. Dandridge. I thought Mr. MacKenzie was full of hot air when he said you would be fair-minded. I guess he was right after all."

To Lauren's surprise, Martin Dandridge laughed. "You just mend and get back on your feet soon, kid. I'll stop by the Bar-T on my way home and let your father know you're well taken care of here." Martin glanced at Alec and added, "I got the impression Frank has some heartburn over your intentions toward his daughter, MacKenzie. I'll tell him what's going on and set his mind at ease."

Alec accompanied Martin Dandridge to the front door.

Martin lowered his voice and spoke just loud enough for Alec to hear. "Watch out for Luttrell. He's dangerous when provoked."

"He's dangerous even when he hasn't been provoked," Alec said. "Lauren is proof of that."

Martin glanced toward the library, his expression drawn. "It might be a good idea if you kept the girl here for a while, at least until we know what Luttrell's next move is going to be. She'll be safer from him here than she will be at home."

When Alec returned to the library, Lauren was holding Martin Dandridge's empty glass up to sniff. She wrinkled her nose. How anyone could stand the smell of the stuff, much less drink it, was beyond her.

Alec took the glass from her and placed it next to his own on a tray on top of the liquor chest. "Well, was facing Martin Dandridge as bad as you thought it was going to be?"

As usual whenever Alec was near, Lauren's heart began beating a little faster and a little harder. She wondered if her nervousness was as apparent on the outside as it was on the inside. "I felt kind of sorry for him. He looked sad when he talked about Eliot leaving."

"I think getting away from his father for a while will be good for Eliot." Alec sat down on the edge of his desk and folded his arms across his chest. "All young men need to separate from their fathers and forge their own identities. If they don't separate physically, they do it by rebelling. It's a necessary part of growing up."

Lauren studied Alec quizzically. To her, he seemed like such a model of perfection that she could not imagine him ever willfully doing anything that smacked of impropriety. "Did you rebel against your father?"

Alec chuckled. "The citizens of Edinburgh have yet to recover from my rebellion, lass. For two solid years, I was an arrogant, bullheaded youth who thought he had the answers to everything. It was a humbling experience to finally realize just how little I actually knew."

Lauren frowned. "I can't imagine Bubba rebelling against Pa. Pa knows just what strings to pull to make Bubba jump like a puppet."

"Your brother will go through the same rite of passage, believe me. And during that time, he will be damn near impossible to live with."

"God, I hope not. Pa will wipe up the floor with him."

Galston appeared in the doorway. "Where would you like luncheon to be served, sir?" he asked.

"In here will be fine," Alec replied.

"And the young lady, sir?"

"Lauren and I will both take our noon meal in the library, Galston."

"Very good, sir."

After Galson left, an awkward silence fell. Lauren felt as if her tongue were tied in knots. She didn't know what to say. All she could think about was having slept in Alec's bed. Why, for crying out loud, had he put her there when there were five other bedrooms in this house? Where had *he* slept? Martin Dandridge's words echoed in her mind: *I got the impression that Frank has some heartburn over your intentions toward his daughter, MacKenzie.* She cast Alec a tentative glance. Just what *were* his intentions toward her? She wasn't so naive that she didn't know what could happen between a man and a woman if they were together for any length of time, especially at night. "How long are you going to keep me here?" she asked.

"No one will force you to do anything you don't want to do. You are free to leave any time you wish. You would be wise, however, to consider staying until your injuries have healed."

The lilting, musical quality of Alec MacKenzie's Scottish accent was having an odd effect on her. It wasn't just her heart that was galloping out of control. Even her thoughts had taken on a life of their own, filling her head with images that she was powerless to stop. Images of Alec . . . at night . . . in his bed . . . without any clothes . . .

She glanced away. "I-I was thinking of Pa," she stammered. "He won't have anyone to take care of him."

"I'm sure your father is managing just fine, lass."

"It's just that it's hard on him not being able to get around like he used to. I mean, after the accident and all . . ." Her voice trailed off. She couldn't think clearly.

Alec studied Lauren thoughtfully. "Who took care of him while you were at the roundup?"

Did he wear a union suit to bed, or did he sleep naked?

Lauren swallowed audibly. "No one. I mean, he pretty much has to fend for himself during the roundup."

"Look at it this way, lass. If you had not been sent home from the roundup, how much longer would you be away?"

"I don't know. Another week maybe."

"Assume you had planned to be away for the coming week anyway. What difference will it make if that week is spent at the roundup or here, recuperating?"

Lauren stared down at her hands. *He slept naked. She just knew it.* "Not much, I guess."

"Then stay the week. When the roundup is over, go home. That way, you'll not be gone a day longer that you would have been otherwise." Alec pushed away from the desk. He crossed the room and sat down on the edge of the table before her. "In truth, lass, I have another reason for wanting you to stay," he said.

The gentle, almost caressing concern in Alec's eyes made every nerve in Lauren's body tingle as if charged with a jolt of electricity, just like the time she had come within a few feet of being struck by lightning. And just like that time, she felt disoriented and off-balance. Her gaze inadvertently dropped from his eyes to the sensuous curve of his mouth, and she imagined him kissing her. On the lips. The way a man kisses a woman he has taken a shine to . . .

"I want to teach you how to defend yourself," Alec said.

Lauren jerked her head up. Her brows knitted. "I already know how to defend myself."

"Lauren, if what I witnessed in town was a fair representation of your ability, I'm afraid you couldn't fight your way out of a broom closet."

Alec's words struck Lauren like a bucket of cold water. Anger flashed in her eyes. "How kind of you to say so," she retorted. She started to stand, but Alec placed his hand on her shoulder, stopping her.

"Unfortunately, the truth is not always kind, lass," he said gently.

Lauren pressed her lips together in a line of resentment and averted her gaze. As much as she hated to admit it, she knew that Alec spoke the truth. She could throw a damn good punch whenever she had to, but hitting her target was more of a matter of luck than skill. Sam Luttrell had come close to pulverizing her on more than one occasion. One of these days, her luck was going to run out.

She fidgeted. "Can you really teach me how to beat up Sam Luttrell?"

"That's not the same thing, lass. Luttrell is bigger and stronger than you. You'd not be able to hold out against him for long. What I *can* teach you, however, is how to throw him off long enough to give yourself time to get away from him."

Lauren toyed nervously with one of the buttons on the front of her shirt. Not only was Alec's argument convincing; at the moment, she really didn't want to leave. Pa was going to be hot under the collar over her being sent home from the roundup, and she preferred to stay away until he had cooled off a bit.

Torn between what she wanted to do and what she felt she should do, she hesitated a moment before blurting out, "All right, I'll stay."

Chapter 6

No sooner had Lauren spoken than she began to have doubts. She didn't even *know* Alec MacKenzie. At least, not well enough to be staying with him. She opened her mouth to retract her decision, but before she could say anything, Alec stood. "Good," he said. "You need time to heal. Besides, while you're here, you can take the opportunity to discover if you really do like to read. My library is at your disposal. Feel free to make use of it."

Lauren's eyes widened in surprise. She glanced at the bookshelves, hardly daring to believe he'd just said what she thought he'd said. "You mean, I can read your books?"

"If you wish. It will pass the hours for you while I'm working."

Lauren felt like a prospector who had just struck gold. "I'd love to! I'll be very careful with them, I promise."

"I'm sure you will. And when you return home, you are welcome to borrow as many as you want."

Lauren's gaze riveted on his face. "You *trust* me?" she asked, incredulous.

"Any reason I shouldn't?"

"No. It's just that—" She broke off, not knowing how to continue. What should she say? That no one else in the valley trusted a Cooper? He was going to find that out soon enough anyway.

Suddenly, she didn't want him to find out. She didn't want him to hear—and believe—all the unflattering gossip that people persisted in spreading about her family. Sure, Pa drank too much sometimes. But so did a whole lot of other people.

" 'Tis what, lass?" Alec prompted gently.

Lauren gripped the arms of the chair. More than anything in the world, she did not want Alec to come to regret his generosity toward her. "N-nothing. I was just surprised, is all. Are you sure you don't mind?"

"If I did, lass, I wouldn't have offered."

Still disbelieving, Lauren caught Alec watching her, his amber-flecked gaze intense and probing. Her heart swelled in her chest. No one had ever trusted her before. No one. It was all she could do to contain her excitement. She didn't want to look too eager or greedy. "Thanks," she said shakily.

Alec smiled. "No thanks required. I'm going to wash up for lunch. You're welcome to browse through the books while I'm gone. Please, lass, make yourself at home."

After Alec left the library, Lauren eased herself out of the chair, wincing at the pain that shot through her body at the effort. For a moment, she wasn't certain whether to be angry with Sam for doing this to her, or grateful. How else would she ever have gotten a chance to stay in this beautiful house and read books that she'd never even thought of reading and have someone as handsome and exciting as Alec MacKenzie take care of her?

She went over to one of the bookcases. She was still plenty mad at Sam, but right now, she didn't want to think about him. She didn't want to think about anything. She just wanted this wonderful dream to go on forever.

From the bottom of the stairs, Alec watched Lauren tentatively touch the spine of a leather-bound volume with her forefinger, and he felt the longing tighten in his loins. He thought of the way she had looked upstairs, with her hair long and loose, and his robe clinging to her damp skin. The longing intensified.

He wanted her.

He gave his head a sharp shake. What was it about Lauren that affected him so? And why, for God's sake, had he insisted that she stay at Duneideann? What he should do is haul her straight home. Now.

He wondered if he had taken leave of his senses.

Chloe Roberts filled a glass with whiskey from the bottle on her dressing table and carried it to Alec, who was relaxing in a chair by the fireplace. His shirt was unbuttoned at the neck and he had propped his feet up on an ottoman.

"That certainly sounds like Sam," she said. "This wouldn't be the first time he's mistreated a woman."

The flames from the hearth cast a golden glow over her skin, softening her face and making her look younger than her years. Her black lace dressing gown hung open, revealing a generous expanse of creamy skin above her corset, and her flaming hair cascaded down around her shoulders. Alec let his gaze roam over the tempting display of flesh as Chloe handed him the glass. "The one who puzzles me is the sheriff," he said. "He refused to go after Luttrell. I don't know if he's colluding with Luttrell, or if there's some other reason. He seems to harbor an unreasonable hatred toward the Coopers, Lauren in particular."

"Of course he hates Lauren. The girl stood in the way of him marrying her mother."

Alec had been about to take a drink. He slowly lowered his glass. "Oh?"

Chloe sat down at her dressing table, facing the mirror. She picked up her hairbrush and began drawing it through her luxuriant tresses. "I don't know the facts firsthand, mind you, but I've heard enough to piece together the story. Marybeth Hayden—Lauren's mother—was the toast of Millerville in her day. A pretty thing she was, and feistier than a year-old colt. Roy Early planned to marry her. They weren't betrothed exactly, but he had his mind made up."

"And Miss Hayden turned him down."

"Not quite. There was a big dance after the fall roundup. As usual, Marybeth's dance card was full. Roy was there—he wasn't the sheriff in those days—as was Frank Cooper. You'd never know it to look at him now, but I've been told that Frank was considered quite handsome in his younger days."

Chloe swept her hair up off her slender neck and began expertly inserting pins into the neat coil. "Well, as the evening wore on, everyone had a bit too much to drink, Marybeth included. One minute, she was kicking up her heels with Frank Cooper, and the next minute they'd both disappeared from the dance. Roy found them in the back of Burroughs' Feed Store. Roy and Frank tangled, and all the while, Marybeth was begging them to stop fighting and trying to get her clothes back on. Don't know who won the fight; it depends on whose version of the story you want to believe. Before long, however, Marybeth was starting to show, and she and Frank were getting hitched. Roy never forgave Frank, or the unborn child."

"Lauren."

"You got it."

Alec shook his head and let out a long, low whistle. "That explains a lot." Whenever Chloe lifted her arms to insert another hairpin, the light from the oil lamp shone through the sheer lace of her dressing gown, giving him a tantalizing view of her shapely figure. He took a sip from his glass, savoring both the whiskey and the view.

Chloe smiled knowingly at his reflection in the mirror. She took the crystal stopper from a bottle of perfume and drew it through the valley between her breasts. "You're having second thoughts about taking the girl in," she said. It was a statement, not a question.

Alec raised his glass toward her in acknowledgment and regarded her through half-closed eyes. "You're reading my mind again." He drained his glass.

"That's what keeps me in business."

Alec stood. Crossing the room, he set his empty glass down on the dressing table, then took the stopper from Chloe and returned it to its bottle. He placed his hands on the dressing table on either side of her and bent down close. An exotic, spicy scent wafted off her warm skin.

Chloe watched him in the mirror, her eyes darkening as he pressed a kiss to her temple. "What are you going to do with the girl?" she asked.

"I haven't decided yet." Alec moved his lips down her neck, then straightened.

Disappointment flickered in Chloe's eyes. She quickly glanced away from the mirror and busied herself straightening the cosmetic and perfume jars on her dressing table. "Are you sure you won't change your mind about staying the night?"

"I need to get back to the ranch. Sly Barnes and I are riding out early in the morning to inspect the installation of the fences."

While Alec put on his jacket, Chloe pulled several strands of hair from her coiffure and arranged them in wispy tendrils around her face. "Don't be a stranger," she said.

Alec stopped in the doorway and looked around him at the decidedly feminine bedroom that was decorated with an overabundance of velvet and lace—not a red satin sheet in sight—and then at the woman, almost a stranger, who seemed to know him better than he knew himself. And for the first time, he began to sense that something vital was missing from his life.

"Thanks for the drink. And for the conversation. You're a good woman, Chloe Roberts."

Chloe's throaty laugh filled the room. "I've been called many things in my life, Alec MacKenzie. A good woman isn't one of them."

"Perhaps it should be. Good night, Chloe."

"Good night, Alec."

Galston took Alec's jacket and hat. "Miss Cooper is in the library, sir," he said in a hushed voice. "She insisted on waiting up for you."

"Thank you, Galston. I'll take over from here."

"Very well, sir. Good night, sir."

Bracing himself against the desire that inevitably surged through him when he was with Lauren, Alec entered the library. He found her curled up on the sofa, sound asleep.

She was wearing his green silk robe over a white cotton camisole and knee-length cotton drawers that were edged with a narrow band of crocheted lace. The robe had ridden up around her knees, exposing the lacy hem of her drawers and baring her slender ankles and shapely calves to his view. She was lying on her right side, with one hand pillowed beneath her cheek. Her lips were slightly parted in sleep, giving her a look of innocence that contrasted sharply with her womanly curves, a pairing of purity and seductiveness that drove him to distraction. He wanted her more than ever. Only now his passion was accompanied by something else, an ache he could not identify, a hunger that gnawed at him, demanding to be assuaged.

He laid his hand on her shoulder. "Lauren."

Her eyes flickered open, and for several seconds she looked confused, as if she couldn't remember where she was. "Mr. MacKenzie," she mumbled sleepily. She pushed herself upright, and her long hair cascaded down around her. "Where were you? You didn't come home for supper."

"I had business to take care of," Alec said stiffly, not certain whether he was more unsettled by her prying or by his body's uncontrollable response to the sight of her hair shimmering in the lamplight. She looked so delectable sitting there in his robe, her expression soft and unguarded, that he was sorely tempted to forget her injuries and take her right there on the sofa.

Lauren rubbed her eyes. "That wine I had with supper . . . it made me sleepy."

" 'Tis late, lass. You should be in bed."

"I need to talk to you. It's about my horse. I don't know what happened to him. I asked Sly, but he said he hasn't seen him."

"I'm sure your horse is all right. He's probably found his way home by now."

"It's just that everything I took to the roundup was in my saddlebags."

"In the morning I'll send someone out to look for him. Right now, however, you need to get to bed."

Lauren got to her feet, holding on to the arm of the sofa to steady herself. "There's something else."

Alec wasn't certain how much longer he could stay in the same room with her and maintain a respectable distance between them. Not trusting himself, he went to the liquor cabinet and poured himself an extra large Scotch. He'd already had more than his usual quota tonight—enough to weaken his defenses, but not enough to impair his abilities. If he was lucky, he might be able to drink himself into insensibility. It might be Lauren's only protection from him. "What is it?" He took a swallow.

"It's about my sleeping in your bed."

The whiskey went down faster than Alec intended, burning a path to his stomach. "What about it?" he asked, trying to catch his breath.

"Well, it was real nice of you to let me use your bedroom, but I thought you might want it back."

"Aren't you comfortable?"

"Yes, but—"

"Then there's nothing to discuss. You'll stay where you are, and I'll stay in the guest room until you return home."

"Wouldn't you rather sleep in your own bed?"

Alec's fingers tightened around the glass. He forced a smile. "The guest room suits me fine. Now be a good lass, and go to bed."

Lauren's brow puckered as she regarded him. "Are you all right?"

"Go to bed!"

She flashed him a resentful look. "All right, I'm going. You don't have to tell me again. Good night, Mr. MacKenzie."

"Good night, lass."

As soon as she left the room, Alec downed the whiskey that remained in his glass and poured himself another. He hadn't drunk anywhere near enough to drown the lust that raged through his veins like a brushfire. Would he rather sleep in his own bed, indeed! Surely the girl wasn't so naive that she didn't know where such questions could lead? Was she oblivious to the effect she had on him?

Of course she was, he realized. That was part of her appeal. It was also what made her so damn infuriating. Never had he known a woman who could arouse him so thoroughly without the slightest awareness that she was doing so.

He put down the glass. The Scotch wasn't helping him keep his mind off Lauren. If anything, it was weakening his resolve to stay away from her. He blew out the lamps and went outside. The brisk night air struck his face, sobering him, but did little to cool his ardor. He started toward the stables, his long, determined strides echoing the intensity of his frustration. He couldn't risk returning to the house until he had his desire under control.

Still smarting from being sent to bed like a child, Lauren took off Alec's robe and laid it across the foot of the bed. She was nineteen years old, for crying out loud! Of course, *he* probably hadn't noticed that. To him, she was probably just a kid, and a troublesome one at that.

Except that the way he had looked at her that

day he helped her free the calf, and then again this morning when she was wearing only his robe, told her otherwise. He had noticed all right. Both times he had stood there observing her in a way that made her feel exposed and vulnerable.

Goose bumps rose on her skin, and she shivered. It was an arrogant look, possessive and assessing, and not at all gentlemanly.

It was the way a man looked at a woman he desired.

Lauren's pulse quickened. Surely Alec didn't think of *her* that way? Hell, she was probably the last person in the world he would ever harbor passionate feelings for. He was handsome and intelligent and sophisticated. He could have any woman he wanted.

Besides, hadn't he just ordered her to go to bed, making her feel like a six-year-old who had overstayed her welcome?

She heard the front door open and close. Curious, she went to the window and pulled back the edge of the curtain.

She saw Alec walking across the yard, his shoulders rigid and his strides purposeful, as if there was a well of pent up anger in him.

Her brows knitted in bewilderment. Something was wrong. Had she said something to upset him? She didn't think so. Maybe something had happened while he was in town, something that would explain why he had stayed out so late.

When he was out of sight, she got into bed, wincing at the pain that shot through her limbs.

The sheets felt cool and soothing against her skin. She ran her hand over them, marveling at their softness and wondering about the man who had given up his own bedroom for her.

He hadn't had to give her his room. He could have put her in a guest room—good heavens, this house had five of them! Yet, he hadn't. He'd put her in his bed, and he had taken care of her himself. And he had gone after Sam Luttrell. No one she knew would have dared take on Sam, least of all for her.

Why, for God's sake, was Alec being so nice to her?

Trying to get more comfortable, she turned gingerly onto her side. For a long time, she lay gazing at the empty pillow beside her. She visualized Alec's head on that pillow, his hair tousled and his skin dark against the white sheets. She ran her fingertips over the pillow, imagining that she was touching his face, then moved her hand downward, over his chest and the flat, hard plane of his stomach—

The tightness that had been gradually building between her legs suddenly became so pronounced she could hardly stand it. She rolled onto her back and stared up at the ceiling, her breathing labored as she waited for the unsettling sensations to pass.

"Prettiest place in the entire valley," Sly Barnes said. "Ned often talked about building a house here, right on top of this very knoll."

Alec looked at the low rolling hills that shimmered a pale gold-green in the morning light.

Bright orange poppies and blue lupines peeked out from the tall grass that moved with the breeze, and the sky was cloudless except for a few feathery wisps near the horizon. Sycamores dotted the knolls, casting long shadows that followed the sun.

It was a beautiful, peaceful spot. He could easily visualize children playing here, their faces tanned and their bodies strong and healthy. His children. And not just boys. He wanted daughters too. In his mind, he saw a little girl, about six years old, running through the tall grass toward him, her fair hair escaping its braids. She had freckles across the bridge of her nose and was missing two front teeth, and her eyes were wide and trusting and . . . blue.

Like Lauren's.

Alec frowned and shoved the image aside. "Why didn't Ned build here?" he asked. "This is an ideal location for a house."

Sly pushed back his hat and leaned forward on his saddle horn. "Just never got around to it, I guess. Then after the missus died, he lost interest in it. Couple of months ago, he sold the place to you."

Both men turned at the sound of a wagon rumbling down the road. It was the wagon carrying the surveying equipment. Two men sat on the high seat. The driver waved.

" 'Bout time Peterson got here," Sly said. "You ready to get started?"

"Aye, that I am. The sooner we can make this irrigation system a reality, the sooner everyone in this valley will benefit."

"It's going to create some much needed jobs, that's for sure." Sly turned his horse toward the road.

Alec lingered for several seconds, taking a final glance around at the idyllic scene spread before him, and again the sensation that something was missing from his life nagged at him. He made a mental note to return to this spot sometime soon. Alone. He wanted to do a little personal surveying, draw some sketches for a house, and think.

Lauren was sitting on the sofa in Alec's library, leafing through a heavy book on the history of Scotland, when she heard someone ride into the yard. She put down the book and went to the window. Alec dismounted and gave his horse over to one of the hired hands, then started toward the front door.

At the sight of him, her heart swelled in her chest and her hands felt clammy. It was happening again, that frightening sense of powerlessness that always overtook her whenever she was with Alec. It hurt to breathe.

She took a deep breath to calm her racing heart and get her churning emotions under control. *You have to stop this,* she scolded herself. *You have to stop letting him affect you this way. Sure, he's handsome and he probably takes the breath away from every female in Millerville who doesn't have anything better to do with her time than fill her hope chest with impractical gewgaws and daydream about the man she wants to marry. But you're not one of those silly, empty-headed females, and even if you were, you're not the kind of woman that a man like Alec MacKenzie would be interested in.*

It was good, practical advice that failed to take into account that she had spent the better part of her waking hours weaving elaborate daydreams in which Alec played a major role. She imagined them spending long winter evenings together in front of the fireplace. His sleeves would be rolled up and his shirt would be unbuttoned at the neck, and she would be wearing a beautiful gown of sapphire blue silk. She would sit on the floor at his feet, her head resting on his knee, while he read aloud to her. Then he would close the book and lean down and gently kiss her cheek . . .

She rubbed her fingertips across her brow in frustration. This was getting ridiculous. She had never indulged in such outrageous fantasies before. But then, she had never known anyone quite like Alec. She wondered if this was how it felt to be in love, then quickly discarded the notion before it had a chance to take hold. Of course she wasn't in love. People in love did incredibly silly things that no sensible person would ever do—such as fuss over their appearance.

Alec entered the library and Lauren was gripped with a longing so acute it hurt. She unthinkingly reached up to smooth her hair, then jerked her hand away when she realized what she was doing.

The self-conscious gesture did not go unnoticed. Alec's gaze riveted on her hair. She had not braided it, he noticed, and was wearing it down, and it cascaded over her shoulders and down her back, soft and shiny and shimmering in the sunlight that streamed through the window. He ached to touch it. Schooling his face into an unreadable mask, he shrugged out of his jacket and draped it over a chair. "I have good news for you. Your horse returned to the roundup."

Lauren came away from the window, her preoccupation with Alec momentarily overshadowed by concern for her horse. "Is he all right? He wasn't hurt, was he? What about my saddlebags? All my stuff was in them."

"Your saddle and saddlebags were both missing, but the gelding had nary a scratch."

"My saddle!"

Alec had been rolling up his sleeves. At Lauren's stricken tone he glanced up. "That's what Mr. Kendrick said."

"Oh, hell. Pa will have a fit when he hears about the saddle. It was his good one, the one he bought just before he hurt his legs."

"Lass, when I found you, you were lying in the bottom of a wash, unconscious. You can hardly be blamed for the loss of your saddle when you were unable even to help yourself."

Lauren raked her fingers through her hair in frustration. "You don't understand. I was responsible for it!"

Alec did not know of anyone in his right mind who would hold Lauren accountable for the loss of that saddle. His one experience with Frank Cooper, however, suggested otherwise. Perhaps Lauren was justified in fearing her father's reaction. "I have extra saddles here at Duneideann that are not being used," he said. "Feel free to choose a replacement for the one that was lost."

Lauren flashed him a smoldering glance. "The Coopers don't accept charity, Mr. MacKenzie."

"It isn't charity, lass. Merely a gesture of consideration to a friend."

Lauren immediately felt guilty about being so thin-skinned. She shifted nervously from one foot to the other. "Can we talk about something else?" she asked.

"If you wish." Alec poured himself a whiskey. "What do you want to talk about?"

Lauren moved to stand in front of his desk. She leaned against it, half sitting on the edge of the broad, polished top. "I don't know. Er . . . what did you do today?"

She was wearing those jeans, the ones that clung to her shapely form like a second skin and left little to the imagination. Alec wondered if she would continue to wear them if she knew what lascivious thoughts the sight of them conjured up in his mind. "Well, first thing this morning Sly Barnes and I met with surveyors. Then, as promised, I rode out to see Archer Kendrick about your horse. The rest of the day I was at the bank, going over different investment strategies to provide financing for the electric power and irrigation projects I want to initiate."

"Those sound like expensive propositions."

"They are. That's why I want my brother-in-law to study the proposals before I commit to anything. James is the financial wizard in the family. I prefer to withhold making a final decision until I have heard his suggestions. He and my sister will be visiting this summer, so I can discuss the matter with him then."

Lauren's eyes widened. "I didn't know you had a sister."

Alec went to a chair and sat down, then stretched out his long legs. He regarded Lauren through half-closed eyes over the rim of the glass as he took a drink of the whiskey. Damn, she was beautiful. Her color had returned and the abrasions on her face were healing nicely. He wondered how her other cuts were healing, and his eyes darkened as he visualized her without clothes. He lowered the glass. "I have two brothers as well, both younger than I," he said thickly. "Ian runs an import-export business in Edinburgh, and Donald is currently going to school in England. Sarah is the youngest." His casual words gave little hint of his true state. The blood pounded in his temples, and elsewhere, infusing him with an acute awareness of how Lauren's presence was playing havoc with his self-control.

Lauren couldn't imagine Alec being a child, much less having siblings. "Are your parents still alive?"

"Very much so." There was an odd catch to his voice. "And so is my father's father. We MacKenzies are a long-lived lot."

Lauren smiled shyly, only she wasn't certain what she was smiling about. She felt her face grow warm, and it was all she could do to stay still under Alec's piercing scrutiny. She glanced up at the painting over the mantel. "Is that your grandfather there, in the skirt?"

Alec chuckled. "That curmudgeon is Alistair MacKenzie, my great-grandfather. And he would roll over in his grave if he heard you refer to his kilt as a skirt. In the Highlands, lass, a man's clan tartan is an emblem of power and strength, one he wears with pride."

Lauren tried to imagine Alec riding into Millerville in a kilt. It would be quite a sight, one that the townsfolk wouldn't soon forget. Still, the kilt did look suspiciously like a skirt. "Do you ever wear one?"

"Aye. When I'm at home with my family, I'm most comfortable wearing one. Here, however, 'tis somewhat impractical."

"It's *dangerous,*" Lauren retorted. "You're liable to get a sandbur where you wouldn't want one."

When they finished laughing, Lauren gazed up at the portrait of Alistair MacKenzie, and her expression turned pensive. "What are they like?"

"Kilts?"

She shook her head. "Your family."

Alec's brow knitted as he pondered her question. "I think you will like Sarah. She has a playful, mischievous sense of humor. She's wonderful with the children she teaches, and they all adore her. At times she can be a little overwhelming. She has a lovable but exasperating habit of trying to plan her brothers' futures, right down to choosing wives for them."

Lauren's stomach flip-flopped. Her gaze riveted on Alec's face. He was watching her intently, his amber-flecked eyes dark and compelling in his tanned face, and the longings she had attempted to suppress erupted anew. She gripped the edge of the desk. "Did she choose a wife for you also?" she asked shakily.

"She tried. She didn't succeed." Alec inclined his head toward the book Lauren had left lying on the sofa. "I see you've been reading about Scotland. There are several less ponderous books on the shelves if that is your interest."

Fully aware he was scrutinizing her every move, Lauren went to the sofa and picked up the book she had left there. "This was the only one I could find that had a map in it," she said. She opened to the middle, where a page printed on heavier paper unfolded to reveal a large map of Scotland, then went to Alec and placed the book on his lap. "I found Edinburgh. But I couldn't find that other place, the one you named the ranch after."

Alec set his glass down on the table and smoothed out the map. "I doubt Duneideann will be on this map, lass. 'Tis but a hamlet, little more than a crossroads." He traced a forefinger across the page. " 'Tis located here, in Wester Ross, about two miles from Loch Maree."

Lauren moved to one side of Alec's chair and leaned forward. A lock of her light brown hair brushed against his forearm, and his body's immediate response to the silken caress jolted him into an almost painful awareness of the carnal urges that churned within him. His gaze fell on her soft rose-hued lips, no longer chapped and split as they had been that day he found her in the wash, and he was seized with an intense longing to pull her onto his lap and kiss her until she was out of breath.

Lauren's brows drew together in concentration. "It sure is out in the middle of nowhere."

"Aye, that it is. Towns are few and far between, as are jobs. 'Tis why my father went to Edinburgh. He loved the Highlands, but he knew there was little future there. 'Tis difficult to coax a living from the thin soil, and few prosper."

"Do the Highlands look like the mountains here?"

"At dusk, when I look toward the mountains, the fall of the shadows and the slope of the land rising abruptly from the valley floor remind me of the Highlands." Alec's gaze lingered on Lauren's profile, only inches from his own, before dropping to her neck, then lower, to the swell of her breasts beneath her flannel shirt.

To keep his hands from straying toward her, he began refolding the map. "There are no saltbush and mesquite groves, or fields of buffalo grass in Scotland," he continued. "Instead, the mountains of Wester Ross are cloaked in heather and lichen and are more often than not shrouded in a chilling mist. But when the sun breaks through the clouds, 'tis a sight one never forgets. The nearer slopes are so green they put emeralds to shame, while the more distant ridges seem to be carved of amethyst. 'Tis a hauntingly beautiful land, ancient and complex, steeped in the blood of rival clans."

Lauren propped her elbow on the back of Alec's chair and cupped her chin in her hand. A dreamy, faraway look crept into her eyes as she tried to imagine the mental picture Alec had painted for her. "I wish I could see it," she mused aloud. "In my entire life, I've never been away from this valley."

I'll take you there someday, Alec thought, then silently cursed himself. *Good God! What can you be thinking?*

He slammed the book shut and stood up with an uncharacteristic abruptness that caused Lauren to jump back from his chair. He handed the book to her. "I'm going to change for dinner," he said curtly.

He picked up his coat and, without another word, strode from the library, leaving Lauren to stare after him in bewilderment and wonder just what she had done to make him so angry.

Sam Luttrell pounded his fist on the table. He was unshaven, and meanness glittered in his eyes. "Damn you, Corrigan! I said I wan' another drink, an' I wan' it now!"

Jack Corrigan reached beneath the bar and felt for the revolver he kept hidden there. "You've had enough, Luttrell. It's not even sundown, and you've already emptied most of a bottle. Go sleep it off, then come back when you're sober."

Sam shoved his chair away from the table and staggered to his feet.

At a nearby table, a hand of poker was temporarily suspended as the participants watched Sam stumble across the room.

He sagged against the bar. "Now, lis'n here, you interferin' old man. Sam Luttrell don' answer to nobody."

"Take it easy, Luttrell. I'm just trying to keep you out of trouble." Jack placed a potmetal token from the bathhouse on the bar. "You'll feel better after you've had a bath and a shave. It's on me."

Sam knocked the token off the bar with an angry swipe of his hand. The token bounced off the wall and rolled across the floor. "I don' wan' no goddamn bath! I wan' a drink!"

Sam started around the end of the bar to help himself, then stopped short when he found himself blinking down the barrel of a Starr .36 six-shot revolver.

Jack Corrigan's forefinger curled around the trigger. "I said, you've had enough," he said quietly. "Give me any more trouble and I won't hesitate to use this."

"Aw, c'mon, Corrigan. I didn' mean nothin' by it." Sam lifted his hands and backed away. Noticing that the other customers in the saloon were watching him, he kicked over a chair. "Whad'ya starin' at?" he demanded.

The men turned back to their card game.

"Take yourself out of here, Luttrell," Jack warned.

"A'right, I'm goin'. I'm goin'." Sam backed into another chair on his way out of the saloon, tripping and nearly falling in the process. "A man can' even get a goddamn drink aroun' here," he grumbled.

Out on the boardwalk, he swore aloud and

squinted into the daylight that stabbed his eyes. He needed another drink. And a woman. If he had a woman, he reasoned, he wouldn't need a drink. On the other hand, maybe he could have both.

Sam untied his horse and managed to climb into the saddle. He turned his horse down Main Street.

When he reached the big white house on the corner of Main and Sacramento, he dismounted and tossed the reins over a fence picket. He stumbled up the front steps.

The door was locked.

He pounded on the door with his fist. "Lissa? Opal? I know you're in there! Open this door!"

No answer. At an upstairs window, a curtain fluttered in the breeze.

Sam beat harder on the door. "Damn you, Chloe! Wha' the hell do you think you're doin', lockin' this door?"

Chloe Roberts pushed aside the curtain and leaned out the window. "We're closed," she called out.

Sam got down off the porch and backed away from the house so he could see the upstairs windows. "Whad'dya mean, you're closed?" he demanded. "You're never closed!"

"You're drunk. And you know I don't let you fellas in here when you're drunk."

"Aw, c'mon, Chloe. You're not bein' fair!"

"Go away, Sam. And don't come back until you're sober and you have money in your pockets."

"Is this man giving you trouble, Miss Chloe?" Sheriff Early asked.

Sam whirled around to find himself facing the sheriff. The sudden movement caused him to lose his balance.

Early caught his arm, steadying him.

"He's drunk," Chloe called out.

Sheriff Early kept a firm grip on Sam's arm. "Come on down to the jail. You can sleep it off there."

"I didn' do nothin'!" Sam protested.

"I know you didn't. I'm just offering you a cot. Unless you have some other place to go."

"Chloe won' let me in."

"You heard her, Luttrell. She's closed." Early steered Sam away from the house. "Come peaceably, and there won't be any trouble. I won't even lock the cell door."

Sam shook off the sheriff's hand. "A'right, I'll go. Jus' keep your hands off."

This is all MacKenzie's fault, Sam thought as he stumbled after the sheriff. If MacKenzie hadn't gotten him fired, Jack Corrigan wouldn't have thrown him out of the Shady Lady, and Miss Chloe wouldn't have locked her door against him.

It was MacKenzie's fault, all right. MacKenzie's and Coop's. He intended to pay back both of them.

Chapter 7

Alec tossed aside the report he had been studying on the feasibility of bringing electric power to southern Pima County, and pressed his fingertips against his closed eyes to relieve the ache that had developed during the past hour. Outside, the wind had picked up, and the occasional slamming of an unsecured shutter hinted at a coming storm.

Lauren had long since retired for the night. His earlier abruptness with her had created an awkwardness between them that lasted throughout dinner. Afterwards, she had mumbled something about being tired and had gone straight upstairs. He had retreated to the library and buried himself in his work.

Or tried to.

He could not stop thinking about Lauren.

He kept remembering the way she had been watching for him at the window when he returned from town. The way her face lit up when he entered a room. The way she blushed whenever she caught him watching her.

The way she looked with her hair spilling down around her shoulders.

The way his body reacted to her, stubbornly defying his efforts to remain unaffected by her presence.

He wanted to make love to her.

He wanted to go upstairs, right this moment, and remove her clothes, piece by piece, until she stood before him naked and unadorned, her only ornament her glorious hair that he longed to bury his hands in. He wanted to pick her up and carry her to the bed and spend hours touching and kissing and exploring every inch of her. And then, when neither of them could wait a second longer, he would part her legs and—

He swore aloud. *'Tis wrong,* he told himself, abruptly shoving the images from his thoughts. Lauren was at Duneideann under his protection, and she was only now beginning to trust him. To cross the line from friendship into intimacy before she was ready would be taking advantage of that trust.

He got up from his desk and went to pour himself a drink. He had certainly worked himself into a fine state tonight, he thought, thoroughly disgusted with himself. Getting drunk a second night in a row might be a convenient solution to his dilemma, but it was hardly a sensible one. If he wanted a woman, all he had to do was ride into town; Chloe Roberts would be more than happy to accommodate him.

Except that he didn't want Chloe, or any other woman. He wanted Lauren. And for the life of him, he couldn't explain why.

There was something about her that went beyond mere physical attraction, something that had touched a place deep inside him that he had not known even existed. An innocence that was more than simple naïveté. Being burdened so young with adult responsibilities made her seem older than other girls her age. Yet in other ways she was still very much a child. A very private, very guarded child. It was as if she had taken the loving, spontaneous, vulnerable part of herself and locked it away behind a wall of antagonism where it would be safe from hurt. He longed to break through that wall, that armor of thorns that did more to isolate than to protect her.

He stared at the amber liquid in his glass, feeling its fire in his veins before he had even taken a drink. Only it wasn't the whiskey that generated such heat in him; it was Lauren. Right or wrong, he wanted her with a passion that he was powerless to fight.

If he didn't get out of this house, he was liable to do something he would later regret.

He put down the glass and turned toward the door, but the sight of Lauren standing in the doorway brought him up short.

She was wearing his silk dressing robe, and her long light brown hair tumbled freely over her shoulders and down her back. Her eyes widened in surprise when she saw him, the velvet black pupils abruptly expanding. His gaze dropped to her mouth, soft and pink and inviting, and the heat in his loins intensified. "Do you want a drink?" he asked thickly, fighting for control.

Lauren glanced at the bottle of whiskey and shook her head. "No, thanks. I just came down to get a book. I-I couldn't sleep."

"I'm finished working for the night. We can sit and talk if you wish."

Lauren's mouth went dry. She clutched the front of the robe closed, acutely aware that she wasn't wearing much of anything beneath it. She hadn't planned on staying down here; she just wanted to grab a book and slip unnoticed back up to her room. To Alec's room, where she couldn't sleep because she couldn't stop thinking about him. She wished now she had changed back into her clothes before coming downstairs. "I-I guess that would be all right," she stammered.

She sat down on the sofa, tucking her legs beneath her, then immediately wished she had chosen a chair instead, or at least the end of the sofa rather than the middle. Alec sat down beside her and stretched his arm along the back. She wondered if he knew she had been thinking about him. She wished he wouldn't keep looking at her mouth because it made her want to look at his, and whenever she did that she started wondering what it would be like if he kissed her.

She shoved her hair away from her face and nodded toward the wall containing Alec's collection of antique armor and weapons. "Those things must be really old."

"Some of them are. That double-edged broadsword on the far end is one of the oldest pieces. It was made in the fifteenth century, and was a favored weapon among the ancient Highlanders."

"Did it belong to one of your ancestors?"

"More than likely it belonged to one of my ancestors' *enemies*. The earliest generations of MacKenzies did little to endear themselves to their neighbors."

"Like the Coopers."

Alec smiled. "You could say that."

The warmth of Alec's smile eased the knot in her stomach. "Do you ever get homesick?" she asked.

"Occasionally. I miss the amenities I was accustomed to in Edinburgh. And I miss my family."

"Why did you move so far away? Couldn't you have stayed in Scotland and had a ranch there?"

"Perhaps. But the opportunity arose to come here, and I took advantage of it. I've always wanted to see America."

"I can't imagine what it would be like to leave Pa and Bubba and go halfway around the world to live." Lauren's expression clouded. Every time she thought about Pa, she couldn't help anticipating what he was going to say when she got home.

"Something is troubling you, lass. What is it?"

She shrugged. "I was just thinking about Pa. He isn't going to like the idea of my staying here."

"Does he think I will take advantage of you?"

"Hell, no. He'd probably welcome that, because he could force you to marry me and then brag to everyone about having a rich son-in-law." No sooner were the words out of Lauren's mouth than she regretted them. She didn't know what had come over her. When she was lying upstairs in his bed, trying to fall asleep, she had started thinking about what it would be like to lie there as his wife, with him beside her. It was only a daydream, colored by a bit of wishful thinking perhaps, but a daydream nonetheless. She certainly hadn't intended to say anything about it. Her face turned red. "I didn't mean that. It just sort of slipped out."

Alec wasn't certain if he was more amused or irritated by the idea of Frank Cooper trying to trap him into marrying his daughter. Either way, the fact that Lauren had thought about it intrigued him. What else did she think about? Was she as innocent as he had assumed? Or did she too lie awake at night, resisting the demons of the flesh?

Lauren nervously moistened her lips. "What I really meant is that Pa is going to be pretty riled up about my not coming home right away. He'll figure that for me to be laid up here, I had better be dead, or damn close to it."

"Lass, Dr. Blakely can attest to the seriousness of your injuries, as can Martin Dandridge. As far as anything else that may transpire while you are here, 'tis for you to decide just how much you want your father to know."

Lauren had the odd feeling that they were not talking about the same thing. She glanced away. "Thanks."

Alec regarded her thoughtfully. "You really don't want to go home, do you, lass?"

The color left Lauren's cheeks. "I didn't say that."

"You didn't have to. 'Tis written all over your face."

A sudden constriction in Lauren's chest made it difficult to breathe. There was an unpleasant ring of truth in Alec's words that pricked her conscience. "I'm starting to feel tired. I think I can fall asleep now."

She uncurled her legs and started to get up, but Alec caught her arm, stopping her. "I hope you are aware, lass, that anything you tell me will remain strictly between us."

Lauren stared at Alec's large hand fastened around her arm and fought a rising sense of panic. She didn't know what she was afraid of, unless it was her own mixed-up feelings. She felt as if she were on the verge of blurting out every fear, every doubt, every troubling dream that had ever haunted her. "I hate to disappoint you," she said unevenly, "but there's nothing to tell. I'm just looking forward to getting out of doing my chores for a few more days. So you can stop trying to read my mind and . . . and . . ." Her voice trailed off.

His hand tightened on her arm. "And do what, lass?"

As if drawn by a force she had no will to deny, her gaze slid downward over the tanned planes of his face to his mouth, and her heart began to pound mercilessly. "Nothing."

Alec's eyes darkened. "Kiss you?" he prompted.

Lauren jerked her gaze back up to his, and her face reddened. "I didn't say that!"

His eyes never leaving hers, Alec slid the fingers of his right hand into the light brown hair that fell like a soft, shimmering veil and gently, but insistently, drew her face toward him until their lips touched.

Desire and uncertainty surged through her at once, as well as the realization that she didn't have the slightest idea what was expected of her in return. Hundreds of times she had thought about kissing, but thinking about it was miles removed from actually doing it. His mouth began to move on hers. Her heart racing, she instinctively leaned a little closer, neither returning nor resisting his caresses, yet hoping desperately that she could figure out what she was supposed to do before he realized she didn't already know.

Puzzled by her unresponsiveness, Alec relaxed the pressure he was exerting on the back of her head and drew back slightly. He saw the confusion and wonder in her eyes, and then he knew. He brushed his thumb over her cheek. "You've never been kissed before," he said gently.

Mortified that he should suspect her ignorance, she shook her head. "That's not true. I've been kissed lots of times."

"Liar."

Before Lauren realized what was happening, Alec lowered her to the sofa and shifted so that he was above her, his knee between hers and his weight bearing her deeper into the cushions. His face was so close to hers that she could see the tiny lines that radiated outward from his eyes and feel the whisper of his breath on her skin. He lowered his lips to hers.

This time Alec gently guided her toward the responses he sought. Without hurry, he molded his mouth to hers, exploring each curve with painstaking deliberation, until he felt her lips soften and begin to yield to his. He ran the tip of his tongue over her lips, then along the crease separating them, urging them to part. When they finally did, he slipped his tongue between them.

Lauren gasped at the unexpected invasion, and her body went rigid with shock. Then gradually her panic gave way to the realization that what Alec was doing to her wasn't as unpleasant as she had first thought. If anything, it was almost enjoyable!

She forced herself to relax, and when she did, Alec deepened the kiss.

His intimate explorations of her mouth caused Lauren's head to swim until she could hardly think. Every nerve in her body seemed to have suddenly become overly sensitive to the slightest stimulation. She was aware of the blood coursing through her veins, of the sound of her own breathing, of the heaviness of Alec's body on hers, of his hand gliding down over her hip and beneath her bottom to pull her closer against him. Her entire body began to tingle with a sweet, yet almost painful, sensation that she had no name for. She felt her will to resist slip away.

As her control weakened, so did her inhibitions. Surprising herself with her own daring, she wrapped her arms around Alec's neck and haltingly touched the tip of her tongue to his.

He clasped her tighter against him, and his kiss become more demanding as his role shifted from teacher to that of lover. He kissed her deeply, thoroughly, awakening responses in Lauren that were utterly foreign to her. The blood pulsed through her veins so fiercely that her body felt as if it had been blanketed in an intoxicating heat. Alec pulled open the green silk robe and slid his hand beneath her camisole, and a tremor of delight reverberated through her as she felt the callused warmth of his hand against her bare skin.

He lifted his lips from hers, and Lauren opened her eyes to find him watching her with tender concern. Beneath her camisole, he continued to stroke her skin with gentle, unhurried movements that made her feel warm and relaxed inside.

Alec felt his heart beating unnaturally hard. Lauren's face was flushed and her eyes dark with newly awakened passion. If he had wanted her before, now he knew he would not be content until he had possessed her completely. His need for her was so great that he doubted his ability to discern whether or not she wanted him to continue. The last thing he wanted was to force her into something she might not be ready for. "Do you want me to stop, lass?"

Lauren swallowed hard. Her conscience told her that a lady did not permit a man who was not her husband to touch her in such a bold manner, but the rest of her never wanted it to end. She shook her head.

Alec groaned. He lowered his head to hers.

This time, she returned his kiss without reservation. At his prompting, her lips parted, her tongue returning his bold caresses with an abandon that both surprised him and further strained his self-control. She slid her hands up his neck and into his hair, clasping him to her as she allowed herself to be carried away by the drunken, dizzying sensations his kisses aroused in her.

As he trailed his lips down her neck, Alec undid the tiny buttons on the front of her camisole, then pushed the thin garment aside.

Her sensations heightened by the sudden coolness against her bare skin, Lauren's breathing quickened as Alec glided his hand up over her breast and began gently rolling the sensitive tip between his thumb and forefinger. Then he lowered his head and drew her nipple into his mouth.

She sucked in her breath as sharp pangs of desire shot through her like thousands of heated arrows. Alec caressed one nipple with his fingers and the other with his tongue, gradually increasing the draw of his mouth until she was writhing beneath him. At the same time, he moved his knee higher between her legs, his thigh exerting a gentle yet persistent pressure against that part of her that was beginning to throb with a fiery ache. She moaned and clung to him, unable and unwilling to resist the wonderful sensations that swept her along like a leaf in the wind, sending her swirling higher and higher into a vast, endless sky.

Suddenly Alec stopped and sat up. He gripped Lauren's arm and pulled her upright.

Her skin still tingling from his caresses, she fought her way up out of the confusion and disorientation that still gripped her. She pulled the robe closed, covering herself. "What's wrong?"

"Nothing." Alec stared across the room, not looking at her. Tension emanated from every muscle in his body. His breathing was labored. "You'd better go up to bed now."

Hurt and humiliated, Lauren caught her bottom lip between her teeth and glanced away. She didn't know what had happened to drive this sudden wedge between them. She swallowed hard. "I'm not a child," she managed to get out over the lump in her throat. "You can't keep sending me to bed every time I do something to displease you."

"I know you're not a child, lass. Believe me, no one is more aware of that fact than I. Please, just go to bed."

Lauren slowly got to her feet, but she still held back. She couldn't leave until she understood why he was sending her away. "Are you sorry you kissed me?"

Alec's gaze riveted on her. The warmth she was accustomed to seeing in his eyes was gone. "It was a mistake," he said curtly. "It won't happen again."

Lauren recoiled from the harshness of his tone. "Maybe it was a mistake for you," she shot back, fighting the tears that choked her throat, "but I'm not sorry it happened. I'll never be sorry it happened."

She spun and bolted from the room.

Alec surged to his feet. "Lauren, wait!"

She did not stop. Alec heard her footsteps on the stairs, then the bedroom door slam.

He swore inwardly. What, in the name of God, had possessed him to kiss her like that? He should have stopped as soon as he realized how inexperienced she was. He should never have let it go as far as it had. What if he had gone farther? What if he hadn't been able to stop at all? The last thing he needed were the complications that were certain to arise from bedding some damn virgin he had no intention of marrying.

He went to the liquor cabinet. What he did need was a drink.

He rapidly downed the whiskey, letting it burn a punishing trail to his stomach, then poured another.

Outside, the wind shuddered through the valley.

Chapter 8

Rain lashed against the windows, and in the distance, thunder rumbled through the valley. In the library, the drapes had been drawn against the storm, and a fire burned brightly in the huge fireplace, banishing the chill.

Lauren lay on her stomach on the thick carpet before the hearth, her head cradled in her arms and her gaze fixed on the dancing flames. An open book lay on the carpet beside her, but she could not concentrate on it. Her mind kept wandering to thoughts of Alec.

She had cried herself to sleep last night.

She tried to tell herself that she had done nothing wrong, but she was having a hard time believing it. Why else would he have dismissed her so abruptly?

Perhaps she should leave. She could get around just fine now, and her injures were healing. She really had no reason to stay any longer except to take Alec up on his promise to teach her how to defend herself.

For all the good that would do, she thought, blinking back the fresh tears that welled in her eyes. She didn't need anyone to teach her how to defend her body; it was her heart that needed protecting. *From him.*

It was crazy. She couldn't believe it herself,

but what other explanation was there? She was in love. *In love.* With Alec MacKenzie, of all people.

It wasn't until he kissed her that she realized it, and by then it was too late. All the daydreaming about him, all the fantasizing about their being together, had merely been masks to hide what she was too afraid to acknowledge all along: that she was falling in love with him. All her life she had wanted to fall in love, yet who would have thought that something that was supposed to feel so wonderful could hurt so much? Instead, she felt as if someone had ripped her heart out of her chest and left it lying on the ground to bleed to death.

And all because he said kissing her had been a *mistake.*

Mistake, hell. He just didn't like kissing her and didn't have the heart to tell her so. It was easier to attribute the kiss to an error in judgment and send her off to bed. Her throat tightened. Why couldn't their kiss have been as wonderful for him as it was for her?

She was so lost in thought that she did not hear Alec enter the library.

"Good morning, lass."

Startled, Lauren pushed herself into a sitting position and hastily wiped her eyes with her fingertips. Before she could respond, Alec turned away and spoke to Galston, who had followed him into the room. "We'll move the furniture out of the center. I want as much of the carpet exposed as possible."

"Very well, sir."

"We'll start with the desk. Take it slow. Don't hurt yourself."

Lauren picked up the book she had been reading and got to her feet. Puzzled, she watched while Alec and Galston moved Alec's massive desk toward the wall. "What are you doing?" she asked.

Alec cast her a cursory glance. The lines on his face seemed deeper than usual and there were shadows beneath his eyes, hinting at a sleepless night—or perhaps one tainted by too much Scotch. "If I remember correctly, lass, I promised someone that I would teach her how to defend herself. Since it appears that this rain has no intention of letting up soon, today seems as good a time as any."

He gave no sign that anything had happened between them last night.

She shifted nervously from one foot to the other. "You really don't have to do this, Mr. MacKenzie."

"I promised you I would." He inclined his head toward the chairs. "You can move those out of the way."

Lauren's throat tightened. She didn't know whether to be hurt or offended by Alec's brusque manner. Either way, being cooped up in the house with him today was liable to put a strain on both their tempers. Why couldn't it have waited until tomorrow to rain?

Glad for something to do to keep busy, she returned the book to its place on the shelf and began shoving the overstuffed chairs toward the wall.

In a short time, they had the carpet cleared of all furniture.

"Will there be anything else, sir?" Galston asked.

"That will be all for now. Thank you, Galston."

"My pleasure, sir." Galston left the library.

Alec went to the wall where his collection of armor and weapons were displayed and removed a mask of metal mesh. "Nothing we do today is going to hurt you, but if you get tired and wish to rest, just tell me."

He spoke not a single word about last night. Did he even remember kissing her? Or had it been so awful for him that he didn't *want* to remember?

"Lauren, did you hear me?"

She jerked her gaze up to his face. "I'm sorry. What did you say?"

A wrinkle of impatience formed between Alec's brows. "If you get tired, tell me, and we'll stop."

She nodded.

He put the mask on.

"What is that?"

" 'Tis a fencing mask, lass, designed to protect the wearer's face from the point of a saber or an épée."

Her eyes widened and her gaze riveted on the assortment of deadly-looking blades on the wall. "You're going to teach me how to use one of those?" she asked, incredulous.

"No," Alec said firmly. He moved to the center of the carpet. "Come here."

Uncertain what he was up to, she went to stand before him.

He took her right hand. At his touch, her defenses crumbled. No matter how much loving him made her heart hurt, she was powerless to resist the potent attraction he had for her. She glanced away and swallowed hard against the lump that had become wedged in her throat.

"Lass, are you all right?"

She took a deep breath and forced herself to met his gaze. "I'm fine. What did you want to show me?"

Alec's gaze searched her face. He knew she had been crying. Her eyes were puffy and there were faint pink splotches on her cheeks. His stomach clenched and he swore inwardly. He hadn't meant to hurt her feelings last night, but if she had stayed in the same room with him a moment longer, he was liable to have done far more than he had. What was it about her that made him want her so badly, that even now was coiling through his veins and undermining his resolve to keep his distance from her? It was as if she had gotten beneath his skin and taken possession of his soul.

He forced the disconcerting thoughts to the back of his mind, but failed to banish them completely. "I'm going to teach you how to use your hands and your feet," he said.

"But that's what I've been using all along."

"Incorrectly, I'm afraid." Ignoring the pained look Lauren shot him, he continued, "What are the most vulnerable areas on a man's body?"

She stared blankly at him. Suddenly the answer to his question struck her at the same time that she became aware of the warmth and strength of his callused fingers wrapped securely around hers. She felt her face grow hot, and her body began to ache with unrelieved longings. "His privates?"

"Aye, that's one area. The knees are another, as are the eyes. There are others, but those are the three we will concentrate on."

That *he* did not seem embarrassed made Lauren even more aware of her reaction to him. She took a deep breath and tried not to let her discomfort show.

Alec molded Lauren's hand into a fist, then opened out the fore and middle fingers to form a vee. "Your goal is to disable your attacker just long enough to allow you to get away from him. The quickest and least expected way is to go for his eyes." To demonstrate, he brought Lauren's two extended fingers toward his eyes. Her fingertips touched the cool metal mesh. "Jab at his eyes with all your strength, lass," he said. "Go ahead. Try it."

Alec's shirt was open at the neck, and Lauren caught herself staring at the tawny curls that peeked out. An image of him barechested flickered through her thoughts, and the longings intensified. She swallowed hard. "I might hurt you."

"You won't. That's why I'm wearing the mask."

"All right, I'll try." Trying desperately to ignore the distracting sensations that were destroying her concentration, Lauren pulled back her hand and stabbed. Her fingers thudded against the metal mesh.

"Harder," Alec said.

She tried again.

"Harder!"

She nervously moistened her lips and stabbed again.

"Harder!" Alec had raised his voice to a shout. He took a menacing step toward her.

Lauren's heart pounded. What did he want her to do? Blind him? She shook her head and started to back away. "I-I can't—"

Alec caught her wrist, halting her retreat. "This is no time to be squeamish, lass. Your reluctance to act quickly and forcefully could cost you your life. Is that what you want?"

Her earlier blush of embarrassment gave way to an even deeper flush of anger and humiliation. She tried unsuccessfully to extract her hand from Alec's grip. "Of course not," she mumbled.

Through the mask, Alec could see her face and the anger that smoldered in her eyes, echoing the fire in his loins. His fingers tightened around her wrist in a subconscious attempt to strangle the passion she aroused in him. "Then do as I tell you," he said sternly. "Don't worry about whether you're going to hurt me." He released her wrist.

She jerked her hand away and massaged her sore flesh. Her mood had deteriorated, and she had to bite her tongue to keep from blurting out something she would likely regret.

Alec took several steps back, then started toward her, his hands raised and poised for attack.

"Pretend I'm Sam Luttrell," he said. "I'm coming after you, and I'm angry. What is the first thing you're going to do?"

Lauren glowered at him. "Run like hell," she retorted.

"Good answer. Always try to get away first if there is any chance at all of avoiding a fight. Assuming there is no avenue of escape, what will you do next?"

Alec's praise mollified Lauren's temper. "Go for his eyes?"

Alec nodded. "Do it."

Lauren started to obey, then hedged. "This is ridiculous."

Without warning, Alec smacked her lightly on the side of the head, deliberately goading her. "Do it," he repeated.

Stunned, Lauren ducked and stumbled backward.

"Remember, I'm Sam Luttrell." Alec smacked her again.

Again Lauren ducked, but this time she had gathered her wits enough to know what was expected of her. As soon as she straightened, she stabbed at Alec's face with her right hand, striking the mask with enough force to send an unpleasant tingling sensation up her right arm.

Still advancing toward her, Alc smacked her again, harder this time. "Again!"

Now there was no holding back. Lauren lunged at him with every ounce of strength she had and drove her extended fingers into the mask.

"Good! You're catching on."

For the next half hour they practiced the exercise, first with Lauren using her right hand and then her left, until her arms began to tire. Then Alec taught her other tactics—how to throw a man off-balance by striking him just behind the knees; how to thwart an assailant who might grab her from behind by bringing her heel down hard on his instep, then using those precious seconds before he recovered to poke him in the eyes. He taught her how to improve her leverage and make her kicks more effective by dropping onto her back.

"Lie down on the carpet and give me your feet," Alec ordered.

Aware of the suggestiveness of her position, she did as he instructed. She was on her back, looking up at him, just as she had been last night on the sofa when he kissed her. The memory of that kiss, coupled with the feel of his strong hands as he grasped her ankles, was nearly her undoing. More than anything, she wanted him to kiss her again, to touch her the way he had last night.

He placed her feet flat against his abdomen, then moved his hands along her legs to cup the front of her thighs. "The muscles here are the strongest in your body," he told her. "Take advantage of them. Use their strength to attack, not to support your own weight."

His hands seemed to burn through her clothing; she was so painfully aware of them that it was almost impossible to concentrate on what he was saying as he showed her the most effective way to kick.

Each time she mastered a step, Alec lavished praise on her. More accustomed to receiving criticism than encouragement, she was wary at first. But gradually her resistance weakened, and she found herself swelling with pride and a sense of accomplishment.

The time flew.

Finally Alec stopped to catch his breath. He pulled off the mask and dragged a sleeve across his sweat-dampened forehead. He looked at Lauren. Her face glowed and her blue eyes shone with a light he had never seen before. Her happiness touched something deep inside him, unleashing far more than simple lust.

Damn, I want you. He hastily shoved aside the unbidden thought.

"We'll go through the steps one more time, and then we'll call it quits. How are you holding up?"

Lauren shoved her hair from her face. "I have a few more bruises than I started out with," she said, laughing, "but other than that, I'm fine."

"Are you ready to go again?"

"Ready when you are."

Alec put the mask back on. "Stand over there," he said, directing her to the center of the carpet. He retreated to the far side of the room. "Pretend you're in town, loading supplies into your wagon. I'll come up behind you."

Lauren nodded, then turned her back on Alec and slipped into the pretense he had suggested.

He strode across the library. Lauren was just bending down to pick up an imaginary bag of flour when he seized her arm and spun her around.

She retaliated with a swift kick to his groin.

It all happened so fast, she wasn't sure what had hit her. One second she was on her feet; the next she was flat on her back, staring up at the ceiling and trying to get her bearings. She raised up on one elbow and pressed her fingertips against her throbbing forehead.

Alec stood, straddling her legs. He shook his head in dismay. "That, lass, is the price of executing a kick from a standing position," he said.

The memory of Alec grabbing her ankle and yanking her off her feet suddenly returned. "That wasn't fair!"

"Do you think Sam Luttrell is going to play fair? Has he been fair to you in the past?"

Lauren answered him with a withering glance.

Alec extended his hand to her. "Get up. We'll try it again."

They practiced the maneuver again. On the fourth try, Lauren managed to place a kick to Alec's stomach that landed him flat on his back. Terrified that she might have hurt him, she scrambled to her feet and leaned over him. "Mr. MacKenzie, are you all right?"

Suddenly Alec's hand shot out and he seized her pants leg, giving it a yank that caused her to squeal in surprise as she lost her balance and pitched forward. She crashed into him, knocking him onto his back and landing on top of him. Before she could get up, Alec wrapped his arms around her, imprisoning her against his chest.

"Damn you," Lauren muttered. Half laughing, half incensed, she lifted her head and opened her mouth to blast him with the full measure of her temper. But when their gazes met, the words died in her throat.

There was no mistaking the passion that smoldered in Alec's eyes, or the intent behind them as his gaze dropped to her mouth.

In that instant, Lauren knew he was going to kiss her again.

He rolled, pulling her beneath him, and his mouth came down hard on hers.

Lauren gasped as a liquid fire blazed through her veins, engulfing her in a dizzying heat and awakening something primitive and demanding in her. She returned his kiss with a fevered urgency, threading her fingers through his hair and pulling him to her. Her lips parted and a moan of surrender shuddered through her as she yielded to the forceful domination of his kiss.

After several moments, Alec tore his mouth from hers and struggled to control his raging passions. He warned himself to slow down, to stop now, before he could not stop at all. Lauren was inexperienced. An innocent. He did not want to frighten her. But he did want her. And he didn't know how much longer he could keep denying himself.

Her lips still burning from his kiss, she gazed up at him through a giddy haze of longing. "Please, don't stop," she whispered breathlessly.

His jaw tightened. He rose to his feet, pulling Lauren with him. A cry of protest sounded in her throat. Before she could get her bearings, he caught her around the waist and swung her into his arms.

She gasped and wrapped her arms around his neck, certain he would drop her. He carried her across the library toward the door and out into the hall, and a new fear began to take root in her mind. Surely when she said *don't stop* he understood that she meant don't stop *kissing her?*

He started up the stairs, and her alarm began to build. She buried her face against his neck and tried to calm her apprehensions. This couldn't be happening. It didn't need to happen. All she had to do was tell him he had misunderstood her, that she really didn't want to do this.

Or did she?

The security of his strong arms around her, the subtle scent of his cologne, the feel of the taut cords in his neck against her face all made it difficult to think.

Alec carried her into his bedroom and laid her on the bed. His bed. The bed she had occupied—alone—every night since her arrival at Duneideann.

Her eyes flew open. She opened her mouth to tell him that she couldn't go through with this, but when their gazes met, the fire in his eyes caused her pulse to leap with excitement. In that moment, she knew that she would never, for as long as she lived, want another man as much as she wanted Alec.

He went to the bedroom door and closed it.

He started to undress, and Lauren's heart began to race when for the first time she saw the tanned sleekness of his torso and the way his muscles contracted when he removed his shirt and placed it to one side.

Suddenly she could no longer bear to lie there, waiting, while he removed his clothes. Or, worse, for him to change his mind. She sat up and took off her shoes, then got to her feet. Acutely aware of Alec's gaze on her, she kept her own averted as she unbuttoned her shirt, then her camisole, and removed them.

Her hair tumbled down around her bare shoulders and brushed against her breasts, causing her nipples to harden. Ignoring the unsettling sensation, she unfastened her britches and slid them down over her hips. Not until she stepped out of them and was completely naked did she finally dare look at Alec.

He had stopped with his hands on the waistband of his trousers and his attention fixed on the flesh that became bared to his view with each piece of clothing that she removed. Standing before him with her shiny hair in disarray, her long legs bare, and her blue eyes wide with an erotic mix of defiance and vulnerability, she was the most enticing creature he had ever seen. Every nerve in his body was as taut as a bowstring stretched to its limit, and the ache in his loins had become too painful to ignore.

He removed the rest of his clothing.

If Lauren's experience in kissing was nonexistent, growing up on a ranch had given her sufficient knowledge of the sexual act to dispel any potential misconceptions about what was going to take place between them. Still, when Alec crossed the room toward her, her knees began to quake so badly that they threatened to fail her.

Their gazes locked, and for one terrifyingly long second, Lauren felt a twinge of fear at the restrained determination in his eyes. Then he buried his hands in her hair and tilted her head back, capturing her lips with a fierceness that stole the breath from her lungs. She slid her hands over his chest, delighting in the rock-hard muscles beneath her palms. She touched his shoulders, his corded neck, the bunched muscles of his back. He wrapped his arms around her, crushing her against him, and kissed her hungrily, passionately, until she felt as if her entire body had turned into a pulsing core of heat.

Taking care to avoid her hip where the skin was still bruised and tender, Alec ran his hands over her back and buttocks. The molten warmth of his hands on her bare skin caused a tremor to shudder through her. He began to knead her buttocks with his strong fingers, and her knees buckled.

Alec lowered her to the bed.

She clung to him, pulling him down with her. He nudged her legs apart with his knee and settled between them. Lauren slid her fingers into his hair, drawing his head down to hers, and her lips eagerly sought his. He teased her lips with his tongue, tasting them, caressing them, then urging them apart so that he could deepen the kiss. He began to caress her breasts.

So many sensations assaulted Lauren's nerves at once that each seemed to intensify the others. The moist warmth of his mouth. His knowing fingers coaxing her nipples into taut, tingling buds. His weight bearing down on her, and the feel of his manhood pressing urgently against the soft flesh of her inner thigh. The sound of the rain drumming against house walls. All those things, and more, honed her awareness of him to an agonizing sharpness. She felt like a bubble, growing larger and larger, quivering with the forces being exerted on it from both within and without.

Then Alec moved his hand from her breast, down over her abdomen and into the silky triangle of curls at the base of her thighs, to stroke a spot so sensitive it felt as if it would ignite of its own accord, and the bubble burst.

Lauren cried out and her back arched as a liquid heat engulfed her entire body.

Alec entered her swiftly.

For several long seconds, the pleasure gave way to pain and confusion. Lauren wasn't certain what had happened. Then Alec began to move within her. The sharp, stabbing pain gradually subsided and Lauren became aware of his manhood deep inside her, filling her, awakening in her something so achingly wonderful that she thought she would die of pure bliss.

Alec thrust faster and harder, driving his hips against hers with uncontrolled force. "I'm . . . sorry," he gasped. "I can't . . . wait." He pressed into her one last time, and his entire body shuddered convulsively again and again as he poured his seed into her.

After the tremors subsided, Alec rolled onto his side, carrying Lauren with him. He folded his arms around her and held her against his pounding heart as he struggled to get both his breathing and his emotions under control.

He didn't know what had happened to him. Never before had he lost control like that. Not only had he climaxed in an embarrassingly short time, but he had been so overcome by his own need that he had neglected to take the time to pleasure her the way he should have. He vowed he would make it up to her.

Beside him, Lauren lay very still, fighting the feelings of emptiness and desolation that had begun to take over as soon as she began drifting back to reality. She did not regret her decision to lie with Alec. Nor was she so naive as to harbor any hopes that he might marry her. She knew in her heart that there could never be anything between them. She also knew that her daydreams had been just that, elaborately embroidered fantasies to help pass the time and dull the sharp edge of loneliness.

So why did she feel so wretched? Why had the comforting warmth that had engulfed her while their bodies were joined evaporated into an aching knot in the pit of her stomach when Alec withdrew? Why did her heart feel as if it were on the verge of breaking?

Alec rose up on one elbow so he could look into her face.

Not wanting him to see how close she was to crying, Lauren started to turn her head away, but he caught her chin and turned her face toward his. His expression was unreadable and his eyes were dark as they searched hers.

He stroked her cheek with his thumb. "I hurt you," he said simply.

She started to shake her head. "You didn't—"

"I did. I wanted you so much, Lauren, that when it finally happened, I lost control. I charged at you like a crazed bull, taking my pleasure at your expense. For that, I'm sorry."

Lauren tried to grasp what he was saying at the same time that her heart vehemently protested any blame on his part. How could she tell him what she was feeling when she didn't understand it herself? Lifting her fingers to his jaw, she traced the sensuous line of his mouth and down his strong chin, reveling in the warmth of his skin. Never in her life had she known a man who was so incredibly handsome or who could make her feel so wonderful and so uncertain at the same time.

"You didn't hurt me," she said. "I just didn't know what to expect, is all. I-I've never done anything like this before. Until last night, I'd never even kissed anyone, even though I said I had."

"I know."

"I didn't want you to think I was ignorant."

"You were inexperienced, lass, not ignorant. There is a big difference." He eased her onto her back and shifted his weight over her. He lowered his head to hers.

She groaned inwardly, unable to bear the onslaught of conflicting emotions that surged through her the instant their lips touched. His hand played lightly over her skin as he kissed her gently, tenderly, without the fevered urgency that had marked his previous kisses, and again Lauren felt desire awaken in her. She curled her hand behind his neck and slid her fingers up into the thick tawny hair at his nape.

I love you, she thought achingly.

Alec eased his arm from beneath Lauren, taking care not to wake her. He got out of bed and drew the covers up over her, then stood for several moments looking down at her.

She was lying on her back, with one slender arm thrown up over her head. Her long lashes cast shadows on her cheeks and her hair tumbled in tangled waves over the pillows and around her shoulders, a disheveled reminder of the fury of their lovemaking only a short time before.

Alec quickly suppressed the urges that reawakened in him, swearing under his breath at his overwhelming desire. He had never before known a woman who could satisfy him so completely, yet leave him aching for more. He could not get enough of her. He still wanted to make love to her. Again and again.

He was just reaching out to touch her cheek when Lauren stirred. She turned her head toward him and her eyes opened. A sleepy smile touched her mouth. "How long was I asleep?"

Alec leaned down and kissed that soft, beckoning mouth. "About an hour. You were exhausted."

Lauren blushed, remembering their last bout of lovemaking. He had lingered over her for hours, exploring every curve of her body and bringing her to one intoxicating peak after another.

Alec straightened. He went to the chair where he had left his clothes and pulled on his trousers. "I'm going down to the kitchen and make us some tea, and perhaps something to eat. Are you hungry?"

Before she could respond, her stomach let out a long growl. She grinned sheepishly. "Does that answer your question?"

Alec winked at her. "Go back to sleep. I'll bring the food up here and you can have it in bed."

He left the room, pulling the door shut behind him.

Lauren's smile faded. She sat up and looked around the bedroom, fighting back the melancholy that settled over her as soon as she was alone.

Damn it all! Why couldn't she have fallen in love with someone else? Why did it have to be Alec MacKenzie? He was the last person in the valley she needed to get mixed up with. For crying out loud, he was trying to ruin the Bar-T by putting up those blasted fences!

Every time she thought of those fences, she felt she was being disloyal to Pa and Bubba by staying at Duneideann. After the first day, she had been well enough to leave if she had really wanted to. To make matters worse, now she was more reluctant than ever to return home. No one had ever treated her as well as Alec did. No one had ever taken the time to talk with her—about books, business, and life in general—or teach her how to fend off an attacker. Pa certainly never had.

Still, Pa was family. And family stuck together, no matter what.

Her throat constricted. Lying with Alec was the second stupidest thing she had ever done in her life.

Falling in love with him was the first.

Alec was halfway down the stairs when he heard Galston say, "I'm sorry, sir. Mr. MacKenzie is busy at the moment. If you wish to return another time—"

"This is important. I'll wait for him." Roy Early had turned to go into the library when he saw Alec on the stairs. "Looks like I won't have to wait long."

Alec swore inwardly. There was no way he could get out of this situation gracefully. He continued down the stairs and extended his hand. "Good day, Sheriff. What brings you out in this foul weather? I would have thought you'd stay inside where it was dry."

Early regarded Alec's bare torso and feet with suspicion. "In case you hadn't noticed, MacKenzie, it stopped raining hours ago," he said wryly.

Galston discreetly excused himself.

Alec motioned toward the library. "You may sit in here. If you don't mind waiting while I get dressed, I'll join you in a few minutes."

Early removed his hat. "That won't be necessary. What I have to say won't take long."

Alec folded his arms across his chest. He

hoped Lauren stayed put and didn't come out into the hall where the sheriff could see her.

As if reading his mind, Early glanced toward the upstairs landing. "I don't see Lauren around anywhere. How's she doing?"

"She's mending."

When Alec failed to elaborate, a look of annoyance flickered across the sheriff's face. After a moment of awkward silence, he cleared his throat. "I saw Martin Dandridge in town the other day. He told me Luttrell no longer works for him. He also told me what his son and Luttrell did to Lauren. I owe you an apology, MacKenzie. That night you came to the Larsons' looking for me, I should have taken your concerns more seriously. At the time, however, I had no reason to believe that Lauren could be in any danger. Usually the Coopers are the instigators of trouble, not the other way around."

Alec said nothing.

"Frank's been worried about her. He wants her to come home."

"You may tell Mr. Cooper that Lauren is safe here. I will take her home when she is ready to go."

"Look, it would be no trouble to take her by the Bar-T on my way back to town. Save you the trip."

"You still haven't told me why you're here, Sheriff."

Roy Early's eyes narrowed and again he glanced at the landing. "I'll get right to the point," he said. "My deputy has arrested the man who shot T.J. Powell."

"Anyone from around here?"

Early shook his head. "His name is Simon Gates. He robbed a bank in Globe and hid the gold in Six-shooter Canyon. Powell nearly stumbled upon his cache when he and Lauren were tracking those wild horses."

Alec's gaze bored into him. He thought of the story Chloe had told him about Early and Lauren's mother, and wondered how the sheriff could let something that happened twenty years ago continue to eat at him after so much time. "Are you going to arrest Sam Luttrell?"

"Let it lie, MacKenzie. Luttrell's already lost his job over this business. What more do you want?"

"I want the man locked up. Barring that, I want him as far away from Lauren as he can possibly get."

"That's not your decision to make. You'd do well to keep yourself out of trouble. I heard how you went out to the roundup and threatened to kill anyone who got near the girl. Folks around here don't cotton to some stranger waltzing in and telling them how to run their lives."

"Sheriff, I may still be a stranger to many of the people in Millerville, but I intend to make my home here. I'm bringing money and jobs and stability to this valley, and I have a vested interest in making it a safe place to live for the people who depend upon me for their livelihood. Now, if you will excuse me, I have work to do."

Early rammed his hat on his head and opened the front door. "I won't take up any more of your time. However, I must insist again that you refrain from taking the law into your own hands. It's my job to uphold the law in this valley. Not yours."

For a moment, the two men stood eye to eye, mutual hatred shimmering between them like heat waves off the desert floor. When Alec finally spoke, his voice was taut with carefully controlled anger. "I suggest you expand your definition of upholding the law to include protecting the safety of *all* the citizens in your jurisdiction, Sheriff. Otherwise, two years from now, I will use every influence I have to ensure that the people of this valley elect a sheriff who will."

After Sheriff Early left the house, Alec paced the hall for several minutes while he got his anger under control. Roy Early had a way of bringing out the worst in him. It didn't matter to him that Early was nursing a grudge against Frank Cooper. What mattered was how he performed his duties as a lawman. His reluctance to enforce the law where Sam Luttrell was concerned had nearly cost Lauren her life. Alec did not want to think about what could happen the next time Sheriff Early allowed his personal likes and dislikes to cloud his judgment.

Once his temper was safely diffused, Alec went into the kitchen. He had promised Lauren tea. She was probably wondering what was keeping him. Had she heard him and the sheriff talking? At least she had stayed in the bedroom.

With the exception of Galston, the other servants and day workers had the day off, so Alec made the tea and sandwiches himself and carried the tray upstairs. He smiled to himself, already thinking ahead to the next time he made love to Lauren.

He knocked lightly on the bedroom door, then opened it. "Lauren?"

She was gone. The bed where he had left her was empty, the sheets rumpled and the coverlet piled in a heap on the floor. Her clothes were nowhere in sight.

Alec put down the tray and returned to the hallway. He checked all the bedrooms and both bathrooms. His heart began to pound with a cold foreboding. He hurried downstairs. "Lauren!"

No answer.

She wasn't in the library or any of the other downstairs rooms.

"Lauren!"

"Is something amiss, sir?"

Alec turned. "Galston, have you seen Miss Cooper?"

"I'm afraid not, sir. Do you want me to look for her?"

Alec raked his fingers through his hair in frustration. "That won't be necessary."

"Very well, sir."

Alec waited until Galston left the room before turning and slamming his fist into the wall. A low, violent oath burst from his lips.

Chapter 9

"Damn it, Coop! What does it take to get through that thick skull of yours? Do I have to hit you upside the head with a two-by-four?"

"Pa, it's wrong! We can't cut Mr. MacKenzie's fences!"

Cal shook his head. "That's not the way of it, Coop." Cal and the others had returned from the roundup just after dawn. "We're not going to cut the fences. All we're going to do is let our cattle onto his land, then put the wires back. He'll never even know."

Lauren swallowed the tears that choked her throat. Everyone was sitting at the table. Her half-eaten breakfast felt like a lead weight in the pit of her stomach. She was beginning to wish that she had never come home. "Pa, Mr. MacKenzie saved my life. He was good to me. I can't go behind his back and do this to him."

"If MacKenzie was so damn good to you," Frank shot back, "how come you walked all the way home from his place yesterday? What did he do to you?"

"I already told you, he didn't do anything to me. I just got homesick, is all."

"Don't lie to me."

"I'm not lying!"

Across the table, Bubba snickered. "I think she's sweet on him."

Lauren glowered at him. "Will you please stay out of this!"

"Shut up, both of you!" Frank snapped.

Bubba's mouth fell open. "All I said was—"

"And I told you to shut up. Get your tail outside and start on your chores."

"But I haven't finished breakfast!"

"Now!"

Bubba swore under his breath and shoved away from the table.

Bernie stood up. "I got work to do. Jimmy, you coming?"

Bernie and Jimmy followed Bubba outside.

Her expression sullen, Lauren absently shoved her food around her plate with her fork.

"It's like this, Coop," Cal said after the others were gone. "Our pasture just won't support our herd through the summer. Unless we drive them cattle up into Six-shooter to graze, we're going to lose them."

"Why don't we just plant more pasture?" Lauren asked.

"Where in the hell do you plan to get money for seed?" Frank demanded.

Cal shook his head. "Coop, even if we could plant, it's too late in the year. That sun will cook the life right out of them seeds. You saw yourself how it is out there this morning. It rained half the day yesterday, and the ground is already hard as a brick."

"There has to be something we can do."

"Next year, maybe," Cal said. "But not now."

"It's just not right," Lauren said. "Mr. MacKenzie is my friend."

Frank's fist landed on the table with enough force to make both Lauren and the dishes jump. "And I'm your father! As long as you live under my roof, you'll do as I tell you."

The screen door slammed, and Bubba ran into the house. "MacKenzie's coming!"

The color drained from Lauren's face. Her heart began to pound.

"What the hell does he want?" Frank grumbled.

"Whatever it is," Bubba said, "he looks plenty mad."

Lauren glanced at Cal and caught him watching her, worry creasing his brow. She put her fork down and pushed her chair away from the table. "I'll go find out."

Frank leveled a warning finger at her. "If you say one word to him about what we plan to do, I'll blister your butt."

Anger and resentment welled inside her. "I won't."

"Just see that you don't."

Her heart lodged in her throat, Lauren went outside. She didn't know what she was going to say. She only hoped that he would understand why she had had to leave Duneideann.

Of course he would understand; Alec MacKenzie was the most understanding person in the world. It was one of the things she loved about him. No one else understood her. No one else even made the effort. Instead, they tried, judged, and condemned without even giving her a chance to defend herself.

But Alec was different. He listened to her. He made her feel as if she mattered. He made her feel special.

He was also the only person in the world who had the power to break her heart.

He was unbuckling his saddle's girth when she came out onto the porch. He hoisted the saddle off of his horse's back, and carried it to the house. He placed the saddle on the front porch, next to a pair of saddlebags. There was no warmth in his eyes as they locked with hers. Lauren's stomach tightened in a strangling knot, and she felt as if she would be sick.

"You may use both the saddle and the saddlebags until you find yours," Alec said. "Your clothes are in the saddlebags, along with the book you were reading, and another one that I thought you might enjoy."

Lauren cast a cautious glance at the screen door. Pa still didn't know she'd lost his good saddle. "Thanks," she mumbled.

Alec was silent for several minutes. Lauren squirmed under his probing scrutiny. She kept her eyes averted.

"You left without saying good-bye."

"I was going to leave you a note, but—"

"Damn you, Lauren! I thought we were better friends than that!"

She recoiled from the anger in Alec's voice, and her gaze riveted on his. Anger snapped in his eyes. He continued in a low, ominous voice.

"I thought we could be honest with each other. I *thought* you trusted me."

"I do!"

"Then why did you run away?"

Again Lauren glanced over her shoulder at the door. Alec's gaze followed hers. A muscle in his jaw knotted. Muttering an oath under his breath, he locked his hand around her upper arm.

"Ow!" Lauren cried out, but before she could protest his grip, he had hauled her off the porch and was halfway across the yard. Repressed fury reverberated in every one of his long strides, and Lauren had to run to keep up with him.

When they were out of earshot of the house, Alec stopped abruptly and spun Lauren around to face him. "I want the truth. Why did you leave?"

Her arm throbbed where Alec's fingers had bitten into the flesh. She tried to rub the pain away. "I left because . . . because I was homesick. I missed my family."

"Like hell you did!"

She winced.

"Lass, I watched you. I saw the way your expression changed whenever you talked about your family. The light in your eyes dimmed. It was as if something inside you shriveled and died. You wanted to go home as badly as you would wish for an outbreak of cholera."

Lauren's chin quivered. There was an awful truth to what Alec was saying, and knowing what her father wanted her to do to Alec's fences made her heart feel as if it would shatter. "I love my family," she said in a low, pain-filled voice.

Alec opened his mouth to respond, then hesitated. He had no right to destroy Lauren's illusions regarding her family, no matter how much they were hurting her. He raked his fingers through his hair and struggled to get his anger and frustration under control. "I'm sorry. I didn't come here to talk about your family, certainly not to make disparaging remarks about them."

Cal and Bubba came out onto the front porch and stood watching them.

Lauren nervously moistened her lips. "Look, I have to go. I have a lot of work to do. The men just got back from the roundup, and I have all their laundry to do, as well as Pa's." Lauren started to turn away, but Alec caught her arm. This time, there was no anger in his touch.

"I'm sorry I lost my temper," he said quietly.

The feel of Alec's hand on her arm brought back a flood of memories and caused her body to tingle with the same disquieting sensations he had aroused in her yesterday when he made love to her. She looked away, not wanting him to see her confusion.

"Lauren, look at me."

Steeling herself against the tenderness and warmth she knew she would see in his eyes, Lauren tossed back her head and eyed him with a defiance that belied the churning uncertainty she felt inside.

Alec brushed his knuckles down her soft

cheek. "I'm also sorry if I've done anything to hurt you," he said. "But I'm not sorry we made love."

Alec knew instantly from the pain that flashed in Lauren's eyes that he had struck a nerve.

She took a shuddering breath. "You said it yourself the first time you kissed me. It was a mistake."

He shook his head. "Nay, lass, 'twas no mistake."

"It was a mistake, and it was stupid. I may be a Cooper, Mr. MacKenzie, but I'm not the kind of girl who goes around lying with men." Sudden tears stung the back of Lauren's throat. "I'm not one of Miss Chloe's girls."

"I never thought you were! My God! Is that how you think I saw you?"

Lauren choked on a sob. "I don't know what to think. All I know is that if I keep on seeing you, we might make the same mistake again, and I can't let that happen. I appreciate your saving my neck and putting me up in your house and all, but I'd be a blooming idiot to pretend that there could ever be anything between us. The only thing you and I have in common is that blasted fence that runs between our ranches."

Alec's brows drew together. "I'm afraid you have me at a loss, lass. What do my fences have to do with our friendship?"

His casual reference to the tumultuous feelings he aroused in her as mere *friendship* cut Lauren to the quick. She jerked her arm out of his grasp. "What do I have to do to make you understand?" Her voice shook. "I can't *be* friends with you. I can't be *anything* with you." She whirled around and bolted toward the house.

"Lauren!"

She didn't stop running until she reached the house. She shoved past Cal and Bubba. Alec winced as the screen door slammed shut behind her.

He swore under his breath. *Dear God, what have I done?* he berated himself. He should have known that making love to Lauren would change the way things stood between them. He had recognized immediately her lack of experience, yet instead of stopping what he should never have started in the first place, he had pressed on, taking advantage of her innocence to satisfy his own longings.

He knew what Lauren wanted. The same things most women wanted: a home and a husband and a family. Things he couldn't give her. He liked her. He enjoyed her company. And she satisfied him in bed. But she wasn't the kind of woman he could consider marrying.

After all these years of avoiding entanglements with any woman who might demand marriage of him, why had he let down his guard this time? Was it because, as Lauren thought, she was a Cooper and therefore unworthy of his respect?

Or was there some other reason that he was unwilling to admit, even to himself?

Feeling a little unsteady, as if someone had yanked the ground out from under him, Alec walked slowly back to his horse. He gathered up the reins.

Cal jerked his head toward the saddle and saddlebags lying on the porch. "Aren't you forgetting something, MacKenzie?"

Alec glanced at the saddle, then at Cal Hoagland's unyielding countenance. "No," he said curtly. He mounted his horse.

Bubba leapt off the porch. He picked up a rock and hurled it at Alec's departing back. The rock missed its mark and skidded across the ground. "You keep away from my sister!" he yelled.

Alec did not look back.

Cal folded his arms across his chest and watched Alec through narrowed eyes as he rode away. An uneasy feeling uncoiled in the pit of his stomach. There was something unnerving about a civilized man who could ride bareback with the ease of an Apache.

By the time Lauren reached her bedroom, she could barely see through the tears that stung her eyes. Slumping against the closed door, she slid to the floor and wrapped her arms around her knees, but the pain that gripped her only seemed to get worse. She pressed her lips together in a futile effort to keep from crying.

Driving a wedge between her and Alec had hurt more than anything she had ever done in her entire life. Yet she didn't see that she had much choice. She couldn't keep clinging to the hope that Alec might someday harbor the same loving feelings toward her that she felt for him.

Even if by some remote chance he did return her affections, what about Pa and Bubba? She couldn't turn her back on them. And she doubted seriously that either of them would look too kindly on her even being friends with Alec. As far as they were concerned, he was the enemy.

Damn it all! she screamed inwardly. It just wasn't fair! Why, of all the men in Pima County, had she fallen in love with the one man she couldn't have?

She dropped her forehead to her knees and burst into tears.

Jack Corrigan set a glass and a bottle of whiskey on the bar in front of Alec. "Don't bother," he said when Alec reached into his pocket. "It's already paid for."

At Alec's questioning look, Jack glanced across the saloon and nodded.

Alec turned around.

At a table on the far side of the saloon, Chloe Roberts was seated with three men, who were laughing and talking in loud tones. Chloe looked past them at Alec and inclined her head in acknowledgment.

"Give me another glass," Alec said.

He took the glasses and the bottle and carried them across the saloon.

Chloe leaned toward one of the men and whispered something to him. He turned and looked Alec over, then nudged the man sitting next to him. "C'mon. Let's go see if we can scrounge up enough hands for a couple rounds of five-card."

The men grumbled among themselves, but they got up and went to another table. Their gazes followed Alec as he sat down on one of the chairs they had just vacated.

"How did you manage to get them to leave peaceably?" Alec asked.

Chloe smiled suggestively. "They know I won't let them in if they start fighting."

"Smart woman." Alec filled both glasses. "Beautiful as well." Chloe's low-cut black lace dress showed off her ample cleavage and her upswept hair emphasized the pale perfection of her slender neck. Alec lifted a glass. "To intelligence and beauty, a rare combination."

Chloe observed Alec over the rim of her glass as she took a sip of the whiskey. The expression in her kohl-rimmed eyes was pensive. "Roy Early came to see me last night," she said.

Alec's hand froze in midair. "Oh?"

"He said he got quite an eyeful when he was at your place yesterday afternoon."

"He saw nothing."

"You bedded the girl, didn't you?"

"Chloe, what happens between Lauren and me is not open to discussion."

"What if you've gotten her with child? Have you thought about that?"

Alec frowned. Lauren's abrupt departure yesterday and her odd behavior this morning had left a bitter taste in his mouth that Chloe's prying did nothing to improve. "Is there a purpose to this conversation?" he asked curtly.

Chloe folded her hands around her glass and eyed Alec evenly. "If Lauren is carrying your baby, what are you going to do about it?"

"I certainly won't abandon the child, if that's what you're asking."

"That's not what I'm asking. I think I know you well enough to realize you wouldn't abandon your own child. But what are you going to do about Lauren?"

Alec glowered at Chloe, his mood deteriorating. "Do you have any suggestions?" he asked sarcastically. He could not believe he was sitting here in a public place discussing his private life.

"Were you her first?"

"For God's sake, Chloe! What kind of a question is that?"

At Alec's outburst, conversation in the saloon stopped, and all eyes turned on them. The muscle in Alec's jaw knotted. "I'm sorry," he murmured. He took a swallow of whiskey.

Chloe lowered her voice so that only Alec could hear her. "It's a very important question, Alec, and well you know it. Women don't have the same freedom as men to 'sow their wild oats.' Women are forever after treated as damaged goods."

Alec set his glass on the table. "I appreciate the drink, Chloe, but I didn't come here to be lectured on how to treat a woman."

He started to stand, but Chloe put her hand on his arm, stopping him. "Alec, wait."

"I have work to do."

"Please?"

At Chloe's pleading look, Alec sat down

again. He did not want to talk about Lauren, but he knew Chloe wasn't going to stop pestering him until she'd had her say. If she didn't say it now, she'd say it the next time he came into town. Or the time after that. "All right, I'm listening. But I'm warning you, Chloe, talking about Lauren Cooper doesn't sit well with me."

"That's because you care about her. If you didn't, you wouldn't be so edgy right now."

"Of course I care about her. I'm not entirely lacking a conscience."

"Alec, we're friends. I think I can be forthright with you."

"That hasn't changed."

"Good. Because you might not like what I'm going to tell you, but you're going to hear it anyway." Chloe's brows knitted. "Millerville is a small town, and small towns thrive on gossip, especially the damaging kind. Once word gets around about you and Lauren Cooper—and believe me, it's already started—there isn't going to be a man in this town who won't think Lauren is easy for the taking. If she's lucky, some man will take pity on her and marry her. More'n likely, she'll end up like me, making her living on her back."

Alec's face darkened ominously. "I would never let that happen to her," he bit out.

Chloe smiled sadly. "I'm glad to hear that. Not that I don't do pretty well for myself, but if the truth be known, I wouldn't wish this life on my worst enemy."

Chapter 10

Sly Barnes let out a long, low whistle as he surveyed the solid black bulls in the livestock pens behind the train station in Tucson. "Those are some good-looking bulls you got there, Mr. MacKenzie. I've never seen the likes of them anywhere in the valley. What did you say they were?"

"Black Angus," Alec replied. His brows dipped and he pointed toward one of the animals. "Except for that one with the curly coat. That one's a Galloway. Sell him."

Sly nodded. "Can do, Mr. MacKenzie."

A lilting feminine voice cut through the dust and din of the stockyards. "If it isn't just like you, Alec MacKenzie, to be so enamored of your precious cows that you forget about your own sister!"

Alec pivoted, surprise frozen on his face as his gaze swept over the fashionably dressed, ebony-haired woman who was standing before him with her hands on her hips, her dark-fringed, deep blue eyes sparkling with a mixture of laughter and righteous indignation. "Sarah!"

With a squeal of delight, Sarah Lachlan hurled herself into her brother's arms. Alec wrapped his arms around her in a hug that lifted her off the ground. Over her head, he saw her husband

James standing a few feet away, grinning. Alec put Sarah down and, placing his hands on her shoulders, set her away from him. As his eyes scanned her smiling face, he felt a pang of homesickness. Sarah looked more and more like their mother every time he saw her. "You look great!" he said, still unbelieving. "You both look great. What are you doing here? I didn't expect you before next week at the earliest!"

James joined them. "We made good time on the crossing. In fact, we'd have gotten here sooner, but your sister insisted on making a detour to New Jersey to see a peep show!"

"Oh, James, admit it. You were as interested in seeing Mr. Edison's factory as I was!"

Alec gripped his brother-in-law's hand. "A peep show?" he asked, fighting to contain his mirth. "Sarah, I'm appalled!"

She rolled her eyes. "Oh, you two! You make it sound so lurid! Actually, Mr. Edison and Mr. Dickson's Kinetoscope promises to be a wonderful teaching tool. Even the most troublesome students will enjoy using the invention. Mr. Dickson is working on a Kinetophonograph so that sound will accompany the moving pictures."

James grinned. "I can see it now. Soon Kinetoscope parlors will be opening around the world. For tuppence, one can view Lillie Langtry's ankles and hear her sing."

"Go ahead and laugh," Sarah said, piqued. "I know you think the Kinetoscope is a useless invention that will quietly fall by the wayside, but mark my words: you're both wrong."

"Lovey, we're just teasing you," Alec said. He hugged his sister again. "Damn, 'tis good to see you both. Have you checked into a hotel?"

"Not yet," James said. "We came in on the same train as your bovine investment there. Even the passenger cars smelled of cattle. I, for one, am eagerly anticipating a hot bath."

"Well, then, let's not delay any longer. Sly, I'm going to leave you to finish up here. If you need to reach me, I'll be spending the night at the Arizona Inn. We'll return to Duneideann tomorrow."

The foreman inclined his head. "Don't worry. Me and the boys will have these fellas out to the ranch by the end of the week. I don't want to drive them too fast; they're not used to this heat."

"Neither am I," Sarah said, fanning herself as they headed back toward the train station. Perspiration had beaded across her upper lip. "Is it always so hot here?"

"Wait until July."

Sarah retrieved a handkerchief from her reticule. "I know what I'm going to do while you two are working."

"Enjoy yourself, I hope," Alec said.

Sarah dabbed at her lip with the handkerchief. "Try to keep from wilting," she corrected.

"Careful there," Lauren said. "That barbed wire will slice right through your hand."

Cal swore under his breath. "Hold the damn light still so I can see."

Lauren bit back a retort. She hadn't wanted to

come here in the first place, and Cal knew it. Pa knew it. What made it even more unbearable was that they didn't really need her assistance on this job. She could not help questioning Pa's motives for making her come along.

While Cal loosened the fence wires, Lauren glanced cautiously around. Although she could not see them in the darkness, she could hear the lowing of the cattle that they had spent all day rounding up. Anger smoldered inside her. She hated the dilemma they were in. While she still felt that what they were doing was wrong, she also had to admit they had little choice. It had not rained since that day she left Duneideann, and already the grass in the lower part of the valley was turning brown and dry. If they couldn't get their herd to higher ground and spread over as many acres as possible, they were likely to lose a large portion of it before the end of summer.

Lauren had not seen or heard from Alec since that god-awful day he had brought her clothes home.

For a week, she had cried herself to sleep every night. Never in her whole life had anything hurt as much as the crushing ache that throbbed in the middle of her chest every time she thought of him. She had hoped that not seeing him would help her get over her feelings for him; instead, it intensified them.

To make matters worse, Pa and Bubba and the hired hands would not stop talking about him.

She was still smarting over her confrontation with Alec in the front yard that same morning when Cal asked her at the dinner table what she had done the whole time she was gone. Torn between wanting to defend Alec and cursing him for being the cause of her misery, she had tried to keep the conversation lighthearted. She told everyone about the things she loved most at Duneideann, about Alec's library, his books, and his collection of antique armor and weapons.

Bubba's face had lit up. "Guns?"

"That, and swords and other weapons. I can't remember their names."

"It's easy to have things when you're rich," Frank said sourly.

Lauren bit back the retort that sprang to her tongue.

"MacKenzie's an odd one," Cal said. "He's not one to run from a fight. Kendrick told me that Dandridge likes him because he's well educated."

"He is," Lauren said, hoping Bubba would get the hint. "He went to the university, but mostly he's self-taught. He buys books on any subject that interests him, and becomes an expert on it. He says a man can teach himself anything he wants to know. All he needs is a desire to learn."

Frank had *harrumphed* loudly. "I already know all I need to know," he said. "And so do you. A woman doesn't need to know nothing outside of pleasing a man and bringing up his children, and don't you forget it."

"Damn it, Coop, will you hold that blessed light still!"

Jolted out of her reverie, Lauren steadied the lantern. "Sorry," she mumbled.

Cal flashed her a cutting glance. "Don't get so fidgety," he said. "I'm almost finished."

Lauren's heart pounded unnaturally hard. "You don't think Mr. MacKenzie will find out about this, do you?"

"Not if we're careful, and stick to our story that we missed these steers during the roundup, and they got caught up here when the fences went up."

In spite of Cal's reassurance, Lauren could not shake the disquieting feeling that Alec would not only find out, but also hold her responsible. He had been honest enough to tell her why he was putting up the fences, and he would think she had deliberately betrayed him.

"Stand back," Cal ordered.

Lauren moved aside while Cal rolled back the strands of barbed wire. When the wires were safely out of the way, Cal put two fingers in his mouth and let out a piercing whistle.

Minutes later, Lauren felt the earth rumble beneath her feet as Bernie and Jimmy drove the cattle toward them. She scrambled out of the way as the first steers reached the fence. Shadows in the night, the cattle moved past her. She pulled her bandana up over her mouth and nose to filter out the gritty dust that filled the air.

Bubba brought up the rear, smacking his rope against his saddle and guiding the strays through the fence opening. After the last of the cattle was inside, Lauren mounted her horse and followed, driving the cattle high up into Sixshooter Canyon. Cal stayed behind to move the strands of barbed wire back into place.

The sun was just streaking over the horizon when the last section of fence was mended, and they headed for home.

"She did what?"

Fully enjoying her brother's discomfiture, Sarah took her time dabbing at her mouth with her napkin before responding nonchalantly, "She interviewed several young ladies of fine character and breeding, and selected the ones she felt would be most appropriate to accompany you to the Fourth of July celebration."

Alec swore aloud.

James began to laugh.

Giving his brother-in-law a lethal glower, Alec shoved his chair away from the dining table and stood. He began pacing. "Damn that interfering, conniving woman! Is there no limit to her audacity? Had I known that she was here this afternoon, I would have returned home for the sole purpose of throwing her out of this house."

Mischief glittered in Sarah's blue eyes as she took a sip of wine. "That's not all. I get to help Mrs. Larson make the final decision regarding your escort this Tuesday at a meeting of the Millerville Women's Junior League."

Alec turned to stare at his sister. "I can't believe you agreed to that."

"I didn't. In fact, I was very careful to tell Mrs. Larson that, *if* you decide to invite a young lady to the picnic, you will want to do the choosing yourself."

Alec's brows dipped. "Thank you."

Sarah inclined her head. "You're welcome."

James chuckled. "Your Mrs. Larson reminds me of Lady Chapman. Remember when she tried to snare you for a son-in-law by arranging for her daughter to be stranded with you after the Wrights' Christmas party so that you would be obligated to drive the girl home, thereby compromising her virtue?"

Sarah frowned. "I don't remember that."

"The plan failed," James continued. "Lady Chapman neglected to take into consideration that Melissa was terrified of Alec and refused to get into the coach with him."

At the sideboard, Alec poured a brandy for James and another for himself. He carried the snifters to the table and sat down. "Lady Chapman," he said dryly, "doesn't hold a candle to Arminta Larson. I could understand it if the woman had a daughter she was trying to foist off on some unsuspecting bachelor, but she doesn't. Arminta Larson meddles for the sheer joy of meddling."

"*Are* you taking someone to the picnic?" Sarah asked.

"Yes. The two of you."

"That's not what I meant."

"I know what you meant, Sarah."

She suppressed a smile. "Mrs. Larson seems concerned that you might be entertaining the notion of asking Lauren Cooper to the picnic."

Alec had been about to take a drink of his brandy. He froze with his hand in midair. The blood began pounding at his temples. He slowly brought the glass back down to the table. "Exactly what did she say?"

Sarah waited until the servants had removed the dishes from the table and left the dining room before responding. "I'm afraid she wasn't very complimentary," she said.

"What did she *say?*" Alec repeated.

"She said that the girl was a hoyden, that she was rude and unprincipled, and that her entire family were social misfits."

The light in Alec's eyes became hard and unforgiving. "Arminta Larson," he said slowly, "is a bitch."

"Working late?"

Alec glanced up from his desk to find Sarah standing in the doorway. He set aside the stack of bills that he had been going through and gave Sarah a tired smile. "Just catching up on the correspondence that accumulated while I was in Tucson. What about you? Couldn't you sleep?"

"I was restless. I heard you moving around down here, so I thought I'd come down and visit with you. We haven't had five minutes alone since James and I arrived."

"That's my fault. I've been preoccupied." Alec stood up. "Have a seat. Would you care for a drink?"

"No. And you don't need one either. You had more than enough at dinner."

Alec had started toward the liquor cabinet. He paused thoughtfully. "You're right," he said.

Sarah settled herself on the sofa. She pulled her dressing robe tighter around her, and tucked her feet up under her. "You always drink too much when something is troubling you."

Alec sat down opposite her. "And what, may I inquire, makes you think something is troubling me?"

Sarah absently twisted a curl around her forefinger. "Is it Lauren Cooper?"

"Sarah, I told you at dinner that there is nothing going on between Lauren and me. She is a neighbor. That's all."

"Alec, this is your sister you're talking to! The person who knows you better than anyone. The only person in the entire world who knows that the real reason you refuse to go fishing is because you can't bear to put a squirmy little worm on your hook."

Alec threw back his head and laughed. "You little minx! You wouldn't have any qualms about using that bit of knowledge against me, would you?"

"Not if it were for a good cause." She smiled demurely. "Are you in love with her?"

"No."

"Liar."

"Sarah!"

"Then tell me about her! Stop being so secretive."

Alec held up his hand, palm outward. "Sarah, enough."

"How did you meet her?"

He shook his head in disbelief. "You don't give up, do you?"

"Just answer the question, Mr. MacKenzie."

Alec leaned back in his chair and observed his sister through narrowed eyes. "I met her in town, in front of the Mercantile. She was buying supplies."

"And?"

"That's all there is to it."

"That's not what Arminta Larson told me."

The nerve beneath Alec's left eye twitched. "Arminta Larson—" he began.

"I know. We discussed Mrs. Larson's sterling qualities at dinner. Remember?"

Alec released his breath in a sigh of resignation. "I helped break up a fight between Lauren and a man named Sam Luttrell. Luttrell and another man ran off her team and trampled her supplies, so Lauren hit him with a can of peaches, then proceeded to pound the tar out of him, until he finally managed to blacken her eye and bloody her nose."

Sarah's eyes twinkled. "Aunt Marian would love her."

Alec's expression gentled. "She would at that," he said pensively. He went on to tell Sarah about what had happened to Lauren at the roundup and about the time she had spent at Duneideann, recuperating from her injuries. Occasionally he paused to repeat something funny that Lauren had said. He was careful to avoid any mention of her last day at his home. He told Sarah about Lauren's family; about the tension that his fences were creating between them; of his concerns about the way Lauren's family treated her. He described Lauren's love for books, and how she had devoured them during her stay there.

As Alec talked, Sarah listened. When he finished, she asked softly, "Are you aware that your eyes light up when you talk about her?"

Alec rubbed his brow in frustration. First Chloe, and now his own sister. He felt as if he was being railroaded into making a commitment he wasn't ready for. "Sarah, I like her. She's bright. She's funny. She's beautiful. But there can never be anything between us."

"Why not?"

"We're not suited to each other."

Sarah was thoughtful for a moment. "Alec, remember the stories Mama used to tell about how her family didn't think Papa was good enough for her because he was the son of a penniless crofter from the Highlands?"

"It has naught to do with that, Sarah. I don't care where Lauren comes from, or who her family is."

"Then what's the problem?"

"I don't know." Alec pressed his fingertips against his closed eyelids. "All right," he said wearily. "Perhaps there is some truth to what you are saying. Perhaps Lauren doesn't fit my image of the ideal wife. What does that make me? Evil?"

"A hypocrite?" Sarah suggested.

Alec glowered at her. "Thank you," he said dryly.

"Alec, from what you've told me, Lauren seems like a lovely girl. And you seem to be very fond of her."

"I am."

"And yet you would destroy her reputation and leave her to the mercy of the local gossip mongers while you go off in search of the perfect socialite."

Alec gripped the arms of his chair. The veins in his temples throbbed and fury snapped like live coals in his eyes.

Sarah leaned toward him. "Alec, 'tis not my intent to pry into your private business," she said gently. "It matters naught to me whether you made love with Lauren Cooper. However, from what Arminta Larson told me, I got the impression that everyone in town believes you did. And *that* does matter."

Alec felt as if the room were closing in on him, suffocating him. He kept seeing Lauren's face the day they had argued, and the stricken look in her eyes when she told him she was not one of Miss Chloe's girls. There was a crushing pressure in the middle of his chest. "Are you saying I should put aside everything I've planned and marry her?" he asked slowly.

"I'm not saying that at all. I'm merely suggesting that you take another look at those plans. If you had truly wanted a model wife, you would have married long ago. God knows there were enough colorless specimens occupying the drawing rooms of both Edinburgh and London for you to choose from. I think what you really want, Alec, is someone who can be a part of your dream for the future here in America, who can be far more to you than just a perfect ornament to be set up in a perfect house. I think you want a woman you can *love*."

Alec abruptly stood up. "I'm getting that drink now. Are you sure you won't have one?"

Sarah shook her head. Her brows knitted as she watched Alec pour himself an all-too-generous portion of Scotch.

Chapter 11

Lauren sat on her horse at the end of the long drive and debated whether to turn back. Coming here had been a mistake, she told herself. She had thought that she'd gotten over her feelings for Alec, but as soon as the Duneideann sign over the gate came into view, the ache in her heart came back full force.

A few days ago, Bernie had run into Alec in town. "MacKenzie asked about you," Bernie told her that night at dinner. "He said to tell you that you're welcome to make use of his library any time you want."

Lauren's mouth went dry, and the food she had swallowed stuck in her throat. She wanted to ask Bernie if Alec had said anything else, but she didn't dare. Everyone was staring at her, and the look Pa gave her was especially disagreeable. Alec MacKenzie was not Pa's favorite topic of conversation.

Perhaps he won't be home, and I can return his books without running into him, Lauren reasoned. She almost hoped she wouldn't see him. She had heard that his prized cattle had arrived, and she dreaded his reaction when he discovered the Bar-T's scrub beef grazing on his land.

On the other hand, the thought of *not* seeing him filled her with overwhelming melancholy. If this was how it felt to be in love, she thought miserably, she wished it had never happened to her. Nothing in her life—with the exception of her mother's death—had ever hurt so much.

One of Alec's hired hands was putting new hinges on the front door of the main house when Lauren rode into the yard. He removed the nail from between his teeth. "How's it going, Coop?"

"Doing fine, Jim. How about you? How's your elbow?"

"Still gives me fits, but it's better." Jim had injured his elbow in a fall while Lauren was staying at Duneideann.

Lauren dismounted and removed Alec's books from her saddlebag. "I came to return these to Mr. MacKenzie," she said. "Is he in?"

"Him and Mr. Lachlan went into town." Jim moved out of her way. "You can go on in. Galston's in there somewhere."

Lauren's heart sank. So she wouldn't get to see Alec after all. It was just as well, she thought. Seeing him was going to make her hurt more. She was never going to get over him if she kept reopening the wound. "I'll just leave the books in his library," she said, fighting to keep the disappointment from her voice.

Inside, there was no sign of Galston. Lauren took off her hat and headed for the library.

The instant she entered the room, memories of what had transpired between her and Alec returned with a rush. Her breath caught in her throat as a wave of intense longing assaulted her senses.

Placing the books on Alec's desk where he would be certain to see them, she started to leave, then hesitated. Just leaving the books without also writing a note to thank Alec for their use seemed rude. She wished she had thought to jot down the note before she left the Bar-T. She knew Alec had writing paper, but she was reluctant to go into his desk. She wasn't sure how he would feel about the intrusion.

Finally, deciding that there was no harm in simply taking a sheet of writing paper, she went around the desk and tried to open the top drawer. It was locked. She tested the drawer below it. It too was locked. She was just reaching for the bottom drawer when a woman's voice said, "I thought I heard someone in here."

Lauren shot upright.

A woman stood in the doorway. She was about Lauren's height, and possibly her age, but that was where the similarity ended. She had dark blue eyes and black hair that had been drawn away from her delicate oval face and arranged in thick, shiny curls. Row upon row of hand-knotted lace adorned the perfectly fitted bodice of a crisp white summer shirtwaist. Its lawn fabric was so fine it was almost sheer, and it didn't have a wrinkle in it. In comparison, Lauren felt slovenly in her rough pants and threadbare shirt. Her face flamed, first with guilt at being caught trying to open a drawer in Alec's desk, then with jealousy.

Biting, mortifying, unforgiving jealousy.

"Who are you?" the woman asked.

"I could ask you the same thing," Lauren retorted, suddenly feeling defensive. She wanted to run and hide. How could Alec kiss her when he already had a woman? And not just any woman either. He had the most beautiful woman Lauren had ever seen.

The woman smiled. "I'm Sarah Lachlan, Alec's sister. You must be one of his friends."

Lauren started to shake her head. "Not really. I just live—" Suddenly she realized what the woman had said. "His *sister?*" she blurted out, relief and surprise echoing in her voice. "You're really his sister?"

"You sound surprised."

For the first time, Lauren noticed that the woman had the same lilting accent that Alec did. She didn't know whether she wanted to laugh or cry. "You don't look like him," she said warily.

Sarah's dark curls bounced as she laughed. "Ian and I look like our mother. Alec and Donald take after our father."

Lauren fidgeted. She didn't know what to say.

"You still haven't told me your name," Sarah prompted.

"Coop—Cooper. Lauren Cooper." Lauren bit her lip. She had been on the verge of telling Sarah Lachlan her nickname when it suddenly struck her that she didn't want to be known by *Coop* any more. *Coop* sounded coarse and vulgar and not quite ladylike. As if it mattered, she thought self-consciously. She didn't exactly look very ladylike. She shoved the hair away from her face and motioned toward the books she had put on Alec's desk. "I was just returning the books Mr. MacKenzie lent me. When you came in, I was trying to find a piece of paper so that I could leave him a note." Suddenly it was imperative that Sarah knew exactly what Lauren was doing at Alec's desk. She didn't want Alec's sister to think she had been snooping through his belongings.

Sarah tilted her head to one side as she regarded Lauren. "Alec must like you very much," she mused aloud.

Lauren shook her head. "Oh, no. He doesn't like me at all," she said quickly. "We're just neighbors, is all. My father's ranch borders this one."

Sarah laughed. "You don't know my brother. Alec doesn't part with his belongings easily. He doesn't even allow anyone else to *touch* them unless he likes and trusts that person completely. You must have made quite an impression on him."

This time there was no halting the fiery blush that consumed Lauren's face. "Listen, it was nice meeting you, but I have to go. Pa will be wondering—"

Lauren was interrupted by the sound of the front door closing. Men's voices filled the hall. She heard Alec laugh, and a terrible pressure filled her chest at the sound. Her gaze darted toward the door. She had not seen Alec since that day he had come to the Bar-T to return her clothes. Suddenly, she wished she had not come to Duneideann.

Alec and a shorter man with dark brown hair,

conservatively dressed in a black suit, entered the library.

Sarah went to the other man and looped her arm through his. "James, I want you to meet Lauren Cooper. Lauren, this is my husband, James."

Lauren gripped her hat. It was all she could do to keep her gaze fixed on Sarah's husband. She could feel Alec staring at her. Not knowing whether to shake hands or acknowledge James Lachlan's presence with a nod, she chose the latter. "I'm pleased to meet you, sir."

James Lachlan inclined his head. "Likewise."

Lauren's gaze wavered, and in the next instant, she caught herself staring at Alec. All the painful feelings that she had been trying to suppress the past few weeks returned with a vengeance, striking her like a blow to the heart. She thought she was going to be ill. "Hello, Mr. MacKenzie." Her voice was a strained whisper.

Alec's golden brown gaze bored into her. "Hello, lass."

The air had become charged with electricity the instant Alec entered the room, causing Lauren's skin to tingle. She averted her gaze, careful to avoid looking at his mouth lest she start thinking about kissing again, and inadvertently ended up staring at his hands, those strong, tanned, work-roughened hands that had touched her so intimately that day he made love to her. She took a deep breath and asked shakily, "How have you been?"

Alec made no attempt to avoid looking at Lauren. He boldly, deliberately allowed his gaze to touch her soft, tempting mouth, the swell of her breasts beneath her shirt, her shapely hips, the juncture between her thighs that made him ache to bury himself yet again in her sweet warmth. "I've been keeping busy," he said thickly. "And you?"

Neither of them noticed Sarah and James leave the room, or heard the soft *click* of the library's double doors being pulled closed.

"All right, I guess. Keeping busy." Lauren's voice shook. She wrapped her arms around her stomach to try to regain control of her emotions. She wished Alec would stop staring at her like that, as if he was remembering how she looked naked. It made her feel naked, and then it made her remember how *he* looked naked. And when that happened, her body had a way of betraying exactly what she was thinking. "I brought back your books. Thanks for lending them to me."

"I'm glad you enjoyed them."

Alec went to the liquor cabinet and poured himself a drink. "Have you had any more trouble with Sam Luttrell?" he asked over his shoulder.

Lauren shook her head. "Nope. He's been keeping his distance." She paused. "Eliot left town."

"I heard." Alec carried his glass across the room. He motioned toward the sofa. "Please, sit down."

"I-I can't stay. Pa is probably chomping at the bit now, wondering where I took off to."

Alec caressed her face with his eyes, steadily, methodically stripping away her defenses. "Stay for a few minutes. There's something I want to ask you."

Lauren's heart started pounding so hard she was certain he could hear it. She had no idea what he wanted of her; she just prayed it wouldn't be something utterly awful, like staying away from Duneideann. If she couldn't see Alec again, she would *die.* "I-I guess a few minutes won't hurt." She left her hat on Alec's desk and went to the sofa. She started to sit down, then stopped as the memory of them kissing on that sofa surged through her thoughts, bringing a fierce heat to her cheeks. Abandoning the sofa, she went to one of the chairs and sat down.

The change did not go unobserved. Wondering what she had been thinking just now to bring a rush of color to her cheeks, Alec sat down opposite her. He knew what entered *his* thoughts when he looked at the sofa. He thought of her lying there in his robe, looking wickedly enticing and claiming that she had been kissed before. He remembered the way she had trembled when he unbuttoned her camisole and bared her flesh to his touch. He thought of how close he had come to making love to her that night, and how much he wanted to make love to her now.

"Lauren, will you do me the honor of accompanying me to the Fourth of July celebration?"

She stared at him, too stunned to respond. He wanted *her* to go to the picnic with him?

Alec felt the longing tighten in his loins. It was when she looked at him like that, her eyes wide and innocent, that his body responded most forcefully, because he knew she was no longer an innocent. He was fully aware of the passion that she was capable of. He laughed softly. "I didn't think 'twas such a difficult question. If you wish, I'll repeat it for you."

"I-I was just thinking, it's over a month away," Lauren said, incredulous. *He wanted her to go to the picnic with him!*

A smile played at the corners of Alec's mouth. "I like to make plans well in advance."

She didn't know what to say. After their argument the last time she saw him, she was surprised he still wanted to have anything to do with her. "Are you sure you want me to go with you?"

"I wouldn't have asked you if I wasn't certain."

She shook her head. "I-I thought . . . I mean, I'd like that very much."

"Good. 'Tis settled then. I'll make arrangements to pick you up—"

"No!" Too late, Lauren realized how sharply she had spoken. "It would be better if I met you here," she hurried to explain. "Otherwise, Pa is going to think up a hundred excuses to keep me at home, and he'll probably end up spoiling the day for everyone." Nor did she want to take the chance that Alec might find out what they had done to his fences. The less contact he had with her family and the Bar-T's hired hands, the better.

"If that's the way you want it."

"I think it's for the best. I'll slip out as soon as I've finished my chores and ride over here."

Lauren caught her bottom lip between her teeth. She couldn't believe this was happening! She began drumming her fingertips on the arms of the chair.

"Is something wrong, lass?"

She shook her head. "No."

"Then why are you so jittery?"

She balled her fists as if it was the only way she could keep her hands still. She avoided his gaze. "I-I was just surprised that you asked me to the celebration, is all."

Liar, Alec thought. Lauren was strung as taut as a bow string, ready to snap at the slightest provocation. Her nervousness, the way she kept blushing, told him that there was something going through her mind other than mere wonderment at being invited on an outing. He had a pretty good idea what that something was. He placed his glass on the table beside his chair and leaned forward, dangling his hands between his knees. "Lauren, I'm not going to pretend that nothing happened between us. Nor am I going to pretend that I don't want us to make love again, because I do. I think you do, too."

Lauren had been gripping the arms of the chair, fighting the panic that welled up inside her as he spoke. "I'd better go," she said unevenly. She started to get up, but Alec placed a hand on her knee, stopping her. The sight of his tanned fingers against her faded jeans caused her stomach to somersault. She slid back down into the chair.

"Lauren, look at me."

Her heart pounded. She didn't want to look at

him again, because every time she did, the heat of his gaze seemed to scorch her soul like a brand, leaving yet another wound that she knew would not heal. She squeezed her eyes shut.

Alec took her chin and lifted it. "Look at me," he repeated firmly.

Alec's touch was making her head spin. She kept thinking of that hand caressing her skin, and against her will her body began to tingle in anticipation of it happening again. Expelling her breath in a sigh that was part aggravation, part confusion and longing, she opened her eyes. She wouldn't let him get to her this time. She *wouldn't*.

His gaze dropped to her lips, and then to the rapidly fluttering pulse in the hollow of her throat before returning once more to capture hers. "I want you to look me in the eye," he said slowly, "and tell me you didn't enjoy our love-making."

The heat from his gaze pulsed with undisguised passion, and Lauren felt her will to resist him slip a notch. "Please, I have to go—"

"Look at me, Lauren. Look at me and tell me you don't want me to make love to you again."

Of course she wanted him to make love to her again. But she was also afraid. Afraid he would tire of her. Afraid he would never love her the way she loved him. Afraid he would use her for his own gratification, then break her heart. Despair welled up in her. She shook her head. "I-I can't . . ."

A look of triumph flickered behind his eyes.

Standing, he took her by the shoulders and pulled her to her feet.

Lauren stiffened. "Mr. MacKenzie, please, all I came here to do was to return your books—"

Alec lightly brushed a finger over her lips, then slid his hand into her hair and drew her toward him. "Call me Alec, lass," he said huskily.

Lauren's heart raced, each beat tripping over the one before it. "Alec," she whispered.

"That's better." He tilted her face toward his, and an involuntary tremor rippled through her as his lips claimed hers. All the desires she had been trying to suppress surged through her with the uncontrollable violence of a flash flood. She groaned and leaned into his embrace, returning his kiss with a hunger that came from deep within her soul.

His arms went around her and he crushed her to him as he possessed her mouth with a savage intensity that scorched her lips and made her head reel. His hands moved down her back to cup her buttocks, and he lifted her higher and harder against his own unmistakable arousal.

No longer in control of either her mind or her body, Lauren made no protest as Alec yanked the tails of her shirt out of her jeans. Beneath her shirt, he moved his hands over her back, along her ribs, and finally up over her breasts, his fingers coming into intimate contact with nipples that were already hard with desire. The rough warmth of his hands on her bare skin caused her knees to tremble so badly that she feared they would give out on her.

Still kissing her, he half lifted, half guided her

toward the sofa and lowered her onto it. He unbuttoned her jeans and worked his hand down inside them, sliding his fingers through the feminine curls and into her wet warmth. She moaned and a tremor shook her entire body.

Alec dragged his mouth away from hers. Struggling to catch his breath, he lifted his head and gazed into her passion-darkened eyes. All the while, his fingers maintained their delicious assault on her senses. "Look at me, Lauren, and tell me you want me to stop," he commanded.

Her lips still burning from his kiss, she swallowed hard and shook her head. "I-I can't . . ."

Alec's gaze holding hers captive, he began moving his fingers faster. "Tell me you want me, Lauren."

The room seemed to tilt and spin as she felt the pressure rapidly building inside her, a liquid heat barely contained in a pulsing knot that had grown so tight it hurt. She couldn't think. "Y-yes . . ."

"Tell me," Alec ordered.

Her breath came in short bursts. "I want . . . you—"

The knot shattered.

A strangled cry tore from Lauren's throat as a bolt of electricity seemed to arc through her, exploding into a thousand brilliant lights. Her back arched and she pressed her body hard against Alec's hand, instinctively seeking relief from the sweet torment he was inflicting on her at the same time that she abandoned herself to the fire that raged through her veins, filling her with an intoxicating heat that washed over her in never-ending waves.

She was so caught up in the dizzying whirlwind that carried her to ever greater heights that she was only vaguely aware of Alec's weight shifting off her, or of him removing her jeans. Until he touched her, she had not realized how badly she wanted—or needed—him. He had a hold on her that she could not shake. For as long as he was near, she would be at his mercy.

She was just regaining control of her senses when he settled between her legs.

Her eyes widened, partly in surprise, partly in pleasure, as he eased into her. No matter how many times they made love, she knew she would never tire of the feel of him inside her.

Ever so slowly, he withdrew nearly all the way. His face was so close she could see the flecks of amber in his golden brown irises and feel the warmth of his breath on her skin. His intense gaze holding hers captive, he hovered on the brink for several agonizing seconds, then drove full length into her.

Lauren gasped, and every muscle in her body went rigid. She wondered briefly if it was possible for someone to die from pure pleasure. Then Alec began to move within her, and she ceased to think at all.

He drove into her again and again. She lifted her hips to meet his thrusts, her body instinctively seeking release from the pulsing ache that had begun to build yet again inside her. "Alec . . . please . . ." she pleaded, not quite certain what she was asking for, yet knowing she would go insane if she didn't get it soon.

She could no longer think coherently. Wildly varying images flickered through her mind, then scattered into an explosion of brilliant colors. Words came to the tip of her tongue, then were gone before she could capture them. Finally she gave up trying. Everything was happening so fast, yet time seemed to slow to a crawl. Every sensation, every emotion, seemed to burn itself indelibly into her memory.

Alec quickened his movements, and her control snapped.

"Alec!" she cried out. She felt herself falling, falling . . .

Seizing her lips in a long, passionate kiss, Alec drove into her one last time.

Lauren's body shuddered convulsively. She unthinkingly sobbed out Alec's name again and again as tremors shook her.

Burying his face against her neck, he gathered her into his arms and held her against his pounding heart. Together, they rode out the storm, then drifted slowly back to calmer waters.

"Pa's been asking for you, and he's mad!"

Lauren hung her bridle on its peg. Her stomach knotted. She had stayed at Duneideann far longer than she had planned. She had also given in and let Alec make love to her. She didn't know what had come over her; it was as if he had cast a spell on her. She took a deep breath and tried to calm her quaking nerves. "Does he know where I was?"

Bubba shook his head. "I sure wasn't going to be the one to tell him. He's been mad as hell ever since he had it out with Jimmy this morning. That son of a bitch quit and went to work for Martin Dandridge!"

"If Pa hears you swearing, he'll scrub out your mouth with soap."

"I'll swear if I want. Didn't you hear me, Coop? Jimmy hired on at the Diamond Cross!"

"I heard you. I just don't believe you." She picked up the new set of books Alec had lent her. "Guess I'd better go see what Pa wants."

Bubba grimaced at the books in Lauren's land. "I thought you were going to give those back."

"I did. These are new ones."

"I wouldn't let Pa see them if I were you. Why do you keep him stirred up anyways? You know how he feels about you wasting time reading them things."

Lauren bit back the retort that sprang to the tip of her tongue. It wasn't Bubba's fault that he was becoming so ornery. Pa kept encouraging him. Even if what Alec said was true, she doubted Bubba was ever going to straighten out.

When Lauren reached the porch, she could hear angry voices coming from inside the house. Moving quietly so no one would hear her, she slipped into the hall and eased the screen door shut, then pressed close to the wall and eavesdropped on the heated conversation that was taking place between Pa and Cal in the dining room.

"Damn it, Frank! This is the second month in a row that you haven't paid us. What in the hell did you expect Jimmy to do? Work indefinitely without any wages?"

"I tol' you, Cal. I'll pay you fellas everythin' I owe you after the auction." Frank's words were slurred.

"That's not good enough."

"If you don' like it, ge' out! I go' too much on my mind to hav'ta listen to yer bellyachin'."

"The only thing you got on your mind, Frank, is enough whiskey to kill a horse. I'm not going to sit here and let you drink yourself to death."

"Hey! Give tha' back!"

Lauren tiptoed up the stairs. When she reached her room, she hid the books under the mattress, then sat down on the bed.

She felt sick to her stomach.

She had known for some time that they were short on cash, but she hadn't realized it was so bad that Pa had fallen behind on paying the men's wages.

Money had always been a problem with Pa. It slipped through his fingers faster than water through a sieve, especially after Mama died and there was no one to keep a tight rein on him. While they usually had enough cash to get by, there was seldom any extra for needed repairs and equipment for the ranch. As a result, the Bar-T's profits had steadily dwindled, year after year, until they were barely staying afloat. Then Pa's accident, and the resulting medical bills, had all but wiped them out. Still, she could have sworn there was enough money left over from last year's auction to pay the men's wages through September. Where had the money gone?

She felt responsible somehow. If she had been home, she might have talked Jimmy into staying on another month. Or at the very least, she might have been able to calm Pa down enough that he wouldn't have gotten drunk.

No sooner had she formed the thought than she began to see the error of her logic. It didn't matter what she did; Pa would have gotten drunk anyway. That was what Pa did best. He got drunk, and he made sure everyone around him was as miserable as he was.

She knew Pa had never been the same after he'd hurt his legs, but that didn't justify the way he treated those who loved him and were loyal to him. Bernie once dislocated his shoulder, but he never snapped at anyone, even though he was in pain for weeks. In fact, all of them had bad days now and then, yet they always tried to get along, whereas Pa . . .

Pa did whatever he felt he could get away with, which was a lot, Lauren realized. She was tired of making allowances for him. It was one thing for her and Bubba and the hired hands to do all the physical labor involved in operating a ranch, and to run errands for him and help him get around. Putting up with his nastiness was something else.

The sound of smashing glass reached her from the dining room. Fighting a feeling of dread, she stood and started toward the door. It wasn't fair for Cal to have to take the brunt of Pa's temper.

She had to go downstairs and do what she could to defuse the situation.

Wait until Pa finds out I'm going to the Fourth of July celebration with Alec, she thought dismally. *He'll probably have an attack of apoplexy.*

That spring was the hottest Lauren could remember. The grass turned brown and dry from lack of rain, and the well fell far below its previous summertime levels. As weeks went by without Alec discovering the Bar-T cattle on his land, Lauren began to breathe a little easier. It was for the best, she told herself. It was enough of a struggle just to keep the remaining cattle fed and watered. Every few days, the men relocated them into a pasture that had not been grazed bare, but their efforts brought little reward. The cattle were as lean as any Lauren had ever seen. Unless they could be fattened before fall, they would be worthless on the open market.

Nothing more was said about the men's wages, but Lauren could feel the tension that hung in the air whenever Pa was around. Nor could she ignore the conversations that suddenly ceased whenever she entered a room. Nothing was said about hiring someone to take Jimmy Smith's place; there was no money to pay an extra cowhand.

Because it didn't seem fair to ask the men to take on extra duties when they were already working without pay, Lauren absorbed as much of Jimmy's share of the work as she could, in addition to her usual chores. By the end of the day, she was usually too exhausted to do anything but fall into bed.

The books Alec had lent her went unopened.

The gossip that trickled out to the Bar-T from town was increasingly devoted to Alec MacKenzie and his guests. Rumors abounded that James Lachlan had connections with wealthy European businessmen and high-level government officials eager to invest in American enterprises. What ordinarily would have been a discreet paragraph in the "Public Notices" section of the *Millerville Gazette* became front page news when Alec MacKenzie and James Lachlan jointly purchased over three thousand acres of land in the Huachuca Mountains. When it was discovered that both men spent a week in Tucson, meeting with geologists and construction contractors, word spread rapidly through the valley that Duneideann was being turned into the headquarters for a large-scale mining operation.

Unemployed miners flooded the valley in search of work. Because there were not enough lodgings in Millerville to accommodate the unexpected influx, tents were erected on the edge of town. Within days, the number of tents in Millerville outstripped the number of permanent residences by two to one.

Angry ranchers descended on City Hall and demanded that all digging be delayed until they had assurances that their ranches would not be adversely affected, only to discover that there were no plans for a mine, and never had been. Yes, the City Clerk told them, Mr. MacKenzie had received permits to begin digging, but not for minerals. MacKenzie was going to blast through the rock and install massive conduits for the purpose of carrying water into the valley. It was the biggest irrigation project ever attempted in the Territory of Arizona, the Clerk said, and everyone in the area would benefit.

Except the miners.

When they learned that no jobs were forthcoming, some of the miners went on a rampage, smashing windows and overturning wagons and terrorizing the townspeople, until they were finally arrested and run out of town. Rumor of a silver strike near Ajo hastened the departure of the remaining men.

Not only were the comings and goings of Alec MacKenzie and his brother-in-law chronicled in the town's weekly newspaper, but those of Sarah Lachlan as well.

"Listen to this," Cal said as they sat on the porch after dinner. He read aloud from the *Gazette*. " 'After luncheon at the Silver Nugget Hotel, Sarah Lachlan and Arminta Larson attended a piano recital given by Miss Letitia Page at the home of her parents, Otis and Cissy Page. Mrs. Lachlan was wearing the latest fashion from the Continent, an elegant tea gown of pale ivory silk and Belgian lace which was much admired by all present.' " Cal shook his head. "Would someone mind telling me what's so all-fired exciting about some fancy tea gown?"

"It depends on the person wearing it," Bernie said. "I hear the lady's a real looker."

"What's so good about her being a looker if she's already married?" Bubba asked.

Bernie laughed. "'Cause you don't have to be the one married to her to do the looking," he said. He glanced at Lauren. "Didn't you say you met her that day you rode out to MacKenzie's?"

Stung by the revelation that Alec's sister seemed to have become cozy with Arminta Larson and her army of followers, Lauren shrugged, feigning indifference. "I met her."

"Well, what's she look like?" Bernie asked.

Normally, this would have been the kind of evening she enjoyed. Even Pa had joined them on the porch, and he wasn't drinking. But the news about Sarah—as well as a disturbing piece of gossip that Cal had brought back from town—had rubbed her the wrong way. "She's pretty," she said, reluctantly answering Bernie's question.

"C'mon, Coop," Bernie prodded. "You can do better than that."

"What more do you want me to say?" Lauren shot back. "She's pretty, all right?"

Frank frowned at her. "What's got you so all-fired prickly tonight?"

"Nothing. I'm just tired." She also felt hurt and betrayed. When Cal had returned from town earlier, he had taken her aside and told her he'd heard at the Shady Lady that she and Alec had gotten mighty cozy during her stay at Duneideann. Now that Sarah was getting in thick with Arminta Larson, she couldn't help wondering if Sarah was the source of the rumors. She pushed to her feet. "I have to go do the dishes," she said. She yanked open the screened door and bolted into the house.

The men observed her hasty departure with a mixture of bewilderment and dismay. "What's wrong with her?" Bernie asked.

Cal turned the page of the newspaper. "Lord only knows."

"Something about Mrs. Lachlan set her off," Bernie thought aloud.

"Maybe she's jealous," Bubba suggested.

Bernie shook his head. "It's not like Coop to be jealous."

"She's just getting uppity," Frank said. "Ignore her. What else does that paper say?"

Cal squinted at the newsprint in the fading light. "Well, it says here that there might not be any fireworks if we don't get any rain between now and the Fourth."

The screen door slammed. Frank Cooper's voice reverberated throughout the house. *"Coop! Where the hell are you? Get your tail down here!"*

Lauren dropped the dirty sheets in a pile on the hallway floor and hurried down the stairs.

At the bottom, Frank leaned on his crutches. His accusing gaze bored into her. "What were you doing?"

Lauren dragged a sleeve across her damp forehead. "Putting clean sheets on the beds."

Frank's brows lowered and he opened his mouth to say something, then changed his mind. He jerked his head over his shoulder. "Get out there and help your brother muck the stalls."

Lauren's eyes widened. "It's Bubba's week to do them!"

"Don't sass me. I know damn good and well whose week it is, but with Jimmy gone, the men need all the help they can get."

Lauren bit her tongue. It wouldn't do any good to argue with Pa anyway. She started to go around him toward the door, but he stuck out one of the crutches, blocking her exit. "You remember what I told you," he said. "If you're going to waste your time with them books, you do it when your chores are done, and not until then. You understand me?"

Resentment threatened to consume her. In spite of the fact that she hadn't had either the time or the energy during the past few weeks to do any reading whatsoever, Pa seemed convinced that all she did was sit up in her bedroom and read. He could stand at the parlor window all day and *watch* her work, and still accuse her of not doing her share. "Yes," she said sullenly.

"Yes, what?"

"Yes, sir."

Frank lowered the crutch. "When you're done with the stalls, I want you to get started on supper. We've eaten late two nights in a row now. I want supper on the table on time tonight."

"Yes, sir."

Lauren sidled past her father and slipped out the door. When she was out of earshot of the house, she gave the ground an angry kick. "I want supper on the table on time tonight," she mimicked. "And when you're done with that, Coop, there's the barn roof and the—"

"What did you say?" Frank yelled.

Lauren clamped her mouth shut and walked faster.

"Damn it, Coop! I'm talking to you!"

Lauren broke into a run. If Pa didn't let up, she was liable to lose her temper and say something that would get her backhanded.

When she reached the barn, she was winded. To her dismay, Bubba was nowhere to be found. Worse than that, he hadn't even started on the stalls. Biting back her anger at being stuck with her brother's chores, she tore the shovel off its nail on the wall and went to work.

It wasn't right, she thought, digging into a pile of straw that was saturated with urine. She already did more than her fair share. And for what? No one cared how hard she worked or how much she did. They just took for granted that she would always be there to cook and clean for them, as well as do the work of two strong men. She wondered peevishly what everyone would do if she just decided to up and leave, the way Jimmy Smith had.

No sooner had the thought occurred to her than she suppressed it. She knew she was being uncharitable, but she couldn't help it. She wished that just once Pa and Bubba and the others would treat her with a little respect, or, barring that, a little kindness.

The way Alec did, a voice in the back of her mind whispered.

Her throat tightened. Those lazy, carefree days

she had spent at Duneideann now seemed so far removed that it was as if they had never happened. Indeed, were it not for the faint scars on her left hip and the front of her thighs, she would have wondered if it had all been a dream.

She missed Duneideann. She missed Alec. She missed their evenings together in front of the fire, and their talks. She missed the way he looked at her when he thought she wasn't paying attention . . . and when he knew she was. She missed the gentle warmth of his hands on her skin, and the way he felt inside her . . .

You have to get over him, she scolded herself when she finally steadied her nerves. *Just because he asked you to the Fourth of July celebration doesn't mean that he has the same feelings for you that you do for him. You'll just make yourself miserable by pining for something you can't have.*

By the time she finished mucking out the stalls and spreading fresh straw for the horses, the sun was going down. Bubba had never shown up. Dinner was going to be late again, Lauren thought dismally. There was nothing she could do about it. Maybe this way Pa would think twice about making her do Bubba's chores again.

Lauren was halfway across the yard when she spotted Bubba at the pump with the hired hands, washing up for dinner. Anger ignited inside her at the sound of their laughter, and it was all she could do not to break into a run. When she got her hands on Bubba, she was going to—

She stopped and the air froze in her lungs. It suddenly hurt to breathe.

There was a fourth person at the pump, washing his hands alongside Bubba and Cal and Bernie.

It was Sam Luttrell.

Chapter 12

Lauren slowly resumed walking. There was an odd ringing in her ears, and the pressure in her chest was so great it felt as if it would explode.

Bernie was the first one to spot her. He nudged Cal. The men suddenly stopped talking. They all glanced her way.

Sam shook the water from his hands and turned to face her, his feet apart as if claiming his ground. A calculating grin spread across his face. "Hey, Coop," he called out. "Where you been all day? I've been looking for you."

Lauren stopped a few feet away. She clenched and unclenched her fists. "What are you doing here?" Her voice shook.

Cal intervened. "Look, this isn't the time—"

"Your old man hired me," Sam said, still grinning.

Lauren felt as if hands had closed around her neck and were squeezing hard, choking her. She glanced at Cal. "Is that true?"

Cal shook his head. "Coop, I'm sorry . . ."

A low oath burst from Lauren's throat. "You sorry son of a—"

"Now, calm down, Coop," Cal cautioned. "Frank has his reasons. If you'd just listen—"

"Like hell I will! Damn you, Cal! You could

have stopped him!" Lauren broke into a run. She ran past them. Sam's laugh followed her into the house.

"Coop!" Cal yelled.

The kitchen door slammed so hard it rattled the windows.

Lauren ran through the kitchen and into the hallway. "Pa!"

Frank hobbled out of the parlor. "What the hell is going on out there? I could hear you yelling all the way in here."

"Pa, how could you hire that bastard?"

"You watch your mouth, girl. You're not too big for a whuppin', and don't you forget it."

Lauren raked her fingers through her hair in frustration. "I'm sorry," she mumbled. She took a shuddering breath and began again, "Why did you hire Sam Luttrell?"

"Because I don't have the money to hire anyone else, that's why. We're lucky Sam agreed to work without pay until the auction."

"But Pa! After what he did to me, how can you—"

"Sam and me, we talked about that. Sam's sorry for what he did, and he wants to—"

"Sorry! Pa, Sam's never been sorry for anything in his life! You know that as well as I do!"

"I don't want to hear any more about it, Coop. He said he's sorry, and I believe him. We need him. He's going to help us get this ranch going again, and make it pay."

"How? What can he do that we haven't already tried?"

"That's none of your concern." Frank hoisted

his crutches up under his arms and started toward the front door.

"Pa, wait." Lauren stepped between him and the door. "If Sam came here volunteering to help us, then he's up to something. I just know it."

Just then, the hired hands trooped in through the kitchen. "What's for supper?" Bubba called out.

Frank wagged a warning finger at Lauren. "Sam's working for us now, and I don't want you causing any trouble, you hear?" He hobbled out onto the front porch.

Bubba appeared in the kitchen doorway, scowling at Lauren. "You didn't cook nothing. What are we supposed to eat?"

Acutely aware of Sam Luttrell standing behind Bubba, watching her, Lauren summoned every ounce of willpower she possessed to keep from crying. She felt defeated. She didn't even have the strength to remind Bubba that the reason dinner was late was because she had just done his chores. "I'll cook something as soon as I've had a chance to wash up," she said woodenly. She started up the stairs.

"But I'm hungry now!" Bubba protested. "Why is supper always so late these days?"

Sam bent down and murmured in Bubba's ear, "Tell you what, kid. Come into town with me, and I'll show you where you can get a hot meal *and* a hot woman."

Bubba's eyes widened, and he gaped at Sam. "Really?"

Lauren froze. "Oh, no, you don't!"

"Yeah, really," Sam said, ignoring her. "How

about it, kid? You up for a night on the town like a real cowhand?"

A grin split Bubba's face from ear to ear. "You bet!"

Lauren gripped the banister. "Bubba, no. You're going to stay right here."

"You can't make me!"

Cal put his hand on Bubba's shoulder. "Just pipe down, mister. Coop's right. There'll be plenty of time for kicking up your heels when you're older and have a little more hair on your chest."

Bubba shook off Cal's hand. "I wish everyone around here would quit treating me like I'm just a kid," he said angrily.

You are just a kid, Lauren thought, but she bit back the remark. "No one's treating you like a kid. It's just that you don't need to be hanging around with the likes of that no-account trouble-maker."

"Well, at least I'm not no traitor cozying up to some stupid foreigner who's trying to run us out of business," Bubba shot back. "Pa's right. You sure have gotten uppity ever since you started reading them dumb books!"

Bubba pivoted and ran back through the kitchen.

"Bubba!" Lauren yelled. She winced as the kitchen door slammed after him with a resounding bang.

Sam's left eye wandered, making it appear as if he was staring past Lauren's shoulder at a spot on the wall. He was still grinning. "Don't worry, Coop," he drawled. "I'll look out for your baby brother." Sam plunked his hat on his head and followed Bubba out of the house.

Lauren choked on a sob. She punched the wall with her fist. "Damn it all," she swore.

Cal sighed. "Just let it lie, Coop. It's not worth getting yourself all worked up over."

"Cal! Sam's taking Bubba to Miss Chloe's!"

"You're probably right."

"But Bubba's only fourteen!"

Cal said nothing. Lauren looked from him to Bernie and back again. Both men were giving her that look that said she was making a big deal out of nothing. Her throat constricted. Gripping the banister so hard her knuckles turned white, she took a shuddering breath. "Supper will be on the table in fifteen minutes. Anyone who has any objection to eggs can cook his own dinner."

Lauren waited until she was safely behind the closed door of her bedroom before bursting into tears.

"Is it possible that the cattle got caught up here when the fences went up?" Alec asked.

Sly Barnes shook his head and squinted at the steers grazing alongside the stream. "There's too many of them. Frank's never owned more than five or six hundred head tops, and they usually don't wander up toward higher ground until later in the summer. I'd say a good half his herd is up here, maybe more."

Alec swore under his breath. He and Sly had ridden up into Six-shooter Canyon to investigate complaints from his hired hands that they were coming across an unusually large number of cattle with Bar-T brands. Even after they drove the strays back onto Bar-T land, more strays appeared, and in greater numbers.

Alec fought a rising tide of anger and frustration. "Do you think Frank Cooper did this deliberately?"

Sly shoved back his hat. "It wouldn't be the first underhanded thing Frank's ever done, and it certainly isn't the worst. If I were you, I'd keep a close count of them bulls you brought here from Scotland."

A muscle knotted in Alec's jaw. He turned his horse around. "Drive those cattle back onto the Bar-T," he ordered. "I'm going to pay Frank Cooper a visit."

Lauren used a long pole to shove the clothes down into the soapy water. The day was hot, and sweat caused her hair to curl around her face and cling to her forehead. Beneath her shirt, her camisole stuck damply to her skin. The fire beneath the washtub sent billows of thick black smoke up into the air. She kept a vigilant eye on the ground around the washtub for stray cinders. The last thing they needed right now was a brush fire. As dry as everything was, it would take only a spark to send the entire valley up in flames.

Even thought it involved backbreaking work, she genuinely enjoyed washday. Not only did she get out of doing her other chores, but standing at the big old tub, stirring the clothes, reminded her of Mama. Mama used to stand in this very spot week after week, tending the wash. She always faced away from the house so she could see the mountains and watch the flowers bloom by the gate in the spring. Mama enjoyed washing too. She always said it was a time when she could be alone to think and dream.

Lauren wondered if Mama had ever thought about Sheriff Early and wished she'd married him instead of Pa. She grimaced. She couldn't imagine having Roy Early for a father.

Now it was her turn to spin dreams and wonder what life held in store for her.

Bubba and Pa were right about one thing: she had changed.

Ever since she stayed at Duneideann, she had felt different, as if she didn't know who she was any more. At one time, she was Coop. She could rope and brand and round up cattle as well as any of the men. She still could, but it was different now. Now she caught herself looking at her hands and wondering if they would ever be soft and pretty. She knew she would never be some society belle who dressed up in fancy gowns and gave tea parties. But she wasn't really Coop any more either.

She was Lauren, whoever that was. Lauren was just as much a stranger to her as Coop. Lauren was insanely, incurably, impossibly in love with a man whose world was so far removed from her own that they couldn't possibly be meant for each other. Yet, even if they did move in the same social circles, she doubted Alec would ever marry her. Why should he?

Why should he pay with marriage for something he had already gotten for free?

She stabbed impatiently at the clothes with the pole. She hated herself for giving in to him, yet at the same time she knew she couldn't trade those memories for all the money in the world. So why couldn't loving him be enough? Why did she want so much more? Why was she always pining after something she was never likely to have?

She stopped stirring the clothes and shoved the damp hair away from her forehead. That was when she saw the approaching rider. Her heart swelled. She would know those broad shoulders and that proud demeanor anywhere.

It was Alec.

Her first impulse was to run into the house and splash cold water on her face and change into a clean shirt. She decided against it. Alec had seen her looking worse than this, and she didn't want to encourage any more snide remarks from Bubba. More than once recently she had been tempted to give her brother a piece of her mind. The only thing that kept her from doing so was her determination not to alienate him even more than she already had. Bubba was spending so much time with Sam Luttrell these days that what little influence she'd had in the past over his behavior was rapidly dwindling. She'd already given up trying to keep him from going into town with Sam. Now it was all she could do to keep him from entertaining everyone at the dinner table with detailed accounts of what the twenty-six-year-old redhead at Miss Chloe's was letting him do with her.

As soon as Alec rode into the yard, Lauren knew from his rigid posture and the unyielding set of his jaw that he was angry. He was more than angry; he was furious. Her muscles clenched. Had he found out about the cattle? Dear God, she hoped not.

He dismounted.

Desire cloaked the anger that shone in his amber-flecked eyes, making them smolder as he walked toward her. Lauren cringed inwardly, and her hands tightened on the wooden pole. There was something powerful and savage in his long strides that sent a shudder of alarm up her spine. She tried to smile, but the attempt fell short. "Hi."

"Hello, lass." He stared at her long and hard, wrestling down his body's lusty response to her while wondering if she knew anything about Bar-T cattle being on his land. Her face was flushed from the heat of the washing fire, reminding him of those other times her face—and her body—had blushed with awakening passion.

Regaining his self-control, he nodded toward the house. "Is your father here?"

"He's out in the barn. Why? Is something wrong?"

"I prefer to discuss the matter with your father." Alec headed toward the barn.

Lauren's heart raced. She had forgotten that Sam Luttrell was also in the barn. There was no telling what would happen when those two confronted each other. Against her better judgment, she left the pole in the washtub and ran after Alec. "Wait!"

He stopped and turned to face her. She nervously moistened her lips. "Maybe it would be better if you just told me what was wrong, and I could—"

"This is between your father and me. It doesn't concern you. I prefer that you stay out of it."

Lauren dragged her fingers through her hair. "It's just that Pa hasn't been feeling good, and—"

"I'm sorry, lass." He pivoted and continued walking.

"Mr. MacKen—Alec!"

He kept walking.

The barn door stood open. Alec went inside. On the far side of the barn, he saw the top of Bubba's blond head over one of the stall partitions. The sound of hammering echoed off the walls. "Mr. Cooper?" Alec called out.

The hammering stopped.

Bubba whirled around to stare at Alec, then backed out of his father's way.

Supporting his weight on the crutches, Frank hobbled into the center of the barn. "A little far out of your way, aren't you, MacKenzie?"

"Mr. Cooper, I wish to speak with you. Is there somewhere we can sit down?"

"I'll stand, thank you."

Bubba positioned himself beside his father. He folded his skinny arms across his chest and eyed Alec defiantly. "If you got something to say, you can say it to both of us." He punctuated the statement by spitting on the ground.

Alec ignored him. "Mr. Cooper, you and I have a problem that needs to be addressed. It concerns your cattle."

Frank held up his hand, palm outward. "Whoa there, MacKenzie. Before you say anything else, maybe I should tell you that you won't be the first man in this valley to accuse me of rustling, and you probably won't be the last.

"I should also tell you that you can search through my cattle any day of the week, and you won't find an altered brand among them. If I had my legs, I'd ride out with you myself, and prove it to you. Instead, maybe my son can go with you, or one of my hired hands."

"Mr. Cooper, I didn't come here to accuse you of stealing, unless you want to include unauthorized use of valuable grazing land in your definition of the word."

Frank scowled. "What the hell are you talking about?"

"A large number of your cattle—I estimate there are close to three hundred head—are on my land. Now, the way I see it, Mr. Cooper, we have two options. You can tell me how they got there and assure me that it won't happen again, and I will return the cattle to you. Or I can keep your cattle in lieu of payment for use of my pasture. Which shall it be?"

Frank's face turned a menacing shade of red. "Why, you thieving foreigner! Just you try to keep my cattle, and I'll get Sheriff Early out here and have you arrested for stealing! I can prove those cattle are mine. Everyone in this valley knows my brand."

Sam stepped out into the open, holding a pitchfork as if it were a weapon. "This man bothering you, Frank?"

Alec stiffened, and his face went rigid with shock. "What in God's name are *you* doing here?"

"I want you off my land, MacKenzie," Frank said. "I want you off now."

A smug look spread over Sam's face. "Want me to take care of him, boss?"

Anger and disbelief sparked in Alec's eyes as they burned into Sam. "You *work* here?"

Bubba balled his hands into fists. "You don't listen too good, mister. My pa just told you to leave!"

"Maybe he just needs a little prompting," Sam said. He started toward Alec with the pitchfork.

"No, don't!" Lauren cried out. She stepped between the two men.

Sam stopped short and lowered the pitchfork. Irritation flashed in his eyes.

Frank pointed a crutch toward the barn door. "You have chores to do. Get your tail out of here."

"Pa, please."

"Out!"

Lauren turned to Alec. Her voice shook. "Alec, please, come outside with me and I'll explain everything to you."

"I told you to get out!" Frank bellowed.

The veins in Alec's temples distended dangerously. His hand snapped around Lauren's arm in a brutal grip. "You're coming with me," he bit out. He hauled her out the door and into the bright sunlight, not slowing his strides until they were well away from the barn.

Lauren dug her heels into the ground. "Alec, stop! You're hurting me!"

He relaxed his grip, and she jerked her arm free. "What is wrong with you?" she cried.

"How long has Luttrell been working here?"

"I—I don't know . . . about a week."

"Damn it, Lauren! Why didn't you come to me?"

She recoiled from the blazing fury in his eyes. "What good would it have done? Pa was the one who hired him. I sure as hell didn't have any say in the matter."

"I don't care who hired him. I don't want the man within a hundred miles of you. Get your things. You're coming back to Duneideann with me."

"I can't do that!"

"I'm not going to permit you stay here as long as Luttrell is here. Get your things now, or leave without them."

Lauren gaped at him. "Alec, you can't just come here and start ordering me around. Besides, you're making way too much of this. Sam is keeping his distance. I swear it."

"For God's sake, Lauren! The man nearly killed you! Or have you forgotten that?"

"No!"

"Well, your father obviously has or he never would have hired him!"

Lauren plowed her fingers through her hair in frustration. "Alec, I don't know why Pa hired him. All I know is that Pa's convinced that Sam is the answer to all our problems, that he's going to help us get out of debt and make the Bar-T profitable again. I don't know how they plan to—"

"By cutting my fences and driving Bar-T cattle onto my land. *That's* how!"

"No! Sam had nothing to do with that. That was already done before Pa hired him."

The muscle in Alec's jaw jerked. "You *knew* about that?"

There was a terrible, crushing weight in the middle of Lauren's chest. "Yes," she choked.

An oath exploded in Alec's throat.

"We didn't have a choice," she continued shakily, trying to make him understand. "Until you fenced it off, our cattle always grazed in Six-shooter Canyon during the summer. There wasn't time to plant new pasture, and even if there was, we don't have the money for seed. All we have left are the cattle, and if they die, we don't have *anything*."

Alec stared at her in disbelief. "Why didn't you tell me this before?"

"It's not your concern."

"No, but *you are*. Good God, Lauren! What kind of friendship do we have if you can't come to me when you're in trouble?"

"That's the whole point! We don't have a friendship. All we have is you coming to my rescue, time after time after time. The amazing thing is, before you came here, I never needed to be rescued. I managed just fine without you."

Alec's expression turned thunderous. "What's that supposed to mean?"

Lauren's voice shook. "I don't know! All I know is that ever since you came into my life, I've been all mixed up about things. I just wish everything could be the way it was before. I'm beginning to wish I'd never met you!"

She started to turn to go back to the house when she saw the flames from the washing fire spreading across the dried grass in the yard. "Oh, hell!" she cried out. She ran toward the fire and began kicking dirt over the flames.

Alec ran past her. He grabbed the pole in the washtub and used it to fish a man's shirt out of the water. The hot water splashed over his hands. He began beating at the flames with the wet shirt.

Within minutes, they extinguished the fire.

When the danger had passed, Lauren wrapped her arms around herself and tried to get a grip on her roiling emotions. She could not stop shaking. All she could think about was how close she had come to letting everything they owned burn down because of her carelessness. If she had stayed by the washtub, if she had not followed Alec into the barn, none of this would have happened.

Alec's chest heaved as he fought to catch his breath. He dropped the soiled shirt into the washtub and dragged his sleeve across his forehead. He glanced at Lauren, and his brow creased with concern. He had never seen her looking so exhausted, or so defeated. It was as if the life had drained out of her, leaving a hollow, joyless shell.

He went to her. "Lauren, I'm sorry about your cattle. I didn't realize that fencing off Six-shooter Canyon would cause you such hardship."

She looked away. "Forget it," she said woodenly.

"I want to help you, lass."

"I don't want your help."

"Lauren, listen to me." Alec placed his hand under her chin and turned her face toward him. "I'll give you enough feed and hay to get you through the rest of the year. This fall, when the weather cools, I'll help you plant more land to pasture so you need not worry about—"

She jerked her head away. "I told you, I don't want your help. And I sure as hell don't want your pity!"

Alec's temper pushed the limits of its restraint. "If you think I pity you, lass, you're mistaken," he bit out. "You're too intelligent to even warrant the emotion. Your problem is that you squander far too much time listening to those who would have you believe otherwise."

He went to his horse and swung up into the saddle. He rode his horse alongside Lauren, then stopped and looked down at her, his expression rigid. "I will have my men deliver the feed tomorrow," he said curtly. "When you come to your senses and realize you'll be better off as far away from this den of thieves as you can get, you can come to Duneideann. You'll always have a home there. Remember that."

Alec turned his horse around and dug his heels into the animal's sides. He did not look back.

"How do you expect me to wrap these bandages if you keep moving?" Chloe asked.

Alec bit back an angry retort and forced himself to keep still while Chloe finished winding the strip of linen around his left hand. He had scalded it when he pulled the shirt out of Lauren's washtub earlier, and now the skin was red and tender.

Chloe tied the ends of the linen. "That salve should numb the skin and keep it from blistering too badly," she said when she finished.

"Thanks," Alec said stiffly.

Chloe put away the medicines and bandages and returned to the kitchen table. It was late afternoon and the house was quiet. Some of the women who worked for Chloe were upstairs, napping, and the rest had gone into town. Chloe pulled out a chair near Alec and sat down. She poured them each a cup of tea. "Do you want to talk about it?" she asked.

"There's nothing to talk about." Alec took a sip of the tea, swearing under his breath as the hot liquid burned his mouth.

"Then why are you so miserable?"

"I'm not miserable. I'm angry. How Frank could hire that man after what he did to Lauren is beyond me."

Chloe frowned. "So Sam is supposed to help Frank turn the Bar-T around," she mused aloud.

" 'Tis what Lauren said."

Chloe shook her head. "Sam's up to something. I wish I knew what."

Alec closed his eyes and rubbed his eyelids with the fingers of his uninjured hand. "I just wish Lauren would get away from there. I don't like the idea of Luttrell being near her."

"Where is she supposed to go? Back to your ranch?"

"I extended the offer. I doubt she will accept."

"Smart girl. The rumors that started circulating about you two the last time she stayed there are only now starting to die down. It won't take much to breathe life back into them, believe me."

"Do you have a better idea?"

"Marry her," Chloe said without hesitation. "That'll get her away from the Bar-T and make an honest woman of her in one fell swoop."

Alec shot her a scathing glance.

She chuckled. "Why not? She's young. She's pretty. She's resourceful. Oh, sure, she doesn't have a pedigree like those expensive cattle of yours, but when it comes to people, breeding doesn't necessarily ensure quality. Besides, you're in love with her."

Alec leaned back in his chair. He tilted his head to one side and regarded Chloe with thinly veiled amusement. "And how, may I ask, did you arrive at the unlikely conclusion that I am in love with Lauren Cooper?"

Chloe smiled knowingly. Putting down her teacup, she got up and went to Alec. She sat down on his lap and wrapped her arms around his neck. "Alec MacKenzie," she said in a low, seductive voice, "you are the only man in this town I want, and I would do damn near anything to have you. You are also the only man in this town I haven't been able to get into my bed. That should tell you something."

At Alec's surprised look, Chloe kissed him lightly on the mouth and stood up. "Finish your tea and get your carcass out of here," she ordered. "I'll be open for business soon, and I can't afford to have nonpaying customers cluttering up my kitchen."

From the dining room window, Frank watched Sly Barnes and several hands from Duneideann unload sacks of feed and bales of hay from the wagons. Cal and Bernie had gone outside to help. Bubba was wolfing down his breakfast so he could join them. Sam was nowhere to be found. He had left sometime during the night and had not yet returned. It was the second time during the week he had been at the Bar-T that he had stayed away all night.

"Pa, your eggs are getting cold," Lauren said. She wished he would come away from the window.

Frank scratched his stomach and chuckled. "It looks like we struck pay dirt this time," he said. Supporting his weight on his crutches, he turned and hobbled to the table. He leveled a warning finger at Lauren. "Let this be a lesson to you, Coop. There's only one way to deal with the rich. You prey on their guilt."

Lauren hated it when Pa talked that way, as if the rest of the world was indebted to him.

Knowing what was going on out in the yard didn't help any. Alec had sent the feed and hay anyway, even after she had told him she didn't want it. She had been hateful to him. She had thrown his friendship back into his face, yet he had kept his promise to help her family.

In her pocket, she could feel the note from Alec that Sly Barnes had discreetly slipped to her. An aching lump wedged in her throat. After all the terrible things she had said to him, he still wanted to take her to the Fourth of July celebration.

Chapter 13

The Fourth of July dawned just like the days preceding it: hot and dry. There had been no rain, and the slightest breeze spawned dust devils that ripped across the parched valley, spooking the horses and making the cattle restless.

"Lighten up, Frank," Cal said at breakfast. "Independence Day comes only once a year. You can let Coop go and have herself a little fun."

"She's got work to do around here," Frank snapped. His eyes were bloodshot and his face gray, attesting to a hangover that wasn't likely to abate any time soon.

Lauren set a plate of pancakes in the center of the table. She glanced up from beneath her lashes and caught Sam watching her. A suggestive grin spread across his face. "It's all right," she said, averting her gaze. "I'll ride into town after I've finished my chores." She still had not told anyone that Alec had invited her to the celebration, and now didn't seem like the right time to divulge that bit of information.

Frank snorted. "You'll ride into town when I say you can, and not until—Jesus, someone get that bacon out of here before I puke!"

Lauren moved the platter of bacon to the

other end of the table and went back into the kitchen to do the dishes.

"Do you think they'll have fireworks?" Bubba asked, talking with his mouth full.

"I don't know, kid," Bernie said. "We still haven't gotten any rain."

"It's no fun without fireworks," Bubba complained.

"That's not true and you know it," Bernie said. "You like the games and the food more than the fireworks anyway."

"I do not!"

"Shut up and eat!" Frank cast a cutting glower at his son, and then around the table. "Doesn't anyone in the house know how to keep the noise down?"

Cal and Bernie exchanged glances.

"You sure you won't change your mind about coming with us, Frank?" Cal asked. "It'll only take a few minutes to hitch up the team."

In the kitchen, Lauren listened in vain for her father's reply as she strained bacon grease into a pail. Judging from the abrupt silence that descended over the dining room, she assumed he had responded to Cal's question with one of his looks.

She was beginning to wish she had never accepted Alec's invitation.

It was bad enough that Pa was being ornery about letting her go. What was she going to say when she saw Sarah? She wasn't even certain she could look at her without telling her what a bloody fool she was for being taken in by that busybody Arminta Larson. There was no telling what Arminta had told Sarah about her. She wondered how many laughs the two women had enjoyed at her expense.

What the hell, she thought, annoyed with herself for allowing the unpleasant thoughts to cloud her spirits. She was going to the celebration to see Alec, and only Alec. She didn't care about Sarah Lachlan or Arminta Larson or anyone else. And she certainly wasn't about to let a bunch of malicious rumors ruin her day.

By the time Lauren finished her chores, Bubba and the hired hands had long since left for town. She scattered the last of the feed corn in the yard for the chickens and went back into the house. Pa was not downstairs. Moving quickly, she dragged the washtub out of the pantry and set it in the middle of the kitchen floor, then closed the door and wedged a chair under the knob. If she hurried, she should have enough time to take a bath before leaving for Duneideann. She had wanted to take one last night after she finished the supper dishes, but with Sam always hanging around the house, privacy had become a rarity.

Thirty minutes later, clad in clean britches and a cotton shirt, her cheeks pink from being scrubbed and her wet hair drawn back from her face and confined into two thick braids, Lauren stood outside her father's bedroom door. Frank Cooper was sprawled fully dressed across the unmade bed, with one booted foot on the bed and the other dangling over the side. His left arm was draped across his eyes. His crutches lay on the floor beside the bed.

Fighting the dread that inevitably welled up inside her whenever she was around her father, she knocked lightly on the doorframe. "Pa, are you awake?"

Frank lifted his arm from his face and opened one eye. "What do you want?"

Lauren debated one last time whether to tell him about Alec MacKenzie's invitation, then decided against it. "I just wanted to let you know I'm leaving now for the celebration."

Frank glowered at her.

"The chores are finished," she continued hastily before he could voice any objection. "I made a fresh pot of coffee for you, and there are new potatoes cooling on the stove if you get hungry."

"You're just going to go off and leave me here by myself, aren't you?"

"Pa, everyone asked you several times if you wanted to come, and you said no."

"You're damn right I said no. I got better things to do than sit out in that hot sun and pretend to get along with a bunch of people who'd just as soon spit on my grave as give me the time of day, and if you had a lick of sense in your head, you wouldn't go either."

Lauren tried to steer the conversation in a different direction. "Is there anything you want me to bring you from town?"

"You haven't heard a word I said, have you? Ever since you started rubbing elbows with that MacKenzie fellow and his kin, you've thought you were too good for the rest of us."

Lauren's stomach clenched. Terrified that she would lose her temper and blurt out something that she would later regret, she pivoted and bolted down the stairs.

Galston opened the heavy oak door. "Good morning, Miss Cooper."

Lauren clutched the books Alec had lent her against her chest. "Is Mr. MacKenzie here? He's expecting me."

"Mr. MacKenzie left with Mr. Lachlan a few minutes ago, but he will return within the hour. He requested that you await him in the library."

Lauren's spirits sank at the news that Alec was not at home. *You're being silly,* she chided herself. *Galston said he'd be back soon*. She took a deep breath. "Thanks."

Just then, Sarah Lachlan came running down the stairs, her dark curls bouncing and her blue eyes shining with excitement. "Lauren, I didn't see you ride up. I've been waiting for you."

Suddenly wary, Lauren glanced at Galston, then back at Sarah. Suspicion clouded her eyes. She didn't trust Sarah Lachlan one bit now that she had become friends with Arminta Larson. "What do you want with me?"

Sarah seized Lauren's hand and pulled her toward the stairs. "It's a surprise. Hurry! We don't have much time."

Lauren dragged her feet. "Mr. MacKenzie wants me to wait for him down here."

"Alec won't mind." Sarah tugged on Lauren's hand. "Come on. Don't be shy. I don't bite."

"I'm not shy," Lauren said, still balking.

Sarah released her breath in a sigh of exasperation. "*Come on!* Alec will be back any moment.

Galston, when Alec returns, don't let him come upstairs, no matter what."

Torn between curiosity and reluctance, Lauren allowed Sarah to pull her up the stairs. "I wish you'd tell me what this is all about," she said peevishly.

"You'll see," Sarah said over her shoulder.

When they reached the top of the stairs, Sarah pulled her down the hall. As they passed the door to Alec's bedroom, Lauren could not resist a glance into the room. A drunken butterfly feeling fluttered in her stomach at the sight of that big bed where she and Alec had made love, and a shiver of desire ran through her.

Sarah pulled her into a bedroom at the end of the hall and quickly closed the door after them. Releasing Lauren's hand, she went to the window and peeked through the curtains, then pulled them shut, making certain there were no gaps between the lace panels.

Lauren's breath caught in her throat as she took stock of her surroundings.

It was not the room's furnishings that caught her eye, but what was on them. Dresses. Dozens of them. Lace dresses and silk dresses and velvet dresses, in the latest styles and in every color imaginable. Lauren had never seen so many beautiful dresses in her entire life. They were draped across the bed, on the chair, on top of the chest of drawers, even over the full-length cheval mirror that stood in one corner of the room.

Sarah laughed. "You need not look so shocked. I know the room's a mess. Let me guess; you're probably a wonderful housekeeper too."

Lauren didn't hear her. She reached out to touch the delicate cutwork embroidery that adorned the front of a white shirtwaist. "It's beautiful," she said, her voice full of awe.

"And so are you," Sarah said lightly, crossing the room toward her. "But we are going to make you even more beautiful."

Before Lauren could say anything, Sarah took the books Lauren was holding and tossed them onto the bed. Then she gripped Lauren's elbow and steered her to a dressing table. She swept away a gown that lay across the chair. "Sit here."

Without thinking, Lauren obeyed. Dumbstruck, she stared at the jumbled assortment of perfumes and cosmetics and jewelry that lay scattered across the dressing table. Did women actually *wear* all that stuff? Did Sarah Lachlan wear all that stuff?

Sarah moved to stand behind Lauren. She took her head between her hands and tilted it so that Lauren was looking directing into the mirror. Then she lifted Lauren's braids off her shoulders and wrapped them around her head and studied her reflection in the mirror. She frowned and her brows dipped. "Mmmm," she murmured.

Lauren bristled. "What are you doing?"

"I'm going to make you so beautiful my brother won't be able to tear his gaze away from you."

Lauren's eyes narrowed, but in spite of her

show of resistance, her heart had begun to pound uncontrollably. "Why would you want to do that?"

Dimples appeared at the corners of Sarah's mouth. "Why do you think?"

A picture of Sarah Lachlan and Arminta Larson laughing over some shared amusement flashed through Lauren's mind, and she felt a flush of humiliation creep up her neck. Hurt and angry, she stood up. "If this is a joke, you can just—"

"A joke!" Sarah's mouth dropped open and her eyes widened in surprise. "Whatever gave you that idea?"

A lump swelled in Lauren's throat, making it hard to talk. "Because damn near everyone in this valley has managed to have a few laughs at my expense, and I'm sick of it! I won't stand for it any more, so you and Arminta Larson can go find yourselves some other sucker to pick on!"

Shock, then horror, then dismay flickered across Sarah's face in rapid succession. She shook her head. "I would never do anything like that to you!"

"I'm going to wait for Mr. MacKenzie downstairs." Lauren started toward the door.

Sarah caught her arm, stopping her. "Lauren, please wait! Are you angry because I had lunch with Mrs. Larson?"

Lauren yanked her arm free. "I'm not angry about anything. I just don't trust you, is all. I don't trust anyone who can be friends with that conniving old witch." Her voice trembled.

"Lauren, the only reason I had lunch with her

was because she knows some people who want to invest in Alec's irrigation system. I did it because I love my brother, not because I am friends with Arminta Larson. Good heavens, I can hardly stand the woman!"

Lauren stared at Sarah, wanting—yet afraid—to believe her. If the thought that Arminta Larson and Sarah had plotted behind her back to humiliate her was unbearable, the realization that she had just made a fool of herself was even more so. "I'm sorry," she mumbled. "It's just that you went to lunch *and* the piano recital with her, and I thought . . . What I mean is—"

"You don't need to explain," Sarah said gently. She took Lauren's hand. "I understand."

Lauren took a shaky breath. "I seem to do that a lot—lose my temper over nothing."

Sarah smiled. "At least you didn't throw a can of peaches at me."

Lauren cast her a startled glance. "Alec—I mean, Mr. MacKenzie told you about that?"

"He did." Mischief glimmered in Sarah's blue eyes. "I wish I'd been there. I'd probably have taken a swing at him myself. I have a pretty mean right cross, you know."

At Lauren's puzzled expression, Sarah laughed, adding, "Alec taught me how to box when we were children."

A tentative smile tugged at Lauren's mouth. "Sam Luttrell *deserved* to get hit."

Sarah squeezed Lauren's hand. "I believe you. Now, sit down and let me get started on what I have planned before Alec comes home and spoils my surprise."

Lauren sat still while Sarah held one dress after another beneath Lauren's chin, then whisked them away before Lauren could even get a good look at them. "I think one of the darker colors will look best on you," Sarah said. "And nothing frilly."

Lauren squirmed on the seat as Sarah held yet another dress in front of the mirror. The dress was raspberry in color and had a delicate ecru collar of tatted lace. She couldn't even begin to imagine how she would look in one of Sarah's dresses, and she couldn't shake the feeling that anyone who saw her in it would laugh at her. Especially Alec. If he laughed at her, she would die. "Maybe I should just wear what I have on," she said uneasily.

"Wait a minute; I have just the thing!" Sarah tossed the raspberry dress aside and went to the wardrobe. She snatched several garments from the wardrobe, then made a beeline for the chest of drawers. "Get out of those clothes."

Though skeptical, Lauren did as she was told, occasionally sneaking peeks at Sarah as she retrieved even more garments from the drawers. *I'll give it a try,* she thought nervously, *but if I don't like it, I won't wear it. I won't allow myself to be the laughingstock of the valley.*

Sarah crossed the room toward her, a pile of clothes draped over her arm. "Those too," she said, inclining her head toward Lauren.

Lauren glanced down at the neatly mended camisole and drawers she was wearing. Inside her wool socks, she self-consciously curled her toes. "Why?"

"Because you're going to wear these instead."

Lauren looked at the dainty silk undergarments that Sarah laid out on the bed, and fought a rising tide of envy. "What's wrong with the ones I've got on? Nobody's going to see them."

"Perhaps not. But if you wear frumpy underclothes, then you're going to *feel* frumpy, no matter how elegantly you're dressed. Besides, these are more fun to wear, and they'll make you feel beautiful."

More than a little embarrassed, Lauren removed her cotton undergarments and put on the ones Sarah insisted she wear instead. The instant the soft silk settled against her skin, a look of wonder transformed her face. She ran one hand down the front of the chemise, unable to believe that anything could feel so soft. Or so decadent.

Sarah smiled knowingly. "I told you so."

Next came a shirt of cream-colored silk that fastened down the front and at the cuffs with tiny pearl buttons, and was adorned at the neck with a narrow black velvet tie that Sarah quickly fashioned into a perfectly balanced bow.

Then Sarah had Lauren put on a skirt of the deepest forest green that Lauren had ever seen. Delight and dismay surged through her at once. "It's too long," she said, unable to keep the disappointment from her voice. "I'm liable to trip over it."

"The length is perfect," Sarah said, frowning as she formed a tuck in the waistband with her fingers. "The waist needs adjusting, but that will take only a minute. My, you have a tiny waist!"

Scrawny is more like it, Lauren thought. Yet the way Sarah said it made it sound desirable. She twisted around to try to catch a glimpse of herself in the cheval mirror. "Are you sure this is going to work? It feels so . . . so . . . I don't know. It feels strange."

"Yes, it will work. I know it will." Sarah chuckled. "Alec isn't going to know what hit him!"

When Sarah finished fixing Lauren's hair and clothes, and even applied a few touches of face paint and powder, Lauren stood in front of the cheval mirror and gazed in mute shock at her reflection, unable to believe that the stylish young woman who stared back was really her.

"You're not saying anything," Sarah prompted.

Lauren shook her head. "What *can* I say? It's beautiful. I mean, the clothes are beautiful."

"*You're* beautiful. The clothes merely accent what was there all along." Sarah hurried to the window and peeked between the curtains. She let out a squeal of excitement. "James and Alec are back!"

Lauren felt the floor move beneath her. Her hands flew to her cheeks. "Are you sure I don't have on too much rouge?"

"I'm sure. It's very natural looking. No one will even suspect you're wearing it. And don't you dare say anything to Alec about it! James doesn't even know I bought it. He's liable to think we're a couple of tarts!"

Lauren giggled nervously. "My hair won't fall down, will it?"

"No, it won't. Now, stop worrying!" Sarah went to the door and opened it. "Are you ready to go downstairs?"

"If Mr. MacKenzie laughs at me, I'll never forgive you."

"Alec won't laugh at you. He might faint, but he won't laugh. I promise."

Alec's voice boomed through the house from the foot of the stairs. "Sarah? Lauren? Are you up there?"

Sarah poked her head out the door. "We'll be right down!"

"Oh, hell," Lauren muttered. This wasn't going to work at all. Alec was going to take one look at her and fall down laughing. She just knew it.

Sarah eyed her quizzically. "Ready?"

"I guess so," Lauren croaked. She wanted to run and hide.

"Then, let's go." As if to thwart any further protest, Sarah took Lauren's arm and maneuvered her toward the door. "Do the shoes still pinch?" she asked.

I don't know, Lauren thought frantically. *My toes went numb a few minutes ago.* "They'll be all right."

"Sarah!" James called out. "If you're not down here in two minutes, we'll leave without you!"

"Go!" Sarah whispered in Lauren's ear.

Bracing herself for Alec's reaction, Lauren took a shaky breath, squared her shoulders, and walked out of the bedroom.

Chapter 14

James peered at his watch and frowned. "Sarah had better not be changing clothes again. I told her she looked fine."

Alec chuckled. "You may as well concede defeat, James. I cautioned you before you married her that you would never be able to break her of that habit." Both men were waiting in the entrance hall, James in a summer weight short coat and black-and-gray-striped pants, and Alec in dark pants and a fawn-colored coat that fit snugly across his broad shoulders.

"It gets progressively worse," James said, returning the watch to his waistcoat pocket. "I can't begin to tell you how many times we have arrived at functions embarrassingly late because Sarah decided at the last minute to—" He broke off and nodded toward the stairs. "Here they come now."

Both men turned toward the stairs at once.

Alec had no trouble recognizing Sarah. With her bouncing dark curls and impish expression, she had changed little since they were children. But he did not immediately recognize the elegantly dressed woman who was preceding his sister down the stairs.

For several long seconds, he stared at the

woman, knowing he had seen her before, yet unable to remember where.

She was dressed in a matching jacket and skirt of deep forest green, which heightened her coloring and made her eyes look astonishingly blue. The skirt lay smoothly over her hips and fell to the floor in elegant folds that moved gracefully as she walked. A cream collar and dainty black tie peeked demurely from the neck of the short waisted jacket, which hugged her exquisite figure as if it had been tailored for her. Her light brown hair was swept up off her slender neck and twisted into a sleek coil at her nape. Wispy tendrils curled softly about her face.

An image of him removing the pins from her hair and letting it cascade down her shoulders flickered through his mind and sent a surge of heat hurtling through his loins. He imagined himself undressing her, circling his hands around that inviting waist, and pulling her to him. He saw himself kissing that soft full mouth and making love to her for hours on end—

Then the realization struck him, and every muscle in his body went rigid with shock. His gaze swept the length of her, taking in every detail of her appearance, before returning to her face. "Oh, my God," he murmured.

Seeing the change in Alec's expression, Lauren faltered. Had Sarah not been close behind her, prodding her down the stairs, she would have turned and fled. As it was, her heart was beating so hard it hurt, and her hands were shaking.

During the time Sarah had been dressing her and styling her hair, she had forgotten about the argument she'd had with Alec the last time she saw him. Now the memory returned full force. She felt more self-conscious than ever. It had been a mistake dressing up like this. A terrible mistake. One she was going to regret for the rest of her life. Feeling like an outlaw on the way to his own hanging, she reluctantly descended the remaining stairs. *At least outlaws don't wear pointy little shoes that cut off the circulation in their feet,* she thought, fighting the urge to laugh out of sheer terror.

His gaze never leaving Lauren, Alec went to stand at the foot of the stairs. She stopped on the bottom step, only inches away from him and her head on a level with his. Her eyes rapidly scanned his face for some sign—any sign—that he was not displeased with what he saw, but his expression revealed nothing of what was going through his mind. *Please, say something!* she screamed inwardly. Just when she thought she could stand it no more, the tiny lines at the corners of his eyes crinkled into a smile and he held out his hand.

Lauren's knees nearly crumpled beneath her in relief.

She took Alec's outstretched hand, her stomach flip-flopping crazily as his strong, tanned fingers closed around hers, and stepped down off the bottom stair. Alec did not release her, but stood there staring at her as if he could not quite believe what he was seeing. When he finally spoke, his voice was oddly strained. "Hello, Lauren," he said thickly.

She gave him a wobbly smile. "Hello, Alec."

He continued to stare at her. A pronounced silence hung between them.

Behind Alec, James cleared his throat. "So this is the plot my scheming wife has been hatching," he said. "I knew you were up to something, Sarah."

"Isn't she beautiful?" Sarah blurted out, no longer able to contain her excitement.

James inclined his head. "She is indeed."

Alec's gaze never left Lauren's. "She's magnificent," he said slowly.

Lauren felt her face grow hot. She was not accustomed to being the object of so much scrutiny, especially scrutiny that was neither belligerent nor condemning. Suddenly shy, she fidgeted and looked away.

Still feeling a little off-balance, Alec glanced at James. "You and Sarah can take the buggy and go on ahead," he said, trying to regain control of the situation. "I'll have one of the men put a sidesaddle on Lauren's horse, and we'll meet you in town."

Lauren felt a twinge of panic, but she wasn't certain if it was at the thought of riding sidesaddle or at being alone with Alec. "I've never ridden sidesaddle before," she said lamely.

"Don't worry," Sarah whispered merrily in her ear. "Alec will catch you if you fall."

Sarah and James left for town. Lauren nervously paced the library while she waited for

Alec to return to the house. She stopped by one of the tall windows that flanked the fireplace and stared wistfully out across the valley. Ever since the day Alec had come to the Bar-T and they had argued, she had been more confused than ever about her feelings for him.

She had seriously considered breaking off all contact with him. She would not borrow any more of his books. She would stay away from Duneideann. It would certainly simplify matters, she reasoned. It would be one less thing for Pa to harp about. And maybe, just maybe, some small measure of peace would return to her life.

Yet, seeing Alec and reading his books were the only things she had ever done for herself, and the thought of giving them up made her feel empty inside, as if a part of her had died. There seemed to be no way to please both her father and herself.

She was still mulling over the problem when Alec returned. Lost in thought, she did not hear him come in.

He folded his arms across his chest and leaned against the doorframe for several minutes, watching her. Sunlight streaming through the window infused her hair with soft golden light, making it shine, and illuminated her profile. It was an elegant, refined profile, guaranteed to turn heads in even the most discriminating establishments. It no longer mattered to him that Lauren didn't have a pedigree, as Chloe put it. He loved her.

After he and Lauren had argued, he had lain awake for hours that night, thinking about what

Chloe had said, and about Lauren and the possibility of spending a future with her. It was the thought of spending the rest of his life *without* her that had finally decided him. He didn't want to lose her to someone else.

The way Roy Early lost Lauren's mother to Frank Cooper, he thought.

"You look beautiful," he said quietly.

Lauren whirled around. "I didn't hear you come in. How long have you been standing there?"

He pushed himself away from the doorframe. "A few minutes. I was enjoying the scenery."

Lauren's face reddened. "Sarah went to a lot of trouble to make me presentable. I got the feeling she didn't want to be seen with me when I was wearing my own clothes."

Alec chuckled. "I doubt that. Sarah's mind doesn't work that way." He stopped in front of her. "Thank you for coming here today. I wasn't sure you'd still want to go to the celebration with me."

"I wasn't sure you'd still want to take me." Lauren fidgeted. "Look, I'm sorry—"

Alec placed a finger against her lips, silencing her. "Don't apologize, lass. You aren't to blame. If anything, I am the one who should apologize. When I saw Sam Luttrell at the Bar-T that day, something inside me snapped. The thought of your father hiring him after what he had done to you turns my stomach."

"I don't like it either. But Pa didn't have much choice. We were shorthanded to begin with, and Jimmy's quitting left us up a river without a paddle. And Sam was willing to work without pay until after the fall auction."

Alec was quiet a moment. If Sam was working without pay, where was he getting the money for his frequent excursions into town? Alec knew Jack Corrigan would never serve Sam liquor without being paid for it in advance, and he was willing to wager that Chloe ran her business the same way. As Chloe said, Sam was up to something. Alec intended to find out what.

"I just don't like the idea of him being anywhere near you, lass. I'll never forgive him for hurting you."

Alec's concern made her feel self-conscious. "I don't want to talk about Sam any more. He has a way of souring everything. Do you think we could go now? I don't want to miss the parade."

"Of course. And I promise, no more talk about Luttrell. Do you have a hat? 'Tis hot out."

"It's upstairs on Sarah's bed. I'll go get it." Lauren started toward the door.

"Lauren?"

She hesitated and turned back. "What's wrong?"

Alec's gaze slowly traveled the length of her. A smile warmed his eyes. "Not a thing," he said.

The smells of beef and corn and chile peppers cooking over mesquite fires filled the air. Children darted between the wagons and buggies that choked the side streets, making passage difficult. Alec quartered their horses at Benton's Livery, and they walked into town. Lauren's shoes pinched something awful, and it was all she could do not to limp.

As they neared the picnic grounds, she caught a glimpse of Bubba hovering near a throng of women who had come from out of town to participate in the festivities. She lifted her hand and waved, and called out to him. Bubba stared at her a moment, then darted into the crowd, disappearing from sight.

Lauren glanced at Alec, wondering if he had found Bubba's behavior odd. "I guess he didn't recognize me."

"You do look different, lass."

She shrugged. "I guess." She removed the wide-brimmed straw bonnet that Sarah had lent her and used it to fan her face. The heat had dampened her hair and caused fine tendrils to curl around her neck. "It sure is hot today. I don't think it was a good idea to wear all these clothes."

Alec took her elbow. "Come with me."

"Where are we going?"

He smiled. "You'll see."

As they passed the barbecue fires, the rich aroma of roasting meats caused Lauren's mouth to water. She hadn't eaten much at breakfast, and now she was famished.

A few yards away, Jack Corrigan was doing a booming business selling cold drinks at a makeshift stand that he had set up in the shade of a tent awning. He grinned when he saw them, and appreciation shone in his eyes as his gaze swept over Lauren. "Good morning, Miss Cooper. If I may say so, you look positively lovely today."

Lauren blushed and shifted uncomfortably. "Thanks," she mumbled.

"Business appears steady," Alec commented. "You picked a fine day for this."

"Couldn't have asked for better. There's nothing like a hot, dry day to stir up people's thirst. What'll it be?"

Alec ordered an ale for himself and a lemonade for Lauren. The lemonade had pieces of ice floating in it. "Let's see if we can find a shady spot to sit down," Alec suggested.

"We don't have much time," she said. "The parade is supposed to start soon."

"Just for a few minutes, while we enjoy our drinks. Don't worry, lass. I wouldn't dream of letting you miss the parade."

Long wooden tables and benches had been set up beneath huge awnings. Because the barbecue would not begin until after the parade, only a few people had already claimed spots at the tables, mostly mothers with babies or very small children and a few elderly men who preferred to sit out the parade. Alec located an empty table. He held Lauren's lemonade while she sat down and smoothed out her skirt. She was not accustomed to wearing a skirt, and felt conspicuous.

Alec sat down beside her.

Lauren sipped on the icy lemonade and watched the other people arrive. She spotted Jake Hanby and Martha Sikes strolling hand in hand, Martha's wispy hair falling out of its bun. She saw some of the cowhands from nearby ranches, and a few of the townspeople, but most of the people who had come to watch the parade were strangers to her. She looked in vain for Bubba, but there was no sight of his silvery blond hair anywhere. Nor did she see Cal or Bernie, although she couldn't help wondering what they would say if they saw her all gussied up.

As Lauren watched the passersby, Alec watched her. Her face was flushed and her eyes sparkled with excitement. Sometimes being with Lauren was like looking at the world through a child's eyes all over again. Nothing seemed to bore her and her observations seldom failed to cast a fresh perspective on even the most common subject. The fact that she pleased him immensely in bed sweetened her appeal. He wondered wryly why it had taken him so long to realize what a treasure she was.

"How are you doing?" he asked.

She cast him a puzzled glance. "I'm fine. Why?"

He gently brushed a tendril of hair from her temple. "I don't want you to get overheated."

The feel of Alec's hand on her face sent a tingle of longing through Lauren's veins. Without thinking, she turned her head and pressed her cheek against his hand. Sheer happiness danced in her eyes. "This isn't Scotland, Mr. MacKenzie. You may as well get used to the heat. Until October, we're all doomed to sweat like stuffed pigs."

Alec threw back his head and laughed. Leave it to Lauren to point out the obvious.

The sound of Alec's laughter drew curious glances. Several people pointed in their direction. Lauren started to say something, then stopped. Her smile abruptly faded.

Alec saw Arminta Larson and her brood of followers bearing down on them. "Damn," he muttered.

Lauren smothered a giggle. "You really should watch your language, sir," she teased. "Swearing is most unbecoming."

He shot her a pained look. "Thank you for reminding me."

Lauren grinned. "That's what friends are for."

Arminta Larson and the other officers from the Millerville Women's Junior League closed the distance between them. "Oh, Mr. MacKenzie," Arminta called out. "Yoo-hoo! Hello there!"

Alec stood up and extended his hand. "Mrs. Larson, how good to see you again. Ladies. You're all looking lovely."

Lauren rolled her eyes. *You're all looking lovely,* she mouthed silently.

Arminta placed one hand in Alec's. "You are so kind to say so, although how we survive this heat is beyond me. I don't remember it ever being this hot on the Fourth." She fanned herself with her handkerchief, and strained to see past Alec. "I see you found someone to accompany you to the celebration. Please, do introduce us, Mr. MacKenzie. I am so looking forward to meeting the young lady."

Lauren set her glass on the table and rose to her feet. "Hello, Mrs. Larson."

Arminta stiffened. She stared at Lauren's outstretched hand in openmouthed shock, making no attempt to take it. She lifted her stricken gaze to Lauren's face, and for a moment, it seemed as if she might swoon.

Lauren withdrew her hand. "Is something wrong, ma'am? Alec, perhaps you should get Mrs. Larson a glass of lemonade. She looks a little peaked."

Arminta fanned herself faster. "No, no, that won't be necessary. I must say, Miss Cooper, you gave me quite a shock. I've never seen you looking so . . . so . . ." She faltered, at a loss for words.

"You look divine," Cissy Page gushed. "Oh, Minta, it's too bad your Harold can't be here to see this. Who would have ever believed that this is our very own Lauren Cooper!"

The other women gathered around Lauren. "I've never seen you dressed like that," Amy Taylor said. "That color is becoming on you."

"I can see you have already met," Alec said. He put an arm around Lauren's shoulders. "And yes, I agree with Mrs. Page; Lauren does look beautiful."

Arminta stiffened. "Well, clothes certainly don't make the man. Or the woman, as the case may be."

Cissy looked shocked. "Minta! What a terrible thing to say. Besides, you yourself have often said that someone should take Lauren aside and show her the proper way to dress. I, for one, think she looks fetching."

"Beauty is as beauty does," Arminta said

stiffly. "And a Cooper in any other disguise is still a Cooper."

Anger welled up in Lauren. She started toward Arminta, but Alec's arm tightened around her shoulders, holding her back. "If you will excuse us, ladies, Lauren and I don't want to miss the parade."

Before Lauren could object, Alec turned her around and steered her away from the women.

She had to run to keep up with Alec's long-legged strides. Finally, she couldn't stand it any longer. "Must you walk so fast?" she blurted out. "I can barely stand in these blasted shoes, much less run in them."

Alec stopped and glanced back at the picnic tables. Arminta and the other officers in the Millerville Women's Junior League were still huddled beneath the awning.

Lauren clenched her hands. "Damn that woman! I wanted to knock her teeth clear to New Mexico!"

"That's precisely what she hoped you would do, lass, give her something more to harp about. Don't let her antagonize you. 'Tis not worth the frustration."

Lauren shook her fist in front of Alec's face. "Just one punch. That's all I want."

Alec took Lauren's fist and carried it to his mouth. He kissed her knuckles. "And what would it have gotten you, lass, besides a bruised hand and a moment's satisfaction?"

She jerked her hand free. "Why do you always have to be so sensible?"

Alec chuckled. "Not always. A few weeks

ago, I wanted to hit her myself. The only thing that saved me from doing so was the fact that she was nowhere around at the time."

Lauren tilted her head to one side and regarded Alec with renewed interest. "What did she do to make *you* want to punch her?"

"She decided to assemble a number of eligible young ladies from whom I might select an appropriate partner to accompany me to the Fourth of July celebration."

Lauren's eyes widened. "She didn't!"

"Aye, lass, she did. Needless to say, I refused her offer."

Lauren shook her head in disbelief. "No wonder she was so shocked to see me with you. She must have thought you'd lost your mind!"

Or my heart, Alec thought. He took Lauren by the shoulders, turned her in the direction of the parade, and gave her a slight shove forward. "I'm beginning to wonder that myself," he joked.

They walked toward town. Several times, Lauren glanced up at Alec and caught him watching her, tenderness and puzzlement on his face. A flush of self-consciousness crept up her neck. *I love you so much,* she thought.

By the time they reached Main Street, the boardwalk was crowded with spectators vying for the best vantage point from which to view the parade. Alec gripped Lauren's elbow to keep from losing her as they worked their way through the crowd. They finally located James and Sarah in front of the Mercantile.

Sarah clutched Lauren's arm. "I never expected to see so many people! Is it always like this?"

Lauren nodded. "Sometimes it's even more crowded. Millerville puts on the best Fourth of July Celebration in this part of the Territory. People come from three counties."

A bugle sounding reveille signaled that the parade was ready to begin.

"That'll be the soldiers from Fort Huachuca," Lauren said. "They come here every year. One year they brought a cannon and shot it off before the fireworks."

"It sounds like fun."

"Oh, it is! They have old guns and sabers from the Apache wars and from the War Between the States, and sometimes they perform mock battles. I got to be a casualty once."

"Not a fatality, I hope," Alec whispered in her ear.

He was standing close to her, his hand on her shoulder; and the protective, almost possessive, gesture made her feel giddy. It was all she could do not to giggle out of sheer nervousness. "No. I just had to lie there and pretend to have a bullet in my arm, and let a medic bandage me up. I remember he had a plug tucked inside his bottom lip, and I kept staring at his mouth and expecting him to slobber tobacco juice on me."

Sarah wrinkled her nose in disgust, but Alec and James laughed. "Lucky for him that he didn't," Alec teased. "I doubt he would have lived to tell about it."

Lauren shot him a withering glance. "Very funny."

Cheers erupted around them as the parade began.

A buggy that had been decorated with red, white, and blue streamers led the procession. Sheriff Early, in his Sunday best, held the reins. Beside him on the seat was a russet-haired woman wearing a wide-brimmed red hat adorned with long black feathers and a red dress that was cut so low her bosom threatened to spill out. She waved to the cheering spectators as they passed.

"Oh, look! That's Miss Chloe!" Lauren said. "Last year, Arminta Larson and the Women's Junior League tried to get her banned from the parade, but when the town council put it to a vote, they not only let Miss Chloe stay in the parade; they voted to let her lead it!"

"Who's Miss Chloe?" Sarah asked.

"She's the local madam," Alec explained.

"Oh?"

James chuckled. "Don't get her started," he warned. "The last time my wife entered a discussion on morality, she nearly assaulted Lady Roxbury."

Lauren's eyes widened. "You did?"

"I did not. But I wanted to. I hate hypocrites, and that woman is a hypocrite of the highest order."

Just then, Chloe waved and blew a kiss in their direction—or rather, in Alec's direction. Sarah and Lauren both stared at him in astonishment, and Lauren felt a twinge of jealousy.

Alec grinned sheepishly. "We're just friends. Nothing more."

Sarah regarded her brother with suspicion, but Lauren fidgeted and glanced away. She didn't even want to think about Alec and Miss Chloe together. Just friends, indeed!

Alec bent down and whispered in Lauren's ear, "Chloe is one of your most outspoken admirers, lass. She set me straight where you are concerned."

Lauren's eyes widened and color flooded her face. The thought of their discussing her was even more embarrassing than the thought of their doing that other thing together. "You talked about me?"

Alec chuckled. "Watch the parade," he ordered.

After Miss Chloe came Martin Dandridge and two other ranchers from the Pima County Ranchers' Association, all on horseback. Martin tipped his hat at them as he rode past. His gaze rested briefly on Lauren, his brow furrowed, and he smiled, but it was a confused smile, as if he wasn't quite sure of himself.

"I don't think he recognized me," Lauren said.

Alec squeezed her shoulder. "You look beautiful, lass."

Her heart swelled in her chest. Standing here with Alec, wearing the loveliest clothes she had ever seen, she felt as if she were dreaming. She even managed to forget about Miss Chloe for awhile.

Carts and wagons and even a mail coach, all decorated with bunting and streamers, rumbled down Main Street, followed by more horses and their riders. Burroughs' Feed Store entry was a completely outfitted Conestoga wagon, its white canvas cover snapping in the wind like a giant sail. Finally, bringing up the rear, were the cavalry soldiers from Fort Huachuca.

"That was fun!" Sarah said as the crowd started to disperse. "What's next?"

"Usually the games and races and the barbecue," Lauren said. "And after that dancing and fireworks, although there probably won't be any fireworks this year because of the drought."

"Arminta told me that last year someone blew up the fireworks display during the parade," Sarah said. "I heard it created quite a stir."

"You might say that," Lauren said dryly, annoyed to have Sam Luttrell brought into yet another conversation. Was there no escaping that man? She glanced at Alec, who winked at her. "If there are fireworks this year," she said, "I'm sure they're being well guarded. At least, they'd better be. I haven't seen Sam anywhere."

"Sam?" Sarah asked.

"Sam Luttrell," Alec said. "He's the one who created the stir." He wondered uneasily where Luttrell was today; he hadn't seen him either.

"Coop! Is that you?"

Lauren turned at the familiar voice. "T.J.!"

Alec extended his hand. "Mr. Powell, 'tis good to see you again."

T.J. shook Alec's hand, then looked at Lauren and let out a long, low whistle. "I hardly recognized you in that getup, Coop. I'll be damned if you aren't the prettiest girl here today. If MacKenzie here wasn't holding on to you like he was scared you'd get away, I'd consider courting you myself. I'd be honored if you'd save a dance for me later."

Lauren cast a sharp glance at Alec, half expecting him to be angered by T.J.'s words. A smile played at the corners of Alec's mouth as he regarded her. "Thanks," she said awkwardly. "How are you feeling?"

"Good as new. I'm glad to see you're doing better too. You were pretty cut up the last time I saw you. Did you hear? Eliot Dandridge left town. His old man wasn't too happy about what him and Luttrell did to you."

Lauren said nothing.

T.J. ran one hand over his jaw. "Listen, MacKenzie, there's something you should know. Can we talk in private?"

"Certainly. James, take Lauren with you and Sarah. I'll meet you at the picnic area."

"I'm dying for something cold to drink," Sarah said. "How about you, Lauren?"

"Sound's good," she replied, glancing from T.J. to Alec and wondering what T.J. wanted.

Alec watched until they were out of sight, then turned to T.J. "Do you want to go somewhere and sit down?"

T.J. shook his head. "This won't take long. It's about those fancy black bulls you brought into the valley."

"Word travels fast," Alec said dryly.

"That's not the only thing that travels fast. Pete Wallace saw one of them in Wilcox last week. The bull had an altered brand that didn't look to be more than a couple of weeks old. The man who had the bull said he'd just bought him from a fellow who had lost his spread and was heading back to Missouri."

"Did your friend get the man's name?"

"Never even saw him in these parts before. Pete was itching to see a bill of sale, but the look in the man's eyes told him he'd already asked too many questions, so he backed off."

Alec swore under his breath. Those bulls were far too costly to be slipping out of his possession so easily. He was going to have a talk with Sly Barnes and try to come up with a way to keep better control over the stock. In the meantime, he intended to find out who the culprit was.

"Got any idea who could be rustling your cattle?" T.J. asked when Alec did not respond.

Sam Luttrell, Alec thought. While he had no proof, he could not help being suspicious of any man who spent more than he earned, and Luttrell had not drawn cash wages since the day Kendrick fired him. Furthermore, the Bar-T bordered Duneideann. Frank Cooper may have considered himself lucky to have acquired a hired hand willing to work without pay until fall, but Alec doubted Luttrell was working without some lucrative form of compensation.

It was also possible that Frank and Luttrell were working together. His own feelings for Lauren aside, it would not be the first time that Frank Cooper had been suspected of rustling, and rumors like that usually contained some kernel of truth. "I have a few theories," he said. "Nothing substantial."

"There's something else, MacKenzie. Something I didn't want Coop to hear. You know how she gets fired up about things."

"What is it?"

"Sam Luttrell. He's still nursing a grudge about getting fired from the Diamond Cross. He blames you. You and Coop. He's been boasting around town about how he's going to get even."

Alec frowned. "Did he say what he intends to do?"

"Nothing specific. Just jawjacking mostly. No one who knows him takes him seriously. All the same, I'd watch my back if I were you. He's been known to pull some pretty mean stunts over the years."

"Thank you for the warning."

"You and Coop saved my life, MacKenzie. I owe you."

At the barbecue fires, Lauren and Sarah and James secured places in one of several long lines that had already formed. Heat rose up off the fires in shimmering waves.

"The food smells wonderful," James said. "My stomach is making quite a commotion."

Lauren's stomach let out a sympathetic growl, and they all laughed. "The food here is the best anywhere," she said. "We've tried cooking beef over a fire at home, but it doesn't taste the same. It's almost as if it demands to be cooked in huge quantities."

Sarah dabbed at her face with her handkerchief. "James, if you don't mind, I'm going to go sit down in the shade. This heat is getting to me."

"You go with her, Lauren. When my errant brother-in-law gets here, we can bring your meals."

"We won't have long to wait," Sarah said. "Here comes Alec now."

Lauren turned back in the direction from which they had come and saw Alec, handsome and self-confident and towering a full head above most of the other men, working his way through the crowd toward them. A sweet, soul-wrenching joy filled her at the sight of him, and her body ached for his touch. His gaze scanned the crowd, then locked with hers, and her heart lurched maddeningly. It was all she could do to stand her ground and not go to him.

"Everything all right?" James asked when Alec reached them.

Mischief glimmered in Alec's eyes. "Couldn't be better," he said cryptically. "You two going to be all right here?"

Sarah muffled a giggle. "Of course we will. Now off with you, and have a good time."

Confusion creased Lauren's forehead. "What's going on?"

"I have a surprise for you." Alec took her elbow. "Come, lass. Our conveyance awaits."

Chapter 15

Lauren allowed herself to be steered through the crowd. "Where are we going?"

"You'll see."

She twisted around for a final glance at James and Sarah, but they were already out of sight. She took several quick steps to catch up with Alec's long strides, holding her hat with one hand to keep it from getting knocked from her head. Her brow wrinkled as she wondered what Alec was up to.

The buggy that James and Sarah had taken to the celebration was parked on the street. At Lauren's puzzled glance, Alec chuckled. "Sarah and James will ride our horses home. Sarah is an excellent horsewoman. Popcorn will be in good hands."

"Do Sarah and James know about this?"

Alec grinned. "They assisted with the planning." He helped her into the buggy and climbed up onto the seat beside her.

A large covered basket sat on the buggy floor. "What's in there?" Lauren asked, curious.

Still grinning, Alec picked up the reins. "If I tell you, it won't be a surprise."

The warmth in his eyes caused Lauren's heart to swell. This had already been the best day of her life, and it was far from over. If she were to die in her sleep tonight, she thought, she would die the happiest person in the world.

Much of the crowd that had filled the streets during the parade had gravitated toward the picnic area. As they drove through town, several people pointed in their direction and stared. Lauren started to shrink away from the unwanted attention, then abruptly caught herself. If Alec wasn't embarrassed to be seen with her, why should *she* be embarrassed?

In an act that was born less of self-confidence than of defiance, Lauren sat up a little straighter, squared her shoulders, and lifted her chin. Let them stare, she thought stubbornly. *She* was the one Alec had chosen to spend the day with. Not them.

As they passed the Mercantile, Lauren spotted Mr. Edrich on the boardwalk talking with Piers Larson. Lauren put on her best smile and waved. "Hello, Mr. Edrich," she called out. "Mr. Larson. Lovely day, isn't it?"

Both men stopped talking and turned to stare as they drove by.

Alec chuckled. "You're enjoying this, lass."

"You're damn—darn—right I'm enjoying it. Did you see the looks on their faces? In fact, I think we should really give them something to talk about. I think we should circle around the block and drive by again, and *this* time you should kiss me right in front of them."

Alec threw back his head and laughed. He was tempted to do just that. He wondered what Arminta Larson would say when she found out that he had kissed Lauren in broad daylight in the middle of Main Street.

He wondered what Arminta Larson would say when he announced that he and Lauren were getting married.

There was only one way to find out.

At the end of the block, Alec turned the corner. Lauren was so busy straining to hear the music coming from the picnic area that she didn't notice where they were going until Alec turned the buggy down Main Street. Again. She shifted uneasily. Surely he had not taken her jest seriously?

As they neared the Mercantile a second time, her heart began to pound. Mr. Edrich nudged Mr. Larson and nodded in their direction. Lauren gripped the edge of the buggy seat. Whatever Alec was up to, it wasn't funny.

He reined in the horse and stopped the buggy right in front of the Mercantile. Lauren's heart was hammering so fiercely it hurt, and she could hardly breathe. "What are you doing?" she whispered sharply.

Alec slid his arm around her waist and pulled her against him.

She gasped. "Alec!"

Grasping her chin, he turned her face toward him and saw the alarm in her eyes before he covered her mouth with his, smothering her protest.

Lauren's body went rigid as surprise and horror and embarrassment shot through her at once. But the feel of Alec's strong arm around her and the heady sensation of his mouth on hers seeped through her resistance, weakening it, and she felt herself caving in to the soul-searing power he held over her.

When he finally pulled his mouth away, she was trembling and out of breath. He held her against his racing heart for several seconds while he got his own emotions under control, then released her and looked past her to the two men standing on the boardwalk, staring at them. He tipped his hat to them. "Beautiful, isn't she?" he asked.

He snapped the reins and the buggy lurched forward. Lauren clutched her hat to her head and struggled to catch her breath. Her cheeks were a bright crimson and incredulity shone in her eyes. "I can't believe you did that!"

Alec battled a smile. When they reached the end of the block, he slowed the buggy. "Shall we make another trip around?"

"No!" Lauren pressed her palms to her flaming cheeks, not sure if she wanted to laugh or cry. "I'll never be able to show my face in this town again!"

Alec urged the horse forward. "Think of the community service we just performed, lass," he said lightly. "We've giving the upstanding citizens of Millerville something to gossip about for months to come."

About two miles outside of town, Alec turned the buggy off the main road and onto a narrow, barely perceptible trail. He glanced at Lauren. "Forgiven me yet?" he asked.

She shot him a fuming glance and fought the rising color in her face. Somehow, she managed not to smile. "I'm still thinking about it," she said. She looked around her. "I've never been this way before. Where are we going?"

The corners of Alec's eyes crinkled. "You'll see."

The farther they drove, the less rocky the ground became. Low hills, dotted with live oak and jojoba, swelled gently around them. A dry wind rustled the tall wheat-colored grass that grew in abundance.

After what seemed like miles, although Lauren knew it couldn't have been that far, Alec guided the horse off the trail and headed for a grassy knoll within sight of the trail.

A grove of towering sycamore trees crowned the top of the knoll. Alec stopped the buggy.

For several long minutes, Lauren sat gazing out across the valley. The wind blew her hair around her face. She brushed it away and turned to look at Alec. Wonder shone in her eyes. "I never knew this place existed," she said. "It's beautiful!"

"I found it by accident when we were surveying for the irrigation conduits. If you continue in that direction and cross over the ridge, you'll be directly above Six-shooter Canyon."

"This land is part of Duneideann?"

"Aye, lass, that it is."

"It's so close, yet it's like some secret place that no one knows about. Can you imagine living up here?"

"Would you like to live here?"

"I'd love it. I mean, if I owned this land, this

is where I would want to build my house. It's so quiet here, so peaceful."

"I've often thought the same thing. 'Tis one of my favorite places on the ranch."

Lauren's expression became pensive. "If it were me, I'd build the kitchen facing east, so it would be filled with light first thing in the morning and so you could see the mountains from the window. And of course, the porch would have to face west so you could sit outside in the evenings and enjoy the sunsets—" She broke off suddenly. "Sorry," she said sheepishly. "I get carried away sometimes."

"Don't apologize," Alec said. "'Tis good to get carried away sometimes." He jumped down from the buggy.

Lauren started to rise.

"Stay there," Alec ordered. He went around to her side of the buggy and extended his hand to her. "Miss Cooper?"

Again, Lauren blushed. "I'm quite capable of getting down by myself," she protested, but there was no disguising the look of pure pleasure that illuminated her face as she put her hand in his.

In as ladylike a manner as she could manage, she stood and climbed down from the buggy.

Just as her feet touched the ground, Alec folded his arms around her and crushed her against him. Before she realized what was happening, his head descended and his mouth came down hard over hers.

She groaned inwardly and leaned into Alec's embrace as his lips claimed hers in a devouring kiss. His hands moved down over her back, scorching her skin through her clothing and igniting a fierce longing that swept through her like wildfire. He teased her lips with his tongue, then parted them and plunged, again and again, in an erotic imitation of a still more intimate act, until Lauren's head reeled and her body felt as if it were floating. When his mouth finally left hers, she sagged against him, her limbs weak and trembling.

Alec brushed his lips against her cheek, then her brow. "I've been wanting to do that ever since I first saw you this morning."

"You already did," she said breathlessly, trying to get her bearings. "In front of the mercantile."

"That, lass, was a mere peck. I wanted a real kiss."

Her wrapped his arms around her and rested his chin on top of her head. Lauren closed her eyes and waited for her heart to calm down. Nothing in the world had ever felt as comforting or reassuring as the solid strength of Alec's arms around her. She wished they could stay like this forever.

Still a little dazed from Alec's kiss, Lauren tilted back her head and gazed dreamily into his eyes. "Thank you," she said simply.

"For what?"

"For making me so happy."

Before he could respond, Lauren's stomach rumbled loudly. Alec drew back his head and eyed her suspiciously. "Unless I misjudged the source of that sound, lass, you're also hungry. When did you last eat?"

"I had a piece of bacon for breakfast."

"That's all?"

"That's all I had time for."

Releasing her, Alec lifted the buggy's hinged seat and took out a blanket. He handed it to Lauren. "Spread this on the ground while I take care of the horse," he said.

While he unhitched the horse and tethered him a few yards away where he could graze undisturbed, Lauren shook open the blanket and laid it on the ground in the shade of a tall sycamore. She dropped to her knees on one edge of the blanket and straightened it, smoothing out the wrinkles. She took off the green jacket, folded it, and set it to one side. Then she removed Sarah's hat and placed it on top of the jacket, touching her hands to her hair to make certain it was still in place. "So what are you going to do with this land?" she asked as Alec joined her, carrying the basket."

He set the basket on the edge of the blanket. "I was thinking of building a house."

Lauren glanced up, surprised. "But you already have a house. A beautiful house!"

Alec sat down beside her. "This is going to be a very special house, lass," he said slowly. There was an odd catch to his voice. "The kitchen will face east . . ."

Lauren stared at him, her gaze held prisoner by his compelling, golden brown gaze.

He took her arm and gently yet inexorably

pulled her toward him. "The porch will face west, toward the setting sun . . ."

He pulled her onto his lap and his arms went around her. Ordinarily she might have suspected he was mocking her, but there was a seriousness in his eyes that quickly dashed any such thought.

His gaze never leaving hers, he reached up behind her and began removing the pins from her hair. Freed of its restraint, her hair, soft and shining and smelling faintly of wildflowers, came tumbling down. "The house," Alec continued, his eyes darkening, "will be a place where I can go when I want to escape from the rest of the world . . ."

Lauren's pulse quickened.

"And be alone with my wife." He paused, then added, "If she'll have me."

Lauren stared at him, not certain she had heard correctly.

His hypnotic gaze bored into hers. "Marry me, Lauren."

Her eyes widened and she suddenly felt unsteady, as if someone had jerked the ground out from under her. *He wanted to marry her?* She touched her fingertips to his mouth, not quite believing he'd said what she thought he had, and terrified to think she might have imagined it. "I-I don't know what to say."

Still holding her, Alec half turned and lowered her to the blanket. He brought his head down to hers. "Say yes," he murmured into her mouth just before he covered it with his. He moved his mouth over hers, devouring its softness as he coaxed her into returning his kiss with an urgency that matched his own. As he kissed her, he tugged at the narrow black tie at her neck, pulling it free, then began to undo the buttons of her silk skirt. He slid his hand inside her shirt to caress her breasts through the thin chemise.

Lauren closed her eyes and let the delicious sensations his touch aroused in her flow through her limbs as he fondled her breasts, lifting and stroking them, teasing the sensitive nipples until they stood erect against the gossamer silk. "Yes," she whispered breathlessly.

Alec smiled and his eyes darkened. "Yes to my proposal? Or to what I'm doing to you?"

Still not quite believing he wanted to marry her, she touched his face. Her hand trembled as she traced her fingertips along his cheekbone, smooth and taut and tanned, and down his face to the strong, chiseled line of his jaw. She lifted her gaze to his amber-flecked eyes, their thick lashes kissed by the sun, and the love she felt for him swelled inside her, filling her with more joy than she had ever thought possible. She sighed contentedly. "Both."

The triumph of victory thrilled through Alec's veins, banishing the last thread of doubt that she would refuse him and stoking his desire for her. He wanted her. No, he *needed* her, like he'd never needed anyone.

He pulled away and sat up.

Confusion flickered across her face and she reached for him. "Alec . . ."

He gripped her hand and pulled her upright. "Take them off," he commanded. She did not have to ask what he meant. Her heart racing, she took off the skirt and the silk blouse while Alec laid his jacket aside and began unbuttoning his shirt.

He removed the shirt.

Lauren's heart missed a beat at the sight of his broad chest and powerful shoulders, gleaming bronze in the dappled sunlight that filtered through the sycamore boughs overhead. She reached out to touch his chest and thread her fingers through the crisp hair, and his muscles leapt reflexively beneath her fingertips. Surprised at his reaction to her touch, and curious to see if she could make it happen again, she glided her hand downward over his chest, over the rippled muscles of his abdomen, toward his belt . . .

He caught her hand, stopping its descent.

Her startled gaze riveted on his, and she saw the desire smoldering in his golden brown eyes. "Nay, lass," he said thickly, easing her onto her back. "This is your day."

He lifted her legs and laid them across his lap, then began unfastening her shoes. She lay there, her hair forming a shimmering pillow beneath her head and her blue eyes trained on his face as he pulled one slender leather shoe off her foot.

She gasped as the blood surged through her foot, bringing both pain and relief. She clutched a fistful of blanket and waited for the fierce tingling to subside. Never again, she swore, would she wear a pair of shoes that didn't fit.

Alec removed her other shoe, and began rubbing her feet. Lauren moaned softly and her fingers tightened on the blanket.

The stark contrast of his tanned fingers against the white silk stockings that encased her shapely feet and calves, in addition to the myriad of expressions that played across her face as he kneaded first one foot and then the other, played havoc with his own rampaging desires. Sweat broke out on his brow and his face grew rigid from the effort of staving off his own release. Determined to make this last as long as possible for Lauren, he slowed his movements, taking his time as he worked his way up her calves, massaging the taut muscles until they were soft and pliant in his hands.

He unfastened her garters and carefully peeled off her stockings, then slid his big hand beneath her bottom and lifted her slightly so he could remove her drawers.

Moving her legs off his lap, he lay down beside her. He pulled down the top of her chemise, baring her breasts to his touch. Lauren's heartbeat quickened and her chest rose and fell with rapid, shallow breaths as Alec's lips forged a smoldering trail down her neck, planting dozens of tantalizing kisses on her heated flesh. He closed his lips around a nipple and Lauren sucked in her breath. She threaded her fingers into his hair and held his head against her breast as the sharp, almost agonizing, sensations of pleasure stabbed through her.

Alec pushed the silk chemise up over her knees. When his fingers touched the bare flesh of her thigh, she unthinkingly parted her legs, allowing him to slip his hand between them. He teased the sensitive skin of her inner thighs until she thought she would go mad with arousal. *I love you,* she cried silently.

He slid his hand farther beneath the silk and into the soft curls at the top of her thighs, and her resistance fled.

As his fingers wrought their magic on her, waves of pure pleasure washed over her, each breaking crest carrying her higher and higher. Gasping, she trembled on the edge of fulfillment, then tumbled into completion, her body quivering with spasms of ecstasy.

As Lauren drifted back down to earth, Alec removed the rest of his clothes. He shifted his weight over her and settled between her thighs, then eased his swollen shaft into her wet warmth. She cried out and opened wider to him, wrapping her legs around his waist and lifting her hips to meet his powerful thrusts. The ache of longing that he had already satisfied began to build deep down inside her once again, tightening into a hot, pulsing knot that felt as if it would explode. Her breath tore from her throat in broken sobs. "Please," she said between breaths.

Alec drove into her harder and faster, and the knot shattered.

Lauren cried out and her back arched as a liquid heat surged through her, pulsing through her veins in shuddering spasms as the world tilted and spun around them.

Alec gathered her to him and held her tightly, savoring the feel of her muscles contracting around him, before driving into her one last time. He buried his face in her neck. "God, I love you."

Lauren fought her way up out of the daze that enveloped her in glorious warmth. "Alec . . ."

He lifted his head to look at her. Her face was flushed and damp, and her eyes bright with unshed tears. "I love you, too," she whispered. "I love you so very much . . ."

While Alec opened the bottle of Bordeaux, Lauren unpacked the basket. There were cold meat pasties. There were thick slices of ripe red tomatoes, sprinkled with coarse ground pepper and sandwiched between slabs of fresh homemade bread. There were deviled eggs and pickled cucumbers and fresh apricots and pears. And finally, there were tiny balls of buttery shortcake studded with chopped pecans and dusted with powdered sugar.

Alec watched Lauren while she set out the food. As she leaned forward to make room on the blanket for one of the dishes, her chemise gaped, exposing her breasts to his appreciative gaze. His arousal was swift, and he felt his hardened flesh strain uncomfortably against his trousers. Lauren looked so fetching sitting there in the silk chemise, her feet tucked beneath her and her beautiful hair down, that he was tempted to forgo the picnic and make love to her again.

Lauren's mouth began to water as she surveyed the feast laid out before them. "This looks wonderful," she said. "With all this, we won't even miss the barbecue."

"I hoped you would like it," Alec said. He poured two glasses of wine and handed one to her.

She took a sip. It was stronger than she expected, and she was unable to suppress a small shudder. She glanced coyly at Alec over the rim of her glass. "Alec MacKenzie, were you planning to get me drunk so you could take advantage of me?"

He grinned and raked a lustful gaze over her scantily clad form. "I didn't need to get you drunk," he reminded her.

Lauren blushed hotly and shot him a scathing look, but her pulse began to race at the desire in his gaze. A hazy warmth was already beginning to spread through her limbs, but whether it was from the wine or the lecherous way Alec was looking at her she couldn't say.

She took a deep breath and picked up one of the tomato sandwiches. "I wanted to thank you for helping Pa with the extra feed. He thinks you owe it to him, but no one else in the valley would have been as generous."

"Lauren, I'm not an ogre. I need to protect my investment, yes, but that doesn't mean I'm out to destroy your father. Far more can be accomplished if people are not working at cross-purposes."

"I wish Pa saw it that way. He'd pitch a fit if he knew I was with you today."

"You didn't tell him?"

"Are you kidding? He says I've become uppity ever since I started seeing you. Maybe he's right. I don't know. I just don't see what's so wrong about . . . us." Her voice faltered.

" 'Tis not easy for you, is it?"

"It's damn near impossible. If I didn't love Pa and Bubba so much, I'd—" She broke off, realizing what she had been about to say, and mortified that she would even think such a thing.

"You'd what, lass? Leave?"

She shrugged. "I've thought about it," she said in a low voice. "But then I wonder who would take care of them. With Mama gone, it's my place to look after them."

"Is it?"

"Who else is going to do it?"

"Has it ever occurred to you, lass, that your father and brother are quite capable of taking care of themselves?"

"But Pa's legs—"

"Your father's legs make it more difficult for him to get around, I agree. But they do not prevent him from doing for himself. And your brother is approaching manhood. He's no longer a child who needs someone to mother him."

"No, he just needs someone to protect him from Sam Luttrell." Lauren sighed. "Sam makes me so damn mad I can't see straight. Sometimes I think he hired on at the Bar-T out of spite, because he knows I hate him."

Alec had his own theories about what Luttrell was doing at the Bar-T, but he didn't want to worry Lauren with them. "If he gives you any trouble, lass, come to me," he ordered. "Promise me you won't try to deal with him alone."

"Don't worry. He won't cause any trouble. He knows no one else in the valley will hire him."

"Promise me."

Lauren's gaze riveted on Alec's, and the concern she saw there smothered any protest she might have made. Alec genuinely cared for her. He made her feel special. *He loved her.* She smiled. "I promise."

Alec leaned back against the tree trunk and drew up one knee. He had not yet tasted the meat pasty he held in his hand. "I'm curious about something, lass. I already know about the situation with your mother and father and Roy Early, and why the sheriff and your father don't get along—"

"Who told you that?"

"I prefer to respect the privacy of my source." Alec bit into the pasty.

The nearly forgotten memory of Chloe Roberts blowing Alec a kiss during the parade flickered through Lauren's mind, and again she felt an unpleasant prick of jealousy. "It was Miss Chloe, wasn't it?"

Alec regarded her through half-closed eyes as he chewed his food. He swallowed. "Jealous?"

"Of course not," Lauren denied. She put down her sandwich and took a swallow of wine—a rather large swallow.

Alec suppressed a smile. "Good. Because you have no reason to be, lass. There is nothing between Chloe and me other than a few drinks and some pleasant conversation."

Lauren felt her insecurities sneaking up on her, threatening to spoil the day. "Did you actually go to her . . . house?" she ventured hesitantly.

"Yes."

Jealousy and hurt streaked through her. "And you didn't—"

"Nay, lass, we didn't. If you don't believe me, you can ask her."

Lauren's eyes widened in horror. "I'm not going to ask her *that*."

Alec chuckled. "She was the one who finally convinced me to marry you."

Shock gave way to bewilderment in Lauren's eyes. "She did?"

"Aye, lass."

"Oh." Lauren didn't know what to think about that.

"As I was saying," Alec continued, deftly circumventing any further questions on the subject, "although I think allowing it to continue this long is absurd, I can understand the animosity between Early and your father. I don't, however, see what fuels this tension between you and your father."

There was an odd tightness in Lauren's chest. She knew that no matter how much she loved her father, or how much she tried to do for him, there would never be a place for her in his heart. Not wanting Alec to see the pain his query had unearthed, she shrugged and said indifferently, "That's easy enough to figure out. All these years, Pa's never been certain I was his."

By the time Alec took Lauren home, the sun had already dropped behind the mountains, turning them a deep purple against the coral sky. The rutted trail that led from the main road to the house was barely visible in the near darkness. "Are you sure you don't want me to go in with you?" Alec asked.

"I'm sure. There's no telling what kind of temper Pa's going to be in after being left alone all day. He'd probably be of a mind to throw you out." Lauren gripped Popcorn's reins. She had changed back into her old clothes, and she missed the luxurious sensation of silk against her skin. "Tell Sarah thanks again for letting me wear her dress. It was really generous of her."

"I'll buy you a hundred dresses if you'll marry me, lass."

Lauren was glad for the cloak of dusk that hid her blush. "I thought Sarah was going to have a heart attack when you told her you had proposed to me. I never saw anyone get so excited."

"Sarah likes you."

"I like her too. A lot. I never used to get along with the girls at school. But Sarah is different somehow." Lauren paused, then added in a low voice, "She wants us to get married before she and James return to Scotland."

"I know."

"But that's only a few weeks away."

"She wants to be there to witness the event." Alec chuckled. "Probably to make certain I go through with it. My family fears I am a confirmed bachelor."

If the idea of getting married had previously filled her with uncertainty, now it made her feel downright panicky. She didn't understand why something she wanted more than anything in the world should scare her so much. "It just seems like everything is happening so fast," she said. "I feel like one of those wooden toy tops that won't stop spinning."

"So do I."

Puzzled, she glanced at him. Alec always seemed so self-assured; she could not imagine him suffering a case of the butterflies. "You do?"

"Aye, lass, that I do. Marriage is not a contract to be entered into lightly. While there are no guarantees, 'tis best to try to find someone you know you can spend the rest of your life with." Alec paused, then added, "I searched a long time for the right woman."

The thought that he considered her to be the right woman caused Lauren's heart to swell with such emotion that she felt as if it would burst. "It's getting late," she said unevenly. "I'd better go."

"I wish you would reconsider my offer to stay at Duneideann," Alec said. "I don't like the thought of you being near Sam Luttrell. I don't trust him."

"Don't worry about me. I'll be fine. Besides, with all the stuff you taught me, Sam's the one who should be scared."

"I hope you never *need* to use any of the skills I taught you, lass. If Sam gives you any trouble, I want you to come to me."

"Alec—"

"Promise me."

"All right. I promise. If there's any trouble at

all, I'll be on your doorstep faster than you can blink."

"That's all I can ask." Alec reached out and brushed his knuckles across her cheek. "Please be careful."

"I will."

He slid his hand into her hair and pulled her head toward his at the same time that he leaned toward her. He kissed her briefly, tenderly. "I love you," he murmured.

She could feel Alec's smile in the darkness, and for the moment, her life seemed complete. "I love you, too."

Lauren was almost at the house before she realized she had forgotten to ask Alec what T.J. had wanted to talk to him about.

Chapter 16

As soon as Lauren rode into the yard, she knew something was wrong. Sheriff Early's horse was tied to one of the porch posts. She rubbed down Popcorn and watered him, then hurried inside.

Frank and Pa and Bubba were all in the kitchen. All three turned to look at her when she entered the room. "Where in the hell have you been?" Frank demanded.

"Take it easy, Frank," Early said. "Coop isn't the one who broke the law."

Frank's face turned livid. "Don't tell me how to treat my own daughter. Coop's long overdue for a whuppin' and that's just what she's going to get if she doesn't come up with some damn good answers."

Lauren moved to stand beside Bubba, who had his hands shoved deep in his pockets and a look of burning resentment on his face. Wondering what they were talking about, and who had broken the law, she glanced from Pa to Sheriff Early and back. "Answers to what?" she asked warily.

"Don't get smart with me, girl," Frank spat. He shook one of his crutches in front of her face. "One word of sass out of you, and you won't sit down for a week. Do you understand me?"

Lauren choked back the protest that welled up inside her. "Yes, sir," she mumbled dutifully.

"Where were you today?" Frank asked again.

"I went to the Fourth of July celebration."

"Don't lie to me!"

"I'm not lying! I did go to the celebration." She nervously moistened her lips. "I went with Mr. MacKenzie, and his sister and brother-in-law. After the parade, Mr. MacKenzie took me on a picnic."

"Mr. MacKenzie took me on a picnic," Frank mimicked condescendingly. "You were supposed to be watching out for your brother!"

Lauren glanced at Bubba. "Did something happen?"

"What do you care?" Frank spat. "Ever since you started socializing with the rich, you couldn't give two cents for your own flesh and blood."

"Pa, that's not true!"

"Your brother was caught stealing," Sheriff Early said. "Money. Jewelry. A gold watch."

"I told you, I *found* the watch," Bubba said sullenly.

"If you'd been keeping up with him like you're supposed to do, this would never have happened."

Frustration and anger consumed Lauren. "Pa, it wasn't my fault! Bubba knows better than to steal. Besides, you didn't even *want* me to go to the celebration!"

"The problem, Frank," Sheriff Early said, "is with Bubba here. If he doesn't learn to keep his nose clean, he's going to find himself behind bars."

"Like hell he will," Frank shot back. "You've been after me and my own like a damn vulture ever since you got elected. I'll be damned if I'm going to stand by and let you ruin my boy's good name just because you don't have anything better to do with your time."

Early shook his head in resignation and rammed his hat on his head. He stopped with his hand on the door and turned back to look at Frank. "Just remember what I told you. The next time your son gets caught breaking the law, it's liable to be a long time before he sees the daylight side of a jail cell."

Sly Barnes and five of Duneideann's hired hands waited until it was fully dark before saddling up their horses. "Anyone in particular we're supposed to be looking for?" one of the men asked.

Sly closed the corral gate. "There's a chance that Luttrell is involved, but no real proof. Just stay in pairs and watch your backs. Rustlers tend to shoot first and ask questions later. I don't want to be going to anyone's funeral any sooner than I have to."

Lauren yanked the last shirt off the clothesline and ran for the house just as a bolt of lightning sliced a jagged path across a leaden sky. The thunderclap that followed rattled the very walls. She dropped the clothes on the kitchen table and closed the window against the wind that drove grit through the mesh screen.

Through the window, she saw a tumbleweed roll across the yard and come to an abrupt stop against the fence. Lightning flashed again, this time so close that her teeth tingled. She flinched at the thunder that exploded almost simultaneously.

She glanced toward the door, wondering if the storm would awaken Pa. She doubted it. He had finished off a bottle of whiskey after his argument with Cal—their third in as many days—and had gone back to bed. She hoped he would stay asleep the rest of the afternoon, or at least until after Cal left. She'd heard enough shouting and name-calling to last her a lifetime.

She had just finished folding Cal's shirts when the kitchen door blew open and Cal came into the kitchen, hunched against the wind. He caught the door just in time to keep it from crashing against the wall, and pushed it shut. Wet spots splotched his hat and shirt. He tossed his saddlebags across the table.

"Raining?" Lauren asked.

Cal took off his hat and dragged a sleeve across his face, blinking at the grit that irritated his eyes. "A few sprinkles," he said. "Not enough to do us any good."

Lauren tried to keep the worry from her expression. The weather had been crazy like this for more than a week now, ever since the day after the Fourth of July celebration. Mornings dawned hot and heavy after a succession of uncomfortable nights that offered little cooling relief from the July heat. By midday, black clouds cloaked the valley, attacking it with vicious bolts of lightning that struck indiscriminately, frying anything that happened to be in their way.

The little rain that accompanied the heat storms was seldom enough to settle the dust. As soon as the clouds lifted and the sun came back out, the rain that did fall rose from the ground in misty tendrils of steam. By dusk, the ground would be even dryer and harder than before. At night, the glow of brush fires started by the lightning could be seen on the slopes of the surrounding hills. They needed rain, and soon.

Lauren handed Cal the pile of clean shirts that she had folded. "I wish you wouldn't leave."

Cal put the shirts in his saddlebag with the rest of his belongings. "Don't see how it can be any other way, Coop. Frank knows it's either me or Luttrell. As far as I'm concerned, he's made his choice."

Lauren crossed her arms defensively. "That just leaves Bernie, and I'm not so sure he wants to stay on either. As soon as you leave, Sam's going to take over the ranch. He's already got Pa hornswoggled, and Bubba thinks he walks on water because Sam takes him down to Miss Chloe's on Saturday nights." In spite of her efforts to control it, her voice trembled.

Cal straightened and looked Lauren in the eyes. His expression was grim. "You want some advice, Coop? Get out of here. I don't care what you have to do to accomplish it, just do it. Go to Tucson and get work in town. Take in washing, if you have to. Just get as far away from the

Bar-T as you can get and don't turn back. There's no future for you here. You'll just sink with the rest of them."

Coming from Cal, who had spent most of his adult life working for the Bar-T, the advice struck a note of alarm with Lauren. "Cal, what's wrong? Is something going on that I don't know about?"

Cal shook his head. "It's best if you *don't* know about it, Coop. You'll just get caught in the middle."

"In the middle of what?"

Cal picked up the package wrapped in brown paper that Lauren had left on the drainboard. "These the sandwiches you made for me?" he asked.

She nodded. "In the middle of what?" she repeated. "Cal, you can't just prick my curiosity like that, then not tell me what you're talking about."

"If I tell you, you'll be in manure up over your head before I'm halfway to Sonoita. I know you too well, Coop. Just pack your things and hightail it out of here before you get sucked into something you can't get out of."

"Cal!"

He buckled his saddlebags and tossed them over his shoulder. "And stay away from Luttrell," he said. "You should know better than anyone what that man is capable of."

"You still here?" Frank growled.

Lauren whirled around to see her father leaning on his crutches in the doorway. He was unshaven, and his eyes were bloodshot. She wondered guiltily how long he'd been standing there. She had not heard him come down the stairs. With his crutches, he usually made enough noise to awaken everyone in the house.

Cal's jaw hardened. "Not for long," he bit out. Thunder drowned out his words.

Lauren glanced uneasily from one to the other. "Perhaps you should wait until this storm lets up," she told Cal. "You don't want to get hit by lightning."

Cal's brittle gaze drilled into Frank. "I'll take my chances."

"Yellow-bellied coward," Frank spat. "Get the hell off my land and don't come back."

"Pa! Don't say that! You and Cal are friends!"

"Tell *him* that."

Lauren winced as the kitchen door slammed behind Cal. "Pa, you'd better go after him and stop him from leaving," she said. "Whatever you two are fighting about, it can't be worth losing a good foreman. Cal's been with you since before I was born."

Frank glowered at Lauren. "One more word out of you and I'm going to knock your goddamn teeth out." He started for the stairs.

Lauren clamped her mouth shut to keep from blurting out what she was really thinking. It was no use trying to reason with Pa when he'd been drinking. Still, the things that Cal said had aroused her curiosity to the point where she could no longer contain the questions that screamed in the back of her mind. "Pa, wait."

Frank stopped.

Lauren took a deep breath. "Cal told me that

if I stayed here, I was liable to get caught in the middle of something I wouldn't be able to get out of. What's he talking about? What are you and Sam involved in?"

A look of contempt twisted Frank's features. "Shut your yapping and fix me something to eat." He shook his head. "I swear, what's a man got to do to get some peace and quiet in his own house?"

Lauren's eyes flew open. She lay in bed, her heart pounding, and wondered what it was that had awakened her. The night was hot and still, and there was not even the slightest breeze to rustle the curtains hanging at her bedroom window.

Then she heard it again, a barely audible creak on the stairs. And then another. As she strained to listen, she heard the faint *click* of the kitchen door catching.

She tossed back the sheet and lowered her feet to the floor. Easing noiselessly out of bed, she went to the window and pulled back the edge of the curtain just in time to see Bubba dart across the yard in the direction of the barn.

She frowned. What was Bubba doing up at this hour? The night sky was still pitch-black, without any of the faint glow that appeared in the east hours before the sun peeked above the horizon. In the distance, heat lightning flickered periodically over the mountains.

As her eyes adjusted to the darkness, she saw Bubba and another man leading their horses away from the barn. Sam Luttrell? she wondered. She didn't think it was Bernie. Bernie would have no reason to sneak out in the middle of the night, whereas Sam could be up to just about anything.

She thought again of Cal's warning. If that was Sam with Bubba, then they were probably up to no good. She just wished she knew what.

Her imagination conjuring up all sorts of possibilities, she went back to bed. Sleep eluded her, however. Just before dawn, she heard the creak of Bubba's footsteps on the stairs as he slipped back into his bedroom.

Several nights later, Bubba and Sam again left the ranch under the cover of darkness, only this time Lauren was ready for them. It was their odd behavior at the dinner table that night that triggered her awareness of what they were up to.

Pa and Bernie had gone out to the corral to check on one of the horses, which had been acting sickly, leaving her and Bubba and Sam in the dining room. She had gotten up from the table and started clearing away the dishes.

Bubba pushed his plate away. "I'm tuckered. I'm gonna turn in early."

Sam stretched and stifled a yawn. "Me too. We had a heck of a day. Got any more coffee in that pot, Coop?"

Lauren had just picked up the coffeepot when she realized that it was Saturday. Bubba would rather die than miss his Saturday night trip to Miss Chloe's. She poured the last of the coffee into Sam's cup. "No ride into town?" she asked Bubba.

He imitated Sam's sprawling stretch. "Naw, not this week."

"I thought you said Lucy was expecting you."

"Sure she is. But she'll wait. Women gotta learn patience. It's good for 'em."

Lauren glanced at Sam and saw him grin at Bubba's puffed-up response. Normally, the men's arrogance grated at her, but there was something different about it tonight that piqued her curiosity rather than her temper. "Lucy might not wait," she suggested. "She might find someone she likes better. She might find someone old enough to shave."

Red flashed in Bubba's eyes. He started up out of his chair. "She better not!"

"Pipe down, kid," Sam said. "She's just trying to provoke you."

Bubba sank back down onto his chair, but his expression remained sullen. Lauren's jab had struck a nerve, and he wasn't inclined to forgive and forget anytime soon. He glowered at her. "You're just jealous 'cause Lucy's prettier than you."

Lauren snorted inelegantly. "Entertaining smelly cowhands who take baths about as often as they go to church does not appeal to me in the least. I'd rather step on a slug with my bare feet."

Sam observed Lauren through half-closed eyes as she carried the dishes to the kitchen. "The problem with your sister, kid, is not that she's jealous. It's that she ain't getting any. It does that to a woman—makes them crotchety.

Pretty soon, they get like Martha Sikes, all dried up and pruny looking."

"That's disgusting!" Bubba retorted. "Who'd want to bed Coop? She's skinny as an ocotillo, and just as prickly!"

Both Bubba and Sam laughed at Bubba's joke. "That's a good one, kid," Sam said when he'd caught his breath. "I'll have to remember that one."

Even though Lauren had left the room, they had spoken loud enough for her to hear. She clenched her teeth, and it took every ounce of self-control she could muster not to march back into the dining room and hurl the coffeepot at their miserable heads.

Still, just the fact that they were willingly forgoing their customary Saturday night excursion into Millerville told her they were up to something. She intended to find out what.

True to their word, Bubba and Sam both turned in early, leaving Bernie to ride into town alone. Not wanting to arouse suspicion, she stayed up and started on the pile of mending that had been demanding her attention for the past week. By the time she finished, Pa had long since gone to bed. She blew out the lamp and peered out the window. The bunkhouse was dark.

Upstairs, she looked in on Pa and Bubba. Both were sound asleep, or appeared to be. She went to her own room. She removed her shoes, but not her clothes. Fully dressed, she lay down on the bed and pulled the sheet up over her.

The wait began.

She wasn't aware of having dozed off until the creak on the stairs jolted her awake. She lay without moving, not even breathing, and listened as her brother tiptoed through the darkened house. As soon as the kitchen door closed behind him, she put on her shoes and went downstairs. She bolted across the yard, managing to duck around the side of the barn just as Bubba and Sam came out, leading their horses. Her heart thumping furiously, she pressed back into the shadows, hoping they hadn't seen her. She doubted either of them would be happy to find out that she was following them.

She waited until they left the yard, taking care to note which direction they were heading, then slipped inside the barn. She put the bridle on Popcorn, but did not bother to saddle him; there was no time.

Not wanting them to hear her coming, she kept the gelding to a steady walk. She wasn't sure how far they had gotten ahead of her, or exactly which direction they would take once they left the Bar-T. All she knew was that they were heading not toward town, but toward Duneideann.

Around her, the tops of the mountains were outlined with an eerie crimson glow that marked the fire line. Patches of flame brightened several places on the slopes where lightning had started isolated fires. Lauren knew the fires were not yet cause for alarm, because the flames would not travel downward. As long as there was no capricious wind to scatter sparks, the fires would stay near the hilltops, where they would eventually burn out. Still, as dry as the timber and grasslands were, it would take little more than a slight breeze in the wrong direction to engulf the entire valley in flame.

Lauren guided Popcorn down into Encina Wash, the dividing line between the Bar-T and Duneideann, and back up the opposite bank. That the wash was still dry told her that no rain had fallen in the mountains. She did not know how much longer this drought could continue. Even the larger, wealthier ranches in the Territory would not be indifferent to its effects. This was the driest summer she had experienced in her entire life.

About a quarter of a mile away from the wash, Alec's fences began. Lauren reined in her horse and looked around, not certain which direction to take. It was too dark to discern a trail in the dirt, and she had not seen Bubba or Sam since they left the Bar-T.

Finally she decided to follow the fenceline away from Alec's house. If she didn't catch up with Bubba and Sam soon, she could either ride back toward the house or return home.

She had not ridden far when she saw the first sign that she was probably on the right trail. The barbed wire had been cut and rolled back, at the same spot where she had helped dismantle the fence the time they had driven the Bar-T's cattle onto Alec's land. Had Bubba and Sam gone up into Six-shooter Canyon?

She was still debating whether to follow them into the canyon or go back home when she heard the snap of a twig in the darkness. Her hands tightened on the reins. She sat without moving, listening, alert. Her heart pounded in her ears. Had they realized she was following them? Sam had tried to kill her once. She wouldn't put it past him to try again.

Whether it was fear or sound judgment that finally decided her, Lauren didn't know. All she knew was that she no longer felt safe out here by herself. She would go home and confront Sam and her brother in the morning. They would probably lie through their teeth, but at least they would be aware that she knew they were up to something. She doubted it would be enough to stop Sam, but maybe Bubba would be scared enough to get out of whatever they were involved in before he got into any more trouble.

She was just turning Popcorn around when the gelding reared back his head and shied to one side. "Shhh!" She patted Popcorn's neck, trying to calm him. "Come on," she whispered. "Let's get out of here."

Just then, a gunshot shattered the stillness.

Popcorn bolted, nearly throwing Lauren from the saddle. Terrified, she clutched Popcorn's mane and hung on for dear life as the gelding broke into a run.

"It's one of the rustlers!" a man shouted. "Don't let him get away!"

Behind her, hoofbeats pounded the ground.

Another shot whizzed past Lauren's ear, so close she felt the sound rather than heard it. Silent screams rose in her throat. Lying close against her horse's neck, she urged him into a gallop, praying desperately that he wouldn't lose his footing in the darkness.

She did not slow down until she was well away and could no longer hear her pursuers behind her.

Struggling to catch her breath, she slid down from the saddle and slumped against the gelding's heaving side. Drenched with sweat and shaking violently, she took the reins and began walking, leading her horse, so he could cool down gradually. She stumbled and nearly fell. She had no idea where she was. She would have to wait until the sun started coming up before knowing which direction to go.

She shuddered, realizing how close she had come to getting shot, and suddenly felt sick to her stomach. *She could have been killed!*

She had recognized the man's voice, but she couldn't remember from where. He was a local. A cowhand, maybe?

It's one of the rustlers!

She couldn't get the man's words out of her mind. Were Bubba and Sam involved in rustling? Terror rose in her throat in dry heaves. Was this what Cal had tried to warn her about?

Lauren put the biscuits on the table. "Bernie get back from town yet?" she asked.

"Haven't seen him." Bubba grabbed two biscuits and dropped them on his plate. "Ow! Those are hot." He stuck his burned fingers in his mouth.

Lauren pulled out her chair and sat down.

"For someone who turned in early last night, Sam's sleeping awfully late."

"We all slept late this morning," Frank said. "I sure as hell didn't see you up at the crack of dawn."

"I was awake most of the night." Lauren looked straight at Bubba. "Just like someone else I know."

Bubba shot her a startled glance.

"What's that supposed to mean?" Frank demanded.

Shaken and exhausted, she had arrived home less than an hour before Bubba. She had been too distraught to relax, however, and had still been awake when her brother finally tiptoed up the stairs to his bedroom. She had heard him drop his boots on the floor.

She forced her voice to remain as steady as the stare she fixed on Bubba's face. "I followed you."

He started up out of his chair. "You had no right to do that!"

"Sit down and shut up," Frank growled. Bubba slumped down in his chair, his expression sullen. Frank pointed his fork at Lauren. "If you know what's good for you, girl, you'll learn to mind your own business."

She turned on her father. "Are Sam and Bubba rustling?"

"Now you listen here—"

"Pa, answer me! Are Sam and Bubba stealing cattle?"

Frank's face turned a congested red. He stood, leaning heavily on his crutches, and plunged his hand down into his pants pocket. He withdrew a fistful of bank notes and tossed them on the table. "You see that?" he bellowed. "There's damn near three hundred dollars there, and all of it from one night's work. Just one!"

Lauren stared at the money in disbelief. Three hundred dollars from a single night's work? Good God, what were they stealing? Golden calves?

Suddenly everything started to fall into place. The reason Sam had come to Pa for a job. Why Sam had been willing to work without pay. Pa's conviction that Sam was going to help them get out of debt. The voice she had heard last night had belonged to one of Alec's hired hands, she suddenly realized. She swallowed hard. "You're stealing Alec's bulls, aren't you? The ones he bought from Scotland?"

"Oooh, Alec," Bubba taunted. "Told you she was sweet on him."

Lauren and Frank both turned on Bubba at once. "Shut up!"

Lauren raked her fingers through her hair in frustration. "Pa, how can you let Bubba get mixed up in something like this? You heard what Sheriff Early said. Bubba might go to jail if he gets into any more trouble. Worse than that, he could get killed. Alec has his men out hunting for the rustlers."

"How in the hell would you know?" Frank demanded.

"They shot at me last night, that's how!"

Frank began scooping the money up off the table and shoving it back into his pocket. His voice shook. "Look, Coop, just mind your own business and don't start asking a lot of nosy questions, and no one will get hurt. Do you hear me?"

"Yeah, Coop," Bubba echoed. "Mind your own business."

There was an odd tightness in Lauren's chest. Never in her life had she felt so much like an outsider in her own home. "As long as I'm part of this family, this ranch *is* my business," she said unevenly. "Sam is going to ruin us. Can't you see that? We've had hard times before, but we always managed to get through them without breaking the law. I want him to leave. I want you to fire him."

Frank glowered at Lauren. "You listen here, Coop. With Cal gone, we need Sam. Unlike MacKenzie, who's doing his damnedest to run us out of the valley, Sam's trying to help us save this ranch. If rustling a few head gives us the money to keep this place going, then so be it."

"But, Pa, they *hang* cattle rustlers!"

"I don't want to hear another word about it!" Frank barked.

"Is there a problem?" Sam asked from the doorway.

Lauren's heart stuck in her throat. She had hoped to be able to talk with Pa and Bubba without having Sam around. "It's nothing," she said.

"She's been spying on us," Bubba piped up. "She followed us last night."

Sam's right eye looked straight at Lauren while his left eye fixed on a spot over her shoulder. His eyelids drooped until he was watching her through mere slits. "Is that so," he said slowly.

There was a veiled threat in both his tone and the way he was looking at her that sent a chill down Lauren's spine. She was beginning to wish she hadn't said anything. Ignoring Sam, she stood and picked up the coffeepot. "I'm going to go make some more coffee."

She turned and walked out of the room. It wasn't until she was in the kitchen that she realized she was shaking. She didn't know what to do. A part of her wanted to go to Alec and tell him what was going on, yet a voice in the back of her mind cautioned her against it. Not only could Bubba go to jail, but Pa as well. If only she could get them to stop before they were caught. She didn't know how she would accomplish that, but there had to be a way.

She was filling the blue enameled pot with fresh water when she felt someone brush up against her. She gasped and the pot clattered into the sink. She whirled around, choking back a scream as Sam pressed his weight against her. She tried to scoot away from him, but he placed his hands on the drainboard, trapping her between him and the sink. His face was mere inches from hers, making his wayward eye seem even more out of focus. Lauren grimaced and turned her head away. She pushed her hands against his chest. "Get away from me!"

Sam caught her chin in his strong fingers and twisted her face back to him.

Fear surged through her. She opened her

mouth to yell, but Sam tightened his grip, turning her cry for help into an impotent whimper. "Shut up!" he growled.

Trying desperately not to panic, Lauren nodded. Sam's face was so close she could smell the stale whiskey on his breath. His grip on her chin hurt. Her heart pounding, she stared at his eyes, wondering if she had the courage to jab him in the face like Alec had taught her. Her stomach turned over. Just the thought of poking him in the eyes made her want to be sick.

Sam released her. "You're getting awful nosy for your own good, Coop," he said in a low, deliberate monotone. "You know what happens to nosy people? They get hurt. Now, you wouldn't want to get hurt, would you?"

Lauren's heart was racing and she was breathing hard. "No," she whispered.

With his knuckle, Sam traced a path along her jaw. It was all she could do not to recoil from his touch. "I've been thinking about you, Coop," Sam continued. "Whenever I can't sleep at night, I think about you, up there alone in your bed, and I remember how you got me and Eliot fired from the Diamond Cross. You and MacKenzie. I think about both of you, and what I'd like to do to you."

Lauren's mouth was so dry it hurt to talk. "What do you want from me?"

"Just be a good girl and keep your nose out of my business, and you won't get hurt. *Comprende?*"

She forced her voice to be calm. "What makes you think I won't go to Sheriff Early and tell him what you've been doing?"

Sam drew an imaginary line across her throat with his forefinger and grinned. "You won't." Dropping his hand, he turned and walked away.

Lauren sagged against the sink. Her knees were shaking and she felt as if she was going to throw up. From the dining room, she heard the scraping of chair legs on the wood floor, then Pa asking, "Is she going to keep her mouth shut?"

"She'll keep quiet," Sam answered.

Lauren's throat constricted. She could not believe any of this was happening. It was bad enough that Pa had hired Sam in the first place, after what he and Eliot had done to her. But to have her own family take sides with Sam against her was more than she could bear.

Perhaps Alec was right, she thought miserably. Perhaps she should consider leaving. Pa and Bubba didn't need her, except to cook and clean and do whatever chores they didn't want to be bothered with. She had been a fool to think otherwise. And while she had been working herself to death to make sure they were taken care of, she doubted that either of them ever gave a thought to what she wanted or needed. If she were to keel over dead right this minute, they probably wouldn't even notice except to complain that there was no one to do for them.

Turning back to the sink, she picked up the coffeepot she had dropped and began refilling it with water. She slowly worked the pump handle, aware that, at this moment, she felt like two different people. A part of her wanted nothing more than to sit down and cry her eyes out, while another part of her felt oddly detached and clearheaded. It was as if she knew what she had to do; she just didn't know if she had the courage to do it.

She stopped working the pump and stared out the window at the sagging fence that did less to restrain the horses than it did to mark the boundaries of the corral. Aside from her mother's memory, what was there to keep her here? The Bar-T was no longer the home she had known as a child. It didn't even feel like any kind of home any more. Cal and Jimmy were gone, and she would be surprised if Bernie didn't leave soon too, if he hadn't already. Pa's drinking had turned him into an unpleasant stranger with whom she could no longer bear to be in the same room.

And Bubba? Until Sam hired on, she had hoped Bubba would outgrow his antagonism. Unfortunately, he idolized Sam and was quickly becoming just like him. Unless something drastic happened to bring Bubba to his senses, he was already well on his way to ruin.

At the sound of laughter coming from the dining room, Lauren's movements slowed until she was moving as if in a dream. Without questioning the sanity of what she was about to do, she added fresh coffee grounds and a handful of broken eggshells to the water in the pot. She put the pot on the stove and checked the fire, then quietly slipped out the kitchen door and headed toward the barn. By the time the coffee boiled over, she would already be halfway to Duneideann.

Chapter 17

"Lass, what is it?" Alec clasped Lauren's arm and pulled her into the house, closing the door behind her.

She wrapped her arms around her stomach and tried to calm down, but violent tremors continued to rack her body. She had made it halfway to Duneideann when she had started shaking, and now she couldn't stop. "Alec, please—" she gasped. Her knees started to give way.

"My God!" Alec swore. He caught her just as she started to fall. He scooped her up into his arms. She wrapped her arm around his neck and buried her face against his cheek.

Sarah came running down the stairs. "Alec, what's wrong? Lauren?"

"Sarah, go into the kitchen and get some wet cloths and some cold water!"

While Sarah ran to do Alec's bidding, Alec carried Lauren into the library and lowered her to the sofa. She cried out and clung to him.

Alec pried her arms from around his neck and hunkered down beside her. He took her face between his hands. "Lass, look at me," he ordered.

Lauren blinked at him. His face blurred and swam before her eyes.

"Lauren, can you hear me?"

"Y-yes."

Alec breathed a sigh of relief. "Tell me what happened. Did Luttrell hurt you?"

She shook her head. "No . . . not that."

"Lauren, talk to me!"

Bit by bit, everything came out, from her following Sam and Bubba, to the confrontation at the breakfast table. When she finished, Alec swore under his breath.

Tears filled Lauren's eyes. "I don't want Pa and Bubba to go to . . . jail . . ." Her voice broke.

A muscle in Alec's cheek knotted. "They won't go to jail, lass. I promise."

He sat beside her on the sofa and put one arm around her shoulders, steadying her as she drank from the glass of cold water that Sarah brought. When she'd had enough, he handed the glass back to Sarah and began wiping Lauren's face with a wet cloth.

Lauren caught his hand. "You don't have to do that," she said shakily. "I'll be all right."

Alec took the cloth from her face. "I'm sure you will be, lass, but I don't want to take any chances." He glanced at Sarah. "Tell Galston to have one of the guest rooms readied. Lauren is going to stay here."

Sarah gave Lauren's shoulder a reassuring squeeze, then quietly left the room.

Alec lifted a lock of hair away from Lauren's face. Her color had returned to nearly normal, but her pupils were oddly dilated. Dark circles shadowed her eyes, confirmation of last night's ordeal. The realization of how close he had come to losing her was only now starting to sink in.

He slowly shook his head. "Every time I think of how narrowly you missed being killed last night . . ." He left the thought unfinished. "Are you sure you weren't hurt?"

"I'm fine. I just . . ." She took a deep breath. "Alec, I'm so sorry. I didn't know they were stealing your cattle, I swear it."

"I believe you."

"How could I have been so stupid? I should have known something was going on. Sam is nothing but trouble. He always has been. I just didn't think it would be anything like this, or that my own family would be involved."

"Lass, how could you have known? I didn't suspect anything myself until the Fourth of July celebration when Mr. Powell told me one of my bulls had turned up in Wilcox with an altered brand."

"Is that what T.J. wanted to talk to you about?"

"Aye, that it was."

Lauren rubbed her fingers over her brow in agitation. "I don't know long they've been at it, or how many of your bulls they've stolen, but I'll pay you back. I promise. Somehow, I'll get the money—"

"Lauren, stop! It's not your fault, for God's sake! I don't blame you."

"But I do!" Her voice broke. Years and years of painful memories welled up in her, clogging her throat and filling her eyes with tears. There was so much pain. The pain of her mother's death. The pain of never being wanted by her own father. The pain of being taunted and criticized by people who called themselves good citizens. The pain of never being quite good enough . . . She took a shuddering breath. "I should have done something, instead of just—"

"What, lass? What could you have possibly done?"

"I don't know!" She squeezed her eyes shut. "I don't . . . know . . ."

Alec's face was rigid with impotent frustration. He didn't know how to make Lauren see that she wasn't to blame for what had happened, and he didn't know how to ease her pain. Never in his life had he felt so damn powerless.

He got to his feet. Sliding one arm beneath her knees, he picked her up. Startled, she grabbed the front of his shirt. "What are you doing?"

"I'm taking you upstairs and putting you to bed. You'll feel better after you've rested."

"I can walk—"

"Indulge me, lass," Alec said sharply. "I don't know what else to do to help you."

Bewildered by his sharp tone, Lauren looped her arms around his neck and rested her head on his shoulder as he carried her up the stairs. The feel of his strong arms around her made her feel safe, and the tension began to ebb out of her limbs. She hadn't realized how tired she was.

They nearly collided with Sarah at the top of the stairs. Sarah motioned to the bedroom across the hall from Alec's and stepped out of the way. "Is she all right?" she asked in a low, worried voice.

"She'll be fine." Alec wished he felt as sure as he sounded. "She just needs some sleep."

He carried her into the bedroom and laid her on the bed.

Lauren's eyes flew open. She had nearly fallen asleep. "Please don't go," she murmured sleepily.

"I won't leave you," Alec promised. He motioned to Sarah, who nodded and quietly pulled the door shut. He lay down beside Lauren and pulled her into his arms, holding her close against his pounding heart. "I'll stay right here, lass, as long as you need me."

After a minute, Lauren sighed and whispered against his chest, "I love . . . you . . ."

He drew back his head and looked down into her weary face. Her long lashes, damp with tears, were clumped together. Her soft rose-hued lips were parted slightly, and her breathing was shallow and even. She was asleep.

He didn't know what he was going to do with her. She had frightened him today, far more than she could ever know. He knew he could not protect her from every danger that came her way, and it would not be fair to try to do so. The only thing he could give was his love, and hope it was sufficient to keep her safe. He brushed his lips against her forehead and gathered her closer in his arms. "I love you too, lass. With all my heart."

The setting sun rimmed the valley with its blood-red aura. From the main house, the glow of small brushfires could be seen along the top of the ridge behind Six-shooter Canyon. Lauren stood at the edge of the terrace, a worried look on her face. On the other side of the ridge was the spot where she and Alec had gone for their picnic lunch on the Fourth of July. Had the place suffered any damage? Worse, what if the fires spread down through Six-shooter Canyon and across the valley? Both Duneideann and the Bar-T could be destroyed.

Several yards behind Lauren, Sarah and James and Alec were seated in comfortable chairs, Sarah enjoying a glass of wine and the men their nightly shot of whiskey. Lauren had declined a drink.

"I'm so excited," Sarah said. "I can hardly wait for the wedding."

"Well, you'll have to wait until the judge is able to fit us into his schedule," Alec reminded her.

"He'll make room for you," Sarah said lightly. "Everyone has time for weddings. They're such joyous occasions."

Concern creased Alec's brow as he regarded Lauren. "Lass, are you going to join us?"

Lauren turned. "I'm sorry. Did you say something?"

"Don't tell me you're getting cold feet already," Sarah teased. "Poor Alec will be devastated if you change your mind."

Alec threw his sister a warning glance. "Sarah, Lauren has the right to change her mind if she so chooses."

Lauren returned to the group and sat down.

"I'm not going to change my mind. I was just thinking about other things."

"Well, I for one am thrilled about the wedding," Sarah continued. "I've always wanted a sister. Are you coming to Scotland for your honeymoon?"

"The grand tour," Alec said. "Edinburgh. Aberdeen. Duneideann—"

"Duneideann!" Sarah grimaced. "Alec, that's out in the middle of nowhere!"

Alec and Lauren exchanged a private look. "'Tis the most important stop," he said. There was a note of finality in his voice that discouraged further questions.

"When you two come to Edinburgh, you are more than welcome to stay with us," James said.

"Thank you," Alec replied. "We appreciate the offer. I think Lauren will like Scotland. I'm looking forward to showing her around."

"Showing her off, you mean," Sarah corrected.

Lauren attempted a smile, but her heart wasn't in it. She caught Alec watching her, his forehead furrowed. "I'm sure it will be fun," she said.

James put down his glass and stretched. "If you will all excuse me, I'm going up to bed." He grimaced. "I'm beginning to be sore where I didn't even know I had muscles. Remind me never to become a rancher. Sarah, are you coming?"

"Be nice to me and I'll give you a backrub," she ventured.

"An offer too good to refuse," James said. He

got to his feet. "Good night, you two. And Lauren, welcome to the family."

Alec and Lauren both stood. "Thank you," Lauren said.

Sarah looped her arm through her husband's. "Good night," she called out.

After Sarah and James went back into the house, Lauren crossed her arms over her stomach and went to stand again at the edge of the terrace. "Sometimes the fires seem so close that you can almost reach out and touch them," she said.

Alec moved to stand behind her. He wrapped his arms around her and pulled her against him. He slid his hand up to caress her breast through her shirt as he tugged on her earlobe with his lips. "What's wrong, lass?" he murmured into her ear.

His steamy breath sent shivers of delight up her spine. She leaned her head back against his shoulder, glad for the diversion of his caresses. The oppressive heat was wearing on her. She could not shake the disquieting feeling that something bad was going to happen. "Nothing."

"You've been preoccupied all evening. What are you thinking about?"

"The fires, mostly. I've never seen them this bad. And it's so terribly dry. I just have a bad feeling about it."

Alec lifted her hair and kissed the nape of her neck. "What else?"

She was silent a moment before answering. "My family."

He sighed wearily. Taking her by the shoulders, he turned her to face him. "Lauren—"

"I know what you're going to say. And you're right. I do worry about them too much. But I can't help it. No matter what they've done, Pa and Bubba are still my family, and I care about them."

"I don't expect you to feel otherwise."

"I just wish I knew what was going to happen to them."

"They won't go to jail. I already promised you that."

"I know, but—"

"I'll go talk to your father in the morning. We'll work something out. Frank may not want my help, but he's going to get it."

Feeling warm and loved and cherished, Lauren slid her arms around Alec's waist and smiled up at him. Her eyes shone in the semidarkness. "Sometimes I wonder what I did to deserve someone as good as you."

"You deserve someone better. Unfortunately, he'd have to fight me for you, and I'm not about to let you go."

He bent his head and covered her mouth with his. He kissed her long and slow, savoring the sweetness of her mouth. It was a kiss that came from deep in his heart, a tender, soul-baring expression of his love for her.

Lauren's arms tightened around him as the gentle warmth of his mouth soothed away her worries, replacing them with a yearning that slowly unfolded and grew within her, until she was trembling with need for him. She didn't want to think about her family, or the possibility that she might never see them again. And the only fire she wanted to think about putting out was the one blazing inside her.

Alec cupped her bottom and pulled her hard against him, the pressure of her body against his arousal increasing both his pleasure and his torment. If he did not stop this now, he wouldn't be able to stop at all. Lauren had had a grueling day, and she needed rest.

But damn, how he wanted her!

Stop! his mind screamed silently. *Stop and put an end to this sweet torture. You'll have the rest of your life to make love to Lauren. Let her have this one night's respite from your incessant demands.*

He tore his mouth from hers, determined to do right by her, but when she slid her palms up and over his chest, he nearly lost his self-control.

"Alec—"

"Nay, lass," he said firmly, removing her hands from his chest and pulling them down to her sides. "No more talk. You need to go to bed. You didn't take a very long nap today."

"But there's something I—"

"If it's about your family, it can keep until—"

"I don't want to sleep in the guest bedroom tonight!" At Alec's taut expression, she slid her hand down his abdomen, over the front of his trousers. In the darkness, her eyes searched his face. Her fingers closed around his throbbing member. "I want to stay with you . . ."

Fire leapt in Alec's veins. He groaned and

crushed her to him, and his mouth descended on hers with a savage hunger that smothered Lauren's startled gasp.

At the open window, the sheer lace curtain moved slightly in the breeze. Alec and Lauren lay on the big bed, their legs entwined. Lauren had fallen asleep with her back to him, her bottom cradled against his thighs and Alec's arm wrapped securely around her waist. Sleep did not come so quickly to Alec, however, and as he lay in the darkness, remembering their lovemaking, that part of him which had filled her only a short time before began to swell and press urgently against the small of her back once again. He could not help wondering how something so deeply satisfying could leave him starving for more.

There had been a difference to their lovemaking tonight, a heightened awareness of each other, and as he poured his shuddering warmth into her, his humble gift to her, he knew a moment of pure bliss, as if something wonderful and miraculous had just occurred.

Pulling the sheet up over them, Alec settled closer to Lauren and buried his face in her soft hair. He was not aware of having fallen asleep until a persistent knocking on his bedroom door awakened him.

Taking care not to awaken Lauren, he eased his tall frame out of bed and went to the door, his bare feet making no noise on the floor. He opened the door.

It was his foreman, Sly Barnes.

"Sorry to disturb you at this time of night, sir, but we got trouble," Sly said. "The fire has spread down Six-shooter Canyon."

Chapter 18

Lauren raised up on one elbow and blinked into the darkness. Alec was sitting on the edge of the bed, pulling on his boots. He was already dressed. "Alec, what's wrong?" she mumbled sleepily.

"The fire is spreading. I need to go—"

"I'll go with you," Lauren said, suddenly wide awake.

She started to scramble out of bed, but Alec caught her by the shoulders and pressed her back down onto the pillows. He leaned over her, his face unreadable in the darkness, but his stern tone was unmistakably clear. "You're going to stay here where I know you're safe," he said.

Lauren's heart pounded. "But you'll need all the help you can get," she protested. "I've helped put out fires before. I know what to do."

"No," he said firmly. "James is coming with me. I want you to stay here with Sarah. She's never experienced anything like this, and she probably won't know what to do if the fire gets too close to the house." He stood up. "I'll be back as soon as I can."

"Alec, I—"

"I'm not going to argue with you, lass. My decision is final. You're staying here." He left the bedroom, pulling the door shut behind him.

* * *

Lauren took the last of the pans from the pantry and piled them on the floor by the sink. "While you fill those," she told Sarah, "I'll go find a ladder."

"And blankets," Sarah called out.

Lauren nearly collided with Galston in the hallway. "The bathtub and the washbasins are all filled with water," he said.

"Thanks." Lauren tried to catch her breath. "Galston, do you know where Alec keeps a ladder?"

"There is one in the garden shed, Miss Cooper."

"I'll get the ladder if you'll round up all the blankets and quilts that you can find and put them by the kitchen door."

"Right away, Miss Cooper."

Lauren bolted through the kitchen. "Be right back," she told a surprised Sarah.

In the garden shed Lauren easily found the ladder. She dragged it across the yard and propped it against the house, then climbed up to the roof to look around.

Below her, Sarah set a kettle of water on the ground outside the kitchen door. "How does it look?" she called out.

"It's pretty dry," Lauren said. "We don't want to waste any water now, but if the fire starts getting close, we'll have to get up here and wet down these shingles."

The sound of thunder rumbled through the valley.

At the top of the ladder, Lauren twisted

around and squinted at the clouds that were rapidly building over the mountaintops. A gust of hot, dry wind blew grit in her face, and she lifted an arm to shield her eyes.

"That's all we need," Sarah said, studying the darkening sky. "More lightning to start more fires."

Lauren pointed across the valley toward the south end of the storm front, where a dark gray sheet stretched between the clouds and the horizon. "Look. It's raining."

Sarah looked. "Do you think it will do any good?"

"I don't know. But it's the most rain we've seen so far. Let's hope it keeps up." She looked toward the storm front one last time before climbing down the ladder. "I'll help you with the pans," she said.

Sly Barnes sprinted across the yard toward them. "Can you two take care of things here?"

"Are you leaving?" Sarah asked.

"We have to move the livestock to safer range. The fire jumped the wash and is spreading through the valley."

There was a terrible tightness in the middle of Lauren's chest. The Bar-T was right in the fire's path!

Four of the hired hands were riding toward the house. One of them was leading Sly's horse. Sly swung up into the saddle and gave final instructions to the men before they rode away.

As soon as the men were out of sight, Lauren started running toward the stables.

"Lauren!" Sarah called out. "Where are you going?"

She didn't hear her. She only hoped she wasn't too late.

The edge of the fire snaked across the desert floor, a wall of flames shooting high into the air before an even higher wall of billowing black smoke. Rabbits and quail and other small animals fled before the advancing conflagration. The earth rumbled beneath the hooves of stampeding cattle.

On the ground, men rapidly shoveled dirt into the hollowed-out hide of a newly killed cow and tied ropes around its front and rear legs. Archer Kendrick wrapped the opposite end of one of the ropes around his saddle horn several times, while another hired hand from the Diamond Cross did the same with his rope. "Move out!" Kendrick ordered.

Kendrick and the other men urged their horses forward. The ropes jerked tight. Slowly they advanced, dragging the cow carcass between them. Kendrick's horse shied as they crossed the line of lapping flames.

Kendrick and his partner dragged the carcass along the edge of the fire, snuffing out much of it as they passed. Other men followed behind them, beating at the remaining flames with slickers and saddle blankets. The heat from the blaze created its own convection, fanning the flames as quickly as the men worked to extinguish them.

Martin Dandridge sought out Alec. "We can't

stop it," he shouted over the din. "It's outrunning us. We're going to lose the Bar-T."

Alec nodded his understanding. "Start burning at the wash and try to turn the fire back on itself," he yelled back. "I'll get Frank Cooper out of the house."

Alec rode hard and fast toward the Bar-T. Frank Cooper wasn't going to like having to leave his home, but he no longer had a choice. Everything they had tried to do to save the ranch had failed. The ground was too dry, and the fire was advancing too quickly.

By the time Alec arrived at the Bar-T, the fire had already burned most of the yard, and flames were licking up the side of the house. Bernie and Bubba had loaded the wagon high with the Coopers' belongings. "We can't get Frank to come out," Bernie yelled. "He says he'll die rather than let anyone drive him off his land."

Alec dismounted. "Where's Luttrell?"

"I don't know," Bernie answered. "He took off this morning after he and Frank got into a fight over some money he says Frank owes him."

Alec looked at Bubba, who was standing by the wagon biting his nails and glancing around with frightened eyes. The antagonism was gone. Now he was just a scared fourteen-year-old boy. "Frank, Junior!" Alec barked.

Bubba turned a surprised gaze on Alec. No one ever called him by his real name. "Sir?"

"Make sure all the animals are out of the barn and the corral," he ordered.

Bubba nodded and ran toward the barn.

"And the chicken coop!" Alec shouted after him. He turned to Bernie. "As soon as I get Frank, I want you and the boy to take the wagon and get out of here."

Alec ran toward the house.

In the parlor and dining room, smoke was wafting in through windows, filling the rooms with an acrid blue haze. "Cooper!" Alec yelled. There was no response.

He ran up the stairs.

Frank Cooper sat on his bed, a bottle of whiskey in one hand and a glazed look in his eyes. He lifted the bottle to his mouth and took a swig, then wiped his mouth with his sleeve and pointed the bottle at Alec. "I'll be damned if I'm gonna let you run me off my land, MacKenzie." His voice was slurred. He was drunk. "You and Luttrell. You're both a couple of no-good thieves. This is *my* land. I'll die here first."

Where flames had already worked their way through to the inner walls, the wallpaper was beginning to curl and blacken from the intense heat. Alec started toward the bed. "No one is going to die," he said. "You're going to get out of that bed and come with me."

"Get out of here, MacKenzie! Get the hell off my land!" Frank hurled the bottle at Alec.

Alec ducked. The bottle, barely missing his head, shattered against the wall behind him.

Driven by a force born of rage, Alec seized Frank by the shirtfront and hauled him off the bed.

Frank's legs gave out and he went down, dragging Alec with him. Alec struggled to regain his balance. "Hold on to me. I'll get you out of here."

Frank clawed at Alec's hands. "Let go of me, you son of a bitch! I'm not leaving."

Alec knew he had no choice. There was only one way he was going to get Lauren's father out of the house. He pulled Frank to his feet, then let go of him.

Deprived of support, Frank swayed and started to lurch. He grasped frantically for something to hold on to.

Alec drew back and plowed his fist into Frank's jaw.

The force of the blow drove a searing pain the length of Alec's arm and through his shoulder. Frank's eyes rolled back in his head. He went down.

Alec caught him as he slumped to the floor. Summoning every ounce of strength that he possessed, he hoisted Frank up over his shoulder. Staggering beneath Frank's weight, Alec carried him from the room and down the stairs.

Just as Alec stepped outside, Bubba barreled into him, nearly knocking him down. *"Pa!"* Bubba screamed.

Bernie caught the boy by the collar and pulled him back. "Get out of the way!" he yelled.

Alec carried Frank to the wagon and dumped him into the back, on top of the kitchen chairs and the bags of flour.

Bubba broke free of Bernie's hold and ran to the wagon. "Pa! What's wrong with you? *Pa!"*

"He'll be fine," Alec said, gasping for air. "Get him out of here. Take him to Dandridge's place."

Bubba began to cry. "What's wrong with him? Why won't he wake up?"

"He will," Alec snapped. "Go on. Get out of here while there's still time."

Bernie climbed onto the wagon box and picked up the reins. "C'mon, kid," he yelled. "Do what Mr. MacKenzie says."

Bubba scrambled up onto the seat. Bernie snapped the reins, and the wagon lurched forward.

Chickens squawked and scattered before the moving wagon.

Still breathing heavily, Alec closed his eyes and waited for the nausea that gripped him to pass. His lungs burned. There was no strength left in his limbs. He wanted to lie down and go to sleep, but he couldn't. Not yet. Not while there was still a chance he could save the house.

He ran to the pump, but there was no bucket. Only a dipper hanging from a string. Where was the damn bucket? He ran into the house.

He hauled the blanket off Frank's bed, then hurried back outside to the pump. He began working the pump handle furiously, letting the water saturate the blanket. Returning to the house, he began beating at the outside back wall with the wet blanket, but the effort soon proved futile. The flames had already climbed too high up the side of the house.

Taking the steps two at a time, he yanked open the screen door and ran into the kitchen. He stopped short.

Sam Luttrell was going through the cupboards, shoving aside cups and plates and utensils. "Where the hell is it?" he grumbled. The kitchen door slammed shut and he whirled around, surprise frozen on his face when he saw Alec.

"What are you doing here?" Alec demanded.

Sam groped behind him with one hand. A slow grin spread across his face as his fingers closed around a knife handle. "I came to get what's mine," he said, a wild-eyed look giving him the appearance of a madman. "Looks to me like I got dealt a better hand than I bargained for." Gripping the knife, he brought his hand around to the front.

Storm clouds and smoke blended into a choking black shroud that pressed down on the valley, blotting out the sun as Lauren rode Popcorn through Encina Wash. Water trickled through the once dry wash, runoff from the rain falling in the mountains. Lauren guided the gelding through the water and up the opposite bank. Her stomach clenched as she saw the devastation spread out before her. Ground that had previously supported brush and tufts of coarse grass was now barren except for a few blackened stumps. Thunder rumbled through the valley.

Her fear reaching the point of panic, Lauren urged her horse forward.

By the time she reached the Bar-T, the house was ablaze, flames leaping from the upstairs windows. Where was everyone? Had they gotten out? What about Pa? He couldn't get around without his crutches. Suppose he was trapped inside?

She jumped out of the saddle, and ran toward the house. "Pa! Bubba!"

The front door stood ajar. She ran inside.

In the parlor and dining room, flames consumed the curtains and roared up the walls. The few remaining pieces of furniture stood out like black skeletons against the blaze. A trail of fire led up the stairs to the bedrooms. She ran toward the stairs. *"Pa!"*

A heavy weight crashed into her, knocking her down. She pushed herself upright, clawing her way up through the thick smoke, when suddenly a pair of arms closed around her, crushing her. Screams of terror rose up inside her in thick, nauseating waves. Strong hands stripped her shoulders and shook her hard. A man's voice sliced through her panic. "Lauren!"

It was Alec!

He turned her toward the door and shoved her so hard she lost her footing and fell. "Get out of here!" he shouted.

Her throat raw, she scrambled to her knees and spun around. "Alec! Where's Pa?" Then she saw Sam. "Alec, look out!"

Sam lunged headfirst, like a charging bull, slamming into Alec with a force that knocked him off his feet.

Lauren screamed.

Alec and Sam, locked in a deathgrip, rolled over and over across the floor.

The men broke apart and Sam rolled to his feet. Alec started to rise, then collapsed on the floor. Sam seized him by the front of his shirt and hauled him upright. He drew back his fist.

There was no time to think. Only half aware of what she was doing, Lauren ran across the room and kicked Sam behind the knees. His legs buckled beneath him and both he and Alec went down. She grabbed a fistful of Sam's hair and twisted hard.

He swore aloud and swung at her, striking her arm with a bruising blow that broke her grip on him. She cried out and clutched her arm. He stood and started toward her.

Fighting the panic that threatened to overwhelm her, Lauren took an answering step backward. She could not tear her gaze away from Sam's eyes, his awful, disconcerting eyes that looked at her and past her at the same time. Her heart pounded. *His eyes!*

He grabbed for her.

With every ounce of strength that she could muster, Lauren jabbed at his eyes with her extended fingers.

Sam screamed and threw his hands up to shield his face. He stumbled backward into Alec, who had just gotten to his feet.

Alec caught him and swung him around. Before Sam could regain his balance, Alec smashed his fist into Sam's face.

Sam staggered backward, toward the stairs.

Alec advanced on him. He hit Sam again and again. Sam fell to the floor. Leaning over him, Alec gripped his shirt and dragged him to his feet.

Lauren shoved her fist into her mouth to keep

from screaming as Alec drove his fist into Sam's belly one last time, sending him reeling into the burning staircase.

His shoulders heaving as he fought to catch his breath, Alec glanced overhead. He swore aloud and turned, and ran straight toward Lauren. "Get out!" he yelled.

She turned and bolted out the door.

Alec caught up with her. Gripping her arm, he dragged her off the porch and out into the yard. In that same instant, blazing timbers crashed to the ground, sending sparks into the air as the house caved in on itself.

Fear exploded in Lauren's chest. *"Pa!"*

Alec wrapped his arms around her, restraining her as she tried to break away. " 'Tis all right, lass. Your father is safe."

Lauren slumped in his arms.

Alec gripped her shoulders, keeping her from falling. "He's safe, lass. Do you hear me? Your father and brother are safe."

She nodded weakly. Alec's face was blackened and streaked with smoke, and his clothes were singed. His knuckles were raw and bleeding.

"Are you all right?" he asked.

"I-I'm fine. But you're not." She reached out to touch the dark stain spreading across the front of his shirt.

He caught her hand. "I'll be fine." His voice shook. "Come here and let me hold you."

She moved into the circle of his embrace, and he folded his arms around her. Tears crowded her eyes and she buried her face against Alec's chest.

He kissed the top of her head. "Thank God you're safe," he whispered raggedly, his throat tight with emotion. His arms tightened around her. He rested his chin on her head, and a blessed numbness crept over him as he stared unseeing at the burning house.

The first cooling drops of rain began to fall, striking his face.

"It has to be something important," Cissy Page said. "Even Martin Dandridge is in there with him."

"Perhaps Judge Kearny is giving him an award for pulling Frank Cooper out of that burning house," Martha Sikes suggested.

Arminta Larson *harrumphed* loudly, making it clear that she thought any attempt to save a Cooper's life was an utter waste of time. Arminta and her army of followers were waiting in front of the courthouse steps for Alec to come out.

"Well, Mr. MacKenzie is a hero all the same," Amy Taylor said. "I can hardly wait to get his story for the *Gazette*."

Arminta frowned. "Speaking of the *Gazette*, where is that photographer? I thought you said he would be here."

"He will, he will," Amy said impatiently.

"Well, the fire should help gain support for Mr. MacKenzie's irrigation project," Cissy said. "Just think how many acres could have been saved if there had been water available to put out the blaze."

"Right now, I'm more concerned with getting

support for our drive to have that painting of Chloe Roberts removed from the Shady Lady. Do you know that *children* see that immoral display from the boardwalk as they walk past the door, not to mention the embarrassment it causes the decent, law-abiding citizens of this town?" Arminta sighed. "Mr. MacKenzie would be the perfect spokesman for our cause. I do hope he agrees to do it."

"Here comes the photographer now," Amy said.

"And not a moment too soon," Arminta replied. She patted her hair into place and put on her brightest smile just as the courthouse doors opened and out came Alec MacKenzie.

Arminta's smile faded. With him was Lauren Cooper, looking sweet and innocent and demure in a gauzy white dress with a cluster of pink rosebuds pinned at her waist.

Martin Dandridge also came out of the building, as did Sarah and James Lachlan, and Bubba Cooper.

Regaining her composure, Arminta stuck her smile back on her face and stepped forward. "Mr. MacKenzie, I am so glad to see you survived your ordeal without any serious injuries. We were all so worried about you."

"I appreciate your concern, Mrs. Larson. But other than a few scrapes and bruises, I suffered no serious injuries." It crossed Alec's mind to tell the woman that perhaps her concern would be better directed toward Lauren, who had just lost her home, but he decided Lauren didn't need the kind of attention Arminta Larson would likely provide.

Arminta glanced at Amy, who was busy scribbling on a notepad. "Did you get that?"

Amy's head bobbed. She kept scribbling.

Alec leaned close to Lauren and whispered gruffly, "Did you invite them?"

She stifled a giggle and shook her head. Still feeling a little dazed over all that had happened, she clutched her left hand with her right, terrified that the gold band around her third finger would fall off if she let go of it.

It saddened her that Pa had refused to come to the wedding, but at least he was alive and unhurt. For that, she was thankful. Martin Dandridge had been there though, and so had Bubba. He had been exceptionally quiet and subdued, and had not bristled whenever either Martin or Alec told him to do something. Martin had told her earlier that nearly losing Pa in the fire had really scared Bubba. Given time, he would come around, he assured her.

On Lauren's other side, Sarah grinned and clapped her hands together in delight as she surveyed the scene before her. "Perfect," she said lightly. "A photographer. Not only can we tell everyone at home that you are truly married, but we'll be able to show them a picture of the handsome couple too."

Arminta Larson took control like a general leading his troops. "Move out of the way," she said, shooing everyone aside. "Give the photographer some room."

"Mrs. Larson, what is going on here?" Alec demanded.

"Why, Mr. MacKenzie, Amy is going to do a feature article on you for the *Gazette*. Everyone in town will be eager to read it, and it will do so much to promote your business enterprises."

Alec opened his mouth to object, then suddenly closed it again. He glanced at Lauren, who was gazing up at him with love and amusement in her eyes, and a mischievous smile tugging at the corners of her mouth. "It would be cruel to turn her down," she said.

Arminta sniffed. "Miss Cooper, I don't know what you are doing here, but I would appreciate it if you would move out of the way so that we may proceed."

Alec put his arm around Lauren's shoulders. "Mrs. Larson, I will be happy to oblige you with your news story. Later. Right now, I wish to go home and spend some time with my wife."

Arminta's mouth fell open. She stared at Lauren. "Your . . . wife?"

"My wife," Alec said. "Now, if you people will excuse us—" With his arm still firmly around Lauren's shoulders, he started toward their buggy.

The photographer emerged from under the black tent he had draped over his camera. "Sir, I haven't taken your picture yet."

"Forget the picture," Arminta barked. "There isn't going to be any story." Pivoting, she stormed away. Whispering excitedly among themselves, the officers of the Millerville Women's Junior League forgot to follow after her—for the first time ever.

"Who's going to pay for my time?" the exasperated photographer asked.

"I will," Martin Dandridge said. He looked at Alec and Lauren, and grinned. "Consider it a wedding present."

"We'll have to hurry," the photographer said impatiently. "I'm running late for another appointment. I want you to stand there, Mr. MacKenzie. And you, ma'am, if you'll just move to the right a bit—"

"I have a better idea," Alec said. Turning to Lauren, he drew her into his arms and lowered his head to hers. "Take a picture of me kissing the woman I love."

Epilogue

The sun broke through the clouds, turning the mountains of Wester Ross a deep purple against the misty sky. Lauren and Alec sat on the grassy bank of a small, swift stream. A picnic lunch awaited them on a blanket. The day was warm and calm, with no chilling wind swooping down off the mountains to spoil their outing.

Alec held the fishing pole in his hands up to eye level so he could see where the line was supposed to be threaded through. His white shirt was open at the neck and his sleeves were rolled up, exposing his tanned forearms. Beside him, Lauren had removed her shoes and stockings, and was dangling her feet in the icy water. She cast Alec a sideways glance, and her heart swelled with pride at the thought that this gentle, strong, handsome man was her husband. More than that, he loved her. *He loved her!*

As he had done every day since their arrival in the Highlands, Alec was wearing his kilt. Although she had reservations about him wearing what looked to her an awful lot like a skirt, to her surprise, he cut quite a striking figure in the MacKenzie tartan. The dark green plaid echoed the colors of the land, and more than once the generous length of soft wool had provided welcome protection for both of them against the biting winds that sometimes sprang up seemingly out of nowhere. Rather than making him look like a greenhorn sissy, there was something oddly mysterious and virile about the tartan.

When the sun came out, Lauren turned her face up to it and closed her eyes, savoring its warmth. Of all the places they'd visited in Scotland on their honeymoon, Duneideann was her favorite. She could easily stay here forever. "I've had the most wonderful time," she said dreamily. "Your family was so kind to me, and it was nice of your brother to come all the way from London to meet me."

Alec glanced up from his task. The look of contentment on Lauren's face warmed his soul. "I knew my family would love you. You captured their hearts—fortunately not the same way you captured mine."

"And what way was that?"

Laughter danced in his eyes. "You didn't tell any of them to go suck an egg."

Lauren burst out laughing. "You're never going to let me forget that, are you?"

"Not on your life. It may come in handy some day when I need to blackmail you into doing my bidding."

Lauren plucked a fistful of grass and threw it at him. "As if it would get you anywhere," she said, grinning. "You're going to have to do better than that if you intend to blackmail me."

She thought of the letter from Martin Dandridge in her pocket, and her smile faded. She couldn't put off reading it much longer, yet she couldn't shake the uncomfortable feeling that it contained bad news. She reached into her pocket.

Alec glanced up at her. "Why don't you just get it over with, lass? Otherwise, 'twill haunt you all day."

She sighed. "You're right." She broke the wax seal and removed the neatly penned page from the envelope. Taking a deep breath, she spread out the page and started reading.

Alec watched her as she read, trying to decipher the content of the letter from the expression on her face, but she revealed little. Finally she folded the paper and returned it to the envelope.

"What did Martin say?" he asked gently.

"Bubba's doing well. He likes working at the Diamond Cross. Mr. Dandridge said he was careful to put him with men he knew would be a good influence on him, and Bubba seems to be coming around. Oh, and he doesn't want to be called Bubba anymore. It's Frank, Junior, now."

"That sounds like a positive change." Alec picked up the bait jar and frowned down into the mass of squirming earthworms. "How is your father?"

"The same. He seems to have lost the will . . . to . . ." Her voice faltered.

"Lass, are you all right?"

"I'm fine. Really I am."

"Lauren—"

"I don't want to talk about him, Alec, and I'm not going to let him spoil our last day here." She took a deep breath and smiled. "I want it to be the most special day of our honeymoon."

Relieved for an excuse to stop fishing, Alec set the pole and the bait jar aside. "I'm starving. Let's see what Mrs. Bates packed in the picnic basket."

"Alec, we just got here! And it's not even lunchtime yet. Besides, you haven't caught a single fish."

"There's enough food in that basket to feed an army. We don't need any fish."

"The fish is to be for our supper," Lauren reminded him.

"Woman, has anyone ever told you you're a nag?" He caught her around the waist, and she let out a squeal as he rolled with her on the grassy bank, pinning her beneath him. "You leave me no choice," he growled, "but to silence you the most effective way I know how."

"Alec! Let me up!"

Burning passion smoldered in his eyes as he gazed down into her sunkissed face. Sliding his hand beneath her skirt to caress her bare thigh, he slowly, deliberately, brought his mouth down to hers.

A giggle that was part laugh, part heady anticipation of what she knew would soon follow, welled up inside her.

The touch of his lips on hers sent a shiver of excitement through her. She closed her eyes and returned his kiss with reckless abandon, surrendering completely to the tumultuous sensations he never failed to arouse in her. She splayed her hands over his back, holding him to her, thrilling at the reflexive movement of his muscles beneath her fingertips.

Alec kissed her mouth, her neck, the sensitive spot just below her ear, all the while working his hand farther beneath her skirt, seeking that other sensitive spot that was hot and tight with desire. She threaded her fingers through the hair at his nape. "I love picnics," she murmured.

Alec tickled her ear with his tongue. "They do seem to hold a special meaning for us," he breathed into her ear.

The sensations he was arousing in her were making it difficult to concentrate on what she wanted to tell him. She felt his hand beneath her skirt, his fingers deftly parting the curls guarding that special place. "That's why I wanted this one . . . to be special . . . That's why I waited until today . . . to tell you . . ."

She sucked in her breath as his fingers slid inside her.

"Tell me what?" he murmured huskily. He began working his fingers inside her, moving them in and out.

She gripped his shoulder, her fingers digging into the bunched muscles. "You're going . . . to be . . . a father!"

Alec froze. He lifted his head to stare into her beautiful, dreamy eyes. "A father?" he asked, his voice strained.

A slow smile melted across his face. "A father," she replied. A naughty look danced in her eyes. She began moving her hips against his hand, continuing what he had started.

His pupils abruptly dilated. He groaned and seized her lips with a devouring hunger that left them burning. When he finally pulled away, his lashes glistened with tears. "I love you, Lauren," he said in his deep Scottish voice.

"Cold?"

Lying in the safe, secure cradle of his arms, Lauren shook her head. She was too happy, too filled with warmth and love, ever to be cold.

Still, Alec pulled the blanket up around her. They were still lying by the stream, but the hour had grown late. Soon it would be time to leave, and the lazy days they'd spent in the Highlands would become precious memories that they would carry with them forever.

"I've been thinking about that piece of land," Alec said in a low voice. "The one where we went on our first picnic."

Lauren tilted her head back so she could look into his face. Fortunately that land had escaped burning.

"I was thinking," Alec continued, "we won't always be able to come to a place like this when we need a holiday, so having a place close to home would be convenient."

"It would be."

"We could build a house. Not a big one, just a place where you and I and our children could go to enjoy a holiday from time to time. A place that would remind us of this."

"There's no stream."

"With the new irrigation system, 'twill be a simple matter to put in a man-made pond. We'll landscape it, and in a year or two it will look as if it has been there all along."

Lauren snuggled against him and trailed her

fingers over his chest. "Are you going to put fish in our pond?" she asked lightly.

Alec snickered. "As long as you don't insist I catch our supper."

She suppressed a smile. "I won't."